# PRAISE FOR THE NOVELS OF BARBARA DAVIS

"Heartfelt and beautifully written."
—Diane Chamberlain, *USA Today* bestselling author of *Pretending to Dance*

"A beautifully crafted page-turner . . . Part contemporary women's fiction, part historical novel, the plot moves seamlessly back and forth in time to unlock family secrets that bind four generations of women . . . This novel has it all."
—Barbara Claypole White, bestselling author of *Echoes of Family*

"Everything I love in a novel . . . elegant and haunting."
—Erika Marks, author of *The Last Treasure*

"A book about love and loss and finding your way forward. I could not read it fast enough!"
—Anita Hughes, author of *Christmas in Paris*

"One of the best books out there, and Davis is genuinely proving herself to be one of the strongest new voices of epic romance."
—*RT Book Reviews* (4½ stars)

"Davis has a gift for developing flawed characters and their emotionally wrenching dilemmas . . . a very satisfying tale."
—Historical Novel Society

"A beautifully layered story."
—Karen White, *New York Times* bestselling author of *Flight Patterns*

# WHEN NEVER COMES

# WHEN NEVER COMES

## BARBARA DAVIS

LAKE UNION
PUBLISHING

Text copyright © 2018 by Barbara Davis
All rights reserved.

Published by Lake Union Publishing, Seattle

www.apub.com

Amazon, the Amazon logo, and Lake Union Publishing are trademarks of Amazon.com, Inc., or its affiliates.

ISBN-13: 9781477808917 (paperback)
ISBN-10: 1477808914 (paperback)
ISBN-13: 9781503950177 (hardcover)
ISBN-10: 1503950174 (hardcover)

Cover design by Kimberly Glyder

Printed in the United States of America

*To Tom—who married me anyway.*
*We've only just begun . . .*

# PROLOGUE

*Monck's Corner, South Carolina*
*August 19, 1986*

*The room is dark but not quite still. A threadbare curtain breathes in and out at the window, shuddering in the sticky Carolina heat. Outside, the hum of night things fills up the quiet, a chorus of moist throats and raspy wings calling through the torn screen.*

*In the bed beneath the window, a girl in a pink cotton nightgown writhes amid tangled sheets. She is a lovely child, raven-haired and pale, a fringe of sooty lashes lying uneasily against her cheeks. Her whimpers turn to tears, turn to wails, turn to shrieks. She is awake but not awake, flailing one moment, rigid the next, stalked by a terror she can neither see nor name. The dreams have come again, her almost nightly companions. But no one is coming to comfort her tonight. Mama has passed out again on the bathroom floor.*

# ONE

The first ring came with the same throat-thickening panic all 2:00 a.m. phone calls produce. Disorientation. Dread. The certainty that something, somewhere, is terribly wrong.

Christine shot up with a gasp, grabbing for the phone on the bedside table. "Hello?"

"Mrs. Ludlow?"

"Yes."

"Christine Ludlow?"

"Yes. Who's calling?"

"Mrs. Ludlow, this is Sergeant Stanley with the Clear Harbor police. I apologize for the call, but we've been knocking for some time now. We need to speak with you."

*Police?* Her pulse ticked up a notch, the skin on the back of her neck prickling with the old familiar warning. "What's happened? What's wrong?"

The voice on the other end of the phone was polite but strained. "We'd prefer to speak in person."

A moment later, she was pulling back the front door, staring at two uniformed police officers. "What is it? Why are you here?"

"I'm afraid it's your husband, ma'am. There's been an accident. His car skidded off a bridge and into Echo Bay."

Christine's chest seemed to seize. "Where is he? Is he all right? What hospital have they taken him to?"

"Your husband isn't in the hospital, Mrs. Ludlow. He . . . didn't survive the accident. I'm afraid we're going to need a next of kin to come down and identify his body."

The silence spooled out as the words penetrated. *Stephen's body. Echo Bay.*

"We'd be happy to drive you," the sergeant continued, his voice full of polite sympathy. It wasn't his first time knocking on a door in the middle of the night, Christine realized dully. How many wives, mothers, lovers, and friends had gotten the visit she was getting now?

It took a moment for the sergeant's offer to penetrate. "No," she replied, feeling strangely detached, as if watching the scene from a long way off. The last thing she wanted at that moment was a ride in the back of a police car. "Thank you. I can drive myself."

The sergeant nodded. "We'll wait while you get dressed then, and you can follow us back to the station."

Christine nodded, trying to wrap her head around what had happened—and the reality of what came next. Bestselling crime novelist Stephen Ludlow was dead, and she needed to go identify his body. But first, she needed to get dressed.

Christine felt the ground tilt as she stepped into the lobby of the Clear Harbor Police Station. The scuffed black-and-white floor tiles, the unforgiving fluorescent glare, the nauseating aroma of burned coffee and stale cigarette smoke, reminded her queasily of another night—another calamity a lifetime ago. She shook it off. *Deal with the calamity in front of you.* If life had taught her anything, it had taught her that.

Sergeant Stanley stepped away to speak to the officer at the front desk, then turned back with an awkward smile and pointed to a row of blue plastic chairs along the wall. "You can have a seat if you like. We've called to have someone escort you down."

Moments later, the stainless-steel elevator doors opened. Christine was startled to see a familiar figure step into the lobby. Daniel Connelly was—*had been*—a close friend of Stephen's, a drinking companion and a regular at his Friday night card games. But he was a homicide detective, and Stephen had died in a car accident. What was he doing here at three in the morning?

"Christine." He took both her hands in his. They were hot and slightly sticky. "I'm so sorry. When they realized it was Stephen, they called me. They thought it might be easier if I was here to . . . explain things."

She frowned. *Explain things?* It was an odd way to put it, a cold, blunt way. She pulled her hands free, trying not to be obvious as she wiped her palms on her jacket. "Thank you, Detective, for coming out at this hour."

"Please, call me Danny."

He was thickset and beefy, with full ruddy cheeks and a head of wiry gray hair. They hadn't met more than a few times, and then only briefly, but she'd never been able to understand Stephen's fondness for the man, beyond the fact that as a homicide detective he'd been an invaluable research contact, always happy to pass along juicy case details in exchange for a box of Cohiba cigars or a bottle of good single malt.

"I guess we should get on with it," he said grimly. "Are you ready?"

Christine nodded. There really wasn't another option when your husband's body was lying on a gurney somewhere, waiting to be identified. She allowed Connelly to take her elbow and steer her toward the elevators, saying nothing as he pushed the button stamped with a well-worn *B*. The basement then. Stephen was in the basement.

When the doors opened again, Connelly stepped out and turned left, leading her down a white-tiled hall lined with windowless blue doors. He stopped in front of the last door on the right and reached for the knob. A dull buzz filled Christine's head as she stared at the engraved metal plate: MORGUE.

Connelly threw her a glance. "You all right?"

The words seemed to come from a long way off, as if they'd been spoken from the bottom of a very deep well. This couldn't be happening, couldn't be real. And yet the look on Connelly's face told her it was very real indeed. Pulling in a lungful of air, she counted to three and nodded. She was aware of Connelly's hand at the small of her back as her feet began to move and wondered if the light but steady pressure was meant to propel her forward or keep her from keeling over backward. No doubt he'd seen his share of fainters.

She experienced a moment of surprise as she stepped through the door. She'd been bracing for unpleasant odors—blood, decay, formalin—but there was only the faint aroma of bleach in the air. It was a small mercy, but a mercy nonetheless. She was determined to keep her eyes moving as Connelly steered her deeper into the room, absorbing it all in one terrible sweep: a high-ceilinged, sterile-looking space with suspended fluorescents and battleship-gray floors.

She avoided the strategically placed drains built into the floor, unwilling to contemplate their purpose, shifting her gaze instead to the trough-style sinks along the back wall. The wall on her right was lined with numbered doors—square stainless-steel doors in tidy rows, equipped with heavy metal hatches. One of those doors would belong to Stephen soon. She turned away, trying to banish the thought, but everywhere she looked there was a fresh reminder of what she was here to do. And then she saw it, a gurney draped with a plain white sheet.

Her breath caught at the sight of it, the air in the room seeming to go cold.

A man in a dingy lab coat stood on the other side of the gurney, his back to them as he scribbled on a clipboard. As if sensing their approach, he turned. He was young, midtwenties, with a pocked complexion and thick, smudgy glasses. He stood there blank faced, as if waiting for some signal.

Connelly laid a hand on her arm. "Are you ready?"

Christine nodded but couldn't find her voice.

His eyes slid to the attendant. "Go ahead, Ryan."

Without expression or fanfare, the attendant reached over to pull back the sheet. Christine braced herself as she forced her eyes to the body on the gurney, the waxy face a bloodless blue white, slack in death but eerily unmarred. He wasn't wearing his jacket, and his top shirt buttons were open, his tie loose and askew. Yes, it was him. Had his face been a ruin she would still have known him. There was no mistaking the Robert Mitchum–style cleft in his chin. And yet there was a jarring strangeness too. The movie star good looks were flaccid now and slightly bloated, leaving behind only a blank husk of the man she'd married eight years ago. The iconic charm and carefully polished charisma that had made Stephen Ludlow an international media darling had been extinguished.

"Yes," she said hoarsely, then cleared her throat. "Yes, it's Stephen." She was relieved when the attendant dragged the sheet back into place, but angled her body away from the gurney just the same. "What happens now?"

"The ME will determine cause of death," Connelly explained. "Though with the icy condition of the bridge, I think we can safely assume the crash will be ruled an accident, death caused by either trauma from the crash itself or by drowning." He paused, letting the words sink in. "I'm sorry to be blunt, but there's really no nice way to say it."

She blinked heavily at him. "No. I suppose not. Do I just go home now?"

"There are papers you'll need to sign. But we were wondering—" He paused to clear his throat, his eyes skittering away briefly. "We were hoping you'd be able to help us with something else."

Christine felt the first icy pangs of uneasiness. Something about the change in his voice, his sudden reluctance to look her in the eye, made her scalp prickle. "Help you with what?"

Connelly looked down at his shoes and sighed. "It's a rather delicate matter, actually. One I wish to hell I could spare you. But the fact is . . ." The words fell away, his eyes straying again, this time to a gurney on the opposite side of the room. "We need your help, Christine."

Uneasiness morphed into dread as her gaze slid along with Connelly's to the nondescript white mound on the second gurney. He was shifting from foot to foot now, his hands thrust deep in his pockets.

"Stephen's wasn't the only body we pulled from his car," he said gruffly. "Unfortunately, no identification was found for the second victim. We were hoping . . ."

The attendant was there suddenly, his blue latex gloves hovering expectantly over the sheet. Connelly gave him a curt nod. No one spoke as the sheet came away, and in the silence, Christine became aware of a clock ticking somewhere. Heavy. Hollow. Like a pulse. And then she found herself staring at a woman.

She was a ghastly shade of white, her platinum hair fanned out from her head in a snarled, sodden halo. There was a gash on her forehead, and a sickening depression along her right temple. Her eyes were open and glazed, a piercing shade of violet with fixed, bottomless pupils. She was also naked from the waist up, her breasts so full and round they couldn't possibly have been formed by nature.

Christine found herself unable to look away. A prostitute? A one-night stand? A casual dalliance or something more? And if so, how *much* more?

Connelly cleared his throat. "Do you have any idea—"

"No."

"I know this is hard, Christine, but please take your time. Look closely."

"I don't need to look closely. I don't know who she is or what she was doing in my husband's car." Her voice broke suddenly, and for an instant, she thought about lunging at the detective. "This is why you're here. Because of her. Because you were Stephen's friend, and they thought you'd be able to get a name out of me. That's what you meant when you said you were here to *explain* things. When you said *things*, you meant her."

"Christine, I know this doesn't look good. I can't even imagine what's going through your mind right now, but we don't know what this means. We shouldn't jump to conclusions."

"She isn't wearing a shirt, Detective."

"And there might be a perfectly valid explanation for that. Maybe when the divers pulled her out of the car, her clothes . . ." He let the words dangle, the look on his face making it clear he'd drawn the same conclusion she had—the only conclusion that could be drawn when a half-nude woman was pulled from a man's car in the middle of the night.

Connelly shifted uneasily, his beefy shoulders bunched. "Was he—do you know if he was . . . seeing anyone?"

Christine glared at him, astonished. "You're asking if I knew my husband was having an affair? Like that's something we'd discuss over dinner?"

"I'm sorry. I thought maybe women had a sense about these things. Women's intuition or whatever you call it."

She eyed him coldly.

Connelly ran a hand through his thatch of gray hair. "Look, I'm just trying to do my job. I've got two years left in homicide, and I'm out. Until then, I do what they tell me. When they realized who they'd pulled out of the bay, they asked me to come down and talk to you. We've got a Jane Doe whose family is going to want to know why she didn't come home tonight, and we can't tell them until we know who she is."

Christine bristled at the inference that it was somehow her duty to help identify the half-nude woman. "I'm afraid I can't help you, Detective. Now if you don't mind, I'd like to go home. You said there were some papers I needed to sign."

Connelly stepped away briefly, returning a moment later with the clipboard Ryan had been scribbling on. He pointed to a line at the bottom then flipped the page, pointing to two additional lines. Christine signed without reading and pushed the clipboard back into his hands.

"Are we finished?"

"For now, yes. You'll get a copy of the report when the ME's finished his examination, and someone will call to let you know when you can come down and collect his things."

Christine stared at him blankly. "His things?"

"Keys. Wallet. Cell phone."

"Right. His things." She turned toward the door, fumbling in her pocket for her own keys.

"Here," Connelly said. "Let me walk you out."

"Thanks, no. I can find my way." She knew she should thank him for coming down in the middle of the night, but somehow she couldn't manage it.

She was almost to the door when he stopped her. "I'm sorry about this, Christine. Truly sorry. Stephen was a friend, but he was also a highly visible public figure. The media's going to want to know what happened. I'll do what I can to keep the details quiet, but I can't guarantee anything."

Christine nodded, then turned back toward the door, not sure whether she should feel gratitude or dread.

# TWO

It was half past four when Christine finally navigated the Range Rover back through the security gate and into the garage. For a time—she couldn't say how long—she simply sat there with the door open and the engine running. The sun would be up soon, the beginning of a new day. There would be people to call, details to handle, but she was too numb to think about any of that now. Instead, she sat in the eerie glow of the dashboard lights, wondering how her carefully ordered marriage had ended in such a spectacular derailment.

She had married an icon, a catch by any woman's standards. Not bad for a girl from the wrong side of the tracks. Stephen Ludlow. Even his name had conjured respect. And if he'd seen it as his job to smooth out her rough edges and make her over into a proper society wife, it was a small price to pay for the stability she had craved. But who was she now that Stephen was gone? A widow suddenly adrift, unmoored from a life that had never quite been hers.

*A widow.*

How was that even possible? Marriage had never been part of her plan. Far from it, in fact. She'd grown up hard and fast, the way most children of addicts did, and had learned a thing or two along the way.

At ten, she learned that no address was permanent, at twelve, that no promise was sacred, and at sixteen, that there was no such thing as safe. There were other lessons too. Lessons that were still etched in her mind—and her flesh.

She dragged back her coat sleeve, and stared at the trio of scars on her wrist, shiny and pale, like a constellation of tiny moons. Her badge of survival. Yes, she'd learned a thing or two growing up, including what happened when you trusted the wrong people.

And then she met Stephen. He was handsome and charming, a rising star in the publishing world. But even more appealing was the fact that he hadn't batted an eye when she informed him, quite emphatically, that children weren't part of her long-term plans. In fact, he'd seemed pleased. He was career minded and so was she. At least that was the excuse she'd given. They were married six months later. It wasn't a storybook marriage by any means, but then she'd never really bought into the whole happily-ever-after myth. Like most whirlwind romances, the early days had been about newness and chemistry, but over time their relationship had evolved into a kind of arm's length alliance, symbiotic and safe, steady. Or so she thought.

She glanced at the clock on the dash. Nearly five. How was it possible that so much could change in the space of three hours? And yet it had. Everything she knew—or thought she knew—about her life and her marriage had suddenly been turned on its ear. She closed her eyes, letting her head fall back against the headrest, waiting for the tears to come. Instead, her head filled with images—a ghost-white face caved in on one side, violet eyes staring at nothing.

*Who was she?*

But she was too numb to ponder that question right now, too sick and too weary to wade through scenarios that all seemed to point to the same terrible conclusion. Exhausted, she dragged her purse from the passenger seat and slid from behind the wheel.

There was a moment of disorientation as she stepped into the kitchen, as if she had accidentally wandered into someone else's home. She was used to the house being empty. For the last few years, Stephen had rarely been home for more than a week at a stretch. There was always somewhere he needed to be, another book tour, lecture, or talk show appearance. But this emptiness felt different. As if with Stephen gone, the house had lost some of its life force.

But then, it had always been Stephen's house. He'd become obsessed with the idea of living in the house Warner Brothers had used to shoot the ending of *Victim's Rights*, his third novel and the first in a series of grittier-than-life box office smashes—so obsessed that he'd made an offer on the place without bothering to consult her. That had been four years ago, about the time she started to realize what a small role she actually played in her own marriage.

She collapsed onto the sofa and unwound her scarf. The sun would be up soon, the morning news hitting the airwaves, newspapers landing on doorsteps. There were calls she needed to make: Stephen's agent, their lawyer, the insurance company. At least there were no family members to contact. Like her, Stephen had been an only child, and both his parents were dead; his father of a heart attack while Stephen was still in school, his mother of a cerebral hemorrhage two years ago. It was a terrible thing to be grateful for, but knowing what she did, she couldn't imagine having to tell his parents about the accident—or face them at his funeral.

She was in the process of unlacing her boots when the kitchen phone rang. By the time she got to it, the call had gone to voice mail. She waited for the recorded message to play out, then picked up when she heard Stephen's agent on the other end.

"I'm here, Gary."

"Tell me it's a mistake, Christine. Tell me what I just heard on the news isn't true."

"It isn't a mistake. Stephen's dead."

"What the hell happened?"

"The police said there was ice on the bridge. His car skidded into Echo Bay."

"Jesus, I'm sorry, Christine. This is . . . I can't believe it. I thought he was on his way to New York for a signing at the Strand. What the hell was he doing up near Echo Bay?"

Christine's grip tightened on the phone. She wasn't going there. Not now. Not ever, if she could help it. "He must have finished early and was trying to beat the weather home. Does it matter?"

"No. I suppose it doesn't. Are you sure there hasn't been some kind of mistake, though? Sometimes the police—"

"I saw him, Gary. They made me go down and identify his body."

"Jesus, God. I'm sorry. That must have been awful."

"It was."

"There are things—" He broke off. There was a brief stretch of silence before he went on. "Look, I'm not trying to be a bastard or anything. Stephen was a friend. But there are things we're going to need to talk about. Details."

"The medical examiner has to finish up before they can release Stephen's body. They didn't think it would be more than a few days. I suppose I could—"

There was an awkward clearing of his throat as Gary cut her off. "I wasn't talking about funeral arrangements, Christine. I meant contractual details, how things work when an author dies. Part of the advance for his next book has been paid out, and now—"

"Now he'll never finish it."

"Yes."

"I don't care about any of that, Gary. I never have. You know that. Just take care of it. Whatever needs to be done, do it."

"All right," he said, willing for the moment at least to let the subject drop. "We'll talk again when you've had some time. I didn't mean to get into this today. I just wanted you to be aware that there needs to be a conversation at some point, not that I have anything to tell you right now. I haven't spoken to anyone at Lloyd and Griffin yet. I'm sure they're still digesting the news like the rest of us, though I do expect my phone to start ringing any minute. My guess is yours will too. Tragedies sell, and the media's going to eat this one up with a spoon, Christine. Just remember, you don't have to talk to anyone until you're ready. Or ever really. Your grief isn't anyone's business but yours. In the meantime, I'll review the language in Stephen's contract about editorial control, and of course the royalties, which, as you know are fairly sizable. I do know he named you as his literary executor."

Christine was too fuzzy to digest what he was saying. "I don't know what that means."

"It means you decide how Stephen's work is handled going forward; copyright issues, movie rights, that sort of thing. But it's nothing you need to worry about right now. Right now, you need to take care of yourself and get through this. If there's anything you need, anything at all, I want you to pick up the phone. I mean it, Christine. Anything."

She was numb as she ended the call. She had only digested about half of what Gary said and wasn't sure she cared about the other half. The truth was she'd never had much of a grasp on how and when Stephen got paid. It had been hard enough when there were only three books. Now there were eleven, not counting *A Fatal Franchise*, which was set to release in eight weeks. The truth was she had no idea how much money Stephen had.

The statements arrived. The funds went into the bank. The bills got paid. As far as Stephen was concerned, that was all she needed to know, and she'd been largely okay with that. She'd never been comfortable talking about money, perhaps because as a freelance editor, she earned so little in comparison. She didn't even know the name of their broker.

The thought of what lay ahead left her exhausted as she mounted the stairs to the bedroom she and Stephen had shared. She desperately needed a shower, but the effort required to strip off her clothes was more than she could muster. Instead, she settled for brushing her teeth and washing her face. She was foraging in the medicine chest for the bottle of ibuprofen when the phone rang again.

The number wasn't one she recognized. She let the call go to voice mail, cringing as a reporter for the *Boston Globe* rambled through polite but curt condolences before finally getting around to business and asking for an interview. The message no sooner ended than the phone rang again. The *Portland Press Herald* this time, followed by the *Times*, the *Mirror*, and the *Dallas Morning News*.

She let them all go to voice mail. The messages were largely the same, a pretense at sympathy followed by a request for an interview with the widow. When the phone rang a fifth time, she turned off the ringer, did the same with the phone in the kitchen, then shut down her cell for good measure. Gary was right. Her grief—and anything else she might be feeling—was no one's business but her own.

Out of habit, she wandered back down to the kitchen and made coffee, then roamed the house with her mug, forgetting to sip as she lingered over things she and Stephen had collected over the years; a handblown glass bowl they had discovered in a tiny shop in Rockport; a lamp made of driftwood designed by an artist from Portsmouth; the Thomas Arvid oil painting that hung in the dining room, purchased on their honeymoon. How long ago it seemed now.

Eight years.

How had they slipped by so quickly? And how had she not noticed that things were changing—that Stephen was changing? Or maybe she'd just *pretended* not to notice.

Determined to shake the thought, she reached for the remote. The screen flared to life; a pair of talking heads behind the WGME news desk, with a bright-red breaking news banner crawling across the bottom. AUTHOR STEPHEN LUDLOW DIES IN CAR CRASH. It was bad enough seeing the words, but when Stephen's face flashed up on the screen—the headshot from the back cover of his last book—she sagged onto the sofa and turned up the sound.

"Police say Ludlow's car skidded off the Echo Bay Bridge and submerged in the chilly waters below. The cause of the accident is still under investigation, but it's believed that ice on the bridge was to blame for the crash. Divers recovered the body just after midnight. Ludlow is best known for his Craig Childress detective novels, several of which have been made into successful action films. Ludlow resided in Clear Harbor, Maine, and is survived by his wife, Christine. The couple had been married for eight years and had no children."

"No," Christine said, clicking off the set when coverage shifted to an apartment fire in Portland. "No children."

As if it was anyone's business. There had been questions, of course. Awkward, intrusive questions she never quite knew how to answer. *No children yet? How long have you been trying? Are you considering in vitro? Because if you are, there is a wonderful doctor at the new women's center in Portland who is having fabulous results.*

She never understood why people, women especially, assumed that every woman on the planet felt a bone-deep need to clone themselves for posterity. If they knew what she knew, seen what she'd seen, they'd know there were worse things than being childless—like having a child you weren't equipped to care for and scarring it for life.

She rose, carrying her coffee mug to the kitchen, then stood staring out the window over the sink. It had begun to snow, lazy flakes drifting down like small white wings. It was the third week of November, a little early for serious snow even in Maine, which meant it wasn't likely to hang around. Still, the sight of it accumulating on the deck was depressing.

Stephen had loved the New England winters. Or rather, he had loved the *idea* of them, of being holed up over the long, frigid months, pecking away in a study with tall windows that overlooked the sea. It was the image he liked, the way he wanted the world to see him.

But then, for Stephen everything had been about image. His career, the house, even their marriage had been carefully crafted to resemble something from the pages of a glossy magazine, as if real life had never quite been enough for him.

Perhaps that explained the blonde in the morgue. And yet, there was no proof that he'd actually been having an affair. Maybe Connelly was right. Maybe it wasn't what it looked like. Either way, the detective had kept his word. There'd been no mention of the Jane Doe on the news.

The sound of a car door slamming suddenly caught her attention. Traffic on Pulpit Rock Road was rare enough in season—locals mostly in their Volvos and Subarus—but after Labor Day, when Clear Harbor emptied for the season, cars were virtually nonexistent, though it wouldn't be the first time a tourist had ignored the PRIVATE ROAD sign and ventured out onto the point.

Curious, she padded to the living room and peered through the curtains, troubled to see that a handful of TV news trucks had gathered outside the front gates, looking like something from a bad sci-fi movie with their giant satellite dish antennas.

When in God's name had *that* happened?

# THREE

It had taken only a handful of days for Stephen's death to go from local tragedy to national obsession, and now, a week later, Christine couldn't turn on the TV without seeing some rehashed version of how the literary community had been tragically deprived of its brightest star. And if that wasn't enough, the number of media trucks outside the gate had been growing exponentially and were now accompanied by a throng of reporters peering through the fence.

She had yet to brave the mob. In fact, with the exception of a phone call to Dorsey and Sons to make arrangements for Stephen's memorial, she hadn't braved anything at all, choosing to remain cloistered, licking her wounds without the intrusion of phones, newspapers, or the Internet. But today she would have to leave her sanctuary. Today was Stephen's memorial.

She had expected to feel something like closure when she woke this morning, or at least the *promise* of closure, but all she felt was dread. She had managed to get through the morning, skipping breakfast to rake through her closet for something to wear to the service. Now, as she descended the stairs, she caught her reflection in the mirror at the end of the gallery, a dry-eyed ghost wearing the suit she had purchased two years ago for her mother-in-law's funeral.

She dreaded the day ahead, queasy at the thought of facing Stephen's friends, playing the grieving widow when the truth was she was quietly fuming. She hadn't let herself be angry at first, passing those early few days in a kind of haze. It seemed wrong somehow, to be angry with someone who had just died. But then out of nowhere she had been struck with a mix of fury and curiosity, propelling her to Stephen's study in search of the usual red flags—suspicious hotel bills, clandestine e-mails, lingerie receipts.

Initially, she had come up empty. But then she noticed a pattern of monthly autodrafts paid to Star Properties LTD. The name didn't ring any bells. For all she knew, Star Properties was one of the publicity firms Stephen used to book events and draft press releases. But there were also regular transfers to an account labeled TRAVEL—$4,000 drafted on the fifth of every month. Not that either was proof of an affair. It was entirely possible the payments were legitimate business expenses or that they were related to Stephen's investments. But her intuition told her they were not.

In the end, it was a photograph that provided confirmation. She'd been sitting at Stephen's desk, exhausted after her search, thinking, as she stared at a collection of photos on a nearby bookshelf, how little Stephen had aged over the years, when she noticed that in one of the shots his eyes were angled toward a small group of onlookers.

And there she was at the edge of the frame, wearing skintight jeans and four-inch heels, her heavily made-up eyes slanting boldly back at Stephen. It was the intimacy of the look that knocked the breath out of Christine, a private moment captured by chance, and for a moment, she found herself trying to remember if there had ever been a time when she and Stephen had looked at each other that way. If there was, she couldn't remember it. Was that Stephen's fault or hers? She couldn't say, but she felt the thought lodge itself in some dark corner of her mind, like a pebble in a shoe that could be ignored for a while but would eventually have to be dealt with.

The case clock on the mantel chimed softly, reminding Christine that she had somewhere to be. But as she grabbed her purse from the kitchen counter, her eyes slid to the phone. She'd been checking her messages all week, hoping to hear back from Connelly, but so far there'd been nothing.

Eleven new messages awaited her when she pushed the button— reporters, colleagues, even offers of sympathy from neighbors who'd heard the news way down in Sarasota or wherever they went when the leaves began to fall. One by one, she deleted them, but paused when a familiar baritone filled the kitchen.

"Christine, it's Gary. Call me when you get this."

She hit "Save" and moved on, in no mood to deal with Stephen's agent. To her dismay, the message that followed was also from Gary. His voice sounded oddly strained. "It's me again. Please call me back so I know you're all right."

Was she all right?

Christine blew out a sigh. She appreciated him checking on her, but it was hard to say what constituted *all right* these days. She jabbed the button again. This time Gary's tone bordered on urgent.

"Christine—Jesus. Where the hell are you? I've been trying to reach you for two days now, and all I get is this damn machine. Call me as soon as you get this. We need to talk."

She rolled her eyes as she checked her watch. She had time for only one phone call before she had to leave, and it wasn't going to be about book advances and movie rights. She needed—no, she *deserved*—to at least know the name of the woman who had died with her husband.

She dialed Connelly's number from memory—after four failed attempts she knew it by heart. Not that she expected to catch him at his desk. He was always out on some investigation when she called, or in the middle of an interview. Today proved no different.

The woman who answered the phone informed her briskly that Detective Connelly was out of the office and promptly shunted her off to his voice mail. She left another message for what it was worth—the fifth by her count—and hung up. Maybe it was just coincidence that he was never available, but part of her wondered if he was purposely dodging her calls. Perhaps he'd learned more than he wanted to and was trying to spare her the truth. If so, he was wasting his time. That ship had sailed.

Christine checked the time once more and picked up her purse. She had a husband to memorialize. But first, she was going to have to navigate her way through the mob of reporters at the gate.

Her palms felt sticky as she backed the Rover out of the garage and down the driveway, then reached for the remote clipped to the driver's side visor. She thought Stephen was just being paranoid when he'd insisted on installing a perimeter fence and security gates—to keep out crazed fans and curiosity seekers, he'd explained—but now she was grateful. Though she doubted he had foreseen a time when the curiosity seekers would turn out to be members of the press clamoring for a glimpse of his widow.

The furor began the moment the gates began to slide back, reporters with notepads and cell phone cameras held aloft squeezing through the opening like a colony of fire ants. Apparently they'd seen the memorial notice in the *Herald* and were hoping to grab a quote as she left the house. The Rover lurched backward as she goosed the accelerator. She held her breath as she continued down the drive, eyes focused straight ahead as she inched past the gaggle of leering faces. Just a few more yards and she'd be home free.

She was about to breathe a sigh of relief when a meaty fist pounded on the driver's side window. She hit the brakes with a strangled yelp, glancing up in time to see a man in a red L.L. Bean parka plaster a newspaper against the glass. Suddenly, horribly, she understood. The reporters weren't here for a quote about Stephen's memorial. They were here to get her reaction to the grisly image staring back from the front page of the *Examiner*—the empty eyes of Stephen's Jane Doe.

## THE NAKED AND THE DEAD: MYSTERY BLONDE PULLED FROM STEPHEN LUDLOW'S CAR

The earth shifted as Christine stared at the headline, a slow, shuddering quake that only she seemed to notice. As if sensing her dismay, the reporters' questions ratcheted up, swelling from hungry clamor to full-blown frenzy. Frantic, she cast about for some route of escape, only to find herself hopelessly cut off from both the road and the open garage door. She was going to have to make a run for it.

They rushed her the instant her foot touched the driveway, like a pack of gulls after a toddler with a french fry. There was no scurrying for the front door. No scurrying anywhere. Instead, she was forced to elbow her way through the crush, eyes fixed desperately on the front door. If she could just get inside and bolt herself in, she'd be safe. But the reporters knew it too and collectively wedged themselves between her and the front steps, so that her only choice was to brave the gauntlet.

Lowering her head, she plunged into the fray, muscling past faces that seemed to blur into a single, greedy entity bent on blocking her path. She was nearly sobbing by the time she reached the front door, so shaken she almost dropped her house key. She had lost her scarf somewhere in the press, and the top button on her jacket was hanging by a thread, but she didn't care. All she cared about was reaching sanctuary.

"Mrs. Ludlow!" A woman's voice suddenly rose above the din. "Do you know the woman they pulled from your husband's car the night he died and were they involved sexually?"

A momentary hush fell as the mob waited for a response. When none came, the questions resumed.

"Can you comment on the fact that she wasn't wearing any clothes when they pulled her from the car?"

"The police are still referring to the woman as Jane Doe. Can you tell us her name?"

"Do you know how long the relationship had been going on?"

"Have there been other women, or was she the first?"

Christine nearly wept as her house key slid home. By the time she pushed inside and shot the deadbolt, she was gulping back tears. She had no idea how long she stood there, too shaken to make her legs move, but suddenly she knew she was going to be sick. Panicked, she dropped her purse and scrambled for the kitchen where she retched over the sink until she was limp-limbed and quaking all over. She'd never been comfortable in crowds, but a mob of reporters hurling questions about her dead husband's mistress was an entirely new level of discomfort.

After splashing her face and pulling a bottle of water from the refrigerator, she wandered back to the living room, careful to steer clear of the windows. Her purse was still on the floor. She bent to pick it up, then froze when she spotted a rumpled copy of the *Examiner* inside, no doubt the work of one of the reporters in the scrum.

Her hands trembled as she smoothed out the wrinkles. The photo had clearly been taken at the morgue. But by whom? And how had it ended up on the front page of a national tabloid? Jane Doe's face stared back at her in grainy black and white, her once vivid violet eyes reduced to a nondescript shade of gray. It took all the strength she had to keep turning pages until she located the actual story: a grisly two-page spread along with another splashy headline:

CAN YOU IDENTIFY THIS WOMAN?

There were four additional photos scattered throughout the article, each more disturbing than the last. The first was an enlarged shot and very blurry, and yet there was no mistaking the crescent-shaped birthmark on the woman's right breast, highlighted now with a circle of bright-red ink. The next two shots were of her face, one taken straight on, the other in profile. The last photo was a shot of her lying on the gurney, the polished toes of her right foot peeking obscenely from the sheet draped over the lower half of her body.

The story itself was no better, full of dark implications and gruesome innuendo, though given the evidence, it was hard to draw any conclusion but the obvious one. Christine stared at the blackout boxes strategically placed over the woman's breasts, certain their purpose had less to do with journalistic discretion than with heightening curiosity. Everything about the piece—the explicit photos, the celebrity name, the untimely death of a beautiful blonde—bore the distinct whiff of erotic tragedy, conjuring names like Mansfield and Monroe, as had no doubt been intended. Only this blonde *had* no name.

Though it was only a matter of time until the press learned her identity and went digging for the rest of the story. Battling a fresh wave of nausea, she reached for the TV remote and began surfing. It didn't take long—only three clicks—to find Stephen's face splashed across the screen. And hers. The picture was from their vacation in Barbados three years ago. How had they gotten it?

"Stephen and Christine Ludlow were married in 2008" the *Entertainment Tonight* anchor was saying as a fresh round of photographs appeared on screen. "By all accounts, their marriage had been a happy one. But recent developments are raising questions about whether Ludlow might have been romantically involved with the scantily clad woman whose photos have now appeared in several tabloids. No identification was found when divers retrieved her body from Ludlow's car. Authorities tell us the investigation into the woman's identity is ongoing. Ludlow's wife has been unavailable for comment. We'll continue to keep you updated on this story as information becomes available."

Christine clicked, then clicked again, running through the list of cable news channels. The story was everywhere. Different talking heads, different photos, but the gist of the coverage was the same. Iconic author dies while cheating on wife with mystery blonde. Only now the story wasn't just about Stephen or even the Jane Doe. It had become about her too.

In the kitchen, she picked up the phone and punched in the number for the Clear Harbor police. This time, when the desk sergeant answered, she refused to be handed off to Connelly's voice mail.

"No, I do *not* want to leave a message," she barked irritably. "I've left messages. Five of them to be precise, for all the good they've done me. So what I need you to do right now is put me on hold and go find him. Don't come back and tell me he's in an interview or out on a case. I'm a case. My dead husband is a case. So unless you want me to come down there and camp out in the lobby, you'll put him on the phone."

There was no response, just a curt click followed by empty silence as she was put on hold. While she waited, she picked up her water bottle and pressed it to her cheek, then her neck, wondering what excuse she'd be given this time. She nearly dropped the phone when Connelly's voice came over the line.

"Christine, I'm sorry. I've been swamped. As I'm sure you've seen, there's been . . . a development."

"Yes, I've seen," she snapped. "I've seen that my driveway is so full of reporters I can't get out to attend my husband's memorial service. I thought you said you could keep things quiet."

There was a long pause, then a gravelly rumble as Connelly cleared his throat. "There was a leak, Christine. It sucks, but it happens. If the brass ever finds out who it was, they'll be fired, but at this point the genie's out of the bottle."

"The genie's out of the bottle? That's what you have to say to me after a reporter just stuck a half-naked picture of your Jane Doe in my face? That's how I found out about the leak. Not a phone call—a mob of reporters on my front steps."

"I didn't mean it like that, Christine, and I'm sorry. But it all just blew up. The pictures are out there, and the media wants to know what we know."

"And what *do* you know?"

There was another long pause, the sound of a heavy breath being let out slowly. "Unfortunately, not much more than we did the night of the accident. We got a few tips this morning after the photos broke. We're checking them out, but in cases like this, you tend to get a lot of crackpots. So far there's nothing concrete. Whoever she was, no one's looking for her. At least not yet."

"So what do I do? I live on a private road, and I can't get out of my house. They're practically camped out on my front porch. I can't even close the front gates."

"I'll send a car around to move them off your property and clear the street. I can't guarantee they won't be back, but for now at least, we can give you a little breathing room."

"And you'll call me when you finally know something?"

"Christine." His voice was annoyingly paternal. "Sometimes the best thing for everyone is to just move on, to remember the good times instead of dwelling on a lot of unpleasantness. A name isn't going to change anything. Why not leave the police business to us, hmm?"

"Because we're not talking about police business, Detective. We're talking about my life. My husband. My marriage. My driveway. So please don't condescend to me. The way I see it a wife's right to know the truth trumps a friend's desire to sweep his poker buddy's indiscretions under the rug. Come to think of it, you didn't seem all that surprised that there was a woman in my husband's car the night he died."

"Christine—"

"You knew, didn't you? Maybe not her name, but you knew there was someone."

Another sigh, this one weightier than the last. "I wasn't sure, but I suspected. He'd let a few things slip now and then. Nothing specific, just . . . things. He never mentioned a name, though, and I never pressed him for one."

"Of course not. That would be breaking the rules."

"Rules?"

"The cheater's club or whatever you call it. All for one and one for all. Isn't that how it works?"

"Look, Christine, I know this hasn't been easy for you, especially the way it all went down, but one thing I do know is that Stephen—"

"Don't!" she snapped, cutting him off. "Don't you dare say he loved me. That isn't why I called, to have you reassure me that a half-naked woman in my husband's car doesn't mean anything. She means something to me. I think I have the right to at least know her name—and I don't mean by reading it in the tabloids. It's been a week, and honestly, I'm beginning to wonder if you're not dragging your feet on purpose."

"What is it you're accusing me of?" The paternal tone was gone, replaced with a gruff wariness.

"I'm not accusing you of anything. All I want is a name. And the number or address of someone who might be able to tell me what was going on between that woman and my husband."

"Look, I don't have the information you want, but even if I did, I couldn't share it with you. Victims have rights, Christine. So do their families. In other words, there are rules. And if we break those rules, we get in trouble. I've put in a whole lot of years here and put up with a whole lot of crap. At this point, all I want is to get out and spend a few years on a little sailboat down in the Keys. I'm not about to stick my neck out, not even for the wife of a friend. I know that sounds harsh, but I have to look out for myself here. Stephen's death wasn't a homicide, which means I'm not even the guy you should be talking to. If anything, it's a missing-persons case, and it's not even that since no one's filed an actual complaint on her. Either way, it's not my purview. Now I need to go do my job. I'll make sure they send that patrol car around, but I'm sorry, that's all I can do."

And just like that Daniel Connelly was gone.

Christine was still leaning against the counter, wondering why she'd just been given the brush-off, when the phone rang. She pounced on it, hoping Connelly had changed his mind. Instead, it was Dorsey and Sons. In the mayhem, she had forgotten that Stephen's friends and colleagues were at that very moment gathering to pay him tribute—and wondering what had happened to the widow.

As it turned out, she needn't have worried. Apparently, the barrage of breaking news had whittled the number of mourners to an awkward handful. But then that really wasn't surprising. Who in their right mind would want to look her in the eye now, let alone gush about what a great guy she'd married?

Using the vaguest language possible, she explained that she had been unavoidably detained and wasn't likely to get there anytime soon. Mr. Dorsey, presumably one of the sons, was delicacy itself as he inquired about how best to proceed. In the end, she advised him to cancel the service but to go ahead with the cremation, which he had agreed to do in tones that could be described only as painfully polite. He hadn't come right out and said so, but she was certain he'd seen the photos. Everyone had by now. Apparently the old adage was true—the wife really was the last to know.

Two hours later, Christine caught the sharp *whoop-whoop* of a police siren out in front of the house. She hurried to the living room window, peering out in time to see a Clear Harbor patrol car inching up the crowded drive, blue lights flashing. The officer stepped out and began waving his arms, gesturing to the No Trespassing signs posted at regular intervals along the fence. There was a brief bit of protest, but eventually the gaggle began filing toward the open gates.

Christine watched as the driveway slowly emptied, and one by one, the news trucks pulled away. When the last truck was gone, she stepped to the control panel in the foyer and closed the front gates, then returned to the window to double-check. She stood there for a time, staring at the empty street, trying to locate something like relief. For the first time in seven days, there was no one camped out in front of the house, no reporters lying in wait.

It took all the energy she could summon to drag herself up to the bedroom and shuck off her funeral clothes. She was thinking about the scarf she had lost somewhere in the driveway when she heard a clatter out on the terrace. Curious, she stepped to the doors and peered past her reflection, stunned to find a reporter pointing a camera at her as she stood there in nothing but a pair of panties.

Too alarmed to scream, she dropped to a crouch, dragging the duvet from the bed and wrapping it around her as she dove for the phone. On realizing he'd been discovered, the intruder abandoned his shot and scrambled for the stairs, stumbling briefly as he hurdled a patio chair, then streaked for the back fence. A moment later, he was gone.

Christine looked at the phone in her hand. Dialing 911 wasn't going to solve anything. She had managed to scare off one intruder, but there would be more, climbing the fence, peering in her windows, rushing her car the next time she tried to leave the house. They would never leave her alone.

Unless she wasn't here.

With an almost eerie calm, she stood and went to the closet, pulled on a pair of jeans and a faded Patriots sweatshirt, then dragged her old weekender from the top shelf. She wouldn't need much: jeans, a few pairs of leggings, a couple of sweaters, her toiletry case from under the bathroom sink. And the contents of the safe.

When her bag was packed, she headed for the study, ignoring the framed photo still lying facedown on the desk as she punched in the safe code, waited for the light on the keypad to go green, then blindly raked the contents into her purse: insurance policies, investment records, passports, birth certificates, and the envelope containing Stephen's emergency cash—in case of a zombie apocalypse, he had once joked. Leave it to Stephen to think he could buy his way out of the end of the world.

She closed the safe and was preparing to leave when she looked down at her left hand, at the ring that symbolized her marriage—a colorless two-carat emerald cut. Nothing but the best for the wife of Stephen Ludlow. It slid easily from her finger; apparently she'd lost weight after a week of subsisting on tea and toast. Her hand felt strangely light, but there was no sense of guilt as she placed the ring on the desk. Stephen had walked away from their marriage some time ago. Now it was her turn.

She held her breath as she peered out the front windows. As far as she could tell, the coast was still clear, no news trucks parked outside the gate, no photographers crouching in the boxwoods. Breath held, she shouldered her bags, stepped out onto the porch, and made a break for the Rover sitting in the middle of the driveway.

Her heart hammered as she scrambled up behind the wheel, locked all four doors, and started the engine. The gates slid soundlessly as she pressed the remote, and then she was through them with nothing but empty road before her.

The exhilaration was almost heady, but unsettling too as the memory of another night—another hastily packed bag, another breathless getaway—came rushing at her. It was hard not to see the irony. At the age of sixteen, she had slipped out of a house in the middle of the night and run for all she was worth. Now, twenty years later, she was running again.

# FOUR

*Christy-Lynn hunches deeper into her jacket as she moves down the puddled sidewalk, kicking herself for not leaving her math and science books in her locker. It's ridiculously cold, even for January, and an icy rain is falling. She keeps her head down, drawn in like a turtle's beneath her oversize hood, limiting her field of vision to the three feet of pavement directly in front of her.*

*Her hands are numb with cold, clenched into fists and thrust deep in her pockets. Her apartment key is there. She turns it over in her fingers, already anticipating the cup of hot chocolate she'll make when she reaches the apartment—if there's any left. At this point, she'll settle for tea. As long as it's hot.*

*She quickens her pace when the sign for the Palm Manor Apartments comes into view, the painted letters flaking off into what might once have been a garden, but is now just a muddy puddle littered with candy wrappers and cigarette butts. Only a few more steps and she'll be inside, warm and dry, with a mug of something hot to drink. And her copy of* The Outsiders.

*It was supposed to be homework for Mrs. Kendrick's English class, but it didn't feel like homework at all. How could reading be work when you got to meet people and go places you'd never be able to go in real life? She smiles as she thinks of Cherry and Ponyboy, the movie-star-handsome Sodapop. They have become her friends, outsiders like her, from the wrong side of town. Except they have one another, and she has no one, a freak loner from an entirely different world than kids who wore name-brand jeans and went home to real houses. It might be nice to belong to a gang—not the drug-selling, gun-toting kind of gang—just a few kids who wouldn't tease her for wearing thrift store clothes and bringing her lunch in a brown paper bag.*

*She's still weighing the pros and cons of gang membership when the rain-drenched quiet is broken by a sharp string of oaths. "Goddamn rain! Every goddamn time I gotta boot somebody out, it goddamn rains!"*

*Christy-Lynn jerks her head up, knocking the hood back from her face as she searches for the source of the swearing, then freezes when she spots a mound of clothing and furniture on the soaking wet steps outside their apartment. And then she's running with the rain in her eyes and a knot in her stomach, running toward a man carrying the mismatched lamps her mother had brought home from Goodwill a few months back.*

*"What are you doing? That's our stuff!"*

*"And that's my apartment," the man says, jerking a thumb at the open apartment door. He's tall and beefy, wearing a soggy wife-beater and dirty gray overalls. "'Less you got six hundred dollars on you. But I'm guessin' you don't—any more than your mama did."*

*"But you can't! She isn't even here!"*

*"I can," he barks back. As if to make his point, he drops both lamps onto the soggy heap of household belongings. The larger of the two rolls off the pile and onto the pavement with a sickening pop as the bulb implodes. "Says so right in the lease your old lady signed when she moved in. Two months late, you're out."*

*A boy carrying an armload of towels and pillows appears in the door-way. He's not much older than she is—fourteen or fifteen—a younger version of his father, with the same yellow hair, hard jaw, and cold eyes. He fires the pillows out onto the pile from where he stands, then aims a hard little smile at her. It isn't the first time he's helped his father evict someone.*

*Eviction.*

*The word fills her with shame. She knows things have been tight, that her mother's been struggling to make ends meet, stretching the groceries with hot dogs and boxed mac and cheese, but she never realized it was this bad. No wonder she's been picking up extra shifts at the Piggly Wiggly. And why she always looks so worn-out, like little by little she's coming apart at the seams.*

*Christy-Lynn is still staring at the sopping heap of their belongings, her gaze locked on a fuzzy purple foot—the stuffed dinosaur her mother had given her for her sixth birthday—when something, a bit of sound or movement, suddenly catches her eye. Her stomach lurches as the curtains part in the window overhead and a pair of faces appear. And they aren't the only ones watching. All around the complex, people are peering through windows or hovering in doorways, looking on as the scene plays out. Their watching makes it worse somehow.*

*She shoves down the urge to cry. What good will crying do? She needs to call her mother, to tell her what's happening, only her boss doesn't like her getting calls at work, and the last thing they need right now is for Charlene Parker to get fired. Besides, there's no way to call. Even if the landlord were to let her back into the apartment—which she was willing to bet he wouldn't—the phone had been shut off weeks ago.*

*The landlord's son appears again, this time with an armload of pots and pans, including the cast-iron skillet her mother uses to make corn bread. He drops them onto the stoop with a clatter, then turns back to take a box his father is holding out. It looks like cleaning supplies from under the kitchen sink, window cleaner, cleanser, dish soap, a half-used roll of paper towels. She watches as the cardboard darkens in the rain, the roll of paper towels slowly wilting.*

It's the paper towels that finally push Christy-Lynn to the edge, the sight of them slumping in the sharp, icy rain is simply too much to bear. They don't have much, a fact that's hard to dispute when everything they own now sits in one ghastly pile on the stoop. Is it too much to ask that he spare their roll of paper towels? A wave of rage suddenly boils up in her, mingled with a throat full of tears she struggles to swallow. It isn't the unfairness of it; if they're really two months behind in their rent, he has the right to evict them. But did he really need to toss their stuff out into the rain while everyone watched?

The son reappears with a stack of plates and mugs. He sets them down on the sidewalk, then drops the dish towels he has wadded under his arm into a puddle. For a moment, she considers charging him, knocking him off his feet and pummeling him bloody, but he's too big for that.

"Your father's a bastard, you know that?" she chokes out instead, hating that she can't keep the tears from bleeding into her words.

He stares at her a moment through the rain, his straw-colored hair plastered flat to his head, then shrugs. "If there's stuff you want, you best get busy." He bends down and reaches into the carton of cleaning supplies, coming up with a box of plastic trash bags. He tosses the box to her without aiming. "If this stuff ain't off the sidewalk in the next hour, it's going in the dumpster."

Christy-Lynn watches mutely as the landlord's son disappears back into the apartment. And then finally, because there's nothing else to do, she stoops to pick up the box of trash bags, rips one from the roll, and begins stuffing handfuls of wet clothes into it.

# FIVE

Wade Pierce stared at the blinking cursor with gritty eyes. It still wasn't right. Three hours on one damn scene, and it *still* wasn't right. Nor was bashing away at it for another three hours likely to fix the problem. It wasn't the scene; it was him. He was edgy and unfocused, buzzy from way too much coffee. Frazzled, he shoved back from the table and padded to the fridge for a Mountain Dew, then opted for a bottle of water instead. The last thing he needed was more caffeine. He took a long pull as he opened the sliding glass doors and stepped out onto the deck.

The air was heavy and gray, thick with the scent of damp ground and distant wood smoke. It was a good smell, an earthy smell. No bus fumes or car exhaust. No reek of trash or piss-soaked alleys. He filled his lungs, scanning the rolling hills that rimmed the town of Sweetwater. The foliage that had set the hilltops ablaze in recent weeks was gone now, leaving behind a landscape that seemed to mirror his mood of late, chilly and barren, devoid of color. Maybe a city boy trying to live off the grid wasn't such a good idea after all. Or maybe he was just sick of his own company.

It had seemed like a good idea at the time—getting away. Okay, running away if he was being truthful. To finally get back to doing something that fed his soul instead of just his bank account. Only it wasn't working. He liked to pretend running off to the wilds to live like a hermit had been about getting in touch with his muse, but it hadn't. At least not entirely.

He'd been hoping for peace, maybe some kind of closure after his abrupt and somewhat volatile departure from *Week in Review*. But coming to Sweetwater hadn't brought him anything remotely close to peace. Instead, he spent the better part of each day questioning the wisdom of chasing a dream he should have buried twenty years ago.

A novelist. After all the lost years, all the sporadic fits and starts, he was back at it again. Which could only mean he needed his head examined. There were guys who were born with the Midas touch, the Stephen Ludlows of the world, karmic alchemists who despite breaking all the rules never failed to turn dross into gold, who with little or no effort enjoyed fame, fortune, and the adoration of millions. Not to mention getting the girl—the kind who stood by you no matter what. And then there were guys like him, who walked the straight line and kept their noses to the grindstone, but always seemed to end up at the back of the line.

Hell, maybe it was time to pack it in and go back to New York, reclaim his reputation as one of the city's premier journalists. Except there really wasn't much to go back to. He'd quit his job and lost his wife pretty much in one go. As for Ludlow, that was ancient history. Holding a grudge about something that happened twenty years ago had been a handy excuse, but it was time to own the choice he'd made all those years ago to walk away from his writing. And so he would stay in this place, where he'd spent every summer of his childhood fishing with his grandfather, and do what he'd come here to do. Win or lose, he would finish the book and take his shot.

Staring out over the lake now, he thought of his grandfather, of sticky afternoons spent on the water, waiting for something to bite. The old man was gone now, God rest his soul, and the cabin belonged to him, though it had been empty for more years than he cared to count. It had been strange at first, being back. He'd spent the first three months getting the place in shape, updating fixtures and appliances, bringing the plumbing and wiring up to code. It was comfortable now, in a barebones, back-to-the-land sort of way. Best of all, there was no television, no phone, and no Wi-Fi. Other than the cell phone he kept for emergencies or an occasional conversation with the mailman, he was blissfully cut off from the world. And that was exactly how he liked it. If there was a blizzard on the way, his phone would alert him, and if it was the end of the world, he'd just as soon not know.

The wind was picking up, swirling the dun-colored leaves at the corners of the deck into papery little tornadoes. To the west, the slow, brooding clouds that had lingered over the hills most of the day had darkened to an ominous shade of pewter. It would storm soon, and he was fine with that. He had nowhere to be and nothing to do, and he wrote better when it was raining.

He had just turned to head back inside when he heard his cell going off. It rang so rarely these days it took a moment to register what he was hearing. Stepping in off the deck, he grabbed the phone from the top of the fridge, expecting it to be Justin saying he was on his way with the cord of wood he had ordered last week.

"Wade! Buddy! How the hell are you?"

Okay, not Justin. Wade scrambled to connect the voice with a face, finally landing on Glen Hoyt, *Week in Review*'s top crime beat writer. They had teamed up on a few pieces—dirty politicians, contractors lining their pockets on the city's dime. When it came to digging up dirt,

Glen was everybody's go-to guy. He had also tried to talk him out of leaving *Review*.

"Glen. What's up?"

Glen barked out a laugh, and for a moment, Wade could see him leaning back in his chair, battered wingtips propped up on his desk. "Yeah, it's me. Just calling to see if you're ready to rejoin the rat race."

"Let me guess, Killian put you up to calling."

"No, but I'm sure our beloved editor in chief would kill to get his hooks back in you. Though after the way things went down, I'm guessing that's not going to happen. You, uh . . . you gave it to him pretty straight."

"Someone had to."

"Maybe, but Jesus, man—calling the guy a blackhearted bastard in front of the whole newsroom? That's a little over the top, don't you think?"

"Truth in reporting."

"More like burning your bridges."

"You only need bridges if you're planning to go back, and I'm not."

"Okay, I get it. But you can't blame me for trying. Place isn't the same since you left. Killian's gone through three guys trying to replace you. The last one was the worst yet. Bastard couldn't lock down a story with both hands and a lug wrench." A brief silence fell. Glen cleared his throat. "So . . . have you heard from Simone?"

Wade winced at the mention of his ex-wife's name. He'd been preparing himself for the question, but it caught him off guard, like a punch you saw coming that still knocked the wind out of you. "Why would I hear from Simone?"

"I don't know. Old times, I guess. She left right after you did."

"No," Wade said flatly. "I haven't heard from her. We don't have much to talk about anymore. The judge tied everything up nice and neat."

"Damn. That sucks. I was hoping you guys would patch it up, though I heard a while back that she was seeing someone."

The silence yawned as Glen's words sank in. *Seeing someone.* Yes, of course she was. It wasn't Simone's MO to fly solo for very long. She needed a wingman, an alter ego to feed off, someone to fill in her blanks. He'd been that for a while.

"What Simone's up to is none of my business, Glen."

"Sure. Sure. I just thought you might, you know, be carrying a torch."

"No. No torch."

"Right. Good. Guy's some hotshot with WKPR. Tall, dark, and hair sprayed. Does the evening news. I think they might be living together."

Wade set down his bottled water and reached into the fridge for a beer. He twisted off the top, tossed it into the sink, and took a long pull. He wasn't sure why the news stung. Simone had always wanted to make the switch from print to television. God knew she had the looks—not to mention the instincts necessary to claw her way up the food chain.

"You still there, man?"

Wade started. "What? Oh, yeah. Just, you know . . . busy."

"Oh good. For a minute there, I thought I lost you. So what's the deal with the book? I know you said you were finally going to finish it. How's that going?"

"Good," Wade replied, hating the lie. "Just polishing, you know."

"Yeah, you were always a polisher. All the *i*'s dotted, all the *t*'s crossed. Every word chosen for maximum impact. Killian really screwed up when he let you get away."

Wade checked his watch, suddenly eager to end the call. "Listen, I'm in a kind of time crunch here with the edits, but anytime you want to come down to the cabin to do a little fishing, you let me know."

"Phone works both ways, man. I'm here if you need me. I mean it. Anything."

Wade ended the call, drained what remained of his beer, then promptly reached for another, hoping to drown the memories of his time at *Week in Review*. Not that it was all bad. In fact, in the beginning it was pretty amazing. The pace had been grueling, but he'd relished the work. He had interviewed POWs and Holocaust survivors; the victims of rape, incest, racism, and mass shootings; the survivors of oil tanker explosions; and wives who lost firefighter husbands when the towers fell on 9/11. And somewhere in there he'd even managed to snag himself a Hearst Award.

But as time went by, the lines between news and sensationalism began to blur, and word came down from on high that human interest was dead. They wanted shock and fear, blood and gore, the gruesome tick-tock of human tragedy, because fear outsold hope and always would.

Things finally reached critical mass when Killian ordered him to interview a survivor from the Crystal Lake Middle School shooting; a twelve-year-old whose mother—a teacher's aide—had been shot and killed while standing just three feet away. That's where he had drawn the line and walked away, though not before letting Killian and an entire newsroom full of reporters know exactly what he thought.

It was a habit he had, saying what was on his mind. Usually without thinking before he opened his mouth and frequently in the presence of witnesses. Not that he regretted a word of what he'd said to Killian that day. There were people who needed a dose of truth now and then. Killian was one of them. Stephen Ludlow had been another.

# SIX

*Clear Harbor, Maine*
*November 29, 2016*

Traffic was virtually nonexistent as Christine pulled onto the highway. Good riddance, she thought as the Rover's headlights swept past the dirty remnants of yesterday's snowfall mounded around the guardrail. She didn't know where she was headed. She only knew there wouldn't be snow on the ground when she got there.

What she needed was a tiny town in the middle of nowhere, preferably one where they'd never heard of Stephen Ludlow, where she could lay low and take stock of what remained of her life. If only such a place existed. It didn't of course. The *Examiner* had seen to that. But with a few days head start, she might be able to disappear until the fervor died down—or some new bit of schadenfreude captured the world's attention.

In the meantime, she needed to put as much distance as possible between herself and Clear Harbor. The only question was how far she'd be able to go before fatigue and the reality of what she'd done finally caught up with her.

Two hours later, she had her answer. Her eyes had begun playing tricks on her several miles back, and more than once, she'd found herself mesmerized by the strobe effect of the highway's broken white lines. She had no idea where she was when she finally stopped for gas, but she was glad for the chance to stretch her legs.

She took a chance on the ladies' room, which reeked of bleach and cherry air freshener, then bought a pair of bottled waters and several packs of Nabs. This wasn't her first rodeo; she had subsisted for days on nothing but water and peanut butter crackers, and the less she stopped, the less likely she was to be recognized. She wasn't sixteen anymore, wasn't flat broke, wasn't worried about seeing her face on a runaway poster, but somehow the stakes felt just as high. In fact, she'd spent a good portion of the drive dusting off her street smarts. Never use your real name. Pick one alias and stick with it. Cut your hair. Cover any tattoos. Lose the jewelry.

As she pulled back onto the highway, she glanced at her hands on the steering wheel, the ring finger of her left hand conspicuously bare. She'd taken care of the jewelry, at least.

The sun was on the wane when she finally crossed over into Virginia. She had eaten the last pack of crackers sometime around noon, and whatever benefit she'd reaped from the hour of sleep grabbed at a New Jersey rest stop had long since worn off. She needed food and sleep, and she needed them soon. Unfortunately, she hadn't a clue where she was. Perhaps it was time to pull out the atlas and just pick a destination.

As it turned out, she didn't need the atlas. She had gone only a few miles when she spotted a billboard for HISTORIC DOWNTOWN SWEETWATER. The name felt familiar, conjuring images of cobbled streets and tiny hole-in-the-wall galleries, a quaint inn with a wishing well in back—and Stephen. Without meaning to, she had stumbled onto one of the tiny towns they had visited on their honeymoon.

They had stayed at a small inn whose name she couldn't recall, had eaten fish and chips at a pub called the Rusty Nail, and then hung around for trivia. They'd been happy then, newlyweds with the whole world before them. What had happened to that couple?

On impulse, she peeled off at the exit and followed the main road through the center of town. Not much had changed. The town was small and picturesque, the sidewalks lined with trendy shops and locally owned cafés. Her mouth watered at the thought of food, but her first order of business was finding a place to sleep.

She pulled into the parking lot of the first inn she saw, an old converted farmhouse called the Fife and Feather. It was small but charming; two stories of clean white clapboard fronted with black shuttered windows and a small porch of weathered brick.

A wreath of magnolia leaves and creamy satin ribbon hung on the front door, reminding Christine with a bit of a jolt that Thanksgiving had come and gone. In the chaos after Stephen's death, the holiday had simply slipped her mind, along with the turkey she had ordered from Longley's. She was still wondering what had become of the unclaimed bird as she stepped into the Fife and Feather's cozy lobby, a snug, low-ceilinged room decorated with shaker furniture and primitive American folk art.

"Hey there!" A pretty blonde stood grinning behind the registration counter. She looked to be in her thirties, but there was an air of prom queen about her too, perky and bright with her messy bun and shimmery pink lips. "Welcome to the Fife and Feather."

Christine ran a hand through her hair, painfully aware of her bedraggled appearance. "I was driving by and saw the VACANCY sign. I'm hoping you still have a room available."

The woman's smile widened as she produced a registration form from somewhere below the counter. "You're in luck. The leaf peepers are gone, and it's too early for Christmas guests. You can pretty much take your pick. What brings you to Sweetwater?"

"I'm, uh . . . just passing through."

"So just the one night then?"

"Yes. Just one night."

"Well, we're happy to have you. I'm Missy Beck, by the way—the owner. And since we're so quiet, I'm going to put you in my favorite room. It was actually the library back when the Holcombes owned it. The bookcases are all original."

Christine didn't have the heart to tell her she wouldn't be paying attention to much of anything except the bed. "Does the inn serve dinner?"

"Sorry. I'm afraid we're limited to breakfast. But I can offer you one of these to take the edge off." She held out a plate of what appeared to be freshly baked oatmeal cookies.

Christine took a cookie, nibbling politely. "I don't suppose the Rusty Nail is still in business, by any chance?"

Missy looked surprised. "The Nail's been closed for years. It's a pizza place now, and a pretty good one if that's what you're in the mood for. I take it you've been to Sweetwater?"

Christine nodded. "Years ago, on my honeymoon."

"Oh, nice. Is your husband traveling with you this time through?"

"No, he's . . . I'm a widow." The word stopped her cold. It was the first time she'd said it out loud, and it surprised her how easily it had slipped from her tongue.

Missy reached across the counter to give her hand a squeeze. "Oh, honey, I'm sorry. And you, so young. Was it sudden?"

"Yes. He was—" She paused, realizing she was about to say too much. "He drowned." It wasn't a lie, but it wasn't the truth either—at least not all of it. She closed her eyes briefly, trying to dislodge the images that had been haunting her for days. *Had he been conscious?*

*Had he struggled, and if so, for how long before the water had finally filled his lungs?*

Missy's gray-green eyes filled with sympathy. "You poor thing. I have a friend who lost her husband a year ago, and I've seen what she's gone through. I know it's hard in the beginning, but it does get easier. Tomorrow will be better, and then the day after that. As long as you have friends, you can get through anything."

Christine managed what she hoped would pass for a smile as she reached for the registration form. She was grateful for the words of comfort. She even wanted to believe them. But if things getting better was dependent on having a circle of friends, she was out of luck. There were a handful of women from the club she had socialized with now and then, most of them the wives of Stephen's friends. A few had even sent cards filled with condolences, but that's as far as it went—and as far as Christine wanted it to go.

"I'm sorry," Missy blurted. "You were asking about dinner, and as usual, I went down a rabbit hole. I'd definitely recommend the Cork and Cleaver. It's right next door, and the food is wonderful. Queenie Peterson owns it. She's a friend of mine, so I'm a little bit biased, but they really do have the best food in town."

Christine nodded vaguely, staring at the line on the registration form asking for her name. She didn't dare use Ludlow. Instead, she picked up the pen and printed the name she'd given up eight years ago when she married Stephen. From here on out, she was Christy-Lynn Parker. Now all she had to do was remember.

"Do I pay you for the room now?" she asked when she had completed the form.

"Tomorrow will be fine. Here's your key. Your room is at the top of the stairs. Breakfast is served until eleven in the room right off the stairs. There are no TVs in any of the rooms, but if you really want to know what's going on in the world, there's a television in the business center. Oh,

I almost forgot—" She paused, wrapping several cookies in a napkin, and passed them to Christine. "To tide you over until dinner. Enjoy your stay."

"Thank you. I'm sure I will."

Christy-Lynn's legs felt leaden as she mounted the stairs and made her way to the end of the gallery. She experienced a profound rush of relief as she locked her room door behind her. Safely and blessedly alone, she let her bags slide to the floor, too weary to do much beyond surveying her accommodations.

It was a bright, spacious room filled with period antiques, including a glorious four-poster bed dripping with vintage lace. And Missy hadn't exaggerated about the bookshelves; they were gorgeous, shelf after shelf stocked with classics bound in worn, jewel-toned leather. Defoe nestled beside du Maurier. Longfellow beside Kerouac. Unlikely friends standing shoulder to shoulder.

The thought brought a smile until she caught her reflection in the bureau mirror. With her stringy hair and rumpled clothes, she looked like a bag lady or an escapee from the local women's prison. What would Stephen say if he could see her now? Nothing good, that was certain. As his wife, her image had been his image, which meant no sweatpants at the market or messy ponytails at the drugstore. But then he wasn't around to criticize anymore. Still, she couldn't walk into a restaurant looking like she'd just crawled out of a dumpster.

Thirty minutes later, she emerged from the bathroom blissfully clean and smelling of the lavender bath gel Missy provided for her guests. The plan had been to dry her hair, pull on fresh clothes, and head next door for dinner, but the effort required to carry it out suddenly seemed Herculean. Instead, she fetched Missy's napkin-wrapped cookies from the pocket of her coat. They might not qualify as dinner, but she didn't have to get dressed to eat them.

She devoured them in minutes, still wrapped in her towel, then lay back against the creamy lace counterpane. Missy's words drifted through her head as she closed her eyes.

*Tomorrow will be better.*
She hoped so.

*Christy-Lynn Parker. Christy-Lynn Parker.*

The name seemed to throb like a drumbeat in her head as she strolled Sweetwater's downtown streets, a reminder that yesterday she had stepped out of one life and into another. It was a strange feeling to suddenly find yourself unmoored from your own life, to open your eyes in the morning and not know where you are, where you're going, or even what happens next. But it was liberating too, in a way, the delicious anonymity of simply blending into the scenery of a small town street. It had been years since she'd been able to blend into the scenery back in Clear Harbor.

She was heading for the corner deli, humorously named the Fickle Pickle, when her fingers began to cramp. She paused, shifting her shopping bags from one hand to the other. Hippie clothes, Stephen would have called her recent purchases. And maybe they were. They were certainly nothing like the sleek designer labels he preferred she wear, or even the cheap working girl separates she had worn in her early days at Lloyd and Griffin. In fact, now that she thought about it, she was surprised he'd bothered to give her a second look back then.

She'd been working as an editor's assistant, still brown-bagging it and driving an old Ford Tempo with wind-down windows when they met—hardly trophy wife material. Stephen had been on his way to a marketing lunch with his editor when she literally ran into him in the hall with an armload of cover posters. He had spoken first, apologizing when the collision had clearly been her fault. It irked her to think of it now—one flashed smile, and she'd gone all tongue-tied. He had canceled with his editor, inviting her for sushi instead, which she secretly hated but pretended to love. Six months later, they were married, and the pretending had become more complicated.

Christy-Lynn shook off the memory, redistributed her shopping bags, and continued on to the deli. She was reaching for the door when she spotted a sign for the Hair Lair next door and changed direction.

An entry chime sounded as she entered the shop. Other than the gum-chewing stylist leaning against one of the shampoo bowls the place was empty.

"Hey there. What can I do ya for?"

Christy-Lynn ran a hand through her shoulder-length hair, suddenly self-conscious. "I'm thinking about going short, maybe adding some highlights. Can you do that?"

"Honey, I can do whatever you want if you've got the time."

"I mean now. Can you do it right now?"

The woman looked around the empty salon and grinned. "I think I might be able to squeeze you in." She stepped closer, running a hand through Christy-Lynn's hair with an assessing eye. "You've got good hair. Color shouldn't be a problem. Have a seat."

Two hours later, the stylist, whose name turned out to be Rena, snapped off her blow-dryer and spun the chair around to face the mirror. Christy-Lynn experienced a moment of confusion as she faced her reflection. It was like looking at a stranger who resembled someone she used to know but had lost touch with. She ran a hand through her hair, shook her head back and forth, savoring the feel of the soft, springy curls against the nape of her neck.

Stephen had liked it long, preferably pulled back in a sleek *Town & Country* ponytail. She had humored him, of course, as she had with most things, but now as she stared at this throwback version of herself, it was as if time had folded in on itself, returning her to the woman she had been before blundering into Stephen with an armload of posters. But that woman had been gritty and independent—a survivor. Was there any trace of her left?

# SEVEN

The sound of canned mariachi music greeted Christy-Lynn as she stepped into the lobby of Taco Loco. She wasn't sure why she came in. She wasn't really hungry, but she wasn't ready to go back to her room at the inn either. And it would appear she wasn't the only one taking advantage of the unseasonably warm evening. The place was jammed, with every table full and several large parties waiting to be seated.

The hostess, a frazzled woman with a headful of blue-black hair, was doing her best to greet guests and manage the wait list. Christy-Lynn had just managed to catch her eye when she heard someone calling her name. After a quick scan of the tables, she saw Missy near the back of the restaurant, waving frantically.

"Oh, my Lord! It is you!" she gushed when Christy-Lynn had finally made her way over. "I wasn't sure at first. Look at your hair! Did you know you were going to do that when you left this morning?"

Christy-Lynn tucked the freshly cropped strands behind her ears, suddenly self-conscious. It was like part of her was missing. "I didn't. I was on my way to grab some lunch when I saw the salon and thought, Why not?"

"Well, I just love it. It's fun and really sexy. Don't you think, Dar? Oh, sorry, I almost forgot. This is Dar Setters. She runs the new age shop on Bond Street. Crystals, candles, that sort of thing. Hey, why don't you eat with us? We just sat down."

Christy-Lynn smiled awkwardly at the blonde seated across from Missy. "Thanks, but I don't want to crash your dinner. I just put my name on the list."

Dar smiled. She was pale and petite, almost ethereal, her head of silver-blonde hair framing her small face like a halo of moonlight. "Don't be silly. Missy was just telling me about you. I'm sorry to hear about your husband."

Christy-Lynn wasn't sure she liked being the topic of conversation but forced a smile. "Thank you. It's awfully nice of you to include me."

"Don't be silly," Missy said, pulling out the chair next to her. "We're not going to sit here and let you eat by yourself. You need to be with friends. Besides, it's margarita night!" Missy's gaze strayed briefly as a waiter in snug-fitting black slacks moved past with a tray balanced on one shoulder. "The scenery's not bad either."

Dar sighed and snapped her fingers. "Focus, Missy."

Missy whipped her head around, feigning innocence. "What?"

"I thought you said you'd sworn off men."

"There's nothing wrong with looking, honey. Especially when looking's all you've got time for. Not that anyone's likely to look back. Guys aren't lining up to date a woman with my particular combination of baggage, and certainly not one with Jamba Juice on her jeans. Speaking of which, where did Marco get to? It's time for another margarita."

Christy-Lynn stole a look at Missy. She was totally gorgeous, outgoing, and appeared to have herself together, a combination that made it hard to believe every man in Sweetwater wasn't jumping through hoops to get her attention. But then, she knew better than most that the face a person chose to show the world wasn't always the real one. Everyone had a story. Not everyone wanted to share.

Missy's attention was still on Marco. She watched until he had disappeared through the swinging kitchen door, then turned to Christy-Lynn with a grin. "He's fun to look at, but I'm pretty sure he's spoken for. Janice over at Bristow's said he was in the other day and bought a pair of ruby earrings, and she's pretty sure they weren't for his mother."

"Poor Missy." Dar sighed. "Foiled in love again."

"Love?" Missy's eyes went wide. "Good grief! Who said anything about love? Like I said, he's nice to look at, but I've got two little boys at home, which is all the testosterone I need in my life at the moment." She feigned a shudder as she turned to Christy-Lynn. "I bought the whole love and marriage T-shirt a few years back but wound up returning it for a full refund, if you know what I mean."

"Defective merchandise?"

Missy wrinkled her nose. "Something like that."

"Sorry."

"Don't be. I'm happy. Mostly. Even if it does feel like my hair's on fire most of the time."

It was the *mostly* that caught Christy-Lynn's attention, but she thought it best not to ask. She'd be gone in a few days, and she had her own baggage to carry. "How old are your sons?"

"Six and eight. Nathan and Christian. Both monsters and both adorable."

Divorced, a businesswoman, and a single mom. Christy-Lynn was impressed. "How do you do it? Run an inn and raise two little boys on your own?"

"Oh, I have help. My parents live close, and I have a great sitter. She's with them now. I feel bad sometimes, leaving them after working all day, but sometimes it feels like all I do is take care of other people. If I didn't get out once in a while, I seriously think I'd lose my mind. Oh, look, Marco's back." She grinned up at him, all but purring. "That for me, sugar?"

He set down Missy's margarita and a fresh basket of chips, then took Christy-Lynn's drink order, flashing an Antonio Banderas smile as he turned to leave.

"Good grief," Dar huffed when Marco was safely out of earshot. "I thought you were going to start stuffing dollar bills down his pants."

Missy's mossy-green eyes gleamed mischievously. "Jealous?"

Dar shook her head slowly, like a teacher with an incorrigible student. "Not everyone's looking for tall, dark, and handsome. Some of us are looking for substance, someone capable of holding a conversation or settling down with a good book."

"Ah, yes. Your soul mate."

Dar picked up her wineglass, glaring petulantly as she sipped. "Go ahead. Make fun. But I'm not the one who married a guy right out of school because I liked the way his jeans fit."

Missy picked up her margarita, chasing her lime wedge around with her straw. "You've got me there. That's what I did, all right. And all I've got to show for it are two beautiful boys I wouldn't trade for the world." She glanced at Christy-Lynn then, smiling one of her brilliant smiles. "Oh, honey, don't worry about us. We're not fighting. This is how we show our love for each other. We're different as night and day, but she knows I'll always have her back, and I know she'll always have mine. You know how it is with girlfriends."

Christy-Lynn nodded, but the truth was she *didn't* know. She'd heard about the bonds of female friendship but assumed it to be the stuff of movies and cable TV, imagining it involved lots of chardonnay and shoe shopping. But now, as she observed the connection between Dar and Missy, she saw that real female friendship bore little resemblance to such trite stereotypes. It was deeper and messier and quite beautiful in its own way. And suddenly—perhaps for the first time—she felt its absence keenly.

But there were reasons for that.

# EIGHT

**Monck's Corner, South Carolina**
**August 9, 1994**

*Christy-Lynn's gaze slides to the girl walking beside her—the new girl. She has a terrible overbite and a head full of wiry red hair. She's also covered with freckles. None of these things are her fault, of course, but that hasn't stopped the kids at Berkeley High from slapping a bull's-eye on her back and labeling her a freak. It isn't fair. You can't help who your parents are—or the genes they saddle you with.*

*She jerks her eyes away as the girl turns to look at her. She's used to being invisible, to simply not being seen, so it's a little weird that Linda Neely has suddenly wandered into her usually empty orbit.*

*It had taken some time for Linda to finally speak, almost two weeks, but eventually, after days of hovering in the lunchroom and in study hall, she had startled Christy-Lynn by blurting out her story. Her family had moved from Norfolk because her father had been transferred to Trident, in North Charleston. She didn't have any friends, and she was having trouble in most of her classes, especially English. Her father was threatening to send her back to private school—the kind run by nuns—if she didn't get her grades up by her next report card.*

*It's hard not to feel sorry for her. After five moves in three years, Christy-Lynn knows what it's like to be the new girl, the one everyone stares at and whispers about. The outsider. But over the years, she's gotten used to it, even gotten good at it if there's such a thing. Which is why it feels weird to be bringing home a classmate to help her with her term paper. It's not like she doesn't have the time—her own paper has been finished for a week—or that she minds really. Words are her thing. She likes the way they feel, the way they taste. It's just . . . weird. New weird. Awkward weird.*

*They're cutting across the parking lot now, past a dumpster overflowing with beer cans and dirty diapers, and cars that haven't moved in months. Christy-Lynn wonders if there's any food in the apartment. She doubts it. There's rarely money for cookies or chips these days. Please, God, let there at least be some real Coke; not the generic stuff her mother brings home when cash is low and there are still five days till payday. Linda Neely might be unfortunate-looking with her freckles and her big teeth, but her Fossil watch and trendy Dr. Martens are clearly not from Goodwill.*

*They're climbing the steps now, three slabs of broken concrete with weeds growing out of the cracks. From the apartment above, Reba McEntire's "Fancy" bleeds through the broken screen, along with the high-pitched wail of a baby. She has always hated the song—just a little too real life for her taste.*

*There's a tug on her coat sleeve as she digs for her key. Linda's eyes are wide, almost disbelieving. "This is where you . . . live? I thought we were just cutting through the parking lot."*

*Christy-Lynn is still trying to think of something to say when she realizes the apartment door is ajar. She nudges it open with her knee and peers in. The curtains are drawn, the TV off. Nothing out of place. She breathes a sigh of relief. Not a break-in then. Just her mother, running late as usual and not paying attention when she left for work.*

*Christy-Lynn holds the door open as Linda steps across the threshold. She's never brought anyone home, and suddenly she wishes she hadn't today. The apartment is shabby and small, and the greasy scent of tater tots and fried onions lingers in the air from last night's supper. She wonders briefly as she lets her book bag slide to the floor what Linda's house smells like. Fried chicken, probably, or pork chops. Biscuits and gravy. Green beans with ham hocks and red velvet cake.*

*Linda is still clutching her book bag, eyes round in the gloom as she slowly takes in her surroundings, and Christy-Lynn is struck by how it must look to a stranger seeing it for the first time. The dingy shag carpet, worn to the jute in places. The rump-sprung couch left by the previous tenants, the battered coffee table that has seen too many moves. The lamp with the dented shade her mother had salvaged from the dumpster after their last eviction. Thank God, at least, the curtains were closed.*

*It'll be better once they get to her room, she tells herself. Not that her room is great, but it's not as shabby as the living room. There are her Beanie Babies—the ones not ruined by the rain—and her precious books, painstakingly scored from library sales and secondhand stores. The kinds of things any fourteen-year-old girl might have in her room. Normal things. She tries not to think about what Linda Neely's room looks like. She doubts her books are secondhand or that her things have ever been tossed into a parking lot. The thought stings.*

*"I thought you said your mother wasn't home."*

*Christy-Lynn turns back to her guest. "What?"*

*"Your mother—I thought you said she'd be at work."*

*"She is."*

*Linda jerks her chin at the floor. "Is that her stuff?"*

*Christy-Lynn follows Linda's gaze to the trail of items strewn on the carpet: purse, shoes, keys, jacket. They look like they've been discarded hastily. But that doesn't make sense. Her mother never misses work. At least not for a while now—not since she dumped Shane Taylor and got hired at the Piggly Wiggly. But Charlene Parker has been feeling a little off lately and looking a little off too, since she started picking up bartending shifts at the Getaway Lounge, burning the candle at both ends to keep the rent paid and the lights on.*

*And then Christy-Lynn catches a whiff of something sour over the lingering aroma of last night's supper. It's acidic and vaguely familiar, like the stench of spoiled milk. She knows that smell, knows what it is and what it means. There's a moan from somewhere down the hall, a low, grating sound that sends a chill down Christy-Lynn's spine. It comes again, louder now, ending in a series of coughs and spluttered retches.*

*Something hot and hideous scorches up into Christy-Lynn's throat as she heads down the narrow hall. Rage. Dread. The awful realization that it's starting all over again. Please, please, let her be wrong.*

*But she isn't wrong.*

*Charlene Parker is draped over the toilet when Christy-Lynn walks into the bathroom. Her hair and clothes are streaked with vomit, her cheeks smeared with a soup of purple eyeliner and melting mascara.*

*"Mama?"*

*Charlene lifts her head, her pale face a ruin. "Baby . . . I'm sick."*

*Her voice is thick and slurred, her eyes unfocused. And then suddenly she's scrambling onto all fours, back arched as she retches emptily into the bowl, heaving as if she's trying to turn herself inside out.*

*Panicked, Christy-Lynn drops down on one knee, doing her best to avoid the splatters of yellow-green goo that seem to be everywhere. The mingled reek of alcohol and bile is overpowering.*

*By the time the retching finally subsides, her mother's face has become a blur. Christy-Lynn swipes impatiently at her tears, but they keep coming, running unchecked down her cheeks. "You promised, Mama. You said no more."*

*Her mother's eyes open slowly, heavy lidded as she drags a hand across her mouth. "Thirsty . . ."*

*It's little more than a cracked whisper, and for a moment, Christy-Lynn's anger turns to pity. She is reaching for the glass on the sink when she notices that her mother is still wearing her bartending clothes—jeans and a skimpy black tank top—instead of her cashier's uniform. Had she not even bothered to come home last night?*

*"Mama, how long have you been here like this?"*

*"Thiiiirrrsty!" Charlene wails like a petulant child. The word rings in the tiled space. And then, without warning, she begins to cry, great ragged sobs that rack her knobby shoulders. "I'm sorry, baby. I'm so sorry." She reaches for the front of Christy-Lynn's shirt, using it as leverage as she curls her body in on itself. "Don't be mad," she croons as she begins to rock. "Please, baby . . . don't be mad."*

*A bit of movement, perhaps an intake of breath, makes Christy-Lynn turn. Linda is standing in the doorway, transfixed by the sight of a grown woman whimpering like a baby on the bathroom floor.*

*Christy-Lynn blinks at her, her throat suddenly full of razor blades. "My mother's sick," she manages, struggling against the fresh round of tears she will not let come. "You'd better go."*

*Linda nods slowly, her expression part horror, part fascination. "Sure. Yeah." She backs slowly out of the doorway, unable to tear her eyes away. "See ya in class."*

*Christy-Lynn says nothing, wondering as Linda backs away how long it will take for the story to spread through the halls of Berkeley High. Then she looks down at her mother, asleep or very near to it, her sticky dark hair fanned out on the bathroom tiles. She had been the prettiest girl in Monck's Corner once—a poor man's Ava Gardner. At least that's how her mother told it. And once upon a time, it might have been true.*

# NINE

Christy-Lynn stared at the sea of papers scattered about her on the bed, documents hastily scooped from Stephen's safe the night she left Clear Harbor. The idea had been to get them into some kind of order. Sadly, they were more of a mess than when she'd started.

Last night's dinner with Missy and Dar had been a pleasant surprise, but when Dar asked if she'd given any thought to what her future plans might be, she had frozen. The truth was she hadn't the foggiest idea. She had her editing business—ten or twelve clients she had cultivated over the years—but that could hardly be described as a life. Come to think of it, she wasn't sure what she had shared with Stephen even qualified as a life.

She'd been living with her head in the sand and not just since his death. But she couldn't just *keep* hiding. Downstairs, Missy was closing up her kitchen and seeing to her guests, while Dar was somewhere downtown, selling crystals and new age books. Life was going on all around her—without her. The time had come to take her head out of the sand and face what needed facing.

The insurance would have to be sorted out, the bank accounts and other financial assets seen to, the house in Clear Harbor closed up and sold. The thought startled her, but she suddenly knew she wouldn't be going back. There was nothing there for her. No family to comfort her. No friends to miss. Nothing but empty memories. It was time to wrap things up and move on. But before she could do any of that, she was going to need Stephen's death certificate.

It took a moment to power up her laptop and connect to the inn's Wi-Fi. The connection was agonizingly sluggish, but eventually she was able to type *Maine death certificate* into her browser's search bar. The page blinked briefly, and a list of options appeared. She clicked on a site for the Maine Division of Public Health and followed the prompts. It all seemed remarkably simple until the RECORD NOT FOUND message popped up in bold red letters. She stared at it a moment, then tried again, only to receive the same message.

Frustrated, she reached for her cell and dialed the Clear Harbor Police Station. She was put on hold while they connected her to the medical examiner's office, but eventually a man picked up, his voice brusque as he droned through a list of questions. And then she was back on hold again. After a few moments, he came back on the line.

"I'm sorry, but that certificate hasn't been filed yet."

"I don't understand. It's been almost two weeks."

"I'm sorry, ma'am. Things have been a little bit backed up."

"Do you have any idea when it might be filed?"

"Not exactly, no. We've got the flu going through the department, and one of the docs is out on maternity leave. All I can recommend is to keep checking back."

Christy-Lynn was about to hang up when she changed her mind and asked to be connected to Detective Connelly in Homicide. He'd blown her off the last time they spoke, but it couldn't hurt to try. Maybe she'd catch him in a better mood.

"Connelly," came a gruff voice, more bark than greeting.

"It's Christine Ludlow, Detective. I just called—"

"Christine? Jesus! Where the hell are you? The media's gone crazy. Half of them have you dead. The other half say you're in a rubber room somewhere after swallowing a bottle of pills. The entire country's looking for you!"

Christy-Lynn bit back her initial response, reminding herself that she was about to ask for his help. "The reason I'm calling is that I just spoke to the medical examiner's office about Stephen's death certificate, and I thought I'd check in and see if you had any new information about his case."

She was almost certain she heard a sigh, the kind that usually accompanied exasperation. "Christine, we've been over this. There *is* no case. It was a car accident, a vehicular fatality."

"It was two fatalities."

"Fine. Yes. Two fatalities. But there's no *case*. There's nothing to investigate. The car skidded on the ice and ended up in the bay."

It was Christy-Lynn's turn to be exasperated. "You know what I'm talking about."

"The woman."

"Yes, the woman. Was that so hard? I think I have a right to know who was in the car with my husband when he died, Detective, even if you don't."

Another sigh. Heavier this time. "We're not doing this, Christine. We're not rehashing why I can't give you her name even if I did know it—which I don't. It's like a goddamn witch hunt around here since those photos were leaked, and the last thing I need is for Internal Affairs to get wind that I've been talking to anyone about it."

"You're saying they still don't know who the leak was?"

"That's what I'm saying, yes. And I sure as hell don't need anyone looking in my direction. Look, I've got to go. I've got work to do. But if I *should* want to call you, where can I find you?"

Hope flickered briefly. Perhaps he would change his mind and pick up the phone when there was less chance of being overheard. But something made her hesitate. Perhaps it was his attitude, or the fear that he might accidentally let her whereabouts slip, but a tiny voice in the back of her head told her it was wiser to err on the side of caution.

"You have my cell if you need me," she said coolly. "Leave a message." She didn't wait for a response before ending the call. She'd had enough of being treated like a nuisance.

Still fuming, she turned her attention to the stacks of paperwork on the bed. She was looking for the name of Stephen's broker when she spotted the letter-size envelope tucked between her birth certificate and marriage license. It was dog-eared and yellow with age, but there was no mistaking it. She hadn't thought about it in years, and now, like a bad penny, it had turned up again. She picked it up, turning it over slowly. It felt almost weightless and yet substantial somehow; a twenty-year-old promise—broken. She wasn't sure why she'd kept it all these years, a reminder perhaps, about the dangers of placing your faith in another person. She wasn't prepared for the sting behind her lids as she peeled back the flap and spilled the contents into her lap.

It wasn't much, a few souvenirs from a day at the fair: a plastic wristband, a handful of faded paper tickets, an old black-and-white photo. She reached for the photo first. It was one of those cheesy sepia shots where you dressed up in period costumes and posed in front of a makeshift backdrop. She traced a thumb over Charlene Parker's image.

She was sporting a feather boa and a tatty hat plumed with ostrich feathers, her head tipped at a saucy angle. Beside her, a young Christy-Lynn grinned gleefully, her front teeth too big for her twelve-year-old face. She had chosen a sequined headband from the musty box of props because it made her look like a flapper from the roaring twenties, and because it matched her mother's costume. But it was the necklace glinting at the base of her mother's throat that held her attention—a mirror image of the one she herself had been wearing when the photo was taken.

There was a fresh ache in Christy-Lynn's throat as she shook the necklace from the envelope and into her palm, recalling the night she had thrown it into the trash and then later retrieved it. Years of being shut up had caused it to tarnish—appropriate, she supposed, given the way things had turned out. She brushed impatiently at the tears suddenly smearing her vision, reminding herself that they were a little girl's tears, and that she wasn't that girl anymore. That girl was gone and had been for a long time.

# TEN

**Ladson, South Carolina**
**October 27, 1995**

*The fair is in town—or over in Ladson, which is as good as the same thing. The kids at school can't stop talking about it. How much of their allowance they've saved up. Which rides they'll go on. Which gloriously greasy foods they'll scarf down—and likely throw up later.*

*It all sounds wonderful.*

*But Christy-Lynn knows better than to entertain any hope of going herself. It costs money to get in, money to ride the rides, money to buy corn dogs and funnel cakes. And there simply isn't any money to spare. Which is why she's surprised when her mother comes into her room on Saturday morning wearing jeans and a sweatshirt instead of her Piggly Wiggly uniform.*

*"Get dressed. We're going for a ride."*

*Something about her mother's smile makes Christy-Lynn nervous. "A ride where?"*

*"That's for me to know and you to find out," she says with a wink before disappearing down the hall.*

*Christy-Lynn stifles a squeal as her mother pulls through the fairground gates. The lot is packed, and they have to park out where the pavement ends and the muddy rows are marked with bright-orange cones. It makes the walk to the admittance gate almost interminable, but she doesn't care. They're at the fair!*

*There's a moment of shock when they finally arrive at the gate, and her mother reaches into her back pocket to produce a thick wad of bills. It's more money than she's ever seen at one time—certainly more than she's ever seen in her mother's hand. Her eyes go wide as Charlene Parker peels off several bills and hands them to the bored-looking man behind the ticket window.*

*"Where did you get all that?" Christy-Lynn asks when the man finishes attaching their plastic armbands.*

*Her mother looks away, stuffing the remaining bills back into her pocket. "Work. Where do you think?"*

*"But I thought . . ."*

*"Hush!" her mother hisses, giving her arm a quick jerk. "You want to go in or not?"*

*Christy-Lynn swallows the rest of her question and nods. She definitely wants to go in.*

*They hit the Ferris wheel first, to get warmed up, then move on to the Tilt-o-Whirl, the Starship 3000, and the Rock-n-Roller-Coaster. By the time they step off the last ride, the world is a wobbly, queasy blur, and Christy-Lynn is giddy with the sights and sounds all around her. They eat barbecue and cheese fries, funnel cakes dripping with butter and powdered sugar, then wash it all down with frozen lemonade.*

*After lunch, her mother finds a stand where they sell beer in plastic cups. They sit under a big white tent filled with picnic tables while she drinks her beer, then orders another and drinks that too. When she finishes her third, they head for the exhibit tents: dressage, rodeo, and bull riding, cook-offs and bake-offs, contests for the biggest tomato. None of these interests her mother. But when they approach a local arts-and-crafts tent, she quickly ducks inside.*

*She hovers before a narrow stall filled with tables of cheap jewelry, fingering a wide bangle set with bits of what's meant to pass for turquoise but is probably just plastic. Next, she picks up an engraved silver band and briefly slips it onto her thumb before sliding it off again and returning it to its black velvet tray.*

*There's something wistful in her face, a kind of longing Christy-Lynn has never seen before, as if she's thinking of all the things she can't have. Christy-Lynn looks away, not wanting her mother to know she has seen her sadness, then turns back when she feels her mother's hand on her arm.*

*"Christy, honey, look at this. It's a mother-daughter necklace!"*

*The necklace dangles from her mother's fingers, glinting sharply in the late-afternoon sun. It's a heart pendant, cut jaggedly down the middle, only there are two chains instead of one. She can't quite make sense of it.*

*"It's supposed to come apart," her mother explains. "See? Right down the middle." She flips it over, then holds it out to Christy-Lynn. "Look! It says 'forever friends' on the back. That's us . . . forever friends." She glances at the price tag threaded through the clasp, then turns to the man behind the table. "We'll take it."*

*"But, Mama, you said . . ."*

*"Hush now, so I can pay the man." She's already reaching into her back pocket for the stack of bills folded there. The man counts back her change, then snips off the price tag. When he pulls out a small gift box, Charlene stops him. "I don't need a box. We'll just put them on. Come here, honey, and hold up your hair."*

*Christy-Lynn does as she's told, still wondering how her mother managed to scrape up enough money to get them through the gate let alone buy a piece of jewelry. The chain feels cool against her skin, foreign. She watches as her mother fumbles with her half of the pendant and then pulls the tabletop mirror closer.*

*"We'll never take them off," her mother tells her with startling fierceness as she stares at their shared reflections. "Whatever happens—no matter*

*how bad things get—we'll always be two pieces of the same heart. Forever friends."*

*Christy-Lynn nods, confused by the edge of determination that has slipped into her mother's tone. Or perhaps it's desperation. She isn't sure, and she's afraid to ask for fear that the spell of this perfect day will be broken. Forever friends. The words flutter through her head like a pair of butterfly wings. Shyly, she touches the glinting half heart at the base of her throat— the first piece of jewelry she has ever owned. Her mother smiles and does the same, and at that moment, Christy-Lynn feels something tug at the center of her chest, as if an invisible cord now runs between them—two pieces of the same heart.*

*As long as she lives, she will never forget this day.*

# ELEVEN

*Sweetwater, Virginia*
*December 12, 2016*

Wade tipped his head back to study the sky, a chilly, cloudless blue, then stretched his legs out across the ribbed bottom of the old cedar canoe. He grimaced as he drew yet another line of red ink across the page, then scribbled a note in the margin. *Tighten flashback or lose?* Or maybe he should just toss the whole thing in the lake and be done with it. Frustrated, he reached for the dented green thermos that had been his grandfather's and poured himself a cup of strong black coffee.

It had taken the old man three summers to build the boat, and Wade had been beside him for all of it, overseeing every plank and rib and painstaking coat of epoxy. Three summers had seemed like an eternity to wait for something they were just going to fish in. Then one day when he was feeling particularly antsy, his grandfather explained that someday the canoe would be his, to fish in with his own children, which was why it had to be built strong, so it would last.

And it had lasted, tucked up under the deck, protected from the elements by several layers of blue nylon tarp. He'd only had to brush out the cobwebs and recane the seats before putting it in the water. He wondered what his grandfather would think if he could see him now, adrift on a chilly December morning, equipped not with rod and reel and a box of freshly tied flies, but with a handful of rumpled pages and a glaring red pen.

He didn't usually edit on paper, or in a boat for that matter, but desperate times called for desperate measures. He'd been hacking and slashing the same four chapters for a week now, and something still wasn't working. He'd hoped a change of venue might help, but so far it hadn't. What he needed was a fresh set of eyes.

That's where Simone had come in handy. Whenever he found himself stalled on a story, bashing at the same handful of lines, he would hand the laptop to Simone. She never suggested any kind of fix—her writing style was too different from his—but she was always able to pinpoint precisely where he'd gone off the rails.

He missed that.

Hell, he missed a lot of things. Like having someone next to him in the morning when he opened his eyes or across from him when he sat down for a meal, someone to fill the quiet that sometimes grew too fraught with memories. The thought brought him up short. Not the gloomy nature of it, but the way he had framed it in his head. Not Simone. *Someone.* Anyone. Was that really how he felt? Had he finally started to let go?

The question came with an uncomfortable jolt of clarity. In letting go of his ex-wife, of what he'd had and then lost, his life would somehow be even emptier than before. The bitterness he'd been nursing, clinging to with such tenacity, would be replaced with . . . nothing.

Would that be so bad? To forget the sting of the day he'd come home to an empty apartment? It wasn't like he hadn't seen it coming.

They'd been having trouble for a while, but things had gone south in a hurry when he started talking about leaving *Week in Review* to chase what she snarkily referred to as a pipe dream. But it wasn't just the money. In fact, looking back, he realized it had never been about the money. He'd never been enough for Simone. But then neither had Kevin. Or Todd. Or Phillip. Perhaps a TV news anchor with good hair would fare better.

# TWELVE

Christy-Lynn stuffed her hands into the pockets of her jacket as she ducked across Main Street. As the last mild days of autumn gave way to chillier weather, Sweetwater's holiday season had shifted into high gear. Wreaths glowed from every downtown lamppost, and tiny white lights had transformed the drilling green into a twinkly winter wonderland.

Not that she'd been paying much attention. She'd been too busy tying up the loose ends of her marriage. After a cursory examination of her finances, it was clear that even if Lloyd and Griffin never sold another Stephen Ludlow novel, there was more than enough money for her to live comfortably for . . . well, forever. But the truth was she wasn't sure she even wanted it. It felt tainted somehow, earned by a man she only thought she knew. What she really wanted—really *needed*—was to shed any reminder that she'd been married to Stephen at all, to erase him the way she had erased so many other calamities from her past.

Maybe she'd donate it all to charity. Or set up an endowment of some kind. But in whose name? Stephen certainly didn't deserve to be remembered as a philanthropist. Perhaps an anonymous donation of some kind. She would have to give it some thought. In the meantime, she had contacted a Realtor to put the house up for sale. She wasn't sure where she'd eventually end up, but for now at least, Missy seemed happy to have her at the inn, and the truth was she was starting to get comfortable. Perhaps a little too comfortable.

She could feel herself settling in, becoming part of the weft and weave of Sweetwater's daily life, and beginning to bond with Missy and Dar. Last night, they had insisted she come along to the annual tree lighting ceremony on the green, and then for pie and coffee after. It had been a lovely night, but she couldn't shake the feeling that she was taking advantage of their friendship by lying about her identity—and why she was really in Sweetwater.

She'd been keeping up with the news, checking in online and on TV every few days. It seemed the worst of the frenzy surrounding her disappearance had begun to die down, thanks in large part to the newly surfaced sex tape of some reality show star and her pool boy. And if the shots taken by the intruder on her terrace had ever shown up anywhere, she never saw them. Now, as she lingered in front of the local bookshop, staring at her reflection in the dusty front window, she wondered if it might not be time to move on.

She was restless. Not bored, exactly, but fidgety and in need of focus. She had wrapped up the last of her editing projects last week, and for the time being had decided to decline any new projects. Suddenly her plate was disturbingly empty.

A sharp clatter jolted Christy-Lynn back to the present. She turned to find Carol Boyer banging on her shop window, waving a wad of damp paper towels in an attempt to get her attention. Christy-Lynn smiled and waved back. Carol owned the Crooked Spine. It wasn't much, a shabby corner shop with outdated titles in the front window and a cramped little café in the back where she'd spent more than one afternoon sipping bad lattes and typing up edit notes, but it was something of a fixture in Sweetwater's quaint downtown.

Carol waved her inside with a conspiratorial grin then beckoned her toward the café. "I've been experimenting," she announced proudly as she slipped behind the counter. "I've been trying to come up with something festive for the holidays, and I think I've finally got it. I know how much you love my lattes, but I was wondering if you'd try one of these and tell me what you think. I'm calling it a noggiato."

Moments later, Carol placed a frothy mug on the counter and sprinkled on a bit of nutmeg. "There you go," she said, beaming. "Give that a try."

Christy-Lynn sipped politely, trying not to shudder as the first sip went down. It tasted like scorched eggnog and was so sweet it made her teeth ache, but she wasn't about to dash Carol's hopes. "It's very . . . festive," she said, trying to sound enthusiastic. "I'm sure it's going to be a huge hit with your customers."

Carol scanned the empty shop with forlorn eyes. Her shoulders sagged. "What customers?"

"Slow afternoon?"

"More like a slow year. It's the middle of December, two weeks until Christmas, and I haven't seen a customer for hours. I don't know what's happened. I've been running this place for twenty-six years, and it's never been like this. I guess people just don't want real books anymore. Rather read on one of those electronic thingies."

Christy-Lynn suspected there was more to the story than the advent of e-readers as she surveyed the worn carpet, scarred shelves, and lumpy armchairs. The place had probably been homey once but now felt like a musty basement.

"Maybe it could do with a bit of a face-lift," Christy-Lynn suggested. "A little rouge and lipstick."

Carol frowned. "Lipstick?"

Christy-Lynn couldn't help chuckling. "It's an expression. It means to spruce the place up. A little paint. Some carpet. Maybe some new chairs up front. And you could brighten up the café a little. Some table-cloths, fresh flowers. It wouldn't cost much."

Carol pulled off her glasses and gave them a wipe with the corner of her apron. "I just haven't got it in me," she said wearily. "It's not the money. It's just . . . I'm tired." She held her glasses to the light, then slid them back onto the bridge of her nose. "I'm seventy-four, and I have two grandbabies down in Florida that I never get to see. But this place has been part of my life—part of this town—for almost thirty years." She was back behind the counter now, filling a small sink with hot water. Her glasses were fogged, her eyes nearly invisible. "I know it's silly, but I hate to think of the place not being here."

"But it would be here. You wouldn't be closing it. You'd just be selling it."

Carol snorted as she turned off the tap. "Who'd buy this place?"

Christy-Lynn was about to suggest she contact a business broker but changed her mind when she considered the likelihood of finding a buyer for a run-down bookstore with outdated inventory and no customers. Throw in the fact that said store was in a tiny town most people had never heard of, and the list of potential buyers dwindled considerably.

"How about me?" Christy-Lynn blurted. The response had come out of nowhere, but the moment it was out, she knew she wasn't kidding.

Carole peered at her through steamy glasses. "You're not serious."

Christy-Lynn considered the question a moment. It was absurd, ridiculous. But why not buy a bookstore and stay in Sweetwater? She'd been in love with books as far back as she could remember, and she was going to need to do something.

"I think I might be," she said finally. "If you are, that is."

"I didn't know you were thinking of staying in Sweetwater."

"I'm not sure I did either. But I've been thinking about what I want to do and where I want to do it. Something about Sweetwater feels right."

Carol's jaw went slack, as if she'd just picked up a rock and found a $1 million scratch-off ticket underneath. "You'd really be interested in my little store?"

Christy-Lynn was as surprised as Carol to realize that she really was interested. In fact, she was nearly giddy at the thought. "I guess everyone who loves books thinks about it at some time or other, but I actually worked in a bookstore when I was in college and loved it."

"Could you make a go of it, do you think?"

Christy-Lynn eyed the place again, this time more critically. It would be a huge undertaking, but it wasn't like she had anything else to do with her time. "I think so," she said at last, the wheels already turning. The renovations would be extensive; new flooring, lighting, shelving. She'd have to gut the café and start over, not to mention hiring a barista who knew how to make a decent latte. The stock was in serious need of updating, and there was nothing to appeal to children, but the place definitely had potential.

"I have a few ideas, some things I think might drive new customers through the door."

Carol shook her head, still trying to digest the sudden reversal in her fortunes. "Well, this is certainly unexpected. I never thought anyone would actually want to buy the place. I have no idea how much it might be worth. It's the property mostly and a little bit of inventory. Can you . . . do you think you'd be able to get a business loan?"

Carol was clearly uncomfortable with having to be so blunt, though it was a perfectly valid question. How to answer was the conundrum. *No worries, my dead husband left me millions* was likely to raise a few eyebrows, not to mention a whole spate of questions she wasn't prepared to answer.

"I think it's doable," she said carefully. "I have some money saved, and there was a little life insurance. I'm not trying to push you one way or the other, but if you're really serious about this, why don't you work up what you think the property and inventory are worth, and we'll get the ball rolling."

Carol nodded slowly, her eyes slightly glazed. "All right then. I guess I'd better go call my daughter and tell her to clean out the spare room."

An hour later, Christy-Lynn wandered into the lobby of the Fife and Feather feeling almost as dazed as Carol had looked when she left the Crooked Spine. Missy appeared with a smile and a plate of freshly baked cookies at the front desk.

"There you are. I was wondering where you'd gotten to. Mama's taking the boys to the movies tonight, and I was thinking of grabbing some pasta. Interested in—" Missy paused midsentence, cookie plate hovering. "What's wrong? You look like you've seen a ghost."

Christy-Lynn shook her head numbly. Was it wise to share her news? Carol might change her mind. Or her daughter could squash the idea of her mother becoming a permanent fixture in her home. The thought brought a pang of anxiety, because at some point during the walk home, she had decided she wanted this very much.

Missy set down the plate and came around to the front of the desk. "Honey, say something. You're scaring me."

"It's fine," Christy-Lynn said quietly. "In fact, it's very fine."

"I don't know what that means."

"It means you're going to be losing a guest."

Missy's expression morphed from concern to disappointment. "You're leaving Sweetwater?"

Christy-Lynn couldn't help grinning. "No, but I'll be needing somewhere permanent to live. I think I just bought a bookstore."

# THIRTEEN

*Sweetwater, Virginia*
*December 31, 2016*

The lunch crowd had already descended on the Fickle Pickle, but Christy-Lynn managed to snag a table near the window. She eyed the sky as she sipped her tea and waited for Missy to arrive. The Weather Channel was predicting a whopping three inches of snow, the equivalent of a spring shower for Mainers, but the report had sent locals scurrying for bread and milk.

The timing was unfortunate, almost certain to put a damper on the evening's festivities. Not that she had any plans of her own. When it came to useless holidays, New Year's had always been at the top of her list. Something about the forced gaiety and tedious resolutions, the pinning of one's hopes on a single stroke of the clock, had always seemed stunningly naive.

But not this year.

For the first time in her life, she was actually looking forward to the stroke of midnight and was chomping at the bit to get to work on the store. And soon she'd have a place of her own to live.

She'd been thrilled to learn that along with the shop, Carol Boyer was looking to sell her house, a small bungalow built in the 1920s that backed up to Sweetwater Creek. The inn was lovely, and Missy's friendship had been an unexpected boon, but it was time to put down some roots.

Both deals were set to close in a few weeks, and she hoped to open the store sometime in April, sooner if all went well. She liked the idea of a spring opening. It felt symbolic, a season of growth and renewal. A time for closing old chapters and writing new ones. She glanced at her wrist, at the trio of moon-shaped scars that had been with her for more than twenty years, a permanent part of her backstory. Was a fresh start—one shaped by choice rather than catastrophe—too much to hope for? She didn't know, but she was willing to find out.

She tucked the thought away, waving as Missy arrived. She looked tired and more than a little frazzled as she unwound her scarf and dropped into the chair opposite Christy-Lynn.

"Sorry I'm late. The dishwasher blew a gasket or a hose or some-thing. I spent my morning coping with a flood. So much for a day off. Oh good, here comes our waitress. I'm famished." She wagged her brows mischievously. "I'm thinking a tuna sandwich with a big old side of pasta salad. Last chance to carb up before the diet starts tomorrow. Speaking of which, what are you up to tonight? Got anything fun planned?"

Christy-Lynn couldn't help smiling. Missy's boundless energy never ceased to amaze her. She was about to answer when the waitress appeared with her order pad and a harried smile. When they were alone again, Missy picked up right where she'd left off.

"So, tonight?"

"No plans. I'll probably just read or work on the café menu."

"You should come over and spend it with us. I hated that you turned me down for Christmas at Mama and Daddy's. No one's sup-posed to be alone on Christmas."

"I told you, I felt funny about horning in on you and your folks. And Christmas has never really been my thing."

Missy shook her head as if bewildered. "I don't get it. How can you not like Christmas? Everything's so beautiful and festive. The music, the decorations, all the yummy food."

Christy-Lynn kept her eyes averted as she spread her paper napkin in her lap. "Let's just say the ghost of Christmas past and I have never been terribly close."

"Sorry," Missy said quietly. "Sometimes I forget how painful the holidays can be for some people. I didn't mean to drag up unpleasant memories."

"Forget it," Christy-Lynn said, fiddling with her silverware. She could feel Missy studying her, waiting for her to say more, and it made her uncomfortable.

It wasn't the bike or the Easy-Bake Oven that had never materialized under the tree—not that there had ever *been* a tree. It was about other things, intangible things like mothers and daughters sipping cocoa and baking cookies, stringing lights and hanging stockings. The moments most people took for granted.

Her own memories were of frozen dinners or boxed mac and cheese, eaten alone in front of the TV while her mother spent the day at the local bar, slinging drinks for tips and then coming home to pass out on the bathroom floor. They didn't write carols about those kinds of things or put them on Christmas cards either.

"Say you'll come tonight." Missy prompted again. "It'll be fun."

"Oh, I couldn't. I—"

"Why couldn't you? It's just going to be me and the boys, and they'll be zonked by nine. We'll order Chinese from Lotus and get sloppy on chardonnay." She paused, grinning. "Okay, I'll get sloppy on chardonnay, and you'll get buzzed on sweet tea, and we'll drool over the adorable but sadly unavailable Anderson Cooper. It'll be fun! Certainly better than working on café menus. And you can finally meet my little guys. Say you'll come."

"All right," she said grudgingly. "But only because you said there'll be guys there."

And because it was better than her inevitable New Year's Eve stroll down memory lane.

# FOURTEEN

*Monck's Corner, South Carolina*
*January 1, 1998*

*Christy-Lynn sits up, blinking heavily in the flickering blue gloom of the living room. The TV is on, the sound turned down. It's how she falls asleep most nights, curled up on the faux leather couch, in case her mother comes home in rough shape and needs help getting to bed.*

*Her eyes are still gritty from sleep. She scrubs at them, then pushes the hair off her face. On the screen, revelers in paper hats are swapping kisses amid a shower of confetti and balloons, a replay she realizes, as the scene cuts away to similar shots from around the world. The New Year has arrived. Not that much will change. At least not for the better.*

*What would it be like, she wonders, to be in the midst of all that excitement—to actually feel like there was something to celebrate? To have the kind of life where there were things to plan instead of things to dread. She's so very tired of the dread. Of the disappointments and the small daily disasters. Pots left to boil dry on the stove. Cigarette burns on the sheets. Rent money vanishing into thin air. Another lost job. Followed by another. And the excuses. She's heard them all by now. Always someone else's fault. It's not that she's keeping score. She stopped that a long time ago. But it's exhausting.*

*The thought quickly evaporates as a sound seeps in through the front windows, the dull thud of a car door followed by a muffled giggle. Her mother is home and, judging by the sound of things, not alone. Out of habit, her eyes slide to the clock on the stove. Two thirty. She's early.*

*A moment later, the front door bangs open, and Charlene Parker tumbles in, smothering another giggle as she hushes her companion. She reels a bit as she stands there, engulfed in a cloud of cigarette smoke and liquor fumes. In the glare of the TV, she looks like a trashy ghost in her skinny jeans and black tank top, one dingy bra strap drooping down her shoulder.*

*"Oh . . ." She blinks at Christy-Lynn, as if she's only just remembered she has a daughter. "Happy New Year, baby!" Her words are thick and slushy, harsh in the quiet. "You remember Jake from the bike shop, right? We've been celebrating!"*

*Christy-Lynn runs her gaze over Jake—tall and lanky with grease-stained jeans and a black leather vest—but can't muster a memory. Last night it was Randy. Tomorrow it would be someone else. They never hung around long.*

*"Did you get dinner?" Charlene asks, fumbling with her purse as it threatens to slide off her shoulder.*

*Christy-Lynn is briefly tempted to ask her mother if she plans to cook but abandons the idea. In her present condition, the snark will only be wasted. "It's two thirty in the morning, Mama," she points out wearily. "I ate hours ago."*

*"Oh," Charlene murmurs, more sigh than actual response. Her eyes are wide and vacant in the gloom, unseeing. She'll crash soon. Hard. And Christy-Lynn doesn't want Jack or Jake or whatever his name is around when she does.*

*Resolved, she slides off the couch and crosses the room, taking hold of her mother's stringy arm. "I've got her now," she tosses at the man in the greasy jeans. "You can go."*

The man's eyes go flinty, and for a moment, he puffs out his chest. He's too drunk to hold the pose though and eventually sags against the door frame. "I look like a damn taxi to you? We was gonna ring in the New Year."

Christy-Lynn fights back a shudder as she glares at him. "In about three minutes, my mother's going to be on the floor, so unless you plan to hang around for that, you might want to ring in the New Year someplace else."

She doesn't care that he's been drinking and has no business climbing back behind the wheel, or that there's a very real chance he'll wrap himself around a tree before he gets home. She just wants him gone and for this night to be over.

"What about you?" he slurs, lumbering a step closer. "I've got some stuff in the car. We could—"

"Go," Christy-Lynn barks before he can get the rest out. "Now. Or I'll call the police." She can't, of course. The phone's been shut off for months. But she's hoping he's too drunk to test the threat. "I mean it. You can leave or deal with the cops."

He holds his ground for what feels like an eternity, his eyes heavy lidded as he sizes her up, as if trying to decide if she's worth the trouble. Christy-Lynn glowers back, prepared to belt out a bloodcurdling scream if he so much as flinches in her direction. Beside him, her mother is weaving precariously. She's going to have to make a choice soon, between letting her mother crumple to the floor and fending off the vest-wearing greaser. And then, mercifully, he wilts.

"Snooty little bitch," he grumbles as he pushes the door open and nearly falls out onto the stoop. "You tell your mama she owes me. Like I said, I ain't no taxi."

Despite years of practice, getting Charlene Parker into bed is never easy. She's a crier when she comes down, whining and clingy, begging for forgiveness between sloppy sobs. But there's always a moment between pleading and oblivion when she becomes quiet, almost docile. This is the window Christy-Lynn waits for. She doesn't bother with her clothes, just drags off her *boots and pulls up the covers, then flips on the lamp and moves the trash can closer to the bed—just in case.*

*She's about to turn away when she notices the vacant hollow at the base of her mother's throat. Her hand creeps to the half-heart pendant at her own throat. "Mama . . . where's your necklace?"*

*There's no answer, no acknowledgment of any kind. Christy-Lynn touches her shoulder then gives it a shake. "Mama?"*

*Charlene's eyes flutter open briefly, unfocused as they swim about the room.*

*"What happened to your necklace?" Christy-Lynn's voice is harsher now, a sick kind of knowing already taking root.*

*"Easy Street . . . Coin . . . something." The words ooze out thick and slurred, but for Christy-Lynn, they're clear enough.*

*"You pawned your half of our necklace?"*

*"Owed Micah . . ." She lifts a hand in the air, flapping it vaguely, then lets it drop back to the bed like a felled bird. "He wouldn't . . ." The words fall away, but Christy-Lynn doesn't need to hear anymore. He wouldn't let her have any more of whatever it was she was into these days. That's what she was too drunk or too high to say.*

*"Oh, Mama . . ."*

*Charlene's eyes open again, glassy and dilated. She yawns, head lolling as she reaches for Christy-Lynn's arm, patting it as if it were a puppy. "Happy New Year, baby."*

*Something hot and bitter rises up in Christy-Lynn's throat as she unfastens her own necklace. She stares at it, coiled in her palm, tarnished after nearly three years of wear. Her mother's words echo in her head, as clear as the day she had spoken them.* We'll never take them off. Whatever happens—no matter how bad things get—we'll always have each other.

*Christy-Lynn swallows a sob. The necklace slips out of her hand with surprising ease, slithering through her fingers and into the wastebasket. She has kept her part of their pact, but it doesn't matter. Half a heart isn't good for anything.*

# FIFTEEN

*Sweetwater, Virginia*
*December 31, 2016*

Missy's house was located behind the inn, a quaint clapboard cottage bordered on three sides by a tidy boxwood hedge. The snow had begun to fall by the time Christy-Lynn arrived, the large wet flakes already clinging to the slate-paved path to the front porch.

Missy pulled back the door with a grin on her face and a wineglass in her hand. "Come on in and kick off your shoes. Just watch your step. Nathan's got LEGOs all over the floor. The place is basically a minefield. Oh, and don't get too close to the tree. I put it up Thanksgiving Day so it's a bit of a fire hazard at this point."

Christy-Lynn followed her to the kitchen. Missy topped off her wineglass and reached for a handful of cheese puffs from an enormous bag on the counter. "What can I get you to drink? We've got lemonade, tea, apple juice, root beer, or Sprite. Oh, and wine, if you've taken up drinking since lunch."

"Sprite works."

Missy shoved the bag of cheese puffs in Christy-Lynn's direction then reached into the fridge for a soda. "Help yourself. It's part of our New Year's tradition—junk food and Chinese. The menu for Lotus is on the counter if you want to look it over. I'm hooked on their lo mein, and the boys always do shrimp fried rice."

Christy-Lynn was scanning the menu, trying to decide between the pepper steak and cashew chicken, when the back door crashed open and a pair of pink-cheeked boys in coats and scarves barreled into the kitchen, making a beeline for the refrigerator.

Missy turned to face them, hands on hips. "Hey, hey, you two. No running in the house. And before you touch anything, hang up your coats and go get cleaned up. But first say hello to our company."

The pair turned in unison, the younger of the two staring with wide blue eyes, the older grinning handsomely, a space where one of his incisors used to be.

"This is Christian," Missy said, ruffling the taller boy's strawberry-blond head. "And the little squirt with the orange lips and fingers is Nathan. I'll give you three guesses who voted for the cheese puffs. Guys, this is Christy-Lynn. She's going to hang with us tonight for New Year's."

"Hello," Christy-Lynn said tentatively, hating the awkwardness she always felt when there were children around. She never knew what to say or how to act, and she wondered if it showed with Missy's boys.

"Do you have a hat?" Nathan asked, scrunching one eye up at her.

Christy-Lynn blinked down at him. "A hat?"

"He means a paper hat," Missy whispered. "For New Year's." She rolled her eyes balefully. "We have horns and noisemakers too. We put them on after dinner since the boys are usually out by midnight."

Christy-Lynn looked at Nathan gravely. "I'm afraid I don't have a hat. Is it mandatory?"

Nathan frowned, clearly baffled by the word *mandatory*. Missy stepped in. "Don't worry, baby. Mama has extra hats. Now the two of you go get scrubbed while I order dinner."

Christian turned on command and darted down the hall, but Nathan lingered, blue eyes fixed shyly on Christy-Lynn. Finally, he slipped away, giggling as he vanished down the hall.

Missy grinned as she grabbed her wineglass from the counter. "Looks like my baby's developed his first crush."

By the time the food arrived, the boys had cleaned themselves up and were sprawled in front of the television, engrossed in what Missy assured her was their seventieth viewing of *Ice Age*.

Missy unpacked the food and portioned fried rice into two small bowls, then carried them to the living room, along with the remaining containers.

They ate sitting cross-legged on the couch, swapping containers and chatting like college roommates, while the boys sat on the floor in front of the TV. It surprised Christy-Lynn just how quickly she'd become comfortable with Missy. She couldn't put her finger on any one quality. Perhaps it was her big heart and her clear-eyed ability to deal with whatever was in front of her. Or the pride she took in the life she had built for herself and her boys. Whatever it was, she was grateful for it.

When they had eaten their fill, Missy stacked the containers and set them on the coffee table. At some point between the fortune cookies and Missy's third glass of wine, the boys had crashed. "Told you," she said softly. "Every year they swear they're going to watch the ball drop, and every year they're out by nine. Give me a minute while I get them to bed."

"Can I help?" Christy-Lynn asked, secretly hoping the answer was no. She hadn't the slightest idea what putting a child to bed entailed. Pajamas presumably, toothbrushes, bedtime stories, prayers. None of which she felt equipped to handle.

"No worries," Missy grunted as she hoisted a limp Nathan onto her shoulder. "When they're like this, it's just a matter of dumping them in the bed and pulling up the covers. Parenting rule number one: never wake a sleeping child."

Ten minutes later, the boys were safely tucked in, and Missy reappeared with a new bottle of wine and a fresh can of Sprite. Reaching for the remote, she sank back onto the couch with a sigh. "And now . . ." she said, flipping to the Hallmark Channel. "It's girl time. We'll do a nice sappy movie, then switch over to Anderson around eleven for the festivities."

Christy-Lynn watched as Missy took a sip from her wineglass then rested it carefully on her knee. Her movements were slightly exaggerated, her speech slower than usual and more than a little slushy. They were signs she recognized only too well.

"Can I ask you a question?" she asked Missy tentatively. "And feel free to tell me it's none of my business."

Missy grinned, waving her glass expansively. "Ask away."

"I can't help noticing that every time we get together, you seem . . ." She paused and took a breath before plunging ahead. "I was wondering why you drink so much."

Missy's chin lifted a notch. "Why don't you drink at all?"

Christy-Lynn recognized the reply for what it was—deflection—but decided to answer anyway. "It's a family thing. My mother."

"She drank?"

"You could say that. She came by it honest, though. Apparently her mother died of cirrhosis when she was twelve. Given my gene pool, not tempting fate seems wiser than just hoping it skips a generation."

Missy's expression softened. "I'm sorry."

Christy-Lynn shrugged. "It's no biggie."

"But you still look for the signs."

"Not purposely, but when I see them, I do wonder. And maybe worry a little. You didn't answer the question, by the way."

Missy stared into her glass, swirling the contents idly. "When you said you wanted to ask me a question, I wasn't expecting that one."

"I'm sorry. I don't mean to pry. I've just noticed that you seem to—"

"Self-medicate?" Missy supplied without blinking. "Yeah, maybe I do. But I am careful. Never more than two if I'm driving."

"And when you're not driving?"

Missy's gaze slid away. "Then I don't really have to count, do I?" She raised her glass to her lips, then seemed to change her mind, setting it aside instead. "It's hard, you know—doing what I do. Two little boys and an inn to run. I'm not complaining. It's the life I chose. And I love it most of the time. But it's nice to step away and just . . . numb out once in a while. To pretend I don't have to hold up the entire world by myself."

"Is that how you feel?"

"Sometimes. I mean, all I do is take care of other people. And you just know there are people out there, women mostly, who think I'm doing it all wrong, who think it's selfish of me to try to run a business *and* raise two boys on my own. They have no idea what I do to make it work—or what I've given up. Hell, I don't even date. Because I swore the day I kicked their father out of this house that my kids would always come first. And they do. I might not be president of the PTA, and the cupcakes I send for class parties might come from Harris Teeter, but my kids are healthy and smart and happy. And just maybe, when they grow up, they'll know how to handle a woman with goals of her own. At least I hope they will."

Christy-Lynn's admiration for Missy ticked up another notch. "I don't know how you do it. I know I couldn't. You have an amazing family and a business you're proud of. So I say screw anyone who says you aren't doing it right. All you have to do is take one look at those boys to know you're doing it *great*."

Missy's expression brightened. "That's sweet of you to say. And you *could* do it. Something happens when you have kids. It's like some switch gets flipped somewhere, and all of a sudden you have these superpowers."

"I don't know about that," Christy-Lynn said, feigning interest in the Star Wars–themed Christmas tree withering in the corner.

"So," Missy said when the silence grew heavy. "Can I ask *you* a question?"

Christy-Lynn dragged her attention from the tree. "I guess it's your turn."

"Why didn't you ever have any? Kids, I mean. I didn't want to pry before . . ."

"But now you do?"

Missy grinned sheepishly. "A little bit, yeah. So what's the deal? You tried and couldn't. You just never got around to it? Your husband didn't want them?"

"I didn't want them."

Missy blinked back at her, clearly surprised. "Oh."

"Weren't expecting that, were you? Which is why I don't talk about it. You worry about people thinking you're doing it wrong. How about people thinking you're defective because you're not doing it at all?"

"Do they?"

"Not out loud, but you see it when you tell them you don't have kids. They assume it's because you can't, because what normal woman doesn't want children?"

"You don't."

Christy-Lynn nodded but said nothing.

"I feel like I should say I'm sorry again, but I'm not sure why. For bringing it up at all, I guess."

"The reason I don't drink—it's the same reason I chose not to have kids."

"Your mother's drinking?"

"Yes. But it wasn't just alcohol. She was into other stuff too. Bad stuff. I decided no kid of mine was ever going to grow up the way I did. I know all about the nature versus nurture argument, that it's not always your genes, that sometimes it's about the role models you grow up with, but since I drew the short straw there too I decided not to risk it."

"Wow."

"Yeah. Now you see why it's not something I share."

"I do. But you should never let anyone make you feel bad about your choices. They're no one's business but your own. No one, and I mean no one else gets a vote."

"Try telling that to the woman who hands you a card for her fertility specialist right in the middle of a cocktail party."

Missy shook her head grimly. "We're not always the most tactful species, are we?" She took a sip of her wine then set the glass aside as if some decision had been made. "You know what? It's about to be a brand-new year so let's make a pact. No more giving a flip about what anyone else thinks. You're starting a new life. Come spring, you're going to have your very own bookstore. Next thing you know, you'll meet someone and be living happily ever after."

Christy-Lynn shot her a look of horror. "Let's leave it at the bookstore, shall we? The last thing I need in my life right now is one more complication."

Missy shrugged, but a sly smile lit her face. "Sometimes complications are really just gifts in disguise."

# SIXTEEN

After a month of wind and rain, spring had finally come to Sweetwater, and Christy-Lynn couldn't have asked for a finer day for her grand opening. Missy had called at the crack of dawn to invite her to Taco Loco for a celebratory dinner, and Dar had pronounced the clear skies and warm weather a good omen. She prayed Dar's intuition proved true. The last three months had been a blur of hammering and sawdust. Battered shelves had been torn out and replaced with new, the original oak floors sanded down and restored, the café demolished, rewired, and rebuilt. She had even carved out a small children's corner at the back, stocked with toys and educational games.

It had been a joy to watch the place take shape. Best of all, every inch of the transformation had been carried out behind paper-covered windows, an idea proposed by one of the two grad students she had hired to staff the store. And now, at long last, it was time for the unveiling.

"It's almost ten!" Tamara, her new barista, called from the café where she was giving the tables a final wipe. "Do you want to pull the paper off the windows, or should I?"

Christy-Lynn's stomach lurched as she checked her watch. What if no one came? Or worse, what if they came and hated it? Sweetwater wasn't exactly big on change. Most of the sidewalks were still paved with brick laid before the Civil War.

Tamara came up from behind, nudging her with an elbow. "Come on, boss. Five minutes. I'll help you with the windows."

Christy-Lynn nodded, but her limbs seemed paralyzed.

Tamara narrowed catlike green eyes. "Oh my God, are you nervous?"

"Try terrified. What if nobody comes?"

"Well, that's just silly. The Crooked Spine is all anyone's talking about. Everybody's dying to know what you've done with the place." She had moved to one of the plate-glass windows fronting Main Street and was slowly peeling off yellowed sheets of newspaper.

Christy-Lynn closed her eyes and pulled in a breath. The butterflies she'd been experiencing all morning had just become a swarm of bees.

"Uh, boss?" It was her new cashier, Aileen, insistently prodding her shoulder. "You might want to look out front."

The floor seemed to wobble as Christy-Lynn opened her eyes. She blinked then blinked again. For a moment, she was too stunned to speak. It appeared the entire town had turned out. "We forgot to clean the windows," she said numbly.

Aileen squinted in her direction. "Seriously? That's what you see? Dirty windows?"

Christy-Lynn shook her head, still dazed. "I had no idea this many people would come out for a bookstore opening."

Aileen grinned, giving her auburn ponytail a toss. "Of course they came out. Like Tom Hanks said in *You've Got Mail*—we're a piazza—a place for people to mix, mingle, and be!" And with that, she headed for the back room. "I'll get the lights."

Tamara came to stand beside Christy-Lynn, arms full of rumpled newsprint. "You did good, boss," she said quietly. "Really good."

Christy-Lynn felt tears threatening but blinked them away. "Thank you. And thank you for all your help. I couldn't have done it without you and Aileen."

"I have to say it's been pretty cool being a part of it. So what do you think? Should we let them in?"

Before Christy-Lynn could answer, the overhead track lights flipped on. The place really did look amazing. "Yes," she said. "Let them in."

The next two hours were a blur as a steady stream of customers poured in, gushing over the changes she had made and thanking her for saving the shop. One woman even snapped several photos with her phone, promising to forward them to Carol so she could see the transformation for herself.

Christy-Lynn savored every word, but as the day wore on, the excitement began to take its toll. She was parched, ravenous, and could feel herself starting to fray around the edges. She glanced at her watch and then at the register. If she hurried, she might be able to swing a deli run.

She had just slipped behind the counter to ask Aileen if she wanted anything when the words died in her throat.

*It can't be. Not here. Not now.*

But there was no mistaking the telltale prickle along the nape of her neck, a kind of antennae she had learned to pay attention to during her street years. There was only one reason for that prickling sensation—danger.

Slipping away unseen was going to be impossible. Instead, she did her best to shrink from sight while keeping an eye on the man at the back of the line. He'd been wearing a dinner jacket the last time she saw him, quite different from the jeans and rumpled Oxford he wore now. But there was no forgetting that profile or the sharply chiseled jaw. Wade Pierce, star reporter for *Week in Review*—in Sweetwater, of all places.

He was holding a cup of coffee, staring down at the cover of Stephen's latest novel as if he'd just unearthed something rancid. She had debated whether or not to carry Stephen's books but decided their absence might seem odd, even conspicuous. And here, by some horrible twist of fate, stood her dead husband's personal Moriarty waiting to purchase a copy of *A Fatal Franchise*.

The line moved, and Wade shuffled closer. Christy-Lynn felt as if she were caught in the path of an oncoming train. He and Stephen had been roommates in college, both creative writing majors until Wade had abruptly switched to journalism. According to Stephen, their friendship had ended just as abruptly, though he'd never said why. Not even after the scene at the Omni.

It had been three years ago—no four. A dinner honoring the recent achievements of several UVA alumni. Stephen was fresh off his fourth bestseller, Wade the recipient of some coveted journalism award. There was a cocktail reception scheduled the first night, and they'd both been drinking. Stephen was in rare form, laying it on so thick even she had to suppress the urge to roll her eyes. He got like that sometimes, dropping names and casually referencing his current position on the *New York Times* bestseller list. But she'd never seen him go out of his way to make someone else feel small—until that night.

And he'd accomplished it in signature style, delivering one of the barbed compliments he loved so well. A sharp smile and a slap on the back, so that no one was quite sure if he was being snarky or magnanimous. Something about Wade being the most talented guy in the class—the second goddamn coming of Ernest Hemingway—and clearly wiser than the rest of them since he'd chosen to use his talents to bang out magazine articles instead of wading into the deep end of the literary pool.

Wade seemed to take it in stride at first, laughing as he set down his drink. Things went downhill from there when he proclaimed in a voice loud enough for the whole bar to hear that he'd take writing articles any day if the alternative was becoming an overhyped hack churning out four hundred pages of crap every year.

She had never seen Stephen's face go so red or been afraid he might actually take a swing at someone. She had stepped between them before things could escalate, informing Wade curtly that a bar full of colleagues was hardly the place to air petty jealousies and that if he couldn't handle a colleague's success he should have stayed home. His jaw had clenched tight, a vessel at his temple throbbing furiously as she stood waiting for him to respond. Instead, he turned and stalked out of the bar. She had scowled as she watched him go, but there was a part of her, even then, that knew he had a point, even if he'd made it badly—and with stunningly poor timing.

"There she is! My favorite bookseller!"

Christy-Lynn jerked her head around, startled to find Missy standing at the end of the counter with a to-go container in one hand and a plastic utensil packet in the other.

"I wasn't sure you'd have time to grab lunch so I popped by with a salad. How's it been going? Are you—"

"Christine Ludlow?"

Wade's voice seemed to slam into her, like an object hurtling at high speed, knocking her off balance. Before she could check herself, she turned, coming face-to-face with a disconcerting pair of amber eyes. He was taller than she remembered and scruffier, his hair messily combed and grazing his collar in back.

"Wade," she said evenly because it was too late for anything else.

"Well, I'll be damned . . . it *is* you. I wasn't sure with the short hair. Don't tell me the great Stephen Ludlow has decided to grace Sweetwater with his presence."

"Of course he isn't here. He's—" Christy-Lynn stopped short, suddenly remembering Missy.

Wade, on the other hand, seemed oblivious, carrying on his half of the conversation as if they were the only two people in the store. "I've got to say, you're the last person I expected to see today. I came into town for some supplies and saw that the place was under new management. Good thing too, or I might have missed the hubby's new novel. And another bestseller. What does that make now—ten, eleven?"

He was being droll and purposely malicious, but at the moment, Christy-Lynn was too busy registering the fact that virtually every eye in the place had just shifted in her direction. The irony was almost too much to wrap her head around. She had been outed on the opening day of her lovely new store—by an award-winning reporter who had despised her husband.

"Christy-Lynn?" Missy stepped closer, running sharp eyes over Wade. "What's happening? Is this guy bothering you?"

*Yes, he is bothering me.* That's what she wanted to say, to scream. But until she knew what Wade Pierce was doing in her store, she thought it best not to antagonize him.

"I'm fine," she said with a calm she wasn't close to feeling. "This is Wade Pierce, a friend of my husband's."

"Your . . ." Missy's mouth fell open, eyes darting from Christy-Lynn's face to the book in Wade's hand, clearly putting the pieces together. "But you said your last name was Parker."

"It was. It is." Christy-Lynn shot her a pleading look. She hadn't wanted it to happen like this, but now that it had, she was going to have to pay the piper. Just not here. And not now.

"Please, Missy, I'll explain at dinner, but right now I need to step away. Aileen, can you hold down the fort?" Without waiting for an answer, she jerked her chin at Wade. "Come with me."

In the café, she glanced around to make sure no one was in earshot, then rounded on him. "All right, what do you want?"

# SEVENTEEN

What did he want?

He wanted to know what Stephen Ludlow's wife was doing in Sweetwater.

He wasn't sure it was her at first. It was the hair, mostly. She was wearing it short now, tucked behind her ears with a fringe of dark bangs falling across her forehead. It worked. So did the gauzy blouse and flowy cotton skirt she was wearing. She looked younger, less buttoned up—or had before she'd opened her mouth.

She was glaring at him now, arms clenched across her chest. Classic hostility pose. But then who could blame her? The scene at the alumni dinner had been an ugly one, thanks to the back-to-back shots of Jameson Simone had urged him to down the minute they hit the bar. She thought it would help take the edge off. Man, had she read *that* one wrong.

Not that whiskey was an excuse for showing out. A smart man would have refused to engage. A smart man would have walked away. But that wasn't what happened. Instead, he'd run his mouth and ended up nose to nose with Christine Ludlow. He'd thought about her from time to time, about how she had rushed to her husband's defense that night, the heat in her voice, the daggers in her eyes. It hadn't been pleasant, but as he stood there taking his well-deserved dressing-down, he'd found himself wondering if Simone would have done the same if the roles were reversed. It had taken three years, but eventually he'd gotten his answer. No.

And now they had chanced to meet again. She was still glaring at him, still waiting for an answer, though he honestly couldn't remember what she'd asked him. "Look, if this is about the reunion, I'm—"

"How did you find me?"

He stared at her, baffled. "How did I . . . what?"

"You can drop the act. I know where you work, remember? Why can't you all just leave me alone?"

"I have no—who is *you all*?"

Her chin inched up, and the familiar daggers were back. "I'm not going to talk to you if that's what you're hoping. There isn't going to be any *exclusive*."

"Exclusive? Christine, I have no idea what you're talking about."

"Really. I suppose you're here on vacation. Because Sweetwater is a mecca for Pulitzer Prize–winning journalists."

"It was a Hearst Award not a Pulitzer, and it was years ago—a million years ago to be exact. And to answer your question, I live here—for almost a year now. Though I could ask the same of you because I sure as hell can't see Stephen hanging out in a place like Sweetwater."

"Is this some sort of game?"

Wade exhaled long and hard, tired of whatever this was. "Okay, clearly I've missed something. Why would I be playing a game?"

"You honestly expect me to believe you walked into my store, today of all days, purely by accident?"

"I do as a matter of fact. Wait, this is *your* store?"

She eyed him sharply. "The whole town's been talking about it. Have you been living under a rock or something?"

"You could say that. I've been squirreled away in my cabin while I finish revisions for a book I'm working on. Why?"

And just like that the fire in her eyes guttered. "Stephen's dead."

Wade struggled to absorb the words, thinking he must have heard them wrong. "My God, Christine. I'm so sorry. Was he . . . sick?"

"His car went off a bridge just before Thanksgiving. It was all over the news."

He stood there a moment, dragging a hand through his hair. "Jesus. No wonder you thought I was being an ass. I wasn't lying before. I really have been off the grid. And I really am sorry. Stephen and I had our differences, but I never wished him any harm. Are you . . . my God, I don't even know what to say. Are you . . . how are you doing?"

"I'm . . . coping."

"So that's what you're doing here? Starting over?"

"Trying to, yes."

"I imagine it's been hard."

"It has. And it just got a whole lot harder."

She was glaring again. Could all this hostility really be about something that happened four years ago? "Look, I didn't mean to dredge up a lot of unpleasant memories. I know what it's like to have to rebuild your life from the ground up. But at the risk of being nosy, why here? Don't get me wrong, Sweetwater and I go way back, but for someone like you, it's a speck on the map."

"I don't know what that means," she said frostily. *"Someone like you."*

*Damn it.* Everything he said seemed to be hitting a nerve. "I just meant it must be a little slow after the life you're used to."

She eyed him coldly. "You don't know anything about the life I'm used to. And Sweetwater isn't just a speck on the map. Stephen and I actually spent a few days here on our honeymoon. He said the two of you used to come here to fish."

"We did. A long time ago. My grandfather had a cabin up on Silver Lake. It's mine now. I guess we all run back to what we know. Nostalgia's a pretty strong motivator."

She straightened her shoulders, meeting his gaze squarely. "Coming here wasn't about nostalgia. It was about necessity."

"Too many memories?"

"Too many reporters. They were camped out in my driveway, waiting to pounce the minute I set foot out my door. I wound up having to sneak out of my own house in the middle of the night."

"And you ended up here. I can see that, I guess. Wanting to be in a place where you and Stephen spent time."

"Oh, that's good," she shot back drily. "Brokenhearted widow returns to honeymoon haven. Tug at the public's heartstrings, and you can sell it as a human-interest story instead of what it really is—none of anyone's damned business. Either way, I'm sure it'll make a great story. Maybe you'll win another award."

"I'm not a reporter anymore."

She blinked at him. "You expect me to believe that?"

Wade felt the familiar pulse flare to life at his temple. "I do, actually. And it's not polite to assume someone's a liar when you barely know them."

She shrugged, a casual blend of hostility and skepticism. "Forgive me, but I've had experience with your type."

"And what *type* is that?"

"The parasitic type, the kind who'd step over anyone or anything to get a scoop. But don't take it personally. It's how I feel about all reporters."

Her words rankled more than he liked to admit; perhaps because they were hard to deny. Yes, he'd walked away from *Week in Review*. But it would be lying to say he hadn't done things that went against his conscience. Still, he wasn't about to let her know she had landed a blow.

"For starters," he said, not bothering to keep the edge from his voice, "the word *scoop* went out with Perry White and the *Daily Planet*, so if you plan to continue bashing me, you might want to bone up on the lingo. And is it impossible to believe some of us went into journalism because we wanted to do some good?"

"Oh yes, tell me all about journalistic integrity. I'm sure doing good was exactly what the guy outside my bedroom window had in mind when he snapped a picture of me in my underwear."

Wade felt his blood begin to simmer. She had every right to be angry—but not at him. "Guys who do what you just described aren't journalists; they're vultures. And I'll thank you not to lump me in with them. I can show you—"

But she held up a hand before he could finish. "I don't want to hear about your awards or sit through a recitation of your portfolio. I'm sure that's what you all tell yourselves on the first day of reporter school—that you're in it for truth, justice, and the American way, but I know what it's like to be on the other side of the camera, to be mobbed by a pack of jackals who don't care who they crush as long as they get the chance to shove a picture of your husband's half-naked girlfriend in your face while the cameras are rolling, so please . . . spare me your indignation."

Wade tried to blink away the images that had just burned themselves into his brain or to at least prioritize them. It was hard to know what to focus on first; the indefensible—not to mention illegal—invasion of her privacy or her casual mention of a half-naked girlfriend. Either way, he found himself seething, disgusted that she'd had to endure that kind of humiliation at the hands of the media—or her husband for that matter. For all he knew, someone from *Week in Review* had been part of the mob in her driveway. Someone like Simone.

"I'm sorry you had to go through that," he told her quietly. "In fact, I'm sorry anyone ever has to go through it, which is why I left *Review*— and New York. I needed to get the taste of it out of my mouth."

Her gaze narrowed. "Just like that, you up and quit?"

"Just like that. I don't own a television, and there's no Wi-Fi at the cabin, which is why I had no idea Stephen was dead, no idea about the girlfriend, no idea about any of it. That's the truth, Christine."

"Please don't call me that." She sounded tired all of a sudden. And looked it too. "I'm Christy-Lynn Parker here, though I suppose it doesn't matter now."

"You changed your name?"

"It's my maiden name. I was trying to fly under the radar, and until you arrived, I was doing fine."

"There was no way I could have known that."

"You weren't lying," she said finally. "You really *didn't* know."

"I really didn't. The picture of the woman—that really happened the way you said?"

"Yes."

"Did you know? Before Stephen died, I mean?"

"No."

He had a dozen questions bouncing around in his head, but he didn't ask any of them. His antenna, finely tuned after God knew how many interviews, told him to keep his mouth shut and wait. It wasn't easy, but eventually she dropped into one of the café chairs.

"They pulled her out of the car," she said quietly. "Naked from the waist up. They asked if I could identify her body."

*Bloody hell.*

And yet he wasn't as shocked as he should have been. Perhaps because Stephen had stopped shocking him years ago. His widow, however, was another story. Her husband's betrayal had clearly rocked her, perhaps even more than she knew, and for an instant, he found himself tempted to reach for her hand.

"Is there any chance it isn't what it looked like?" he asked instead. "That Stephen and this woman weren't actually . . . involved?"

"No. I don't know who she was, but there was a photograph in Stephen's study, and a bunch of unexplained bank drafts, every month just like clockwork. I haven't had a chance to dig through it all yet, but I'm pretty sure I know what I'll find. The police don't even know who she is. At least they didn't when the morgue photos surfaced a week later."

"Leaked?"

She nodded. "Front page of the *Star Examiner*."

Wade closed his eyes briefly, wishing to God he didn't know what he knew. He could imagine the celebration only too well, the inevitable strutting and chest bumping that came with that kind of score. And with photos, no less. He'd seen Simone bask in the glory of an especially juicy takedown piece, never once considering the people on the other end of those stories. It had sickened him then, and it sickened him now.

"A celebrity. A tragedy. And a half-naked mystery woman," he said, recapping. "That certainly explains the driveway full of reporters, but not how a tabloid got hold of morgue photos."

"Stephen had a friend on the force, a detective by the name of Connelly. He promised to do what he could to keep it out of the papers. Apparently someone had other ideas."

"Who?"

Christy-Lynn shrugged. "They're working on it. Or so they say. To be honest, I haven't called in a while. They don't seem very eager to talk to me."

"No, I don't suppose they would be. It had to be someone inside, probably someone in the ME's office. They don't want the public knowing that."

She sighed and shook her head. "It doesn't matter."

"Doesn't it?"

"Stephen's dead. And so is his wife as far as I'm concerned. I'm Christy-Lynn now."

"Except, I just blew your cover. I really am sorry about that. I wasn't expecting to see you, and then there you were. What are the odds?"

"Yup. Today's my lucky day." She flashed a brittle smile as she pushed back her chair and stood. "I knew someone would recognize me sooner or later. I just hoped it wouldn't be a reporter."

"It wasn't."

"So you say."

"It's true," he said, holding up three fingers in a kind of scout salute. "You have my word of honor."

She eyed him squarely, ignoring his attempt to lighten the moment. "We'll see. I'd like you to go now. We're closing soon, and I'm going to have to explain you."

Wade pushed to his feet, still trying to get a bead on the emotions she was struggling to keep under wraps. Fear. Anger. Those were easy. But there was something else too, something he couldn't put a name to, despite being keenly aware of its pull. "It was good to see you again," he said, extending a hand. When she didn't take it, he withdrew it and stuffed it into his pocket. "Right. I guess not."

He turned and headed for the door, leaving the unpurchased copy of *A Fatal Franchise* on the table. He would read it, of course, at some point. Just like he read all of Stephen Ludlow's novels. Not because they were great. Or even good. They were neither. He read them because he was still trying to figure out what all the fuss was about.

# EIGHTEEN

Christy-Lynn held her breath as she watched him go, releasing it only when she saw him climb into a dusty black Jeep and pull away. It was almost closing time, the store empty. Behind the counter, Aileen and Tamara stood whispering, their heads bent close. Tamara took a step back when Christy-Lynn's gaze settled on her. Aileen turned her attention back to the register, eyes averted as she cracked open a roll of dimes and spilled them into the cash drawer.

It was Tamara who finally spoke. "You okay, boss?"

"Yes," Christy-Lynn said quietly. "I promise I'll explain all that eventually, just not right now."

"Why don't you take a break?" Aileen suggested, handing her the takeout container Missy had brought by. "Eat your salad."

"Or I could make you a nice chai," Tamara offered. "We'll be closing soon. You could just hang out in the café and, you know, collect your thoughts."

Christy-Lynn managed a grateful smile. She appreciated their concern, but at the moment, collecting her thoughts was the last thing she wanted. "Thanks. I think I'll just go straighten the shelves."

It was a relief to disappear into the rows of books, like losing herself in a forest. If only she could stay there and continue to hide. But the truth was out now, which meant hiding was no longer an option. Unless she decided to pick up and run again—but to where and for how long? For all Wade's protests, he could at that very moment be spilling his guts to one of his reporter buddies, and come morning, the press would be back at her heels.

But even worse than the prospect of a renewed media frenzy was the memory of Missy's face as she stood there holding her salad and slowly connecting the dots. Even now, she and Dar were sitting at Taco Loco, sipping margaritas and digesting the fact that they'd been lied to.

She had a lot of explaining to do.

Taco Loco was in full swing when Christy-Lynn arrived. Missy and Dar were already seated, unsmiling as they sipped their drinks, and she found herself grateful for the boisterous Saturday night crowd. Less chance of a scene—she hoped.

She had rehearsed several versions of an apology on the way over but had come up empty. There was simply no way to pretty up what she'd done.

"I can imagine what you must think of me," she began gravely. "But I never meant to lie to you. When I first came to Sweetwater, I was . . . well, I don't know what I was, really, except exhausted. Things were so crazy after Stephen died. And then the pictures leaked, and everyone wanted to know who the woman was—including the reporters. I became a prisoner in my home. And then one day I caught a reporter outside my bedroom window, pointing his camera at me while I stood there in my underwear. That was it. I packed a bag and snuck out of the house. I drove until I couldn't drive anymore—and ended up here."

There was a long stretch of silence when she finished. Missy was shaking her head, staring into her nearly empty margarita glass, while Dar fiddled with the crystal pendant she was never without. Christy-Lynn held her breath, waiting.

It was Dar who finally spoke. "It must have been awful. To be trapped like that. Spied on in your own home. No wonder you left. You must have been beside yourself."

Christy-Lynn felt herself relax but was determined to tell the rest of the story. "It was like having a target on my back. My picture was on the news and in all the tabloids, the phone wouldn't stop ringing, and the house was surrounded. I knew they'd never leave me alone, that no matter where I went they'd hunt me down. Which is why I was so relieved to find Sweetwater. It seemed like the perfect place to hide. I used my maiden name because I was afraid they'd find me. I told myself it was okay since I wasn't staying. And then one thing led to another, and I didn't want to leave. I should have told you sooner. I wanted to. Instead, I let the lie get bigger."

"Bastards," Missy muttered as she banged down her glass. "How dare they put you, or anyone, through that."

Christy-Lynn blinked at her. "You're not . . . mad?"

"Oh, I'm mad," Missy assured her. "But not for the reasons you think. I'm upset that you didn't think you could trust us with the truth. But I guess I get why you were scared."

"I'm sorry. Truly. Today when you came to the shop—"

"You were white as a sheet. I thought you were just tired, and then I saw the guy standing there holding that book, babbling on about your husband, and I didn't know what to think. I hope you don't mind, but I did a little snooping online after I left the store. I couldn't believe it. Those hideous tabloid pictures. And then to be hounded like that." She scowled as she reached for her glass. "Bastards."

"Can't you sue them or something?" Dar asked with uncharacteristic heat. "I don't care how famous your husband was or who was in his car when it went off that bridge. There are just some things that aren't anybody else's business. Like you in your underwear, for Pete's sake. They didn't print that, did they?"

"I don't think so. At least I never saw it. The morgue pictures were bad enough."

Missy was shaking her head again. "How on earth did they get hold of them? Shouldn't they have been . . . I don't know . . . confidential or something? I mean, for pity's sake, she wasn't wearing a shirt. Who wants to see that?"

Dar pulled a face as she reached for a chip. "Are you kidding? People can't get enough of that kind of trash. They don't even care if it's true as long as it's juicy."

Missy sat with arms folded, chin jutting peevishly. "Trash is exactly what it is."

Christy-Lynn stared at them in disbelief. "You're both being so nice. I thought you'd be furious. Not that you wouldn't be justified. I lied to you."

Missy gave her hand a pat. "Of course you did, honey. You were doing what you needed to. And who's to say we wouldn't have done exactly the same thing if we'd been in your shoes?"

Christy-Lynn's throat tightened. "I don't know what to say."

Missy shot her a wink. "Say you see Marco around here somewhere. We're supposed to be celebrating, and my glass is empty."

The mood lightened considerably when the appetizers and a fresh round of drinks arrived at the table. The banter had nearly returned to normal when Missy looked up from her nachos, blotting her mouth with exaggerated daintiness. "All right, I think it's time one of us asked what we've both been wondering since learning the truth about your dearly departed."

Missy's countenance was suddenly somber. Christy-Lynn put down her fork, bracing for whatever might be coming. "Okay."

"How much did the bastard leave you?"

Dar covered her mouth, smothering a giggle while trying to look stern. "Missy! Didn't anyone ever tell you it's impolite to ask someone how much money they have?"

"Oh, like you haven't been dying to know!"

"That isn't the point," Dar barked, still fighting laughter as she turned to Christy-Lynn. "I'm sorry about her. You don't have to answer if you don't want to."

But Christy-Lynn took no offense. "It's all right, really, though the truth is I'm not entirely sure what it all added up to. Stephen always handled that end of things, and after he died, there was so much to take care of. Then I was trying to get the store open. There are still some accounts I have to sort out."

"But you're loaded, right?"

"Missy, that is none of our business!"

Christy-Lynn couldn't help laughing. "Yes, I suppose I am."

"I'm not going to lie," Missy said, picking up her fork again. "I did wonder what kind of life insurance policy would pay for the store and a house. Now I'm wondering why you don't just coast a little. There's so much you could do with money like that."

Christy-Lynn reached for her iced-tea glass, fiddling with the straw. "I know this is going to sound crazy, but I've actually been struggling with the idea of spending it at all. I have the store now and the bunga-low, but that money came from the sale of our house in Clear Harbor. The rest of it, all the investments and the money Stephen earned from his books, is just sitting there piling up. I know it's mine legally, but after everything that's happened, I don't know. Stephen had an opinion about everything. Where we lived. What we ate. Even how I wore my hair. Because I let him. I guess I just want this to be about me, about what I want." She shrugged. "I want to do this myself, to build it from the ground up. Does that make sense?"

Missy smiled softly. "Of course it does. In fact, it's why I bought the inn. Finding myself divorced with two little boys felt like standing at ground zero. I had no idea what my life was supposed to look like. I just knew I needed a plan, fast. So I bought the inn. It was my compass; a direction I could point myself in every day and say this is who I am now, this is what I do. The store is your compass. It'll feel scary for a while, and you'll just know you're in over your head. And then one day when you aren't paying attention, you'll realize it's going to be okay. That's a pretty good day."

Christy-Lynn found herself blinking back tears. She liked the idea of finding her compass, of it someday being okay. "Thank you—both of you—for being so supportive. I'm not sure I deserve it, but I'm grateful."

"Oh, hush," Dar shot back. "It's what friends do. What I really want is to hear about the guy who came into the store. How do you know him?"

"His name is Wade Pierce. He was Stephen's roommate in college. For a while, at least. They had a falling-out."

"What over?"

"I don't know. Stephen never wanted to talk about it, and when Stephen locked something in the vault, it stayed there. I always assumed it was a woman."

"Well, I can certainly see that," Missy said, batting her eyes coyly. "He was rather hunky. At least six three, with great shoulders. A nice face too, if you like them scruffy."

Dar wrinkled her nose. "No thanks. I had a scruffy one once, used to give me beard burn. What does he do, Christy-Lynn?"

"He's a reporter."

Missy's expression hardened. "No wonder you went white as a sheet when you saw him. If the press is still looking for you, he could be trouble."

"Lucky for me, the public has a short attention span. For now at least, they seem to have moved on to greener pastures. And with any luck, it'll stay that way. Besides, he claims he's quit the news business.

He's supposedly working on a novel and living in a cabin up by the lake, apparently without television or Wi-Fi. He didn't even know Stephen was dead until I told him."

"You know," Missy said, tapping her lower lip thoughtfully. "I think my father knew his grandfather. Grayson Pierce his name was, but he went by Grady. According to Daddy, he was a real craftsman. Built that cabin with his own two hands. He died a few years back. I didn't know anyone was living up there. It's in the middle of nowhere though, so I suppose it would be a good place to write. No neighbors and smack-dab on the lake."

Christy-Lynn shrugged. "I don't know anything about his family or the cabin, except that he brought Stephen there a few times to fish back when they were still friends."

"Rotten luck having him turn up and spoil your big day." Missy's gaze narrowed suddenly. "You don't think he'll cause trouble, do you?"

"He could if he wanted to, but I'm hoping he doesn't. He claims he's through with that part of his life. He said he had to leave New York to get the taste of it out of his mouth."

Missy grunted, clearly not convinced. "I'd still watch my back if I were you."

Christy-Lynn offered a noncommittal nod. It was hard to find fault with her advice, but she couldn't help feeling a little guilty about the way she'd gone after Wade in the café, lumping him in with the mob in her driveway when the truth was, apart from his dislike of Stephen, she knew almost nothing about him.

She had assumed—judged. And tonight she had arrived at Taco Loco expecting the same from Missy and Dar. Instead, they had rallied around her, accepting her story at face value and without judgment. It seemed she had a lot to learn about this friendship business.

# NINETEEN

Christy-Lynn checked her watch, hoping it wasn't too late for an impromptu visit. She'd been halfway home after dinner with Missy and Dar when she decided she needed to set the record straight. Unfortunately, directory assistance had no listing for a Wade Pierce, which appeared to back up his story about living off the grid, but also meant having to drive all the way up to Silver Lake in the dark, armed with nothing but Missy's vague description of a lakefront cabin in the middle of nowhere.

Thankfully, the description turned out to be spot-on and enough to get her where she was going. But now, as she stepped up onto Wade's front porch, she was having second thoughts. Yes, she'd been ratty, had even resorted to name calling, but under the circumstances that was hardly surprising. Maybe she should just scurry back to the Rover and forget the whole thing.

Before she could make up her mind, the door swung open. Wade made no attempt to hide his surprise. "Christine. Sorry . . . Christy-Lynn. I thought I heard someone pull up. What are you doing here?"

"I'm sorry. I hope it's not too late to come by."

"Um . . . no." He was holding a mug, and the smell of coffee drifted out onto the porch. "Come on in. I just brewed a fresh pot if you're interested."

"No. No, thank you. I won't be long. I just wanted to talk about this afternoon."

"Can we talk in the kitchen? I need a refill."

Christy-Lynn surveyed the cabin as she followed Wade through to the kitchen. It was small, but the open plan and vaulted ceiling gave it a surprisingly spacious feel. There was a stairway in one corner and a roomy loft overhead. If she craned her neck, she could just glimpse the foot of an unmade bed.

"Are you sure I can't pour you one?"

"No, thanks." Her gaze drifted to the expanse of moonlit water beyond the sliding glass doors. "Quite a view."

"Yes."

An awkward silence spooled out as they stared at each other. Finally, Christy-Lynn found her tongue. "About today. I may have been out of line when I said what I said."

Wade's shoulders seemed to relax, though not completely. "Forget it. I caught you off guard."

"It's just that I've been trying to put everything behind me, and when you showed up out of the blue, all I could think of was the circus starting all over again."

He sipped slowly, as if mulling over her words. "You assumed the minute I left the store I would pick up the phone and tip off an old friend."

"Something like that."

"Do you always assume the worst about people or is it just me?"

Christy-Lynn wasn't sure how to answer that, though it was certainly a fair question. Perhaps it was a little of both, though his bristly manner at present was hardly helping his case. "Look, I came to apologize, but you're not making it easy."

Wade scrubbed at the scruff along his jaw. It wasn't a look Stephen could have pulled off, but on Wade, it worked. "I did offer you coffee."

Christy-Lynn ignored the remark. She wasn't in the mood for humor. "Just let me say what I came to say, and then I'll go. I'm not an idiot. I know you had some kind of ax to grind with my husband, and I'm sorry I jumped to conclusions this afternoon. I shouldn't have. But it's hard not to think that all of this isn't enormously satisfying for you."

"Whoa." Wade set down his mug very slowly. "For someone trying to apologize, that's a pretty harsh accusation. You're saying I'm taking some sort of perverse glee in all this?"

"I'm just stating the facts as I see them. I don't know what happened between you and my husband all those years ago. He never would tell me. I just assumed you fell for the same girl—and that you lost."

Wade's expression hardened. "I assure you the bad blood between Stephen and me had nothing to do with losing out on the homecoming queen."

"You're not going to tell me either."

He picked up his mug, giving it a swirl. "No."

"Fine. Here's what I came to say—I know there's nothing stopping you from picking up the phone. In fact, I'm pretty sure you could make a nice buck if you wanted to, but—"

Wade cut her off with a huff of his own. "First of all, *real* journalists don't pay for stories. It's not what you call . . . ethical. Second, I'm not in the habit of ratting out friends."

Christy-Lynn's chin lifted a notch. "Stephen wasn't your friend. You've made that clear, even if you won't say why."

"I was talking about you."

"Oh." The statement knocked her a little off balance. "Well, I'm not your friend either, am I? And you *were* a reporter, presumably one who still has connections, though until you actually pick up the phone, I guess I'll have to give you the benefit of the doubt."

"Well, it's not exactly warm and fuzzy, but I'll take it. And I wasn't lying when I said I was done with that life, Christy-Lynn. It cost me a great deal to walk away, but I did it. Because I was tired of looking in the mirror and not liking what I saw. I wanted to do something worthwhile, something that made me remember who I was before they got their hooks in me. Except, I'm still not sure I know. Sounds crazy, doesn't it? Not knowing who you are?"

She had been staring out over the lake. She turned to face him. "Actually, it doesn't. Sound crazy, I mean. Sometimes things happen, things we can't control, and it knocks us down—hard. Getting up isn't easy." She turned back toward the glass. "Sometimes it's impossible."

"The woman," Wade said quietly. "The one in the car with Stephen when he died. That's what you meant by things we can't control."

"Yes."

"And what else?"

"Nothing." She shrugged, stepping away from the door. "I don't know. Questions. The kind that creep in when the initial numbness starts to wear off. How long had it been going on? Did he love her?" She paused, hugging her arms tight to her body. "Was it my fault?"

"Did you just say *was it your fault?*"

Her eyes slid from his. "Men cheat because they're trying to make up for something they're not getting at home."

"Who the hell sold you that load of crap? *Cosmo?*"

The harsh response startled her. It also got under her skin. "Okay, you're the expert on male behavior. Why do you think he did it?"

"Because he was Stephen. And because he thought he could get away with it."

She avoided his gaze, running her eyes around the small kitchen; knotty pine cabinets with wrought iron hardware, a plate rail over the sink stacked with thick brown stoneware. "I could've been a better wife," she finally blurted. "Maybe that's why he went looking. Because I wasn't enough."

Wade shook his head, either annoyed or baffled. "Men like Stephen don't cheat because they're missing something at home, Christy-Lynn. They cheat because they're missing something inside, so they take what they want and make it theirs, because they need to fill up all that empty space. That's what this woman was. A space filler, something he wanted and took. It wasn't about you."

She stared at him, weighing his words. "How do you know?"

"Experience."

He'd said it without flinching, as if there was no other answer possible, and suddenly she realized this was what she'd come for. Not to deliver some grudging apology, but to connect with someone who had known her husband, another human being who knew the man—perhaps the *real* man—she had married.

"Thank you," she said quietly.

"For what?"

"Listening, I guess. There are so many things I don't know, so many questions without answers. I haven't really talked to anyone about any of it, unless you count Detective Connelly, and he's not doing much talking these days."

"Have you thought about going over his head?"

"I've threatened to."

"Threatening isn't doing."

There it was again, the undisguised rebuke she had detected earlier, plucking at nerves already exposed and raw. "I've been a little busy getting the store open," she replied coolly. "But the last time I spoke with him, he assured me I'd be wasting my time."

"How long ago was that?"

"I don't know. A few months."

"So that's it? You just took his word? A few minutes ago, you said you had all kinds of questions, and now you tell me you haven't spoken to him in months. It's none of my business, but maybe it's time to ask yourself if you really *want* to know."

Christy-Lynn felt her spine stiffen. He had a way of locking on her eyes, holding them until she wanted to squirm. A natural trait, she wondered, or something he had cultivated as a reporter? Either way, it was unnerving.

"And what is that supposed to mean?"

"Just that sometimes not knowing is easier than coming face-to-face with the facts. Believe me, I have some experience with this. The facts may suck, but they're still the facts. Pretending they're not never works."

"You think I'm pretending?"

"I think you're hiding. And I get why. Just don't be surprised if you reach a point where it stops working."

*Hiding.* It was the perfect word for what she'd been doing. Dodging uncomfortable truths while pretending to be too busy to pick up the phone. Because what then? Knowing the truth meant having to do something about it, didn't it? She'd have to process it, somehow. Own it. Live with it. Was she prepared to do that?

"I think I'd better go."

"I'm not judging, Christy-Lynn."

"Aren't you?"

"Just . . . observing."

"It's hard to tell the difference."

Wade ran a hand through his hair, smiling awkwardly. "Look, I'm not *trying* to be a jerk. I just seem to have knack for it. As you've probably guessed, I have a habit of stating my opinion whether it's wanted or not. For what it's worth, I usually mean well."

Christy-Lynn stood looking at him. If he was hoping for a laugh, he had sadly misjudged his audience. He'd struck too close to the bone, and they both knew it. "I think it's best if we just keep our distance," she threw over her shoulder as she crossed to the front door. She had said her piece. She just wanted to leave and forget the conversation ever happened. If that meant she was hiding, so be it.

Wade watched the Range Rover's taillights fade from sight. He'd certainly mucked that up, managing to turn an apology into a confrontation because he couldn't keep his opinion to himself. But it was she who had opened the door; all he did was walk through it. And in spite of their history, which amounted to exactly one alcohol-induced dissertation on the shortcomings of her husband, he really had wanted to help.

She was in a bad place, questioning her worth as a wife and a woman, blaming herself for things that weren't even close to being her fault. Because she'd made the mistake of getting mixed up with a bastard. Was it possible to be married to Stephen Ludlow and not know who he was underneath? One thing was certain—he'd left his footprints all over Christy-Lynn.

Behind all the icy stares and prickly responses, she was glaringly fragile, like a broken bit of china that had been haphazardly mended. One careless move and she would shatter. Not that all those fissures were necessarily her husband's doing. It was possible that she'd earned them long before meeting Stephen, and that he had merely capitalized on them, sensing an easy mark and then moving in. In fact, the longer he thought about it, the more convinced he was that that was precisely how it had gone down. Not that it mattered. She'd made it crystal clear that their truce—all twelve minutes of it—was over.

Wade's question continued to fester as Christy-Lynn drove home. Could he be right? Did she really *not* want answers? The accusation rankled. Not because he had no right to make it, but because part of her knew he was right.

It had been months since she checked in with Connelly. Yes, she'd been focused on the store, busy with the renovations, but with the opening finally behind her, would she resume her quest for answers? And what did any of it matter really? Stephen was gone, and she had started a new life. Even the media had moved on. Why shouldn't she do the same?

Maybe Wade's theory was right. Maybe the affair hadn't been about her at all, but about Stephen's enormous ego and his sense of entitlement. But what if he was wrong? What if it was something else, something missing in *her* that had actually driven her husband into another woman's arms? The thought should appall her—and did. To buy into the fiction that she was somehow responsible for her husband's infidelity was an affront to betrayed women everywhere. And yet there it was, the pebble in her shoe demanding at long last to be dealt with.

Her thoughts were still churning as she pulled the Rover into her driveway and cut the engine. After the events of the day, it was a relief to turn the key and step through the door of the 1920s bungalow she now called home. It wasn't grand, but then she hadn't wanted it to be. In fact, it was rather shabby, the rooms still crowded with Carol's furniture and knickknacks, the bath and kitchen sadly dated. There simply hadn't been room in her brain to tackle renovating the shop and the house simultaneously. Now, with the opening behind her, she could finally start thinking about making the bungalow a home.

Just not tonight.

At some point during the drive home, her head had begun to throb. The opening had exceeded her wildest hopes, and she had managed to smooth things over with Missy and Dar, and yet she couldn't shake the niggling suspicion that Wade Pierce wasn't through complicating her life. But she'd have to think about that tomorrow. At the moment, she didn't have the energy to do more than swallow two ibuprofen, peel out of her clothes, and fall into bed. She sighed as she slid between the sheets and clicked off the bedside lamp, her limbs suddenly leaden as she drifted toward a strange and watery dreamscape.

*The water is icy, a million needles prickling at her skin. And murky. Like tea or dirty dishwater. There is a light in the distance—no, a pair of lights—dismal points in the watery gloom. Lying lifeless along the bottom is a hulk of cold, bent metal. A woman's face looms behind a square of glass, blue-white and familiar, her pale hair fanned out like a halo around her head. She floats there with eyes closed, a grisly mermaid, the sunken place at her temple strangely bloodless. And then suddenly her eyes are not closed. They're wide and glassy, vivid violet through all that water. And then the blue-tinged lips begin to move. The words are garbled and indecipherable, but there is a sense of despair in the empty eyes, of desolation and loss as her lips continue moving, as if she is trying to impart some terrible secret. A confession? A prayer? An apology come too late? There is no way to know. And then without warning, the violet eyes are shuttered, the blue lips suddenly quiet. All is still again beneath the waves. But Christy-Lynn does not swim away. Instead, she remains, floating, waiting—willing the dead violet eyes to open again.*

# TWENTY

Christy-Lynn stared at the stacks of papers on her desk but couldn't make herself focus. The dream had come again last night, as it had nearly every night for the last five weeks—since the night she'd gone up to Silver Lake to see Wade.

She was no stranger to dark dreams—she had suffered night terrors well into adolescence—but this was different, the images so disturbingly vivid they often left her gasping and drenched with sweat. But the dreams had begun to take a physical toll too. She'd been lethargic of late and punchy, the by-product of being afraid to close her eyes for fear of being jolted awake in the wee hours.

It didn't take a PhD to figure out what had conjured that first dream—or to understand why she was *still* having them. Wade may have strayed into prickly territory, but his observations had thrown a floodlight on things she'd been trying very hard not to see—primarily that she had purposely been ducking questions about Stephen's Jane

Doe. And now, more than a month later, she still hadn't plucked up the courage to pick up the phone.

On impulse, or perhaps out of defiance, she reached for her cell. For better or worse, it was time to stop wondering. "I'd like to speak to Detective Connelly," she said briskly when a Sergeant Wood answered on the second ring.

"I'm sorry, ma'am. Detective Connelly is no longer with the department."

For a moment, she thought she'd heard him wrong. "Did you say he's no longer with the department?"

"Yes, ma'am."

"What does that mean?"

There was a pause, as if he didn't quite understand the question. "It means he's not here, that he's taken early retirement."

"When?"

"First of the year, I believe. Is there someone else I can connect you to?"

"No—yes! I'd like to speak to whoever has taken over Detective Connelly's cases."

"And may I have your name?"

"Christine Ludlow. I was Stephen Ludlow's wife, and I was hoping . . ."

"One moment, please."

The line abruptly went silent. A moment later, there was a new voice in her ear. "This is Captain Billings, Mrs. Ludlow, with the Office of Public Affairs. How can I help you?"

"Are you Detective Connelly's boss?"

"Not exactly, though I did outrank him, if that's what you're asking."

Christy-Lynn fumbled for a response. The truth was she didn't know what she was asking. She was still trying to wrap her head around the fact that Connelly was gone when she was almost certain he'd told her he was still two years from retirement.

"Mrs. Ludlow?"

"Yes, I'm sorry. I was hoping to speak to whoever was handling Detective Connelly's cases. I've been trying to get some information about my husband's accident. Particularly about the woman who was in the car with him that night."

"Your husband's case was closed months ago, Mrs. Ludlow. There was no indication of foul play, and the tox levels all came back within legal limits. The ME's finding was accidental death by drowning."

"And the woman?"

There was a brief stretch of silence. "The woman?"

"Yes, Captain, the woman. I'm sure you remember her. Her pictures were in all the tabloids thanks to someone in your department."

The captain cleared his throat, a halting, awkward sound. "Yes, of course. That was . . . unfortunate. But I'm afraid we're not releasing any information with regard to the second victim. It's a rather sensitive matter, after all, particularly in light of your husband's high visibility, and the family has a right to privacy. Perhaps it would be best to simply . . . let it lie."

Christy-Lynn's blood began to simmer. "It's a little late to be worrying about sensitivity, don't you think? And where was all this concern for privacy when the press was camped out in my driveway, passing around photos that someone in your department leaked?"

"Mrs. Ludlow." His voice was sharper now, more like a lawyer's than a police captain's. "There has been no confirmation that those photos were leaked by anyone in this department, though I do understand how difficult this must be for you. And despite what you might think, we take a family's right to privacy very seriously. Which is why we won't be releasing any information we may or may not have on a second victim."

"And what about my rights as a wife? Do you not take those seriously?"

"Forgive me for sounding unfeeling. I don't mean to be. But that really isn't our concern. I hope you'll understand. Goodbye."

There wasn't time to protest before the line went dead. Christy-Lynn stared at the blank phone screen with a mixture of confusion and annoyance. They were clearly eager to put the leak behind them, but where did that leave her?

Her hands shook as she scrolled through her contacts for Connelly's cell number. If the good detective was no longer a member of the Clear Harbor police force, he might finally be willing to help.

Unfortunately, the number was no longer in service, which seemed odd. She could see a home phone being disconnected if he had moved, but most people kept their cell numbers, didn't they? Her next call was to directory assistance, but the home number they gave her turned out to be disconnected as well. She remembered him saying something about a sailboat in the Keys, but trying to locate Connelly on one of the forty islands that comprised the Florida Keys would be like looking for a needle in a haystack.

She was still contemplating what to do next when Tamara appeared with a tall to-go cup in her hand.

"What's that?"

"A triple-shot latte," Tamara said with an unmistakable air of pity.

"Do I look that bad?"

"Nothing a little caffeine and concealer won't fix. By the way, you have a visitor."

Christy-Lynn smothered a sigh. At this rate, she was never going to get to the invoices. "Who is it?"

Tamara flashed a grin. "I'll give you a hint—tall, dark, and scruffy."

"Wade's here?"

"Of course he's here. He's here all the time—as if you didn't know."

"Yes, but not to see me."

Tamara rolled her eyes, as if she were dealing with a particularly dense child. "Yeah. Whatever. Anyway, consider yourself informed."

Wade was in the café when she stepped out of the back room. He nodded as she approached. "Hello."

"Hello."

His eyes narrowed slightly. "You okay? You look tired."

"Yes, I've been told. What's up?"

"I came to ask you to lunch."

It took a moment to process the words, and she still wasn't sure she had it right. "What?"

"I said I came to ask you to lunch."

"Why?"

It was hardly a gracious reply, but she was too surprised to search for the Miss Manners response. They saw each other several times a week— or perhaps avoided each other was a more accurate way to describe the curt nods that passed for a greeting whenever they happened to make eye contact in the café. How had they gone from that to lunch?

"I'm proposing a truce. I've decided it's silly that we keep bumping into each other and never know what to say."

"I don't keep bumping into you," Christy-Lynn pointed out coolly. "You keep coming into my store."

"Fair enough. Sometimes I need a change of scenery, and this works. So what do you say? Lunch?"

"I'm working. Or trying to. It's not going very well."

"Anything I can do to help?"

"Not unless you want to unpack and shelve three boxes of books."

"Tempting, but I'll take a rain check."

"So it was more of a hypothetical offer then."

He grinned, suddenly looking very boyish. "Something like that. Maybe we can do lunch another time?"

Christy-Lynn gave him a half-hearted shrug. He was obviously intent on clearing the air between them, though after so many years, she wasn't sure why he cared. Maybe he was one of those guys who needed to be liked. She, on the other hand, was perfectly willing to keep him at arm's length. "Yeah, maybe."

She watched him leave, waiting until he had climbed into the Jeep and driven away before turning back to Tamara, who was quietly grinning from ear to ear as she pretended to wipe down the counter.

Christy-Lynn shook a finger at her across the counter. "I know what that smile's about, and you can get that idea right out of your head. We don't even like each other."

"He's hot though, isn't he?"

"I'm not paying you to ogle the customers."

"No," Tamara said, smirking. "But it's a nice perk."

"Hey, what's going on in here?" Aileen had appeared, a feather duster in hand. "You're not supposed to be having fun without me."

"I don't know about fun," Tamara said saucily. "But I'm pretty sure the boss has an admirer."

"No, the boss doesn't," Christy-Lynn snapped. "Now get to work, both of you. I'll be paying bills if you need me. And no whispering behind my back, or I'll know."

She could hear Tamara and Aileen already giggling as she walked away. For weeks now, they'd been making snide remarks about the frequency of Wade's visits, though they clearly had the wrong idea about his motives. It was understandable, she supposed, seeing what they wanted to see. They were young and still starry-eyed, too naive to know that true love and happily ever after were the stuff of fairy tales—and that sometimes the line between frog and prince got pretty blurry.

# TWENTY-ONE

*Monck's Corner, South Carolina*
*April 12, 1998*

*It usually starts over cigarettes—who smoked the last one, whose turn it is to buy—and eventually shifts to beer. Tonight's sparring match is no different, the petulant sniping, the petty slurs, the raised voices escalating into full-on tirades. Christy-Lynn is in her room, nose buried in a history book, U2 on full blast to drown out the ugliness going on in the kitchen.*

*It's hardly a new occurrence, although Derrick, the latest in her mother's recent stretch of live-in losers, is louder than the last few. He scares her sometimes when he drinks, which is most of the time. He swears and throws things and is quick with a slap when her mother talks back. It's better when they're both high—or at least quieter—but that's only when there's money for a score. They've been on COD status with their dealer since her mother lost her job at the Piggly Wiggly.*

*Borrowing.*

*That's what her mother had called it when they caught her skimming money from the register. Her boss had called it embezzlement and fired her. The only reason she wasn't locked up is because he dropped the charges when she told the police she had a little girl at home that she was raising on her own.*

*They're letting her pay it back fifty dollars at a time. Except she isn't having much luck finding another job. Someone from the Piggly Wiggly must have let the cat out of the bag, which means it's just tip money from the Getaway Lounge and whatever Derrick brings home when he's sober enough to work.*

*Christy-Lynn puts in as many hours as they'll give her at the doughnut shop. It's not much, but it helps with food and maybe the lights. Not the rent though. That's past due again. Two months. But no one talks about that. Because no one knows what happens next. And they don't seem to care. They just drink and fight and get high.*

*The yelling from the kitchen ratchets up again, unintelligible except for the occasional string of profanities bleeding under the door. Christy-Lynn cranks up the music another notch and returns to her history book. She knows only too well the folly of intervening in her mother's squabbles. Not that she hasn't tried. For her efforts over the years, she's been kicked, slapped, and punched in the head. But that isn't the worst of it. The worst is that her mother always ends up resenting her the next day, as if she'd rather wake up with a black eye or a broken jaw than risk driving away her latest Prince Charming.*

*Suddenly, over the rhythmic grind of "Bullet the Blue Sky," comes the shattering of glass, three explosions in rapid succession, followed by a howl of rage, and then a bloodcurdling shriek. Christy-Lynn's history book tumbles to the floor as she scrambles off the bed and down the hall toward the wartorn kitchen. But she's already too late.*

*Charlene Parker is sprawled on her knees like a heap of broken kindling, a bloody hand clutched to the left side of her face. Christy-Lynn stares in horror at the steady ooze of red trickling through her mother's fingers and onto the grimy kitchen floor. Above her, Derrick stands with legs wide apart, weaving a little on his feet.*

"What did you do?" Christy-Lynn demands, eyeing the paring knife still clenched in his fist. "She's covered with blood!"

The blade in his hand is bloody too. Derrick looks down at it, as if surprised to find it there. "Bitch threw a bottle at me," he growls, revealing bloody gums and a missing incisor. His lip is split like a ripe plum, his chin smeared with blood.

He takes a step forward, but Christy-Lynn is there, blocking him. "Get away from her," she hurls at him. "Or I'll do more than that!"

Charlene is sobbing, flailing drunkenly as she struggles to rise, then slips again in the rapidly growing slick of blood. "You cut me!" she wails raggedly. "You cut my face, you drunken bastard!"

It takes some doing, but Christy-Lynn manages to pull her mother to her feet. She's snarling now and sobbing, the front of her T-shirt smeared a bright, gory red. Christy-Lynn feels a cold whirl of panic, a faintly metallic tang at the back of her throat. She's never seen so much blood—her mother's blood—and for a moment, the room sways as she registers the damage.

The left side of Charlene Parker's face has been flayed from cheek to chin, revealing a gaping span of quivering pink flesh beneath. There will be a scar, Christy-Lynn notes dimly. Her mother's beautiful face is in ruins.

And then there are sirens wailing outside the apartment complex, blue lights flashing coldly through thin curtains. Fists begin to pound on the apartment door, mingling with Charlene's desperate wails.

"Police! Open up!"

"Help me!" Charlene bellows over the pounding. "He's trying to kill me!"

Derrick looks down at the knife in his hand, and for a moment, Christy-Lynn is sure he's about to lunge at one of them. Desperate men do desperate things. Instead, he drops the knife, frantically casting about for some alternate route of escape. Before he can manage a step, there's the shriek of splintering wood, and then the police are exploding through the door, guns drawn like on TV. Christy-Lynn's legs wobble with relief at the sight of them. For once, she's grateful for nosy neighbors.

*Derrick stands stonily as he's handcuffed and read his rights. Christy-Lynn watches with a kind of savage satisfaction. She's glad he's going to jail, glad he won't be hanging around anymore, freeloading off what little they have. But her satisfaction is short-lived. The medics have arrived and are in the kitchen examining Charlene, starting an IV and tending to her face. The police are in the kitchen too, reading Charlene her rights. Assault, they explain. Not self-defense. Because she threw the bottle at Derrick before he came at her with the knife and not after.*

*Christy-Lynn is allowed to ride in the ambulance, but when they arrive at the hospital, she's told to have a seat in the waiting room. She can only watch helplessly as they wheel her mother away. It's nearly 5:00 a.m. before she's allowed to see her.*

*The room is cold and smells of antiseptic. Its stillness after the clamor of the waiting room is unsettling. Charlene lies very still in the slightly raised bed, a tube in her arm, her left cheek swathed in gauze. The doctors have sewn up her face.*

*Her lids flutter open. "Baby . . ."*

*Christy-Lynn stares down at the bed, and for a moment, her mother's face goes blurry. She used to be the most beautiful girl in Monck's Corner, and now—*

*"Does it hurt?"*

*"Not now." Charlene's fingers creep to the bandage on the left side of her face. Her nails are still crusted with blood. "They gave me . . . something. Numb."*

*"Did they say when you can come home?"*

*Charlene closes her eyes, turning her head as a pair of tears squeeze from beneath her lashes. "I don't think I'll be coming home, baby. Not for a while, at least. I'm in some trouble."*

*Trouble. The word hovers ominously in the quiet. "But Derrick—"*

*"It isn't just tonight, Christy-Lynn."*

*"The money you took from the Piggly Wiggly?"*

*She nods, sighing heavily. "And . . . other things."*

"What things?"

"Things I didn't want you to know about. It has to do with a guy I know. An . . . arrangement we had."

"Sex?" Christy-Lynn asks softly.

"Yes, sort of."

"So you could get drugs."

She nods again, eyes skittering away. "And one night I got caught. It didn't amount to much—solicitation, first offense. But it all adds up, and now . . ."

"You'll go to jail?"

"That's how it's looking."

Christy-Lynn takes an involuntary step back. "What about me? Did you tell them you had a daughter?"

"There are places . . ."

"No!"

"It'll only be for a few months," she promises in the wheedling, petulant voice she hauls out when she's made a mess of things. "A year at the most. It'll be over before you know it. And when it is, we'll be together again. We'll move away, start somewhere new. It won't be so bad, you'll see. You'll even be able to visit me."

But Christy-Lynn has stopped listening. She doesn't want to visit her mother in jail or move somewhere new when this is all over. Because it will never be over. It will only start again in a new town, with a new set of problems, and probably a new dealer.

"I'm sorry, baby," Charlene whispers, reaching for her daughter. "So sorry."

"I know, Mama," she says quietly, ignoring her mother's outstretched hand. "You're always sorry."

# TWENTY-TWO

*Sweetwater, Virginia*
*May 1, 2017*

Christy-Lynn eyed Wade's Jeep in the driveway as she lifted her hand and knocked a third time. He was clearly home. Was he ignoring her? Paying her back for snubbing his lunch invitation? If so, it probably wasn't a great time to ask for a favor.

She knocked again and waited, almost relieved when there was still no answer. It had been a crazy idea anyway. She was about to step off the porch when she heard a door slam somewhere around back. She weighed her options—suck it up and ask what she'd come to ask or leave with her pride intact and no hope of getting the answers she now knew she wanted.

Skirting the remains of last winter's woodpile, she made her way around the back of the cabin. Wade was coming down the deck steps, a red nylon tote slung over his shoulder as he headed for the small wooden canoe beached at the waterline. He had one leg in when he spotted her. He straightened and stood staring at her, a hand raised to shield his eyes against the lowering sun.

"Hello," she said awkwardly, as if she'd been caught trespassing.

"Have you changed your mind about lunch?"

She ducked her head sheepishly. "I came to talk."

"About a truce?"

Christy-Lynn smothered a groan, too weary to spar. "Can't we just . . . talk?"

"Get in the boat."

Christy-Lynn's eyes went wide. "What?"

"If you want to talk, you'll need to do it on the water."

She laughed, though something told her he wasn't kidding. "I'm not really dressed—"

"We won't be waterskiing or anything. Kick off your shoes and leave your purse. You'll be fine."

Christy-Lynn eyed the canoe warily, asking herself again just how badly she wanted Wade's help.

"What's wrong? Can't you swim?"

"Of course I can swim."

"Then what's the problem?"

When it became clear he had no intention of relenting, Christy-Lynn dropped her purse and kicked off her ballet flats. Wade steadied the boat as she stepped in, instructing her to keep both hands on the gunwales— which she assumed meant the sides—as she inched her way forward, then turned and carefully lowered herself onto the narrow cane seat.

A moment later, Wade was pushing away from shore, settled across from her as they headed smoothly out onto the water. For a time, neither spoke, Wade paddling with close, easy strokes, Christy-Lynn marveling at the echo of sunlit clouds mirrored in the lake's glassy surface.

"It's beautiful." She took a deep breath, feeling herself relax as she filled her lungs with pine-scented air. She hadn't meant to say it aloud. In fact, she didn't realize she had until Wade met her gaze.

"Yes, it is. So?"

"So . . ."

He shrugged, his face blank as he pulled the paddle out of the water and laid it across his knees. "It's your meeting."

Christy-Lynn nodded. "Yes, I guess it is." She paused to regroup, then began again. "The last time I was here you said something. You said I might not really want to know the truth about the woman in Stephen's car."

"Yeah, sorry. I had no right to say that stuff. Your grief is none of my business."

"No, it isn't. But that doesn't change the fact that you were probably right. The longer I thought about it, and about what I might learn, the more I realized I was afraid."

"Of what?"

Her eyes were fixed on her lap, fingers pleating and unpleating the hem of her skirt. "Do you have any idea what it's like to learn your spouse's darkest secrets from a pack of reporters? To be the last one to know he's been leading some kind of double life?"

"No, but I can imagine."

She lifted her chin. "Can you?"

"I think so, yes."

"Mrs. Ludlow, do you know the woman they pulled from your husband's car the night he died and were they involved sexually? Do you know how long the relationship had been going on? Have there been other women, or was she the first?" She held his gaze, fighting tears that were more about anger than self-pity. "And those were the polite questions. But the worst part was I couldn't have answered them if I wanted to. And it made me ashamed. How could I not know what my own husband was up to? And then when you said what you said the other night, about me not *wanting* to know, I was ashamed all over again. Because I realized you were right. I didn't want to know. Not really."

Wade reached for the red tote and unzipped it, producing a paper towel and a bottled water. "Here," he said, pushing the paper towel into her hands. "You're leaking."

"Sorry." She felt foolish as she blotted her eyes. "I didn't come here because I wanted you to feel sorry for me. I just wanted you to understand."

"I get it. I do." He was foraging in the tote again, pulling out a variety of leftover containers, peeling off lids and balancing them on his lap. "Because I've seen it firsthand. The news business was different when I got in. It used to be about real news. Now it's about voyeurism and the public's need to revel in the suffering of others. The human fallout doesn't enter into it. It's about ratings, circulation, copies sold."

She dabbed at her eyes again. "And that's why you quit?"

"Yes. It had been coming for a while, but things reached critical mass when they asked me to interview a kid who'd just watched his mother die at the Crystal Lake shooting. So here I am."

"Writing your book?"

"Trying to, yes. Want some dinner?"

Christy-Lynn blinked at him, surprised by the abrupt change of subject. For a moment, she considered pressing for more, but something in his expression warned her off. Instead, she surveyed the makeshift picnic spread out on his lap: cold chicken, fresh fruit, and what looked like potato salad.

"Go on," Wade prompted, holding out the container of chicken. "There's plenty."

She chose a drumstick and began nibbling, not because she was hungry but because she wasn't ready to tell him why she had really come.

"This is delicious," she said between bites, an awkward attempt at small talk. "Where did you get it?"

Wade glanced up, looking mildly insulted. "I didn't *get* it. I made it."

"Well then, I'm impressed."

He shrugged. "Not much to it actually. Lemon, olive oil, some rosemary, and a little garlic. Marinate it for a couple of hours, then throw it on the grill. The potato salad, on the other hand, is from the deli. If it isn't some form of pasta or something I can toss on the grill, I'm fairly hopeless."

Christy-Lynn found herself smiling. "I'm still impressed. I don't think Stephen knew how to turn on the oven."

"My ex-wife's idea of a home-cooked meal was coffee and a Twinkie. She was a whiz with a takeout menu, though." He reached back into the tote, producing a fork, and handed it to her along with the container of potato salad. "Sorry, there's only one. I wasn't expecting company. You go first."

They ate in silence as dusk settled around them, the quiet broken only by the occasional splash or a birdcall from high in the trees. After a few bites, she wiped the fork with her paper towel and handed it back to Wade, along with the potato salad, watching as he dove in with gusto.

"So," she said, trying to sound offhand and failing miserably. "Are you still . . . connected to any of the people you worked with at *Review*?"

Wade looked up and stopped chewing. "We're going *there* again?"

"No," she said quickly. "But yes, a little. I was wondering if you might . . . be able to help me."

He suddenly looked leery. "Help you how?"

Christy-Lynn clamped her hands between her knees and glanced away. "I called the Clear Harbor police this afternoon. They said Daniel Connelly has taken early retirement. So I did what you said and went over his head. Or tried to. No one would tell me anything. Not even her name. So I was wondering . . ."

"If I could get one of my parasitic reporter pals to dig up the dirt on her?"

Christy-Lynn felt her cheeks go hot. "I suppose I deserved that."

"I was merely pointing out the irony of the situation in case you had missed it."

He was enjoying himself immensely, and she supposed he had a right to that. "You don't have to explain it to me," she told him sheepishly. "I'm aware. In fact, I almost didn't come. But I was out of options.

So here I am, sitting in your boat, eating crow. If you'll just row me back to shore, I'll go."

"Paddle."

"What?"

"You don't row a canoe. You paddle. Oars are attached. Paddles aren't."

"Fine. Then will you *paddle* me back to shore?"

"No."

Christy-Lynn's eyes widened. "No?"

"I have some questions first."

"Such as?"

"Such as, what do you plan to do with the information you're asking for?"

She scowled at him, confused by the question. "I don't plan to do anything with it. I just want to know who she was. My husband died with a half-naked woman in his car. I have a right to at least know her name, even if the police don't agree."

"And how will her name change anything?"

"It won't. But at least I'll have some closure."

"Knowing the name of your husband's mistress will give you closure?"

Christy-Lynn squirmed on the narrow cane seat. He was doing it again, studying her, probing for more than she wanted to tell. And he was good at it. "I'm not planning on causing trouble if that's what you're asking."

"It is, in part. You're asking me to do something I normally wouldn't consider. But I do think you have the right to know her name, even if I don't understand your *need* to know it. If I agree to do this, I have to know you're not going to use the information to hurt someone."

Her chin came up a notch. "I don't want to hurt anyone. I just want to close the door on that chapter of my life. I thought that was what you *wanted* me to do."

"Where does what I want come into it? I just asked a question. But I'm starting to think there's something else going on, something you're not telling me."

"Like what exactly?"

"I don't know, but it's there. And this isn't just the journalist in me talking. I can feel it. What's really going on?"

"A dream," she said grudgingly. But the words were almost a relief as they left her lips. "Almost every night. It's her . . . under the water. Her eyes are open like they were in the morgue photos, only she isn't dead. She's blinking and her mouth is moving like she's trying to talk to me, only I can't hear what she's saying." Christy-Lynn closed her eyes, trying to keep the quaver from her voice. "I want it to stop."

"And having a name will make it stop?"

"I don't know. I just thought . . ." She shrugged, wiping at her cheek with the back of her hand. "I honestly don't know what I thought. Never mind. It was a stupid idea."

"I'll make a call."

The canoe rocked lightly as Christy-Lynn jerked her head up. "You will?"

"There's a guy I used to work with at *Review*—Glen Hoyt. He's a crime beat writer. The old-school type with plenty of contacts. He might be . . . helpful."

"Thank you."

"You do know you're probably not going to like what you find out, right?"

"Yes."

"And you're okay with that?"

She returned his gaze frankly. "Honestly? I can't imagine learning anything worse than what I already know."

Wade grunted darkly as he began to pack up the food containers. "First rule of journalism—never assume you've seen the worst."

# TWENTY-THREE

*Sweetwater, Virginia*
*May 9, 2017*

Christy-Lynn juggled an armload of cookbooks, nearly dropping them all as she reached for the phone. "Good afternoon. The Crooked Spine."

"Since when does the boss answer the phone?"

The sound of Wade's voice caught her off guard. "Since Aileen's out having a root canal and next Sunday is Mother's Day. They're running me ragged around here."

"Sounds like it. Are you getting any sleep?"

"Here and there," she said, trying not to sound evasive even as she avoided the question. "What's up?"

"Actually, I had a phone call this morning. I have some information."

"Oh . . ." The news nearly knocked the breath out of her, but it was what she wanted, wasn't it? All the gritty details?

"If you've changed your mind—"

"No. No, I haven't changed my mind. I just . . . didn't expect to hear back so soon. It's barely been a week."

"I told you, my guy has connections."

"Oh . . . right." Christy-Lynn pulled in a deep breath and let it out slowly. "Okay, I'm ready."

"I'm not sure doing this over the phone is a good idea, especially with you at work. Come by the cabin after you close up."

Christy-Lynn felt her stomach clench, like the sensation you got when you looked down from the top of the Ferris wheel and realized just how far the drop was. He wouldn't tell her over the phone? What had he found out?

"Is it that bad?"

"I just think it would be better if we do it in person, when you'll have time to process."

"All right then. I'll see you as soon as I lock up."

It was nearly seven by the time she pulled into Wade's driveway. He was already at the door when she stepped onto the porch, a kitchen towel over one shoulder, a wooden spoon in his hand. "I thought you forgot about me."

"Sorry. We had a few last-minute customers, and then there was a ton of stuff to reshelve." The mingled aromas of garlic and oregano enveloped her as she followed him inside. "Oh no, I'm screwing up your dinner again."

"Our dinner. Please tell me you like spaghetti."

"I love spaghetti, but I didn't come to eat. I can come back, really."

"Don't be silly. You're here, and there's enough to feed a small army. Besides, we're not discussing anything until you've been fed." He turned, heading back to the kitchen. "If you get any thinner, you're going to disappear on me completely, which would stink since I think we're actually on the verge of becoming friends."

Christy-Lynn found herself grinning. When had he become charming? "So I'm being blackmailed?"

"Precisely."

She had no choice but to follow him to the kitchen where a pot of sauce bubbled on the stove. She watched as he dropped his spoon in then lifted it out for a taste. "I think I might just have pulled it off."

"I thought you only tackled things you could cook on the grill."

"Well, I cheated a little. I started with the bottled stuff, then doctored it up. But I think it's pretty good. The salad's made. All I need to do is throw the pasta in to boil."

Christy-Lynn eyed him warily. He was too cheerful, too chatty. It set off warning bells in her head. "Is this your way of softening whatever you're about to tell me? A high-carb meal?"

"Actually, it's my way of avoiding work. My writing day pretty much sucked, so I thought I'd try my hand at cooking instead."

Christy-Lynn wandered to the small bistro table in the corner as he wrestled with a box of vermicelli. His Mac was there and open, a Word document up on the screen. She had just begun to read the opening lines of chapter eighteen when Wade snaked an arm past her and lowered the screen.

"Please don't read that."

"Sorry. Force of habit. The editor in me, I guess. I should have known you'd be the protective type. A lot of men are."

"More like the embarrassed type," he corrected with a scowl. "Not one of my better efforts, I'm afraid. In fact, I meant to delete the whole scene."

"It isn't as easy as it looks, is it?"

"What?"

"Writing the great American novel."

"I take it that's a shot about my lack of reverence for your husband's work?"

"No. Just an observation. You did call him a hack though, which is a pretty harsh thing to say to a man who's cranked out a dozen bestsellers."

"*Cranked* being the operative word."

Christy-Lynn bit back her initial response, confused by a knee-jerk need to defend Stephen despite the validity of Wade's criticism. Habit, she supposed. Or misplaced loyalty. Like the night she had unloaded on him in the bar at the Omni.

"It doesn't really matter now, does it? Can't we just drop it?"

Wade gave the pasta a quick stir then set down his spoon. "I just think if you're going to put a hundred thousand words on paper, you should take the time to choose the *right* ones, instead of just grabbing the ones on the bottom shelf. Writing should be about quality not quantity."

"I agree with that. In fact, I tell my writers the same thing. But there's a lot less time to reach for those top-shelf words when you're writing to contract. Deadlines are real, and if you want to keep getting paid to write books, you treat them as sacred. It's a matter of finding the line between efficiency and integrity and then walking it. It's tricky."

"Did Stephen walk that line?"

"What do you mean?"

"Do you think your husband cared about integrity?"

Christy-Lynn stared at him, wondering if she'd lost the thread of the conversation. "Are we talking about writing or something else?"

"I'm talking about both—about everything. Integrity isn't something you have in some parts of your life and not in others. You either have it, or you don't. I'm asking if you think Stephen did."

Christy-Lynn was both startled and confused by the intensity in his tone. "Under the circumstances, I'm not sure I'm the right person to ask."

"You were married to him. That makes you the perfect person to ask."

"I can tell you he was dedicated to his career, that he worked all the time and never missed a deadline. He started every morning at five and worked past midnight a lot of nights. Sometimes he'd even go off and check into a hotel somewhere so he could—" She stopped midsentence, letting the words trail away. "Except he wasn't working, was he? He was with her."

Wade dropped his gaze to the floor. "I didn't mean to dredge up—"

"Your pasta's about to boil over," she said flatly, cutting him off and effectively ending the conversation. The sooner they got through dinner, the sooner she would have her answers.

They ate out on the deck or at least attempted to. Thirty minutes in, Christy-Lynn gave up the pretense and pushed back her plate. "I'm sorry. I just can't."

"You didn't like it?"

"No, it's fine. I'm just not hungry." It was the truth. She was too keyed up to eat. In fact, she wasn't sure she had tasted a single bite of what was on her plate. "I'm sorry. You went to all this trouble, and I'm being rude."

"Forget it. It gave me a chance to eat off real plates instead of wolfing down my food over the sink. That's what guys do, by the way, when they live all alone in the woods. They turn into cavemen."

"Do you actually like living up here all by yourself?"

He leaned back in his chair, propping a leg on the corner of the table. "Never really thought about it. It is what it is, I guess."

Christy-Lynn squinted one eye against the sun as she continued to study him. His answer had been just a little too nonchalant to be convincing. "I don't think I knew you were married the first time we met, but I seem to remember there being a woman with you—sleek, brunette, very glam."

"Simone."

"What happened there?"

"I think the question you're looking for is, *Who* happened?"

"There was someone else?"

"Someone *elses*," he corrected drily. "Plural. She was ambitious. I'll give her that. But not very good at covering her tracks. To be honest,

I think she stopped bothering. When I finally confronted her, she told me she was glad I knew, that I'd become a self-righteous bore, and she didn't know why she ever married me."

Christy-Lynn winced, a mingled pang of pity and guilt. It had never occurred to her that he might have suffered a few heartaches of his own. Or that when he spoke about infidelity he was speaking from experience. "I suppose it would be hard to save any marriage after that."

He eyed her grimly. "The phrase 'all the king's horses and all the king's men' comes to mind." He reached past his water and grabbed his beer instead, draining it in one long swallow. "It was inevitable, I suppose. We weren't a couple. We were a team. Work was what we had. Maybe all we had. When I left *Week in Review* that was gone. It's taken me a while, but I've come to terms with it."

She studied him a moment, the tight lines around his mouth, the rapid tick that had begun to pulse at his temple. "Have you?"

He looked away, but not before a shadow darkened his face. "I thought we were supposed to be talking about Stephen."

Wade's words felt like a glass of icy water poured down her back. She pulled in a lung full of air, then pushed it back out very slowly, hands braced on the arms of her chair. "Yes, we are. So let's have it."

"Her name was Honey Rawlings."

Christy-Lynn sat very still, letting the name play over in her head, and for one terrible moment, she was back in the morgue, staring down at the chalk-white face from her nightmares, beautiful and bloodless. *Honey.*

"Did your . . . source happen to mention how they met?"

"I'm afraid not. But we do know she was from West Virginia—a little spit of a town called Riddlesville." He pulled a folded sheet of paper from his shirt pocket and laid it open on the table. "It appears she still has family there. A grandmother named Loretta, and a brother, the honorable Reverend Ray Rawlings. We did manage to find an address for the grandmother, but if either of them has a phone, it isn't listed.

Not sure if that's new since the accident or not. It could be, though. Apparently the family's a bit sensitive about Honey's involvement with a married man. The brother has threatened to sue the entire state of Maine if his sister's name ever leaks in connection with your husband's, which is why I'm guessing the police have been so tight-lipped."

Christy-Lynn stared at the scribbled notes—Honey Rawlings of Riddlesville, West Virginia. She had expected to feel . . . something. Relief. Closure. Anything. But Wade was right. Nothing had changed. Nothing at all. Still, he had done what he promised.

"I don't know how to thank you. I was—"

"There's more."

Christy-Lynn leaned back in her chair, waiting.

"Your contact at the station, the detective friend of Stephen's—"

"Connelly."

"Yes, Connelly. He was the leak. Apparently, he talked one of the maintenance guys from the morgue into snapping some shots of Honey with his phone. Word on the street is they each netted five figures. Hence, the detective's so-called early retirement."

Christy-Lynn shook her head, still trying to digest the news. He claimed to be Stephen's friend, and the whole time he was lecturing her about policies and procedures he'd been scheming to make a buck off the death of her husband.

"So that's it? He's just allowed to retire?"

"My guess is he was told to clean out his desk and allowed to slink off to Florida like the reptile he is. And just like that, it all goes away."

Christy-Lynn shook her head, disgusted. Another body blow, and one more thing that wasn't what it seemed. Suddenly she was exhausted, too tired or disillusioned to vent the frustration roiling in her chest. "Is that all?"

Wade seemed surprised by the question. "Isn't that enough?"

"I was hoping your guy might have learned when it started or how they met."

"Sorry. If you want those kinds of details, you're going to have to talk to her family. He did do all the standard legwork though, ran the usual searches through Factiva and Lexis, even talked to one of his guys."

"One of his guys?"

"An investigator. At least that's what he calls them. A little shady, but they aren't shy when it comes to turning over rocks."

"And?"

"And nothing."

"Nothing?"

"No arrests. No public records. Sketchy work history—waitressing mostly, a stint at the local grocer. He did manage to dig up an old yearbook photo from Riddlesville High, which he e-mailed to me if you really want it, but that was the extent of it. It would appear Miss Rawlings kept a pretty low profile before hitching her wagon to Stephen's."

Christy-Lynn stared down at the spaghetti congealing on her plate as she absorbed the information, trying to make sense of her disappointment. Wade had been right. She'd been kidding herself, thinking a name would be enough. She wanted more, needed more. But what exactly? Did she even know?

"Sorry," Wade said, interrupting her thoughts. "That last crack was indelicate."

"Yes, but factual. It seems your friend was very thorough. I was just hoping—" She paused, shaking her head. "I don't know what I was hoping."

"The things you want to know aren't something a reporter or PI is going to be able to get at. No one will. You understand that, right?"

Christy-Lynn picked up the page of notes, running a finger thoughtfully along one of its creases. "I could talk to the grandmother—to Loretta."

"Christy-Lynn . . ."

"She's a woman. She'll understand me needing to know."

"No. She won't. Her loss is different than yours. She lost a grand-daughter, not a philandering husband."

Christy-Lynn folded the paper and laid it in her lap. "I just want the dream to stop."

Wade said nothing for a moment, as if weighing his next words very carefully. "Before, it was just her name. Now it's where they met and how long ago. There's a point where wanting to know becomes something else, Christy-Lynn."

She heaved a sigh. "I know. I know. It's crazy."

"No. Not crazy. But painful. And not just for you. The woman just lost her granddaughter. Think about how you'd feel in her shoes."

"It's not like I'd be badgering her. We'd just . . . talk."

"Woman to woman, you mean?"

There was no mistaking his sarcasm. Christy-Lynn stood and moved to the railing. "You don't understand."

"No, I don't. Because we talked about this when you first came to me. I told you I needed to be sure you weren't going to use whatever you found out to cause trouble. And here you are, thinking about doing exactly that."

Christy-Lynn turned to face him. "Yes, here I am. And I meant what I said. This isn't about causing trouble. It's about a ghost—a woman whose name I don't know, whose face I see every time I close my eyes."

"I understand the pain you must be feeling. What I don't under-stand is how you think what you're talking about is going to fix any of it? Stephen's dead. Honey's dead. And you're here in Sweetwater, starting a new life. Maybe that needs to be enough."

She forced her eyes to his, her throat burning with the effort it took not to tear up. "What if it isn't?"

"Did you love him?"

"What?"

"Before all this—did you love Stephen?"

Christy-Lynn's mouth worked soundlessly, sensing a trap in the question. "He was my husband," she said finally.

"So a ring, a piece of paper? That's love?"

"It was a commitment." She shifted her gaze toward the lake where a pair of egrets waded near shore. "Or it was supposed to be."

"It takes two people to make a commitment work, Christy-Lynn."

"I suppose."

"Are you going to contact Loretta Rawlings?"

She thought about the question. He was right. Of course he was right. About all of it. So why couldn't she let it go? "I don't know," she answered finally. "I know you think I shouldn't, and you're probably right, but I need some time."

"Time for what?"

She looked at him then, shaking her head. "I don't know that either."

# TWENTY-FOUR

*Sweetwater, Virginia*
*May 18, 2017*

It had taken Christy-Lynn more than a week to make her decision. A week of grappling with her conscience, of weighing a wife's right to know against a grandmother's right to grieve in private, of struggling with her promise to Wade.

*Honey Rawlings.*

She had waited for the stab of jealousy the first time she heard the name, had braced for the squeeze in her chest, the heaviness in the pit of her stomach, the things any red-blooded wife should feel. But it hadn't come. Instead, she'd felt only an obsessive curiosity. And shame that she had been so blind, so gullible, so unplugged from her own marriage.

Had Stephen really been that good at covering his tracks, or had she simply stopped paying attention? She cringed as she recalled Wade's point-blank question. *Did you love him?* Her response couldn't have been more tepid if they'd been talking about her mailman.

It was hard to deny that their marriage had lost some of its spark over the last few years. As the demands of Stephen's career took center stage, their lives had intersected less and less, until they seemed to have little to talk about. Toward the end, even their sex life had become more about habit than passion. But that was normal, wasn't it? For things to settle into predictable patterns, for the *sameness* to set in?

The truth was it had been the sameness she most enjoyed about her life with Stephen, the sense of stability that came with knowing every morning when she opened her eyes exactly what the day would hold. But they had also enjoyed a lifestyle she could never have imagined growing up—money in the bank, a stunning home, travel, and a fashionable social circle. She had never stopped to wonder if it was enough for Stephen.

And that was why she was going to West Virginia, to learn what the missing piece might be. Because a sparse background check and a high school yearbook photo weren't enough. And because her own attempts at online sleuthing had turned up even less. But then they would. As Wade had pointed out, the things she wanted to know weren't likely to show up on a Google search. She had no idea what she'd find when she got to Riddlesville or what she hoped to come away with when she left. Answers, perhaps. Closure, hopefully. And a way forward.

She had arranged store coverage for the next three days and was already packed, but now, as she popped in to make sure Tamara and Aileen had gotten the doors open without any hitches, she couldn't help wondering if the trip to West Virginia was a mistake.

She was reaching for the door, her mind a million miles away, when she barreled into Wade as he stepped onto the sidewalk with a cup of coffee in his hand.

"Oh no!" Christy-Lynn stared at his dripping shirt in dismay. "You're soaked. I'm sorry. I wasn't paying attention."

Wade seemed surprised to see her but took the coffee dripping down his shirtfront in stride, blotting the stain absently with a soggy paper napkin. "I didn't expect to see you. Tamara said you were taking a few days off."

"With Mother's Day over, I thought it would be a good time."

"You're going, aren't you? To see Loretta Rawlings?"

She forced herself to meet his gaze squarely. "Yes."

"You weren't going to tell me?"

No. She wasn't. She'd thought about it, feeling she owed it to him after he had helped her, but in the end, she had decided against it. "I knew you'd try to talk me out of it."

"I already tried that. Clearly, it didn't work. And you don't need my approval."

"No, I don't. But I wish you could understand why I have to do this. I'm not going to Riddlesville to break Loretta Rawlings's heart."

"I know you're not. And it's not *her* heart I'm worried about."

Christy-Lynn wasn't sure how to respond to that, and so she said nothing at all.

"Take care of yourself," Wade said, his voice suddenly gentle. "It's a long way to West Virginia."

"I made it here from Maine."

"True enough. Still . . ." He reached for the cell phone peeking from the side pocket of her purse and began tapping the screen. After a moment, he handed it back. "All right. I'm in there. Just in case you get sleepy while you're driving. Or if you just want to talk."

She smiled awkwardly. His concern was both touching and unsettling. "I'll be fine."

"Yes, you will. Just the same, I'll leave mine on."

Riddlesville was a gray and gritty town, made all the more dismal by the steady drizzle that had been falling all afternoon. Christy-Lynn couldn't help cringing as she drove through the derelict downtown—block after block of run-down buildings, vacant storefronts, and dirty sidewalks. She was relieved when she finally reached the stop sign at the edge of town, though what awaited her on the other side proved no less depressing. Ramshackle houses with crumbling chimneys and sagging porches, yards choked with broken baby strollers and cast-off recliners—all reminiscent of a childhood she'd just as soon forget.

Organized neighborhoods eventually gave way to a more sparse landscape, lots pocked with rusty trailers and rotting barns. Christy-Lynn's stomach clenched when she spotted the sign for Red Bud Road. She'd been driving for hours, wondering if she'd ever reach her destination, but now that she was close her doubts began to resurface. How did one go about broaching the subject of adultery with a grieving grandmother?

Christy-Lynn followed the deserted clay track for more than a mile, wondering if she'd missed a turn or misread the sign. Finally, she spotted a small clapboard structure set back from the road, the yard a rough patch of sparse brown scrub. She let her foot off the gas, approaching at an idle, certain now that she had made a wrong turn.

The place was little more than a shack with a listing front porch and a roof patched in places with squares of weathered plywood. In the side yard, a cracked kiddie pool contained several inches of slimy green water, and there was an old Chevy slowly rotting around back, the rear windshield caved in, back tires flat to the rim. Surely no one lived here. But the number on the mailbox matched the one on the paper Wade had given her.

She pulled into the drive and got out, picking her way along a weedy track meant to pass for a path to the porch. Skirting a cluster of mismatched pots filled with pink and white geraniums—the only signs of life in an otherwise abysmal landscape—she mounted a set of creaky steps, took a deep breath, and knocked before she could change her mind.

It was some time before the door opened, but finally a wizened face with eyes the color of old chambray appeared through a narrow opening.

"Yes?" The voice was creaky with age and unmistakably wary.

"Are you Loretta Rawlings?"

"Who wants to know?"

"My name is Christine Ludlow, Mrs. Rawlings." The name felt strange on her tongue, foreign after so many months as Christy-Lynn Parker. "My husband was Stephen Ludlow. Does that name mean anything to you?"

The door eased open another few inches. The old woman stood looking her over, heavily stooped at the waist and shoulders. "You've come then," she said hoarsely. "I wondered if you would."

"I'm not here to cause trouble, Mrs. Rawlings. I just . . . there are questions. About your granddaughter and my husband. I was hoping we could talk."

The old woman glanced back over her shoulder, as if she might have something on the stove. Christy-Lynn tried to peer inside but could make out nothing beyond an old plaid couch and a floor lamp with a yellowed shade.

"Give me a minute, and I'll be out."

She closed the door then, leaving Christy-Lynn standing on the porch. Moments later, she returned with two glasses of lemonade. She wore a scruffy wool sweater despite the afternoon heat. "There," she said, nodding toward a pair of plastic chairs. "We'll sit there." She handed Christy-Lynn a glass that was already beginning to sweat, then fumbled in the pocket of her housedress, eventually producing a soft pack of Basic Menthols and a disposable lighter.

She eased stiffly into one of the chairs, waiting until Christy-Lynn had taken the other to withdraw a cigarette from the pack and clamp it between her lips. Her hands, blue-veined and skeletal, trembled as she lit it. "Hope you don't mind. I don't smoke in the house anymore."

"No. Not at all."

Christy-Lynn studied the woman as she took that first long pull, her leathery cheeks caving in as she dragged in a lung full of smoke and then exhaled it with a faint rattle. It was impossible to guess her age.

She was skin and bone, all joints and sinew, her skin the texture of old parchment. Somewhere in her eighties was probably a safe bet, though she could have been younger. Something told her life had been less than kind to Loretta Rawlings.

For a time, Christy-Lynn said nothing, balancing her untouched lemonade glass on her knee and wondering where to begin. In the end, it was Mrs. Rawlings who broke the silence.

"Ask what you came to ask," she said in her flat, phlegmy voice. "I'll do my best to answer."

"I know how uncomfortable this must be for you, Mrs. Rawlings. It's uncomfortable for me too. But there are things I feel I have a right to know, like the precise nature of your granddaughter's relationship with my husband."

Loretta Rawlings turned her head, her hazy eyes unsettlingly steady. "You don't need to mince words, Mrs. Ludlow. I've been around a long time. Not much shocks me."

Christy-Lynn nodded, wishing she could say the same. "All right then, was your granddaughter having an affair with my husband?"

Loretta took another long pull on her cigarette as she mulled the question. "I'd stopped thinking of it that way, but I suppose that's what it was. No way around it really, since it was you wearing the wedding ring and not my Honey."

The blunt answer left Christy-Lynn scrambling for a response. She had expected something else, a defense of her granddaughter's behavior, excuses, justification. Instead, she had answered the question head-on. "Can you tell me how long they were . . . how long they *knew* each other?"

She seemed to give the question some thought, tracing a shaky finger around the rim of her glass. "I suppose it must be almost four years now. It was right after the book about the plane crash. Honey loved that book. When she heard they were making it into a movie, she convinced herself that if she could just meet the author she could talk him into giving her the part of Sandra. Used to walk around practicing her lines like she was moving to Hollywood any day."

"Your granddaughter was an actress?"

Loretta smiled sadly. "My granddaughter was a dreamer, Mrs. Ludlow. And determined to get out of this town." She turned her face away, her voice suddenly thick. "She got half her wish."

Christy-Lynn squirmed as the moment stretched, sad and more than a little awkward. "I'm sorry you lost your granddaughter, Mrs. Rawlings."

"No one calls me Mrs. Rawlings. Call me Rhetta. And thank you for that. It's big of you to say after . . . everything. How did you find out?"

"I was asked to identify your granddaughter's body at the morgue."

Rhetta's head snapped around, eyes flashing. "Bastards," she growled, flicking her cigarette off the front porch and into the weeds.

"Yes."

Silence descended again, a moment of shared anger punctuated by the dreary patter of drizzle. Rhetta fished out another cigarette, putting it to her lips with an unsteady hand. "The pictures were awful," she said, staring out into the yard. "That's how I found out she was dead. I was standing in line at the IGA, and there she was, splashed across the front page like one of those movie stars from the 1950s."

Christy-Lynn silently cursed Daniel Connelly for his greed. "I'm so sorry," she said softly, because she was. "I'd hoped you hadn't seen them."

"We get the papers here just like everyone else. I saw your picture a few times too. It must've been terrible being in the middle of all that."

"It was. I had to move. I live in Virginia now."

Rhetta lit her cigarette then blew out a long plume of smoke. "I'm sorry your life got turned inside out because of Honey. I told her nothing good would come of it. I told her the first time she brought your husband around."

Christy-Lynn felt the words like a physical blow. It never occurred to her that Stephen would have come to Riddlesville. "You've met my husband?"

Rhetta blinked at her through a lingering cloud of smoke. "Of course I've met him."

"Here?"

Rhetta's weathered face puckered with a sour smile. "We weren't what he was used to, but he came around when he could."

"I'm sorry. I just thought—"

"I know what you thought. I thought it too, at first. All that money and those fancy clothes. Never a hair out of place. I couldn't think what a man like that would want with Honey. But then, people aren't always what they seem."

Christy-Lynn allowed the remark to sink in, trying to decide if it was aimed at Stephen or Honey. She was about to say that she'd learned that lesson the hard way when a shadow darkened Rhetta's face. She had gone still, her head inclined toward the door, as if she'd caught some faint sound.

And then Christy-Lynn heard it too, a high-pitched keening that seemed to be drawing closer by the second. There was a sudden look of alarm as Rhetta tossed her cigarette over the rail and struggled to her feet. Before she could reach the door, it opened and a small face appeared.

"Nonny!"

She was a tiny thing, pale hair pasted stickily to her head, eyes luminous with panic. Rhetta reached for her, scooping her up into her arms with a harsh rattle of breath. "Hush now," she crooned against the child's wet cheek. "I'm right here. Nonny's right here."

The girl quieted almost immediately, though her breath still came in muffled shudders, her face burrowed in the crook of Rhetta's shoulder. Christy-Lynn's heart squeezed as she watched the scene. She recognized the aftermath of a nightmare when she saw it. And judging by Rhetta's practiced attempts to soothe her, it probably wasn't the first episode.

She was curled in Rhetta's lap now, pulling furiously at the thumb in her mouth. Rhetta patted her back gently, crooning against her cheek. "That's my big girl. We have company."

The child turned to look at Christy-Lynn, her mouth suddenly still around her thumb, as if noticing her for the first time. She was lovely, a pale fairy of a girl with hair like corn silk and enormous violet eyes.

*Her mother's eyes.*

Something cold and slippery roiled just south of Christy-Lynn's ribs as she inventoried the child's features. Heart-shaped face, skin like a china doll's—and a prominent dimple in her tiny chin.

*Stephen's chin.*

Rhetta's eyes locked with Christy-Lynn's. "This is Iris."

The porch seemed to shift, the soft thrum of rain receding as she stared at Stephen's little girl. The one she had vowed to never have. The one Honey had given him instead.

# TWENTY-FIVE

"We'd better go inside," Rhetta said, struggling to get out of her chair with Iris clinging to her. "No sense airing the family laundry on the front porch."

Christy-Lynn looked up and down the deserted road, wondering who on earth might overhear them, but it wasn't worth the argument. She stood, worrying briefly that her legs might buckle as she turned to follow Rhetta inside.

The living room was small and cluttered, the air thick with stale cooking oil and decades of old smoke. She eyed the sagging curtains, the ancient television stacked with dog-eared copies of *TV Guide*, the cheap bric-a-brac covering every available surface. It was like a secondhand shop where no one ever bought anything.

Rhetta jerked her chin toward the old plaid couch. Her lips had gone a funny shade of blue, and she was huffing like an old tractor. "Have a seat. I need to get her quieted down, and then I'll be back. Meantime, drink your lemonade. You don't look so good."

Christy-Lynn did as she was told, easing numbly onto the edge of the couch. In the kitchen, Rhetta kept up a soothing stream of chatter as she bathed Iris's face and neck with a cool cloth. When she was finished, she stripped off her damp T-shirt and replaced it with a clean one from the wicker basket on the counter, then set the child down in front of the television with a small dish of fish-shaped crackers.

By the time Rhetta settled into the lumpy green recliner, she was an alarming shade of gray. "I'm sorry about that." Her head lolled back against the chair. "I didn't mean for you to find out like this. In fact, I didn't mean for you to find out at all."

"Why?"

"No need to kick you while you're down. You've been through enough."

"I came because I wanted to know the truth."

"And now?"

"I still want to know."

She sighed, clearly exhausted. "Then I suppose you'd better ask your questions."

"She's Stephen's," Christy-Lynn said, fighting to keep her voice even. She didn't need confirmation. She just needed a moment to sit with the truth of it. Of all the uncomfortable things she had expected to learn, the possibility of a child had never crossed her mind.

Rhetta was nodding gravely, her weathered face full of sympathy. "She's a good girl, poor thing, but she's having a hard time. We both are. There are some things you just can't prepare yourself for. But then, I suppose you know about that."

Christy-Lynn was barely listening, her attention fixed on the flesh and blood proof of her husband's infidelity. It was jarring to see the features of both Honey and Stephen mingled in one tiny little face, perhaps because after a few minutes, it became impossible to say which features were her mother's and which were her father's. Finally, she managed to drag her eyes away. The sooner she had her answers, the sooner she could leave.

"Stephen and Honey . . . do you know how they met?"

Rhetta groaned, as if the memory was painful. "A book signing over in Wheeler. She saw in the paper that your husband was going to be there, and that was that. Shameful, that girl. I think she thought he'd give her the part right there on the spot. He didn't of course—that's not how it works—but something must have happened. Next thing I know she was flying with him to California to meet some director or other. She ended up as an extra, I think they call it. No lines, but she was convinced that sooner or later she was going to be a big star. Maybe that's what he told her, or maybe it's just what she wanted to believe."

Christy-Lynn closed her eyes, trying to dispel the images suddenly filling her head. She knew Stephen had fans. He had a ridiculous following on social media, and his signing events were usually standing-room only. She just never thought of those people as potential threats—and certainly not threats to her marriage. Though now that she did think of it, it wasn't that surprising. When it came to turning on the charm, no one was better than Stephen.

"Was your granddaughter in love with my husband?"

Rhetta looked mildly startled. "She was twenty-five years old. What on earth did she know about love?" She sighed, closing her eyes again briefly. "Though I suppose she thought she was. She certainly wouldn't listen to anything I tried to tell her. I warned her what would come of messing with a married man, talked till I was blue in the face. And then one day she came home and said she was pregnant. There wasn't much sense talking after that. The damage was done."

"Yes, I suppose it was," Christy-Lynn said, wishing she'd never asked. But she had asked, and now there was nothing to do but sit stonily as Rhetta unraveled the time line of Honey and Stephen's affair.

"Don't get me wrong. I love that little girl to pieces, but I'm a bit long in the tooth to be raising a child. I've already raised three, God help me, and only one of them mine. Theresa—that was Honey's mama—got herself pregnant by the first boy who offered her a ride in his truck, then ran off and left me to raise her daughter. Only saw her twice after that—the first time she'd gotten herself in a mess and needed money. The last time was to leave me with Ray—Honey's brother. And now there's Iris."

"How old is she?"

"Three in March—the seventeenth."

Christy-Lynn worked out the math as her eyes slid to the little girl in front of the TV. She had been conceived in July. Of course. Stephen had been in LA that summer, consulting on the screenplay for *An Uncommon Assassin* and rubbing elbows with director Aaron Rothman. And Honey apparently.

"Are you all right?" Rhetta asked. "You look a bit rattled, not that I blame you. This must all come as a terrible shock, as if you haven't had enough of those already. Can I get you something stronger than lemonade? Made right over the county line. My son would throw seven fits if he knew I kept a jar in the house, but every once in a while, you need a little kick to set you right. I'd be happy to pour you a drop."

Christy-Lynn shook her head. It would take more than a drop of West Virginia moonshine to set her right. "No," she managed finally. "No, thank you. I don't . . . I'm sorry. I have to go." And just like that, she was off the couch and moving toward the door, suddenly desperate to put as many miles as possible between herself and Riddlesville.

Rhetta got to her feet with a bit of effort. "I'm so sorry about all of this. You seem like a nice woman, certainly not one who deserved to learn what you did today. I know it's too late, but for what it's worth, I'm sorry Honey caused so much pain. She wasn't a bad girl, just . . . selfish."

Christy-Lynn fumbled for a response but could find none. With a curt nod, she stepped out onto the porch, nearly tripping over the geranium pots as she scrambled down the steps and back to the Rover.

She started the engine and managed to make it all the way back to the main road before slamming the car into park and slumping over the wheel. She had come for the truth, and now she had it. Four years.

They'd been together four years. And there was a child. The reality was simply too much to grasp.

The shaking hit her all at once, confusion mixed with disbelief coursing through her like poison. Stephen—a father. It was inconceivable, the idea utterly foreign to her concept of the man she had married, the one who hadn't batted an eye when she said she didn't want children. But there was no denying it. One look at Iris with her dimpled chin and violet eyes was all the proof she needed.

Had it—had *she*—been planned? Or was the pregnancy an accident, the by-product of one careless night when passion had eclipsed reason and caution had been thrown to the wind? The thought made her stomach knot, but it was better than revisiting the possibility, as inexcusable as it might be, that the thing that had ultimately driven Stephen into the arms of another woman was the one thing—the *only* thing—she had ever denied him.

The thought brought a clammy wave of nausea, and for a moment, she thought she might actually be sick. Lowering the window, she sucked in a dizzying breath. She needed to get herself together. She couldn't just sit in the middle of the road and go to pieces, and at the moment, she was dangerously close to doing just that. She needed to get out of Riddlesville—now.

She was reaching for the gearshift, thinking about calling Missy as she had promised to, when her cell phone went off. She dragged it from her purse and answered without looking, wondering if there really was such a thing as telepathy.

"Missy, I was just about to call you."

"It's not Missy."

"Wade?"

"I was worried about you."

Something about the simple words caused Christy-Lynn to crumple. She let out a gut-wrenching sob, unable to check the sudden torrent of tears flowing down her cheeks.

"Talk to me, Christy-Lynn. What's happened? Are you hurt?"

Was she hurt? It was such a ridiculous question she hardly knew how to answer. "No," she finally managed, gulping down a fresh sob before it could fully form. "Yes . . . I don't know."

"Where are you?"

"I'm here." She paused to wipe her nose on the back of her hand. "I saw her, talked to her."

"And what else?"

"He has a daughter," she blurted. "Stephen and Honey had a daughter."

"Jesus . . ."

"Iris. Her name is Iris." She closed her eyes, slumping forward to lean her head against the steering wheel. "She's three."

"Christy-Lynn, you can't be sure. It could be—"

"No, it couldn't. She's his. I'm sure of it."

"I'm so sorry. I don't know what to say."

"There's nothing *to* say."

"So how did you leave it?"

"I didn't. I just got up and walked out. Rhetta . . . Mrs. Rawlings said she'd answer any questions I had, but then there was Iris, and I couldn't sit there another minute. I just . . . left."

"Where are you now?"

"I'm in the car, about to head back."

"Christy-Lynn, you can't. You've been driving all day. You've got to be exhausted."

Her throat ached, and she could barely breathe. "I can't stay here."

"Please promise me you won't drive tonight. Find a motel and get some sleep. You can leave first thing in the morning." When she said nothing, he prompted her. "Promise me."

"Yes. Okay. I'll find a motel."

"And some food, since I'm guessing you haven't eaten. I'll check on you in the morning."

"You don't need to."

"I'll check on you in the morning," he repeated firmly.

"All right then." Her thumb was poised to end the call when she hesitated. "Wade?"

"I'm still here."

"Thank you."

"No sweat. Get some rest."

Christy-Lynn's room at the Conner Fork Day's Inn was clean and quiet. She dropped her bags on the bed, stripped out of her clothes, and headed for the shower, determined to scrub away the lingering traces of stale grease and cigarette smoke still clinging to her skin and hair.

She had no idea how long she stood there under the scalding stream or how long it took to finally cry herself out, but eventually she emerged from the bathroom, pink-skinned and spent. She donned a T-shirt and leggings, then flipped on the television, hoping to numb out with an old movie, but it was no use. Like a video on an endless loop, the day's events kept replaying in her head, and the facts couldn't be denied.

Stephen and Honey had a little girl, and that little girl was now an orphan. She had assumed Ray Rawlings's motives for wanting to keep his sister's sins under wraps had to do with shielding the family from scandal. But maybe it was more than that. Maybe it was about protecting an innocent little girl. The moment Honey's name was made public the reporters would swarm. It would be only a matter of time before they stumbled onto Iris—a child with a famous father and a mother who wasn't his wife. Had Stephen given a second thought to what might happen to his daughter in such a case?

And suddenly it was there—the question she'd been trying not to ask herself. How had Stephen taken the news that he was going to be a father? Had he been angry? Horrified? Or was it possible the idea of a child had actually appealed to him, that in some dark and ambivalent corner of his alpha male psyche, part of him longed to leave a piece of himself to the world?

Or maybe the questions she should be asking weren't about Stephen at all, but about herself? Was there some part of her—some broken or missing part—that had prevented her from seeing that Stephen needed more? Had she been so busy trying to outrun her own scars that she had missed the signs? Or had the affair been exactly what it looked like, a midlife crisis with a celebrity-struck, surgically enhanced blonde, the child a mere afterthought? Was it only obligation that had bound them together, or had it gone deeper? The only two people who could answer those questions were dead.

But there was Rhetta.

She had come to Riddlesville for answers, but there was still so much she didn't know, things she'd never gotten around to asking. Was she really willing to go back to Sweetwater without knowing all of it? And if so, why had she bothered to come at all? The question continued to churn long after she had slipped between the thin hotel sheets and switched off the light.

*The water is icy, a million needles prickling at her skin. And murky. Like tea or dirty dishwater. There is a light in the distance—no, a pair of lights—dismal points in the watery gloom. Lying lifeless along the bottom is a hulk of cold bent metal. A face looms behind a square of glass, blue-white and familiar, pale hair fanned out around her head like a halo. She floats there with eyes closed, a grisly mermaid, the sunken place at her temple strangely bloodless. And then suddenly, her eyes are not closed. They're wide and glassy, vivid violet through all that water. And then the blue-tinged lips begin to move. It's a strange thing to be aware that you're dreaming, to know what's coming and not be able to wake yourself or at least look away. A surreal and terrible déjà vu. Except tonight the dream is different. There's a new face peering out at her through the glass, a tiny face with vivid violet eyes—a small, bright echo of the other. She does not speak at first. Her mouth is closed, silent. And then she begins to cry, a miserable wail through all that water—Nonny! Her face is suddenly filled with terror, her hands splayed in panic against the glass. It's too much to see, too much to hear. And then, with lungs near bursting, she is swimming away from the tiny face, the terrible wail growing fainter as she claws her way madly toward the surface.*

Christy-Lynn sat bolt upright in bed, drenched and gulping for air, the echo of Iris's pale face still fresh in her mind. Please God, not the child too. Her heart battered her ribs as she dragged her eyes to the clock on the nightstand, the numbers glowing blue in the unfamiliar dark: 11:15.

Kicking off the sheets, she padded to the bathroom, sponged her face and neck with cold water, then stripped off her sweat-drenched clothes and climbed back into bed. She was about to reach for the TV remote when she spied her phone charging next to the bed. She pulled up Missy's number, then peered at the clock again. It was long past the boys' bedtime, which meant Missy was probably already passed out, exhausted after a day at the inn, followed by an evening of baths and homework. On impulse she scrolled down to Wade's number. He'd put it there, after all, in case she needed to talk. And she did.

He picked up after a single ring. "Please tell me you're not driving."

Christy-Lynn dragged the sheet up reflexively at the sound of his voice, covering her bare breasts. "No, I'm not driving." There was a pause. He was waiting for her to say more, except she didn't really have any new information since the last time they'd spoken. "I ate," she said lamely.

"Good. But why aren't you asleep?"

"I'm sorry. It's late. I shouldn't have called."

"I didn't mean that. I just meant I was hoping you'd get some rest."

"Not going to happen, I'm afraid."

"Can't sleep?"

"Ghosts," she said quietly. "She showed up in the dream tonight too."

"The little girl?"

"Iris," she told him softly. "Her name is Iris. And yes. I can't stop thinking about her. There's so much I don't know, things I never got the chance to ask."

"At the risk of sounding heartless, why would you want to know anything else?"

Christy-Lynn raked a hand through her bangs. How did she make him understand when she didn't understand herself? "Honestly, I'm not sure I do. But I'm here now, so I was thinking . . ."

"Oh, God . . ."

"I was thinking about going back. If Rhetta will still talk to me after the way I walked out. I'm just not sure I can handle seeing Iris again."

"Then maybe you shouldn't. Maybe it's time to just let this go and come home like you said you were going to."

"I don't think I can. Not until I know the rest of it."

"The rest of what, Christy-Lynn? They had an affair. What else is there?"

"What else is there?" she echoed, aware that she sounded faintly hysterical. "There's a child. One Stephen never told anyone about and never bothered to provide for. Never once did he bring up the idea of us having a baby. Not once in eight years. But he had a daughter with Honey. Did the child mean anything to him, or was she just a mistake, an accident he wasn't willing to own?"

Another sigh, softer this time. "Why are you doing this, Christy-Lynn? Torturing yourself like this? It's over."

Christy-Lynn closed her eyes, knees hugged to her chest. "I know you don't understand. You couldn't. And you don't need to. But there are reasons I need to know what happened and why, things I need to figure out. So for me, it *isn't* over. Why do you care anyway?"

"Because it's what he did—what he *always* did. He swooped in, took what he wanted, and then made it someone else's fault. And now I see you falling right into it, taking the blame because he was a snake. You deserve better than that."

The remark took Christy-Lynn by surprise. "How do you know?"

There was a long pause, as if he were hunting for an answer. "I don't know," he said finally. "I just do. Look, you're tired. Try to sleep if you can and then come home. You've got something here, something that's yours. Maybe that's what you should focus on. Not the past. And not someone else's mistakes. The future."

"All right."

"Call me when you get on the road."

"I will."

But even as she ended the call, she knew she wouldn't be heading home first thing in the morning.

# TWENTY-SIX

If Rhetta was surprised to find Christy-Lynn standing on her porch again the next morning, she hid it well. She was still in her house-coat and slippers when she answered the door. "I suspected you'd be back."

Christy-Lynn ran her tongue over her lips, her mouth suddenly dry. "About yesterday—I'm sorry about walking out like that. I was just . . ."

The sound of cartoons mingled with the aroma of frying bacon drifted out onto the front porch. "I've got breakfast going for Iris if you're hungry."

Christy-Lynn shook her head. Food was the last thing on her mind. "No, thank you. I just have a few more questions."

"Yes, I thought you might." She pulled back the door and stepped aside. "Come on in then and let me get her fed."

Iris sat cross-legged in front of the television, clutching a bedrag-gled teddy bear to her chest. Her hair was still sleep-tangled, her eyes glued to the screen. Christy-Lynn fought down a shudder as snatches of the previous night's dream came flooding back. That tiny face, frantic behind the glass. What in God's name was she doing here?

"Coffee?" Rhetta offered as Christy-Lynn followed her into the tiny kitchen.

"Yes. If it's ready."

Rhetta filled a thick brown mug and set it on the table along with a spoon and a half gallon of milk. "Sugar's there if you take it."

Christy-Lynn took a seat, pouring a splash of milk into her mug as she watched Rhetta crack a single egg into a bowl and give it a quick scramble before pouring it into the pan. Her hands trembled as she worked, but she moved with the ease of a woman who had prepared her share of breakfasts. Moments later, she turned the egg out onto a plate, added two slices of bacon, and disappeared into the living room with Iris's breakfast.

She was a bit winded when she returned, her lips parted and grayish. "I don't like for her to eat in front of the television," she said, filling a mug for herself and joining Christy-Lynn at the table. "But this way, we'll have the kitchen to ourselves."

"Thank you."

"Well, it's not the kind of talk a child should hear, is it?"

"No, I suppose not."

Rhetta splashed some milk into her coffee, then dropped in a heaping spoonful of sugar. "So," she said, still stirring. "Here we are again."

"Yes. Here we are. A friend of mine thinks I'm crazy for coming here. He doesn't understand why I need to know all the gritty details."

"No, a man wouldn't. But I do. You need to make sense of it."

Christy-Lynn nodded, relieved to at last be understood. "Yes."

Rhetta's eyes slid away, watery blue and suddenly full of memory. "I was married once, a million years ago. Men haven't changed all that much since my time. Women either. We still try to make everything our fault."

"I guess what I really need to know is . . . why."

"Good luck figuring that out."

"Now you sound like Wade."

"Your friend?"

"Yes. He thinks I'm a glutton for punishment, and maybe I am. It's certainly a strange thing to be confronted with—the child of your husband's mistress."

"I didn't mean for you to find out about Iris. That was an accident. She's been through enough without having to figure out who you are. She doesn't understand where her mama's gone, not that her mama was around all that much."

"Where was she?"

Rhetta sighed, a hoarse, tired rasp. "Who knows. With him, somewhere. I told you Honey had her heart set on being an actress. Where she came up with that idea, I'll never know, but that was her dream. She took a few acting classes in high school and at the community college, even did a commercial for a furniture store here in town. She wasn't very good, but she was pretty, and I guess she thought that was enough because off she went to find him." Rhetta rose and shuffled to the counter, returning with the coffeepot to top off their mugs. "Groupies, they used to call them in my day, but that was for singers and movie stars. I didn't know writers had them too."

For an instant, Christy-Lynn was transported back to the day she bumped into Stephen in the hall at Lloyd and Griffin. If possible, he had been even better-looking than the author photo on the back of his novels, and with his polished smile and easy patter, he had positively oozed charm. It wasn't hard to imagine a girl like Honey, ambitious, starry-eyed, and desperate for a ticket out of Riddlesville, succumbing to that combination—as she herself had.

"My husband had a way of collecting people," she said finally. "Like a magnet. I used to think it was unconscious. Now I realize he knew exactly what he was doing. Funny what you can see in the rearview mirror."

Rhetta let out another sigh. "I thought she'd stop seeing him when she realized he didn't actually have much say about who got to be *in* the movies, but she didn't. Maybe it was the money. He bought her nice things, took her nice places. It turned her head. I guess it would any girl's. At least any girl from Riddlesville. She got all that with Stephen, along with a nice car and a fancy apartment somewhere. Pretty soon, she didn't even look like Honey—with those store-bought boobs and all the designer clothes. She'd disappear for a while then come back just long enough to rub her new life in everyone's face. Especially the old crowd down at the IGA where she used to cashier. She'd spend a little time with Iris, but mostly it was about showing off. And then off she'd go again."

Christy-Lynn was still digesting the fact that Stephen had set his mistress up in an apartment when she remembered the autodrafts she had discovered on his bank statements. Star Properties LTD. Not a publicity firm then; a property management company. And what about the $4,000 transfers each month?

"Was my husband paying child support?"

She had put the question a bit bluntly, and for a moment, Rhetta seemed genuinely surprised. "I don't know if you'd call it that. At least I never did. It was more like an allowance. He would put money in Honey's account every month. Quite a lot of money. It made me ashamed that she took it—there are names for women who take money from men—but then Iris came along, and I couldn't afford to be all high-and-mighty. Children need things. Lots of things. And a government check only goes so far."

Christy-Lynn felt a sharp stab of remorse. She'd never stopped to consider that Stephen's death might spell disaster for Iris and her great-grandmother. "Is she . . . are you all right? Money wise, I mean?"

Rhetta stepped away, sliding the pot back onto the burner. "We'll manage," she said firmly. "We'll have to."

"You mentioned a grandson."

"Ray," she said, suddenly looking very tired. "He never thought much of Honey. Very pious, my Ray. Reverend of the Living Water Tabernacle. His wife, Ellen, plays the organ on Sundays. And oh, wasn't she green with envy when Honey started popping up in church with all her fancy clothes. And Honey loved every minute. I know that sounds petty. And it is. I'm not making excuses for the girl. What she did was wrong, but I'm guessing you have no idea what it's like to grow up in a town like this, to see how the rest of the world lives and know there's no chance you'll ever have that kind of life—or much of any life, really, unless you count raising a passel of kids in a double-wide. But Honey knew it. So did her mother. Which is why I suppose they both got out the first chance they got."

For one terrible instant, Christy-Lynn flashed back to the night she had been ushered into a hospital room to find her mother lying there with her face sewn up, promising that when she got out of jail things would go back to the way they were. In her whole life, she'd never been more afraid than the night her mother made that promise. Yes, she did have an idea what it was like. Much more than an idea. In that, at least, she and Honey had had something in common.

Rhetta was back in her chair now, stirring sugar into her freshened mug, her eyes clouded and far away. Christy-Lynn watched her for what felt like a long time, trying to figure out the best way to frame her next question.

"Did they ever talk about getting married?" she said finally, because there *was* no best way.

"You mean was Stephen planning to ask you for a divorce?"

Christy-Lynn looked down at her hands, wrapped a little too tightly around her mug. "Yes."

"Not that I ever heard. And I'm not sure Honey really cared about a ring. I think she liked having all the benefits of being married to a rich man without any of the responsibility. That's why Iris coming along knocked her for such a loop."

Christy-Lynn gnawed at her lip, weighing another awkward question. "You don't think she got pregnant so Stephen would marry her?"

Rhetta's eyes widened. "You mean to trap him? Good grief, no. It was Honey who ended up getting trapped with that baby. Stupid girl.

She talked about, you know . . . not having it. It was Stephen who talked her out of that."

Christy-Lynn let the words sink in. The question reared its head again. Was it possible Stephen hadn't been as okay with her choice to remain childless as he had pretended? It was a haunting question, one she'd never have an answer to.

"How often did he see Iris?"

"Not very often near the end. But you know what his schedule was like. Always jetting off somewhere. And he was living two lives, wasn't he? It couldn't have been easy, keeping it a secret from the whole world—and you." Rhetta set down her mug and looked Christy-Lynn in the eye. "You never suspected even a little?"

"Not even a little," she answered flatly, pretending the old woman's gaze didn't unsettle her. "Did he seem . . . fond of Iris?"

Rhetta lifted her shoulders then dropped them with a sigh. "It's hard to say. He treated her more like a doll than a daughter, something pretty he could pet and hold on his lap. He used to call her his best girl. I don't think Honey liked that too well. She didn't like sharing him, even with Iris. It's terrible to say, but I think she would have eventually stopped coming to see Iris altogether. And in time things would have gone south with Stephen. Honey always did have a short attention span."

"Four years isn't that short," Christy-Lynn pointed out drily.

"I suspect Iris was the reason for that. Your husband could have lived without Honey. And she could have lived without him. But children have a way of changing things. They turn your life inside out—your heart too. Honey was just too young and selfish to know it. My fault I guess, since I brought her up."

Christy-Lynn considered Rhetta's words as she pushed away her mug. She'd been nothing but forthcoming, neither defensive nor secretive, though not quite apologetic either.

"You're very blunt about all this."

Rhetta seemed surprised by the observation. "What else can I be? This was only ever going to end badly, but when you've been around as long as I have, you realize people have to make their own mistakes— sometimes big ones—before they figure out they're getting it wrong. Trouble is, they usually figure it out too late, and someone else is left holding the bag. All Honey cared about was having fun. She knew I'd take care of Iris—and I will for as long as I can."

On cue, Iris toddled into the kitchen clutching her teddy bear. "Juice."

"All right. I'll get you some juice."

Rhetta clutched the edge of the table as she shoved herself out of her chair, her slippers scuffing the worn vinyl as she went to the refrigerator. Her hand trembled as she filled a plastic sippy cup, then snapped on the lid. "There you go, sweetie."

But Iris had lost interest in juice. She was too busy staring at the stranger in her kitchen, her wide violet eyes full of questions.

Rhetta took the forgotten sippy cup from Iris's hand and set it on the table, then took hold of her shoulders. "This is Christy-Lynn, honey. She's a friend . . . was a friend . . . of your daddy's."

Iris cocked her head to one side, a tiny V of confusion forming between her pale brows. Rhetta caught Christy-Lynn's eye as she grabbed a rumpled pack of cigarettes from the counter. "Come on then," she said, taking Iris by the hand and nodding toward the door. "Let's get you outside in the sunshine for a bit."

Christy-Lynn recognized Rhetta's words for what they were, code for *Nonny needs a cigarette*. She followed reluctantly as Rhetta herded the child onto the porch and then down the front steps, unearthing a plastic bucket and shovel from somewhere and putting them in Iris's hands.

"We'll be right up here," she promised, lumbering back up the porch steps. "Right here where you can see us."

"Is Mama coming?"

Rhetta pressed a hand to her chest, her eyes closing briefly. "No, baby. Mama isn't coming. She had to go away, remember?"

Iris's chin began to quiver, her little face threatening to crumple. "Want Mama."

"I know you do, little one. So do I. But she's watching us." Rhetta squinted up at the sky, pointing to a tuft of white cloud. "From up in heaven, remember? And she loves to watch you play. Can you do that for Mama? Can you play?"

Iris nodded, but her face was a dejected blank as she turned away with her plastic shovel. Rhetta reached into her housecoat pocket, cellophane crinkling as she fished out her cigarettes. She fumbled one out of the pack then eased into the chair beside Christy-Lynn's. "It's hard looking at her, isn't it?" she asked when she'd lit her cigarette and taken the first pull.

"Very."

"It's hard for me too." Her voice crackled. She took another long drag, blowing out the smoke on a long sigh. "She barely talks anymore. Just a word here and there when she wants something. Poor thing. She's so confused. She's started having nightmares since Honey . . . since the accident."

Christy-Lynn nodded but said nothing.

"I'm tired, Mrs. Ludlow. And I'm not . . . equipped. I didn't expect to be raising another child at my age, and my doctors aren't exactly full of good news these days. I don't know how much longer . . ."

Christy-Lynn cut her off before she could finish. "Surely Ray and his wife—"

"They've already said no. And I suppose I can't blame them. They can barely keep body and soul together as it is, and there's another mouth coming in the fall. I don't know how Ellen will manage. She can't keep up with the four she has, let alone five. There just isn't room for Iris."

"What will happen if . . . ?"

"When," Rhetta corrected, squinting at Christy-Lynn through a freshly exhaled haze of smoke. "There's no if. Only when."

"And Iris . . . ?"

"Social services, I suppose, unless Ray backs down. And I don't see that happening."

Christy-Lynn felt her chest squeeze, as if her rib cage was suddenly filled with stones. "You mean foster care?"

Rhetta's breath shuddered as she looked away. "I know it's a hard thing, but there's nothing else . . . no other way."

Christy-Lynn remained quiet, partly because she didn't trust her own voice. She was sixteen when she entered the foster care system. She couldn't imagine what it would be like for a child Iris's age, especially when that child was already showing signs of coping issues.

"You can't mean Ray would actually let his own niece go to foster care. If it comes down to it, if something happens, they'd take her, wouldn't they, rather than let her end up with strangers?"

Rhetta's eyes were moist now, her face full of misery. "He told me I had better take care of myself because there was no way he was having Honey's brat in his house. As if it was Iris's fault her parents weren't married."

Christy-Lynn was stunned. "What about Christian charity? About *suffer the little children*? Isn't that what he's supposed to believe?"

Rhetta shook her grizzled head, as if bewildered. "I gave up trying to figure out what that boy believes a long time ago. But you can ask him yourself if you want. That's him coming up the road, and it looks like he's brought the whole brood. I forgot they were coming by to pick up some muffins I made for the church bake sale."

Christy-Lynn looked up in time to see a faded maroon van coming down the road in a cloud of dun-colored dust. "I'll go," she said, instantly on her feet. She didn't want Rhetta to have to explain her presence. "Oh, my purse and keys are inside on the kitchen table."

Rhetta pushed to her feet with startling swiftness. "I'll bring them out."

To her dismay, Christy-Lynn found herself alone on the porch, watching as the van pulled up and the doors swung open. The children tumbled out first, rawboned and pale, whooping like wild things as they scrambled in all directions. Ray appeared next, coming around to open the passenger side door for his wife. She was matchstick-thin but for her swollen middle, carrying a foil-covered casserole dish as she waddled toward the house a few paces behind her husband.

Christy-Lynn averted her gaze, wishing Rhetta would reappear so she could leave before things got any more awkward than they already were. In light of Rhetta's revelations, she didn't trust herself to hold her tongue.

Iris had been playing with her shovel in the dirt. She looked up, shrinking visibly as her uncle moved past without so much as a glance in her direction. The cousins came next, swarming across the yard. Iris ducked as the oldest, a boy with stained jeans and greasy blond hair, stepped over her as if she were a puppy.

Ray stared up at Christy-Lynn from the bottom step of the porch, a slight man with sharp shoulders and long, stringy limbs. Beside him, Ellen Rawlings ran her gaze over Christy-Lynn in one long, dismissive pass.

"Afternoon," Ray said coolly. "You here to see Rhetta?"

Before Christy-Lynn could respond, Rhetta reappeared, her purse in one hand and a plate of cling-film-covered muffins in the other. She handed the purse over, her eyes full of apology.

"This is Mrs. Ludlow, Ray. We've just been chatting about your sister—and your niece."

Ray snorted, a blend of disgust and dismissal. He closed one eye, as if drawing a bead on Christy-Lynn. "That so? You come all the way from Maine to talk about my sister?"

"I live in Virginia now, and I'm here—"

"I know why you're here," he shot back. "And I'll tell you the same thing I told the police when they came sniffing around. I see my family's name in the papers, I'll sue everyone from here to kingdom come. We're good, decent people, Mrs. Ludlow, just trying to raise our kids and live our lives. Your beef was with my sister, and since she's dead, I'd say you're all done here."

Christy-Lynn lifted her chin, meeting his gaze squarely. She would probably have disliked Ray Rawlings on sight, but knowing he was capable of turning his back on a child cemented her revulsion. "You mentioned raising your kids. Does that include Iris?"

"She's not my kid."

"She's your flesh and blood, a part of your family."

"She's an abomination is what she is. Born in sin, and *no* part of my family."

Christy-Lynn stared back at him, dumbfounded. "So that's it? You'd let your own niece end up in foster care because of something her parents did?" She knew she was overstepping her bounds but couldn't seem to help herself. It was impossible to look at Iris and not see herself. She might have been sixteen when she entered the foster care system instead of three, but that was just math.

"The wages of sin, Mrs. Ludlow. Right there in the good book. The Lord shall visit the inequities of the father on the children."

"Praise His name," Ellen murmured coldly as she pushed past Christy-Lynn and disappeared inside the house with her casserole dish.

Rhetta glared at her grandson. "For God's sake, Ray, the child's right there. And Mrs. Ludlow is company."

Ray shrugged. "Not my company."

As if sensing she'd become the topic of conversation, Iris dropped her shovel and raised her eyes to Christy-Lynn. Christy-Lynn looked away quickly, tormented by the silent plea in the child's violet gaze.

"I need to get back," she told Rhetta. "Thank you for the coffee and . . . everything. I came for answers, and now I have them—or as close as I'll ever get. That couldn't have been easy for you."

Rhetta nodded, her eyes suddenly awash with tears. "It's only what you deserved, though I'm not sure I've done you any favors with the truth."

Christy-Lynn wasn't sure either but reached for Rhetta's hand just the same, giving it a squeeze before she turned to descend the steps. Ray made no move to get out of her way, forcing her to sidle past. She was heading for the driveway when she heard footsteps behind her. Before she knew what was happening, Iris had launched herself full force, arms locked tight around her knees, clinging like a limpet.

Rhetta scurried down the steps after her. "I'm sorry," she said uncomfortably. "She doesn't like it when people leave. She never knows who's coming back and who's not."

Christy-Lynn nodded, an ache suddenly clawing at her throat. What kind of future would this child ever have? With a caregiver in decline and an uncle who wanted nothing to do with her. One day Rhetta would fall ill, or worse, and the county would come for her. A woman with sensible shoes and a vague, practiced smile. And Iris would disappear, swallowed up by a system too flawed to protect her. It was too terrible to contemplate. But as Christy-Lynn backed out of Rhetta's driveway, it was all she *could* contemplate.

# TWENTY-SEVEN

*Goose Creek, South Carolina*
*June 27, 1998*

*Christy-Lynn turns off the water and steps from the shower. Her reflection stares back at her from the steam-mottled mirror, dripping wet and unnaturally still. Her eyes are enormous in her face, great pools of bewilderment.*

*It's been eight weeks.*

*Eight weeks since Charlene Parker was arrested. Eight weeks since the caseworker drove her back to the apartment she shared with her mother and told her to pack her things. Eight weeks since she had been shuffled off to a suitable foster home.*

*It isn't a bad place, a two-story colonial out in the cookie-cutter suburbs, the kind of house she always wanted to go home to after school. The furniture is new, the phone works, and there's plenty of food in the fridge. But it isn't home. At least it's not her home.*

*They call it a receiving home, a temporary place to stick new kids until they decide where to park them long term. The people who run the receiving home, Jean and Dennis Hawley, like to brag that they specialize in teens, but Christy-Lynn isn't so sure.*

There are two other kids living with the Hawleys now. There were three until last week, when the girl who shared Christy-Lynn's room—a thirteen-year-old named Dana whose entire left arm was crisscrossed with a web of fine white scars—got hold of a razor blade and nearly bled out on the bathroom floor.

Christy-Lynn had watched from her bedroom window as they loaded the girl onto a stretcher and then into an ambulance, siren screaming as the flashing red lights sped away into the darkness. Even if she lived, she wouldn't be coming back. Not to this house.

Down the hall there are two other residents, a pair of brothers, Terry and Todd Blevins, whose parents died when their trailer exploded while they were cooking up a batch of meth. They're the thickset, sullen sort—mouth breathers, Dana called them—and Christy-Lynn is careful to give them a wide berth. She doesn't like the way the oldest brother's eyes follow her, lingering just a little too long for comfort.

The one thing they have in common is that none of them have any hope of finding a forever family. Forever family. It's the stomach-turning term some caseworkers use for adoption, as if they're corgis or cocker spaniels instead of human beings. Kids who end up in foster care already have two strikes against them, but toss in the potential for alcohol, drugs, and unwanted pregnancy, and a teen's pretty much guaranteed to remain in the system until the clock runs out, and they're finally kicked loose on their eighteenth birthday, often without a job or a cent to their name.

Not that Christy-Lynn wants a forever family. It's too late for that. She only wants to be left alone, to finish school, then find a way to get into college so she can get a decent job and never have to depend on anyone but herself. But she's in a holding pattern now, caught in a bureaucratic limbo where every kid is treated the same—a mouth to feed, a soul to save, a government check to collect.

But it's how things are. Nothing to do but wait and wonder while her mother serves her time. Her lawyer—the one the court appointed—was saying three years, maybe eighteen months with time off for good behavior.

*And then what? Would she keep her promise when she got out? Or would it just be a repeat of the same old nightmare, like the movie* Groundhog Day *where Bill Murray wakes up every morning to the same old hell?*

*The thought of going back to that life sends a chill through her. Not that she'll have much choice if it comes to that. Eighteen months from now, she'll still be a minor. They'll make her go back to her mother, and that will be that.*

# TWENTY-EIGHT

*Sweetwater, Virginia*
*June 3, 2017*

Wade pulled up Christy-Lynn's number once more and hit "Send." His last three calls had gone straight to voice mail, and he'd had to settle for leaving a message, asking only half jokingly if she was upside down in a ditch somewhere. He was surprised this time when she actually picked up.

"Hey, it's Wade. I thought you were going to call me."

"I know. I'm sorry. I just wasn't in the mood to talk to anyone."

"You went back, I take it?"

"I had to."

"If you say so."

"Please don't be snarky."

Wade instantly regretted the remark. She sounded as if she'd been crying, her voice dull and ragged. "Sorry. Tell me what happened."

"I don't think I can. Not now. I just walked through the door, and I've been driving all day. I'm beat."

"Sounds like you need a meal and a good night's sleep."

"There isn't much in the house, and there's no way I'm going back out. I'll settle for a hot bath and good night's sleep. That work for you?"

"Right, I get it. I'm nagging. Go then. Get in your tub."

Forty-five minutes later, Wade found himself standing on Christy-Lynn's front porch with a bag of takeout from Lotus. He'd be lucky if she didn't dump it over his head, but he was willing to risk it. She had looked a bit frayed around the edges the day she left, and the last forty-eight hours couldn't have done her much good.

He was still trying to come up with an excuse for popping by unannounced when she opened the door, wearing a white terry-cloth robe cinched at the waist. Her hair was wet, and she smelled of shampoo, like rainwater or the sea.

"Hello," he said thickly. "How was your bath?"

"What are you doing here?"

"I brought food." He held out the bag as proof. "I wasn't sure what you liked, so I got an assortment. There's lo mein, shrimp and vegetables, and cashew chicken. Oh, and soup. You sounded like you needed soup. It's on top, and it's hot, so be careful."

She took the bag, looking dumbfounded. "There's ten pounds of food here."

He smiled sheepishly. "Leftovers."

"Wait," she said as he turned to go. "You're not staying?"

"I'm not here to invite myself to dinner. I just wanted to make sure you got some food."

"I'm inviting you. Just watch where you walk. It's kind of a mess in here."

Wade navigated a maze of cardboard boxes as he followed her through the living room. The place looked like a warehouse, jammed with furniture, knickknacks, and half-packed cartons. "What's going on? Are you moving?"

"Redecorating. Carol was in such a hurry to get to Florida she left almost everything behind, and with the store opening, I haven't had time to get through it all. I've been packing most of it up for Goodwill, which explains the boxes. I'm thinking about updating the bathroom and kitchen. I want to hang on to the vintage feel. Missy thinks her cousin Hank might be able to handle it. There's just so much to get rid of first."

Any first-year reporter could see what was going on. She was keeping up a steady stream of conversation, moving around the room so she wouldn't have to look at him. It was classic avoidance, and after the last two days, she had a right to that. Tonight, they'd talk about what she wanted to talk about.

He peered into one of the nearby boxes, eyeing chipped plates and battered pots and pans. "I know about having to get rid of stuff. When I moved to the cabin, there was a ton of my grandfather's stuff to clear out. It was weird, sorting through broken mugs and stray gloves, wondering when he thought he was ever going to need any of it."

Christy-Lynn was unpacking the takeout containers, removing their cardboard lids and setting them out on the table. She paused to look at him. "Maybe it wasn't *about* needing them. People hold on to all kinds of things, silly things, even broken things, because of the memories attached to them."

Wade studied her as he digested her words. In the kitchen light, her face looked puffy and mottled, her eyes raw and red-rimmed. She'd been crying, for hours by the look of it. "I'm more of a clean break guy myself. People like to dig up the bodies, anguish over mistakes. What's the point? The water's poisoned. There's no cleaning it up after it's done. The only thing you can do is walk away—and set fire to your bridges."

Christy-Lynn stared at him, clearly mystified. "Am I supposed to know what that means?"

Wade shrugged the question off. As usual, he'd said too much. Not everyone saw the merits of a scorched-earth policy. "It doesn't mean anything," he said finally. "It's just an expression. A work thing."

It was a lie, of course. In leaving New York, he'd set fire to more than just his career. He really had tried to make it work with Simone, though in retrospect he couldn't imagine why he'd bothered. He had shelved his writing and knuckled down at *Review*, earning a shelf full of awards and all the perks that came with them. For a while, he had even convinced himself they were happy. But neither of them had been able to sustain the illusion. The truth was a happy ending had never been in the cards.

An awkward silence fell as they swapped containers and spooned out portions, the quiet heavy with unasked questions and surreptitious glances. Finally, Christy-Lynn set down her fork and looked at him across the table. "This isn't working, is it?"

Wade looked up from his eggroll. "What?"

"Us not talking."

"I'd be lying if I said I'm not worried about you."

Her face shuttered suddenly, as if she had tucked her emotions away for safekeeping. "You don't need to be. I found out what I wanted to know, and now I'm going to get on with my life, like everyone's been telling me to."

Her robe had loosened, offering a glimpse of pale shoulder. He forced his eyes back to her face. "Why don't I believe you?"

She shot him an unconvincing smile, waving a vague hand at the mess in the living room. "Look around. This is what getting on with my life looks like."

"That's the external stuff. I'm talking about the internal stuff."

Christy-Lynn picked up her fork again, eyes on her plate as she toyed with a sliver of carrot. "I'm working on that part. The last two days have been . . . hard, but I finally got all the whens and wheres. Now I can move on."

"What about the whys?"

She shrugged. "He was a man. She was a woman. The why speaks for itself."

"And the girl? Iris?"

"Inevitable, I suppose."

He looked at her, not bothering to hide his skepticism. "So that's it? You're ready to just . . . move on?"

"Yes."

Wade raked a hand through his hair, wondering who she was trying to convince, herself or him. "Look, I know I've been telling you to stop torturing yourself, but I didn't mean like this. You can't just pretend you don't have feelings if you do."

Christy-Lynn tossed down her fork with a clatter. "Of course I have feelings. But what am I supposed to do with them? There's no way to walk it back, is there? No way to put the genie back in the bottle. No one to even rail at since Stephen's dead. There's just this little girl with no parents!"

The words rang sharply off the walls of the kitchen, shimmering hotly in the small space. Wade watched her, startled and uncertain as she went very still, head lowered, a hand pressed to her mouth. She was shaking visibly. Eventually, she opened her eyes. He pushed back his plate and folded his arms on the edge of the table.

"What happened today, Christy-Lynn?"

Her eyes slid away, looking everywhere but at him. "He wanted her," she said softly.

"Honey?"

Her eyes drifted back to his, weary and full of sadness. "Iris. Honey considered . . . not having her, but Stephen changed her mind. I wasn't expecting that." She wiped the sleeve of her robe across her eyes, then bounced out of her chair. "Coffee?"

Wade blinked at her, startled by the abrupt change of subject, and by a newly improved view of her left shoulder. He dragged his eyes away to check his watch. "Sure. Why not? I'm basically immune to caffeine at this point."

He watched as she scooped coffee into the basket, his professional sonar pinging off the charts. He could feel the carefully checked emotions, tamped down good and tight but bubbling hard beneath the surface. Anger mixed with confusion wrapped in betrayal. But there was something else too, something he couldn't quite put a finger on.

She returned to the table a few moments later and handed him a mug. "Sugar only, right?"

She had tightened the belt of her robe so that her shoulder was no longer exposed. He wasn't sure if he was relieved or disappointed. "You've been paying attention. I'm flattered."

"You've been drinking coffee in my café for two months now."

"True enough. Now sit."

He was surprised when she actually dropped back into her chair without protest, her mug cradled between her palms.

"What's going on? What haven't you told me?"

"We didn't have kids," she said simply.

Wade looked at her over the rim of his mug. He wasn't sure what he'd been expecting, but it wasn't that. "How is that relevant?"

"It just is."

He waited, watching as she blew on her coffee, then sipped slowly. She was still stalling, tossing out lame responses, but she was getting there.

"I was the one who didn't want kids."

"And Stephen did?"

"If he did, he never said so. We talked about it before we got married—about not doing the family thing—and he seemed fine with it, maybe even a little relieved. But he could have changed his mind. Some men do."

Wade sat with the words a moment, mentally tugging at several loose threads. "You're saying if you'd had a baby Stephen wouldn't have cheated?"

She shrugged. "They say a man with kids is less likely to cheat because he has more to feel guilty about."

Wade paused midsip, stunned by what he'd just heard. "That may just be the biggest load of crap I've ever heard. Guys who cheat don't do it because they're dying to be family men, Christy-Lynn. They do it because they're alley cats."

"What about you? Did you want . . . my God, I never even thought to ask. Do you *have* kids?"

"No. But I wanted them eventually. I mean that's part of it, right—raising a family? But our lives were so crazy. That's one of the reasons I wanted off the media merry-go-round. I wanted to slow things down, see what else life had to offer. Simone had other plans. No way was she slowing down to change diapers."

"You could have though," Christy-Lynn pointed out. "You could have been a stay-at-home dad."

"And I would have. I was ready for a change. But that wasn't the life Simone signed up for. We never had the conversation before we got married. I guess she thought I felt the same way she did about the job. She loved the sleuthing, camping out in front of some guy's apartment in hopes that he'd sneak out for cigarettes or a newspaper, and then bam. Full-scale ambush."

"Yes, I know the drill."

"Sorry, I forgot. I used to think she was just dedicated, you know? Change-the-world dedicated. But as time went on, I saw another side of her, a darker side. The chase, the constant adrenaline rush. It became like a drug for her, and I didn't want any part of that. Which is why I eventually walked away. Stephen could have done the same if he wasn't happy. Instead, he snuck around behind your back and fathered a child with another woman, a daughter you still wouldn't know about if he hadn't driven off a bridge with a half-naked woman in his car."

"Thanks for the recap," Christy-Lynn said dully.

Wade sighed, mentally kicking himself. *Nice going, jackass.*

"I'm sorry. I was just trying to make a point, which is that none of this is your fault. There was something about Stephen, something that made it okay to cross whatever line he wanted, even if it meant hurting people. He did it to me back in college. And now he's done it to you. I couldn't understand it back then. How could he stab a friend in the back and never bat an eye? Now I realize it was his pattern. I also realize it had nothing to do with me. Or you. It was him. He didn't care about anyone but himself."

"He cared enough to persuade Honey not to end the pregnancy," Christy-Lynn said as she rose to refill her mug. "I can't help thinking that if things had been different Iris might have been our daughter, and there would never have been a Honey Rawlings."

Wade eyed her with open skepticism. "How would that have worked? You didn't even want kids, remember? In fact, it sounds like you gave the matter quite a lot of thought, though you never said why."

"No, I didn't."

"And you're not going to."

"No," she said flatly. "And it's water under the bridge now, isn't it?"

Wade nodded. "Fair enough. And I wasn't judging. I was just curious."

"I know you weren't. It just gets old, you know? Always defending your choices. No one ever imagines your reasons might be well thought out, that it might actually be the least selfish choice you'll ever make. Not all of us believe our lives are meaningless unless we reproduce."

"Of course you don't."

Christy-Lynn sighed, running a hand through her hair. "It's just a sore spot for me right now." She set her mug on the counter and crossed to the sliding glass door, arms folded over her chest as she stood facing her own reflection. "I can't get her face out of my head. She has Stephen's chin, that crazy dimple right in the middle. But she looks like Honey too. She's beautiful."

Wade let out a very long breath, lost as to how to respond. "I can't imagine how hard all this must be."

She turned back to him, her face near crumpling. "She barely speaks. Did I tell you that? Since the accident, she barely says a word. And she has nightmares. She's afraid everyone's going to leave her. And she's right. Rhetta's got to be eighty, and she isn't well. And her uncle . . ." Her voice choked down to a whisper. "There's a good chance she'll end up in foster care."

The tears came in earnest then, sliding silently down her cheeks, as if she was entirely unaware of them. Wade stared at her in astonishment. How was it possible that after everything, she could stand there gulping back tears for the child who embodied her husband's betrayal?

He swallowed a groan, scrambling for something to say that wouldn't come off sounding pompous or condescending, but came up empty. And so he let her cry. Because she needed to, and because he didn't know what else to do.

Feeling helpless and desperate to make himself useful, he began closing up the takeout containers, gathering plates and silverware. After a few moments, Christy-Lynn blotted her eyes on the sleeve of her robe and moved to the sink. Neither spoke as they did the dishes, but the rhythm of the simple domestic act seemed to smooth the tension. When the dishes were stowed and the counters wiped, she turned to him.

"I'm sorry about tonight. You came over and did this nice thing, and all I did was weep into my soup. It's all I seem to be doing lately—crying."

"I'd say under the circumstances you're entitled, although I do prefer you when you're not crying." He reached for the takeout bag on the counter, preparing to toss it when he noticed it wasn't empty. "Hey, look, we forgot the fortune cookies." He handed her one, then tore into his, snapping it in half to fish out the small bit of paper.

"Do not confuse activity with accomplishment." He scowled as he crumpled the fortune and dropped it into the bag. "Appropriate for an aspiring novelist, don't you think? Now you."

Christy-Lynn made a face as she handed him her cookie. "You read it."

Wade fumbled with the wrapper, dropping crumbs all over the clean counter in the process, but eventually managed to liberate the tiny scrap of paper. "Salvation lies in doing the thing that frightens us most." He cocked his head. "Mean anything?"

"Not really. But everything frightens me lately."

He studied her a moment, shaken and vulnerable in her oversize robe. So beautiful. And strong in ways she hadn't begun to grasp. "I think you must be one of the bravest women I know," he said with an intensity that startled him.

Christy-Lynn seemed startled as well, her smile fragile and yet strangely incandescent. Suddenly, Wade found himself fighting an overwhelming desire to touch her cheek. It had probably been a while since she'd been touched, held—kissed. It had been a while for him too.

*Jesus!* What was he thinking? He took a step back, horrified by the direction of his thoughts. Support, empathy, even friendship were perfectly acceptable reactions to her situation, but he'd just gone down a completely different road, and he needed to do a U-turn ASAP.

Christy-Lynn reached for his arm as he prepared to step away. Her fingers were still cool from the dishwater. "Thank you for the food. You've been very . . . kind."

Before he could stop himself, he took her hand, pressing the bit of paper that contained her fortune into her palm. "I meant what I said. You really are one of the bravest women I know. You'll get past this. I promise. In the meantime, if you need someone to talk to or just someone to eat takeout with, you know where to find me."

# TWENTY-NINE

*Sweetwater, Virginia*
*June 10, 2017*

With summer approaching, Christy-Lynn had shifted her energies from the store, which was humming along nicely, to transforming the bungalow into a real home. Now, as she eyed the remaining cartons in the living room, she could finally see the light at the end of the tunnel. With any luck, she'd have them sorted by the end of the day.

She thought of Wade's reaction the other night—*Are you moving?*—and felt a twinge of guilt. She'd been avoiding him since the great Chinese food debacle, going so far as hiding out in the back room when he stopped by the store for coffee.

She should have called the next day to thank him for the takeout, but she hadn't been able to make herself pick up the phone. It felt like the kind of thing you did after a date, not after lapsing into a crying jag over soggy eggrolls. She had never been the type to go to pieces, and yet that's exactly what she'd done with Wade. But she hadn't been able to get Iris out of her head. In fact, she still couldn't.

She had no idea how much a social security check for someone like Rhetta might run, but it couldn't be much. Certainly not enough to raise a child on. And now that Stephen was dead, the monthly allowance he used to give Honey had stopped, which meant there were things Iris would have to do without. Things like books, doctors, medicine—a roof that wasn't patched with plywood.

The thought infuriated her. That Stephen had died without a will should have surprised her but didn't. Death was for mere mortals, not bestselling authors with adoring fans and millions in the bank. But all that should have changed when Iris came along. And maybe it had. It was a long shot, but maybe he'd made some separate arrangement to provide for Iris that his lawyer had purposely omitted from their conversations and had yet to execute.

She dug her phone out of her purse and pulled up Peter Hagan's number. She was surprised when the receptionist put her straight through. "Peter, it's Christy . . . Christine."

"Christine, it's good to hear from you. How've you been getting along?"

"I'm fine. Look, I have a question. I know Stephen didn't have an actual will, but I was wondering if there was some piece of paper somewhere, something you didn't tell me about."

"I'm sorry?"

Christy-Lynn tried to analyze his tone. Was he playing dumb? Purposely being coy? "I know about Iris," she said flatly.

"Who?"

"Iris Rawlings. Stephen's daughter."

There was a long pause, though she couldn't say whether it was of the awkward or confused variety. "Peter?"

"I'm sorry, Christine. I have no idea what you're talking about."

"Look, you don't need to protect him anymore. I know everything."

"Then you obviously know more than I do. If there's a daughter somewhere, Stephen never mentioned her to me."

"How do I know you're not lying?"

"You don't. But I'm telling you as a friend that Stephen never approached me about any kind of estate planning. Not for you and certainly not for a child."

"Do you know the name Honey Rawlings?"

"I'm afraid not. Should I?"

"She was the woman in the car with Stephen the night he died."

"I wasn't aware that she'd been identified."

"She hasn't—officially. But that was her name."

"And how do you know that?"

"I just do. And I'd like to keep that between us."

"Of course, but where are you going with this?"

"Stephen and this woman had a child, Peter. A little girl named Iris. So I thought maybe he'd made some kind of provision, in case anything ever happened. She's living with her great-grandmother in West Virginia, but with Stephen gone, there's no money. It's terrible."

"Christine." Peter paused to clear his throat and perhaps frame his response. "Let me caution you in the strongest terms against getting involved here. For starters, you have absolutely no way of knowing if this little girl—"

"Iris."

"Yes, all right, Iris. We have no way of knowing if Stephen is actually Iris's father. Your concern is admirable, but you have no idea what kind of people come out of the woodwork when someone of Stephen's stature dies. For all we know, this is just some hard luck story conjured up to con money from you. It happens all the time."

"This isn't a con, Peter. I'm sure of it."

"How?" he said, clearly frustrated. "How can you possibly be sure?"

"Because I know my own husband's face when it's looking back at me."

"You've . . . seen her?"

"Last weekend. I drove to West Virginia. Iris is Stephen's daughter."

"And that," Peter said tightly, "is exactly the kind of thing you shouldn't be saying out loud. It could be seen as an admission of paternity and open a lot of very expensive doors. I'm sure your heart is in the right place, but there are established ways—legal ways—to handle these things, and until we avail ourselves of those, I strongly suggest you remove yourself from the situation."

"I don't need a test," she shot back. "And no one's asked me for a dime."

"Christine, please. As your lawyer, I'm telling you this could get sticky."

"It's long past sticky, Peter, but thanks. I found out what I needed to know."

He was still talking when she ended the call.

In the kitchen, she retrieved one of the blank note cards Carol had left in the drawer near the phone and began to write.

Rhetta,

I wanted to thank you again for your kindness the other day. I know my presence was an unwelcome reminder of your loss, and that our conversation must have been as painful for you as it was for me. Our losses are not the same, but the pain we feel is real, and I regret that our paths had to cross in such an unpleasant way. Please accept this small token of my appreciation, and my best wishes for you and Iris. It cannot make up for the loss you've suffered, nor is it meant to. But I do hope it will help make the care of your great-granddaughter a little easier.

Regards,
Christine Ludlow

When she finished the note, she made out a check for $10,000, then slipped it inside the note card, trying not to think about Peter Hagan's reaction should he get wind of the gesture. Legally, Stephen's estate didn't owe Iris a cent. But legal obligations and moral ones were two very different things.

# THIRTY

Christy-Lynn's stomach heaved as she passed the Riddlesville town limits sign. She was clearly out of her mind, but someone had to talk some
sense into Rhetta Rawlings, and since the woman didn't have a phone,
that meant a road trip.

She'd been stunned to receive Rhetta's note, thanking her in thin,
spidery script for her kind wishes, but explaining that she couldn't possibly accept charity from the woman her granddaughter had wronged.
But how could it be charity? Iris was Stephen's daughter, his own flesh
and blood. That he hadn't bothered to plan for her future didn't change
the fact that the check—and so much more—was absolutely Iris's due.

She had no trouble finding Rhetta's house this time, though she'd
hoped her memory of the despair hanging over the place had been exaggerated. It hadn't. But then, that's why she was here—to help alleviate
some of that despair.

Rhetta's eyes shot wide as she opened the door. "What on earth?"

"You don't have a phone," Christy-Lynn blurted as if that explained everything. "Is this a bad time?"

"I'm afraid I don't understand. Bad time for what?"

"I'm here about the check. I want to explain."

Rhetta shuffled back a few steps, an unspoken invitation for Christy-Lynn to come in. Iris was stretched out on the living room rug, head bent over a coloring book. She looked up when Christy-Lynn walked in, her pale face guarded.

"Iris, honey?" Rhetta said in her phlegmy voice. "Do you remember Christy-Lynn? She's come back to visit Nonny."

Iris made no reply, not so much as a blink from those wide, luminous eyes.

Christy-Lynn managed to find a smile. "Hello, Iris," she said gently, afraid the child might bolt like a frightened deer. "That's a lovely fish you're coloring. Pink fish are my favorite."

Iris glanced down at the pink crayon in her fist as if surprised to find it there.

"She's having one of her quiet days," Rhetta whispered apologetically. "Let's go into the kitchen. I just finished making a pitcher of tea."

"I promise I won't be long," Christy-Lynn said when she spotted a large stockpot bubbling on the stove. "I know it's almost dinnertime."

Rhetta's gnarled hands shook as she wrestled with the tea pitcher, sloshing a fair amount onto the counter as she filled two glasses, then handed one to Christy-Lynn. "I have to say, I didn't expect to see you again."

"I didn't expect to be here, but when I got your letter, I knew I had to come. I'm wondering why you sent back the check."

"I told you in the letter. We can't take your charity."

"But it isn't charity. It's no different than the money Stephen used to give Honey to help with Iris."

"It absolutely *is* different." Rhetta's chin wobbled with something like defiance, her blue eyes suddenly clear and sharp. "That was Stephen's money, his to do with as he pleased. But he's not here anymore, which means that money legally belongs to you. We've got no right to it."

"Rhetta," Christy-Lynn said, lowering her voice to blunt her frustration. "As I'm sure you know, my husband was a very wealthy man. It isn't right that he never bothered to provide for his daughter. I'm trying to correct that—if you'll let me."

"It isn't right."

"It is. In fact, it's the only thing about this whole situation that *is* right." Christy-Lynn reached into her purse for the check and slid it across the vinyl tablecloth. "Please . . . take it."

Rhetta closed her eyes, giving her grizzled head a firm shake. If possible, she looked even wearier than she had the last time, worn thin by the day-to-day trials of caring for a child with emotional problems.

"It isn't money that girl needs," she said, tracing a yellowed thumbnail through the sweat on her tea glass. "She needs someone who's going to be there for her. Even when Honey was alive, she didn't have that."

"She's lucky to have you," Christy-Lynn said feebly.

Rhetta glanced up from her glass, pain etched in the lines on either side of her mouth. "But for how long?"

It was Christy-Lynn's turn to avert her gaze. It was the elephant in the room, after all. The question about what would happen to Iris when Rhetta was no longer able to care for her.

"Been thinking about it a lot since your last visit," Rhetta said heavily.

"And?"

"And nothing." Her lower lip began to quiver. "She's a handful, poor thing, between not talking and not sleeping. It's not her fault, but when you get to be my age, it's a lot to manage."

Without thinking, Christy-Lynn reached for Rhetta's hand. "That's why you need to take the check, Rhetta. You could get some help in, maybe find a counselor to help Iris cope with everything that's happened. Things would be easier for you both."

"Who would I get around here?"

"Maybe there are people at the county who could help or at least suggest someone you could hire. A kind of home health aide."

A look of horror rippled over Rhetta's weathered countenance. "Just what I need, a bunch of government do-gooders knowing I'm too old to take care of my own. Next thing I know, they'll be swooping in to take her. I'm not saying it won't come to that someday. It may well. But I'll be dead when it does, and it will be . . . out of my hands."

Christy-Lynn fought back a shudder. She was right. Old, infirm, and living well below the poverty line, Rhetta Rawlings wouldn't be anyone's idea of an ideal guardian, kin or not.

"Maybe Ray could put out a few feelers at church for someone to help with meals, laundry, that kind of thing."

Rhetta snorted. "He doesn't even want me bringing her to church. As far as he's concerned, Honey's already brought enough shame to the Rawlings name—as if a Rawlings ever amounted to anything in this town."

Christy-Lynn experienced a fresh wave of disgust for Ray Rawlings. "He doesn't want his niece going to church?"

"Not his church, no. Says he doesn't need me sticking Honey's brat in everyone's faces, reminding his congregation what she was. His own sister—" Her voice broke. She looked down at her glass.

"Rhetta, that's terrible."

She blinked hard as she turned to stare out the kitchen window. "I used to think he'd change his mind, that his heart would soften toward Iris in time, but it hasn't. And it won't. He means what he says." She shook her head, eyes closing briefly. "So where does that leave Iris?"

"I don't know, Rhetta. I wish I did. But at least take the check. It won't solve everything, but it'll help you get by until you figure things out. And before you say it, this isn't charity. It's hers or should have been. Plus a whole lot more. Please, say you'll take it."

The tears that had been trembling on Rhetta's lower lashes finally spilled over. "Mrs. Ludlow . . ." Something like a cough escaped her as she dropped her head into her hands. "I don't know how . . . your astonishing kindness . . ."

Christy-Lynn slid a hand across the table, capturing both of Rhetta's, her fingers gnarled and startlingly fragile. "Please don't cry, Rhetta. We'll find someone to help you look after Iris. I promise. And you need to call me Christy-Lynn."

Something, some sound or bit of movement, seeped into Christy-Lynn's awareness. She peered over her shoulder and saw Iris hovering in the doorway, eyes glued to the women holding hands across the tiny kitchen table.

Rhetta noticed her too and quickly mopped her eyes. "Iris, baby, I didn't hear you come in. Do you need some juice?"

Iris stood there a moment with her hands behind her back, as if she were trying to puzzle something out. Finally she inched forward, hesitant but clearly determined on some course of action.

"What is it, Iris?" Rhetta asked, clearly mystified by her great-granddaughter's behavior. "What have you got there?"

Iris didn't answer. Instead, she took another halting step, then whipped a sheet of paper from behind her back and held it out to Christy-Lynn. "Pink fishes are my favorite too," she blurted in lispy toddlerese, before scurrying from the kitchen.

Rhetta sat speechless, a hand pressed to her mouth as she stared at the messy pink Nemo her great-granddaughter had just bestowed on Christy-Lynn. "Six words," she said quietly, counting them off on gnarled fingers. "That's the most she's said at a stretch in I don't know how long."

Christy-Lynn wasn't sure how to respond, or how to process the unfamiliar wave of emotion she had just experienced. "She was just mimicking me," she told Rhetta sheepishly. "Because I told her I like pink fish."

Rhetta was smiling, the first genuine smile Christy-Lynn had ever seen cross her face. "She likes you."

"She was just being sweet. She doesn't even know me."

"Oh, I think she does." There was a strange gravity to Rhetta's words, an unsettling weight that made Christy-Lynn go very still. "Children know things, like who's kind and who's not, who's genuine and who's not. She knows exactly who you are, Christy-Lynn." Rhetta's voice fractured again, and she cleared her throat. "We both do."

# THIRTY-ONE

Christy-Lynn shot straight up in bed, adrenaline still pumping like needles through her limbs. It took a few moments for the stark physicality of the dream to fade—not that it ever did entirely. The swimming faces and garbled words were always within easy reach, a dark and watery backdrop to her waking hours. She had hoped convincing Rhetta to accept the check would end or at least reduce their frequency. Instead, the dreams seemed to be coming *more* frequently, leaving her too wired to go back to sleep and in a near zombielike state the next morning.

Eventually, her heart began to slow, and she noticed the steady drum of rain against the windows. Lying back, she closed her eyes, willing her mind to quiet, but it was no good. Every nerve in her body was on alert, like violin strings tuned too tightly.

Still shaky, she slipped out of bed and padded to the kitchen for her ritual cup of Earl Grey. As she waited for the water to heat, she stared at the bright-pink fish grinning at her from the refrigerator door. In her wildest dreams, she couldn't have imagined a day when there'd be kiddie art tacked up in her kitchen, and yet there it was.

She turned away as the microwave dinged, then frowned as she caught what sounded like muffled mewling coming from the other side of the sliding glass doors. When the sound came again, she stepped to the door and peered out. It didn't take long to spot the source of the commotion.

"Well, well. What have we here?" Without thinking, Christy-Lynn eased back the door to get a better look at the miserably drenched feline. "Looks like someone forgot their foul weather gear." Too late, she realized her error. Mistaking sympathy for an invitation, the cat squeezed between her ankles and bolted into the kitchen with another strangled yowl.

Christy-Lynn eyed her sodden guest with dismay. "I'm afraid you've knocked on the wrong door, sir. It's not personal. Pets just aren't my thing."

The cat was unmoved, continuing to stare up at her with pitiful amber eyes. She heaved a sigh, her resolve beginning to falter. She hadn't forgotten what it was like to be wet and cold and have no place to sleep.

"All right. All right. You can spend the night but don't get any ideas about making it permanent. And I hope you're not expecting dinner because I'm fresh out of cat food."

Another yowl, followed by more golden-eyed pathos.

"Fine," she groaned, heading for the fridge. "I have milk. But that's it."

She filled a saucer then stood by as the cat greedily emptied it. How long had it been since the poor thing had had any real food? In the pantry, she located a can of tuna, opened it, and turned it out onto a second saucer.

By the time the Earl Grey finished brewing, both dishes were clean, and her guest had turned his attentions to matters of appearance. Christy-Lynn carried her mug to the living room and settled on the love seat to observe the stray's careful ablutions. She was surprised when after only a few minutes she felt her lids grow heavy. She let them close, melting against the cushions. Perhaps if she slept here instead of in her bed, the dream wouldn't find her.

She woke several hours later to a flood of warm yellow light spilling through the living room windows. Stiff and dazed, she sat up, confused as to why she was waking up on the love seat instead of her bed. And then she spotted the orange-and-white fur ball curled on the arm of the love seat, and the events of the previous night drifted back.

As if sensing her eyes, the cat lifted his head, blinking up with a blend of curiosity and sleepy annoyance, then stood, stretched, and jumped to the floor, making a beeline for the kitchen and the sliding glass doors.

"Just like a man," Christy-Lynn muttered drily, pulling back the door to let him out. "Slinking away the minute the sun's up."

She watched as he darted down the back steps and disappeared from sight, then went to make coffee. Missy would be by in a few hours for lunch, her first guest since Hank had finished the kitchen updates, and she wanted everything to be perfect.

Missy was late as usual but looked flawless in a sleeveless tunic and white linen slacks. She pressed her lips to Christy-Lynn's cheek as she stepped through the door, leaving behind one of her signature fuchsia lip prints. "For you," she said, handing Christy-Lynn a small gift bag brimming with tissue paper. "Just a little gift to mark the milestone. You can open it after I'm gone if you want. But right now—" She paused, grinning as she held up a plastic grocery bag. "I brought stuff to make mimosas. And before you say no, I got sparkling cider for you. Or you can just drink plain old OJ, but it's not nearly as much fun without the bubbles."

Missy whistled appreciatively as they walked into the newly remodeled kitchen. "I still can't believe what you've done with this place. I know I saw it while the work was going on, but now that it's finished—wow."

Christy-Lynn couldn't help beaming. It was her favorite room since the renovations. "Thanks. The farm sink and vintage hardware were Hank's ideas. He completely nailed the look I was after."

Missy was wrestling with the champagne cork now, the bottle wedged between her knees. She flinched as it released with a clean, sharp pop. "Did you ever decide what to do with that spare room?"

Christy-Lynn thought of the room next to her bedroom, crowded at the moment with the leftover bits and pieces of her decorating efforts. "Not yet, but I'm leaning toward an office. I was thinking about picking up a few editing projects again. I miss my writers. And the truth is, with the shop up and running and the bungalow mostly finished, I have too much time on my hands."

Missy had located two champagne flutes and was pouring the orange juice. "Maybe you should think about filling that time with some fun. There's a guy who works with Daddy, a CPA. Nice-looking. Divorced. No kids."

Christy-Lynn shot her a look. "Why don't we have some lunch?"

Missy feigned a pout. "All right, I get it. Time to change the subject."

"Exactly." Christy-Lynn pulled two shrimp and avocado salads from the fridge and headed for the deck. "Speaking of kids, where are the boys today?"

"On a campout with the neighbor's kids." Missy handed Christy-Lynn a champagne flute and settled herself into one of the deck chairs. "What is it about boys sleeping in tents?"

Christy-Lynn smiled. "I can't help you there, but it must be nice to have some alone time."

Missy gave the question some thought then shrugged. "You'd think so, but I actually miss the little monsters. The house is too quiet when they're gone, and I'm not sure I know what to do with alone time anymore. I know it's crazy, but I like running around with my hair on fire. There's nothing I wouldn't give up for my kids, but I guess it comes with the territory."

"Not always," Christy-Lynn said more gloomily than she intended.

Missy's expression softened. "You mean your mother."

Christy-Lynn waved the remark away. "Forget it. I didn't mean to get all maudlin. I just haven't been sleeping well lately."

Missy's gaze narrowed. "I'm guessing that's not because you've been binge-watching the last season of *Game of Thrones*."

Christy-Lynn considered changing the subject but knew better than to think she'd get away with it. "There's been . . . a development."

"What kind of development?"

"A little girl," she blurted quickly, like ripping off a bandage. "Stephen and Honey had a little girl."

Missy sat frozen, absorbing the news with a faintly stunned expression. "Well," she said finally. "He really *was* a bastard, wasn't he? How did you find out?"

"I've seen her—at Rhetta's. It was like someone knocked all the air out of me. All I could see was Stephen and Honey looking back at me."

"Sweet Jesus," Missy breathed, reaching for Christy-Lynn's hand. "And you've been carrying this around all by yourself. Why? You know I'm always here for you, don't you? That you can tell me anything?"

Christy-Lynn nodded. She *did* know. But in the three weeks since she'd learned of Iris's existence, she hadn't been able to work her into the conversation. Except with Wade, of course, but that was only because she'd blurted it all out in a moment of weakness.

"I guess I've been processing," she said finally. "It's embarrassing, finding out your husband fathered a child with another woman and managed to keep it a secret for three years. And if his car hadn't gone off that bridge, I *still* wouldn't know."

Missy huffed so hard her bangs fluttered. "Look, I know you're upset, honey, and you have every right to be, but you have absolutely nothing to be embarrassed about."

Christy-Lynn shrugged half-heartedly. She wanted to believe the words. But wanting and believing were two different things. Stephen had been no saint. She'd come to terms with that, but her willingness over the years to turn a blind eye to his character flaws was hard to deny. She'd been content with the status quo, happily ensconced in a false sense of security, and in her blissful state of oblivion had enabled an affair—and by extension, the birth of a little girl whose childhood eerily mirrored her own.

Missy was looking at her, waiting for the rest of the story—because of course she knew there was more. The woman was like a bloodhound. And so it all came tumbling out—the stomach-dropping moment she had first seen Iris, the check Rhetta had been too proud to accept, the awful moment Ray Rawlings had called his niece an abomination.

Missy was still shaking her head when Christy-Lynn fell silent. "My God. A little girl with no parents, and that poor woman with a child to raise at her age. I honestly don't know who to feel sorrier for."

"It's awful. The house they live in looks like it would blow over in a stiff breeze. There's no yard, no phone, no neighbors close by. But the worst is Honey's brother refusing to take Iris if something happens to Rhetta. She could end up in foster care."

Missy looked thoughtful as she smoothed the creases from her linen slacks. "I know it's awful, honey, but at the risk of sounding heartless, it really isn't your problem. This is her parents' fault, and it's up to her family to deal with it."

Christy-Lynn stared at her lap, wadding her napkin into a ragged ball. "He called her an abomination, Missy. An abomination born in sin. Her own uncle called her that." She swallowed convulsively, her heart aching at the unfairness of it all. "None of this is Iris's fault, but she's the one who'll pay."

Missy let out a long sigh. "You're up to your neck in this, aren't you?"

Christy-Lynn nodded, though deep down she knew the ache in her chest wasn't only for Iris. For some terrible, twisted reason, fate had conspired to put this little girl in her path, an unwelcome reminder of the childhood she'd been trying to outrun for decades. And now, for better or worse, there was no going back.

"Yes," she said finally. "I am. Am I crazy?"

"Yes," Missy answered without a moment's hesitation. "I don't know a woman alive who'd give a rat's behind about a kid her husband fathered with his girlfriend. But you do—so that's that. What are you going to do?"

"I don't know. It's a drop in the bucket, but I finally got Rhetta to cash the check. She called a few days ago to let me know she finally has a phone and to thank me again. I can't make her understand that in every way that matters that money *belonged* to Iris."

"Hate to break it to you, honey, but not many people would see it that way."

Christy-Lynn remained quiet as she sipped her fizzy orange juice, weighing the wisdom of what she was about to say. If Missy already thought she was crazy, what would she think when she heard the rest? "I've been thinking about setting up a trust," she blurted. "For Iris."

Missy's gray-green eyes widened. "Seriously?"

"You know I've never been comfortable with all that money. It's just sitting there, piling up month after month. Why not give it to her?"

"What? All of it?"

"I don't know, but a good chunk. She'd have money for doctors, tutors, schools—hell, a decent roof over her head."

Missy shook her head dolefully. "For now, maybe. But you said it yourself, Rhetta isn't long for this world, and her uncle doesn't want anything to do with her. Money might come in handy today, but it's only a short-term fix. I hate to say it, but it sounds like foster care may be the best option. At least the poor thing will be looked after and have a shot at a happy home."

*A happy home.*

Christy-Lynn looked away. She'd said it so casually, as if going into foster care was some sort of solution. But then she couldn't expect Missy to grasp the reality—or the horror—of what such a future might mean. People who grew up with puppies and swing sets would never understand that the foster care system, well-intentioned though it might be, could quickly become the stuff of nightmares for those trapped in it. Or that a child like Iris, with nightmares and inhibited verbal skills, would be starting with two strikes against her.

"I realize it doesn't fix the long-term problem. It's just . . . what I can do."

"Have you discussed the idea with Rhetta?"

"Not yet. I need to do some homework first. And then I'll have to convince her to let me do it. I can't even imagine what Wade's reaction will be."

"What's Wade got to do with it?"

"He caught me off guard the day I met Iris, and I ended up blurting out the whole story. He knew Stephen. I thought he might have some kind of insight."

"And did he?"

"He says Stephen had no conscience."

Missy scowled. "Hard to argue with him there."

"He thinks I'm too invested, that I'm setting myself up for more heartache and should just let it all go."

"And what do you think?"

"I agree with every word. I *should* just let it go. I'm just not sure I can."

"Then I guess you'd better get started on that homework."

Christy-Lynn blinked at her. "You don't think it's a bad idea?"

Missy's smile was tinged with sympathy. "This is your business, honey. It's not my place to tell you how to handle it. I just want what's best for you. Speaking of which . . . you said something before about not sleeping well. Are you taking care of yourself?"

"It's no big deal really."

"But it is. Sleep is a girl's best friend. And there's no reason to do without. My doctor wrote me a prescription for some pills last year when I had some stuff going on, and they worked like a charm. I have a few left if you're interested. I know you're not big on the chemical thing, but it might help you get caught up."

"No, but thanks for the offer. I'm sure things will smooth out once I make a decision about Iris and the trust."

"You know, you might want to talk to Dar. She carries all kinds of oils and teas—all natural stuff. Maybe she could recommend something to help take the edge off without having to pop a pill." She lifted her glass, draining the last of her mimosa, then stood. "I'm going inside to fix us another round. When I come back, I'll have your present."

Christy-Lynn didn't want another mimosa. She didn't want to open her present either, but she didn't have the heart to tell Missy no. Instead she sat quietly, staring down at the creek. She had just tossed the wadded remains of her napkin onto her plate when something caught her eye. She turned to find herself being observed by a pair of sleepy golden eyes.

"Well, well. Look who's back. Couldn't live without me, eh?"

If the cat objected to her sarcasm, he gave no sign as he sashayed toward her, tail held high. He was about to take a second turn around her ankles when Missy reappeared.

"I didn't know you had a cat."

"I don't. He just showed up last night, ravenous and dripping wet."

"Did you feed him?"

"Just some milk and a can of tuna."

"Then you have a cat."

"Oh, no, I don't," Christy-Lynn countered firmly. "I've never even had a goldfish. But you could take him. The boys have been pestering you for a pet."

"Yes, they have. They've been pestering me for a dog. And since there's zero chance I can pass off an orange tabby as a golden retriever, I'm afraid he's yours."

Christy-Lynn glowered at the cat. "Don't go getting comfortable, mister. I am *not* keeping you."

Missy chuckled as she handed Christy-Lynn a gift bag brimming with silver tissue. "Maybe, but he appears to be keeping *you*. That's how it works, by the way. You don't pick them. They pick you. Now open your present."

"I wish you hadn't done this."

"It's no big deal but hurry up. I'm dying to know if you like it."

Christy-Lynn reached into the nest of tissue, groping blindly until she located a small box. She felt self-conscious as she lifted the lid and then her breath caught. "Oh, Missy . . ."

Against the box's black velvet interior lay a bracelet adorned with a trio of silver charms: a tiny house with a porch and chimney, an open book, and a to-go cup inscribed with the word *latte*.

"Missy, you shouldn't have, but I love it. The charms are perfect."

"They represent the pieces of your new life. There's one for the bungalow, another for the store, and one for the café. It's up to you to fill up the rest."

There was no missing the unspoken message. *It's time to get on with your life.* It seemed to be the general consensus these days. And she really was trying. She was a million miles from her life in Clear Harbor. But the ghost of that other self was still with her, anchoring her to the past, clouding the future.

She fingered the charms one at a time, carefully chosen symbols of the life she had begun to create for herself. "Sometimes it feels like none of it's real, Missy, like I'm just pretending. I can't let myself settle into it. There are still so many things I need to sort out, pieces of myself I haven't been able to put back together."

"I know, baby, but it'll come."

"When?"

"When you're ready."

"What if I'm never ready?"

Missy set down her mimosa, her expression suddenly stern. "I don't believe in never, and neither should you."

A tiny *V* appeared between Christy-Lynn's brows. "How can you not believe in never? It's just a word."

"No," Missy said firmly. "It isn't. It's all the doors we keep shut. It's the places we won't let ourselves go, the things we won't let ourselves have or be, because we don't think we're good enough or strong enough for more. I know because that used to be me. And then I became a single parent, and I realized I didn't have time for nevers." She paused, her smile thin and tremulous. "All I'm saying is don't live a smaller life than you deserve."

Christy-Lynn nodded, the appropriate response when a friend gave you good advice. And it was good advice. For most people. But then most people knew what they wanted—and what they deserved.

# THIRTY-TWO

Christy-Lynn crossed the street when she spotted the sign for the Moon Maiden. After three straight nights of waking up in a cold sweat, she had decided to take Missy's advice and talk to Dar.

A set of brass bells jangled as she pushed inside the dimly lit shop. The space was cool and quiet, the air scented with sandalwood. Dar appeared from the back, pale haired and nymphlike in a flowing skirt of hyacinth-hued silk and a filmy white blouse. She deposited an armload of incense packets on the counter and reversed direction when she saw Christy-Lynn.

"Hey there! What brings you by?"

"Missy said I should come see you for something to help me sleep."

"Ah." Dar's expression morphed into something more clinical. "Then you'll need to tell me a little bit about the kind of trouble you're having. Do you have trouble falling asleep? Or staying asleep?"

"The latter mostly."

"Are you on any medications?"

"No. None."

"Caffeine?"

"Well, I own a café, so I probably consume more than I should, but I've cut back over the last few weeks and haven't seen any real difference."

"What about your stress level? Anything new there?"

Christy-Lynn's gaze slid to a nearby bookshelf. The title of a particularly thick volume seemed to jump out at her. *The Language of Dreams.* She'd never been much for all the symbolic woo-woo stuff, things like enneagrams, past life regression, and zodiac signs, but suddenly the subject of dream interpretation was an intriguing one.

"Christy-Lynn?"

"I'm sorry, what?"

"I asked if you were under any stress."

"Oh, you know"—Christy-Lynn's eyes strayed back to the dream book—"there's always something going on at the store."

"Are you interested in dreams?"

"Oh, no. I was just . . ."

"It's a hobby of mine, reading people's dreams. I'm fascinated by the whole inner landscape thing, how our deeper selves are always sending us messages."

"You think that's what dreams are? Messages from our deeper selves?"

"Sure. What else? The soul, the psyche, whatever you want to call it, has a way of looking out for us, even when we're not paying attention. They come when our minds are quiet, when we have no choice but to listen."

"I guess that makes sense. You can't run away when you're asleep."

"No," Dar said gently. "At least not for very long. So do you want to tell me what's really going on? Are you having dreams? Is that why you can't get back to sleep?"

Dar's eyes, so keen and calm, were suddenly unsettling. "Did you glean that with your psychic powers?"

"No dark art required," Dar assured her. "You keep looking at *The Language of Dreams*, and pardon the expression, but you look like you've seen a ghost—or like you've been dragging a few around with you. Please don't take offense. It's just that I've been there, and I know it's no fun."

*Dragging around ghosts.*

If there was a more apt description for the dreams she'd been having, she couldn't think what it might be. "I've been having nightmares," she said quietly. "Basically the same dream for months now. I'm exhausted."

"Well then, that's different." Dar crooked a finger. "Come with me. I was going to suggest valerian root, but I think a little insight will do more good than tea."

She led Christy-Lynn to a small reading area at the rear of the shop where a stick of incense in a leaf-shaped holder gave off a thin tendril of blue-white smoke. She smiled as she sat, patting the settee beside her. "Why don't we talk a little? Sometimes that's all it takes. Looking at it when you're wide awake, saying it out loud, can help you see where the dream is coming from—and the message it has for you."

"So we're back to the message," Christy-Lynn said uncomfortably.

"There's no way to get around it really. Dreams are like public service announcements from your soul. The only way to get past them is to pay attention to what they're telling us. If you'd like to share, I might be able to offer some insight."

Christy-Lynn pulled in a breath then let it out very slowly. "I'm underwater," she began tentatively. "At the bottom of the bay. Stephen's car is there. He's in it. So is the woman who was with him the night he went off the bridge. It's just the two of them at first, dead in the car. But then the woman's eyes open, and she starts talking, only I can't make out what she's saying. I just know she's trying to tell me something."

"What do you think she's trying to say?" Dar prodded gently.

"I don't know. That she's sorry about stealing my husband maybe. Except it doesn't feel like that. It feels like something else. I just don't know what."

"Is that all of it?"

"It was in the beginning, but a few weeks ago, I found out Stephen and Honey had a child—a little girl named Iris—and now she's showing up in the dream too. She's in the car, and she keeps pushing at the windows, screaming for Nonny—her great-grandmother—but she isn't there. It's just me, and instead of helping her, I swim away."

Dar's eyes were full of sympathy. "You poor thing. After everything else, there's a child to cope with. No wonder you're exhausted. You obviously feel some kind of sympathy for this little girl, but I'm wondering . . ."

Christy-Lynn's head came up slowly. "Wondering what?"

"If there isn't something else going on, something that may run a little deeper. Like why you'd want or need to take that kind of responsibility on your shoulders." She paused, smoothing her skirt over her knees. "In dreams, water generally represents the subconscious, so when someone tells me they've been dreaming about water, my first thought is something's being repressed. Do you think there are things you might need to start looking at, things you've been trying to hide from?"

Christy-Lynn was tempted to dismiss the question, but that wasn't going to make the dreams stop. "Maybe," she answered finally. "But why now? After all these years?"

Dar folded her hands in her lap and smiled softly. It was the kind of smile mothers saved for children who asked impossible questions. "I can't tell you that. What I can tell you is there are places in our minds where we lock up all the things we don't want to remember, like a musty basement filled with all the stuff we don't want anyone—including ourselves—to see. We think it's safe, that we're safe. And then one day, for reasons we can't begin to fathom, something yanks those doors open, and all our psychic junk comes tumbling out."

Christy-Lynn huffed in frustration. "It's all this stuff with Iris and Stephen."

Dar seemed to consider the answer. "Maybe. But it's easy to reach for the obvious. Even comforting. I know this stuff with your husband's been hard, and it probably feels like that's all that's going on, but it could be something else. You said you swim away in the dream. Maybe there's something you're afraid of, something further back. Or it could be something that hasn't happened yet, something you're *afraid* will happen. Is any of this striking a chord?"

Of course it was.

Christy-Lynn nodded. "I just wanted it to be something else."

"The memories are uncomfortable?"

"Yes."

"Then I think it's a good place to start. Your higher self is telling you it's time."

Christy-Lynn felt her shoulders tense. "Time for what?"

"To let the memories catch up with you. You're never going to outswim them. Why not drift a little and see what comes up? You might even try a little meditation before bed. Ask the dreams to come. Ask them what they're trying to show you. Remember, they're just memories. They can't hurt you unless you let them."

The jangle of bells alerted Christy-Lynn that a customer had entered the shop. Relieved, she shot to her feet, happy to end what was quickly becoming an uncomfortable conversation.

On the way to the front, Dar pressed a packet of tea into her hands. "Try the valerian root anyway. It might help."

"Thank you. For the tea and for your time. What do I owe you?"

"Don't be silly. It's a gift between friends. And I hope our talk helps. Just remember, I'm no expert. Everything I said could be total crap."

Dar's advice played over in Christy-Lynn's head as she walked back to the Crooked Spine. *Stop swimming and let the memories catch up . . . They can't hurt you unless you let them.* It was a fine sentiment, wise and well meant. She just wasn't sure she could do what Dar was asking. In her experience, memories could hurt very much.

# THIRTY-THREE

Christy-Lynn stared at the page of the bullet-pointed notes she had scrawled during her call with Peter Hagan. *Inter-vivos trusts, custodians, successor trustees, scheduled disbursements.* Her head was still spinning with all the legalese, but at least she had some idea what the process would entail.

Peter was still hedging on the idea, sticking to his earlier recommendation that they quietly petition for a paternity test, even hinting at one point that she hire an investigator to check out *these people* before making what may turn out to be a costly mistake. He'd hate to see her take such an imprudent step only to have regrets later. There might well come a time when she needed the money herself. She had nearly laughed at that. No one needed the kind of money they were talking about.

He had also expressed concern that as a woman her judgment might be clouded since there was a child involved. She had assured him, coolly and firmly, that there was nothing wrong with her judgment, and that since Stephen hadn't bothered to provide for his daughter, she intended to do it, and he could help her or not. He had ended the call with a promise to get started on preparing the paperwork and to be in touch in a few days.

It all sounded fairly straightforward. Once the paperwork was completed and the signatures affixed, everything was pretty automatic. There was only one problem, and it went back to what would happen when Rhetta passed away. Who would direct the disbursements and oversee the spending then? Was she willing to take on that role, to tether herself to Stephen and Honey's daughter for the next fifteen years? She honestly didn't know. What she did know was that there was a little girl living in a shack in Riddlesville, West Virginia, whose life was teetering on the brink of disaster. Someone somewhere had to step up and do the right thing.

She was spared a flash-forward to what might lay ahead for Iris when Aileen poked her head in the door. "Customer asking for you, boss."

Christy-Lynn found Wade standing in the café, laptop case slung over one shoulder. He looked more tan than he had the last time she saw him, and he was clean-shaven. His hair had that just-cut look.

He broke into a smile as she approached. "Hey, stranger. Long time, no see."

"It's not like I'm hard to find. I practically live here. You're the one who's been scarce."

"I've been keeping my head down, working on the novel. I'm determined not to let it break me."

"Butt in chair, as I tell my writers. So what's up?"

"I wanted to check on you."

"On me?"

"You were upset the last time we talked. I wanted to know how you were with . . . things."

"Ah, that. Well . . ." Christy-Lynn shifted her gaze, feigning interest in whatever Tamara was doing behind the counter. She wasn't sure why she was hemming and hawing all of a sudden. It wasn't like she'd withheld much when it came to Honey and Stephen. In fact, she was surprised at how much she'd been willing to tell him. So why was she reluctant to share this new idea? Unless it was because she was afraid of what he might say. "I've, uh . . . I've been doing some thinking."

"About?"

"Do you have plans for dinner?"

The invitation clearly caught Wade off guard, though not necessarily in an unpleasant way. He grinned, a wickedly effective blend of boy and rogue. "What did you have in mind?"

"I was hoping I could bounce something off you. I need some advice."

"You want advice from me?"

"I do."

Wade scratched his head then glanced at his watch. "Sure. Okay. You want to meet somewhere after work?"

"Can we do it at my place? We can do Lotus again, or I'll cook. I owe you a meal. In fact, I think I owe you several."

"I'll take my chances with your cooking. Seven all right?"

"Fine."

"Can I bring anything?"

"An open mind."

His brow wrinkled, but the smile was back. "I'll see what I can do."

Wade felt slightly sheepish as he knocked on Christy-Lynn's door with a bouquet of daisies in his fist, like a tongue-tied teen on a first date. He straightened awkwardly when the door opened. "My mother taught me to never show up for dinner empty-handed. And since you don't do wine . . ."

"Thank you. They're sweet."

She had changed since he last saw her. She wore a breezy floral skirt now and a tank top that showed off tawny arms and lots of shoulder. There was a dish towel tucked into the waist of her skirt, and she was barefoot, a silver chain winking at her ankle. She reminded him of a gypsy, beautiful and just a little untamed. He cleared his throat, determined to shake the thought. The last thing he needed was a crush on Stephen Ludlow's wife.

"Come on in. Dinner's on the stove."

He whistled softly as he stepped into the living room, surprised by the transformation since his last visit. "The place looks great. You really did a nice job."

"Thanks," she said, heading for the kitchen. "I need to finish the sauce. Can you take care of the flowers? There should be a vase under the sink."

When he had finished with the daisies, he stepped to the stove, inspecting the preparations over Christy-Lynn's shoulder. "Smells amazing. Is that Alfredo?"

"I hope that's okay. There's salad too."

Moments later, the pasta was on the table, and they were ready to eat. They sat at opposite ends, the vase of daisies between them. Wade experienced a pang of déjà vu as they sat silently picking at their salads. They had done this before, eaten in awkward silence in her kitchen, only the food had been takeout last time, and he had invited himself.

Tonight she had invited him. For advice of all things. Curiosity prickled along the back of his neck. The old reporter instinct, he told himself, like the tingle of a phantom limb—the need to get at her story. But the truth was he didn't just want to know Christy-Lynn's story. He wanted to know *her*. To know what went on behind those pensive hazel eyes when she thought no one was looking.

Stephen's betrayal had knocked her for a loop, not that he was surprised. It was Stephen's way to leave a trail of destruction in his wake. But there was something else going on, something she was holding back. He'd spent half a lifetime combing through the ruins of lives rocked by tragedy, chronicling the survivors, their losses, and their heartaches, and Christy-Lynn was a textbook survivor, tough, guarded, and behind the aloof and sometimes thorny facade, achingly fragile.

Off in the distance, a rumble of thunder sounded, a low growl that seemed to roll in over the hills. He glanced out the sliding glass doors. A bank of bruised clouds crouched against the western horizon, and a stiff breeze had kicked up, rocking the treetops and turning them silver. There was a storm brewing.

Christy-Lynn seemed not to notice, preoccupied with twirling pasta around her fork. As usual, she wasn't actually eating much.

"This is delicious," Wade said, hoping to spark some sort of conversation. "Family recipe?"

"No. There was a place back in Clear Harbor—Zia Rosa's. The best Alfredo I've ever tasted. Rosa gave me her recipe."

"She *gave* it to you?"

"People were always doing things like that for Stephen. They loved him."

"You mean they loved having a celebrity as a customer. I'm guessing there are signed photos of Stephen Ludlow tacked up on restaurant walls all over the Eastern Seaboard."

"And LA," she added drily. "Don't forget LA."

"Did you mind it? The fame I mean."

Christy-Lynn pretended to go back to her pasta. "I didn't care as long as I didn't have to participate. Stephen loved the attention. He never got tired of being recognized. I, on the other hand, preferred to remain hunkered down with my laptop. Which is why Stephen traveled by himself most of the time—or so I thought. Turns out I had that part wrong."

Wade put his fork down and wiped his mouth. "I'm sorry. I know that sounds trite, but I really am."

"Everyone is." Her eyes slid from his as she reached for her water glass and took a deep swallow. "I don't blame them. There really isn't anything else *to* say. But I'm tired of people feeling sorry for me. Frankly,

I'm tired of feeling sorry for myself. You were right. It's time to move on, to take charge of what's happened instead of wallowing in it."

The remark surprised him, but he was glad to hear her say it. "I think you're right. In fact, I know you are. You've done an amazing job with the store. The whole town's talking about it. And I really think . . ." He never finished the sentence, distracted when an orange-and-white cat sauntered into the kitchen and made straight for his legs.

"Who's this?" he asked, reaching down to give the cat a pet.

"His name is Tolstoy—because he insisted on curling up on a copy of *Anna Karenina* one night while I was reading."

"A Russian cat. And literary. I like it."

"He showed up one night in the middle of a storm. He's basically been here ever since. He certainly seems to like you."

"Yeah, it's a thing I have. Animals love me. Kids too." He shot her a lopsided grin. "It's the grown-ups I have trouble with, as you've no doubt witnessed."

"I take it that's a reference to the alumni dinner?"

Wade rolled his eyes. "Talk about first impressions. Simone knew I was edgy about seeing Stephen again. She thought a little Jameson might loosen me up." He raked a hand through his hair then shook his head. "Boy, did it ever."

"Will you tell me what happened between you and Stephen?"

"No point, really. It was a long time ago. Besides, you said you wanted to talk to me."

Christy-Lynn stood abruptly, carried her plate to the sink, and then busied herself with preparing a pot of coffee. When she finally pressed the brew button, she turned to face him. "I've been thinking of setting up a trust for Iris."

Wade stared at her, letting the revelation land. She'd said it so plainly, without any kind of preamble, as if giving away fists full of money to your husband's love child was the most normal thing in the world.

"What kind of trust?"

"I want to set it up so Stephen's royalties automatically go into it. There would be monthly disbursements to pay for living expenses, school, whatever she needs. And then later college if she wants it."

He said nothing for a time, running through the possible pitfalls in his head. It wasn't a short list. Finally, he stood and carried his plate to the counter. Christy-Lynn was avoiding his gaze, fussing with mugs and cream and sugar.

"Have you thought this through, Christy-Lynn? I mean *really* thought it through?"

"I had just hung up with Stephen's attorney when you came into the store today."

"So . . . that's a yes."

"It's the right thing to do, Wade. I don't want Stephen's money. Or anything that reminds me of him."

"His daughter isn't a reminder?"

"Yes," she said, not looking at him as she filled two mugs. "She is. Every time I look at her, I see Stephen. And Honey. And it hurts. But someone has to take responsibility for the man's child."

"And you think that *someone* is you?"

"You didn't see where she's living, Wade—how she's living. She's three years old. She's going to need things. Who's going to give them to her? Rhetta? That bastard uncle of hers? If I can make sure she grows up with a decent roof over her head, with an education and some sense of opportunity, why *wouldn't* I do it?"

"Sounds like you've made up your mind. Why bring me into it?"

"I don't know really. Because I've told you everything else, I suppose. And because I knew what you'd say but wanted to hear it anyway. You may not believe it, but I value your advice, even if I don't always take it. I don't want to do something stupid, but I do want to do what's right."

She spooned a bit of sugar into one of the mugs and handed it to him, then doctored her own and wandered into the living room, leaving him to follow. There was another growl of thunder—a long, low rumble that vibrated through the floor and walls, followed by the splat of rain-drops against the front windows. Christy-Lynn pulled back the curtains, peering out briefly, then settled herself on the love seat.

"So let's have it," she said flatly. "Give me your opinion."

Wade dropped down beside her, sipping thoughtfully while he tried to corral his thoughts. "What you're talking about is incredibly gracious," he said, choosing his words carefully. "I'd just make sure you're looking at the whole board. Right now this little girl is all you can think about, and that's laudable, but what about down the road? There's a chance you could end up regretting this—or maybe resenting is a better word."

Christy-Lynn stared into her mug, thoughts clearly churning. "It's just money," she said at last. "Money I don't even want."

Wade looked at her hard, wondering if she'd thought about the long-term implications of what she was proposing. "Christy-Lynn, if you do this thing, if you set up this trust, you're tying yourself to that girl—to Stephen's daughter by another woman—for the next fifteen years. Are you really prepared to do that?"

Her chin came up sharply. "Don't you think I've asked myself that? The truth is I don't know. I just know I'm not prepared to stand by and do nothing."

"What did the attorney say when you told him what you wanted to do?"

"Exactly what you'd expect a lawyer to say. That I'm jumping the gun. That I'm letting my emotions get in the way. He thinks I should hire an investigator to check out Honey's family, to make sure I'm not being scammed."

Wade tugged thoughtfully at his lower lip. "It's not the worst idea I've ever heard. You're talking about a lot of money. It never hurts to be careful."

Christy-Lynn let out a sigh. "Exactly what am I supposed to inves-tigate? Rhetta Rawlings is an octogenarian who lives in a shack and chain-smokes generic cigarettes. What do you think she's going to do with the money? Buy a Cadillac? Put in a pool? So what if she does?"

"And the uncle?"

Christy-Lynn didn't bother to hide her disgust. "Reverend Rawlings is far too pious to dirty his hands with Stephen's money. He's more concerned with distancing himself from his sister's sins."

"Don't be so sure, Christy-Lynn. Money changes things. Especially people. Look, I'm not trying to tell you what to do. It's your decision. All I'm saying is don't rush into it while your emotions are still raw. Take some time and think it through before you pull the trigger."

Christy-Lynn nodded somberly. "That's why I asked you over tonight, to be my sounding board. But right now my head is starting to throb. Do you think we could talk about something else?"

"For instance?"

"I don't know. Your book. We've never really done that."

"What do you want to know?"

"I don't know. Anything. How long have you been working on it?"

"Twenty years, give or take."

Christy-Lynn's eyes went wide. "Twenty years?"

"Give or take. I started it back when I was in college and then—" He paused, clearing his throat roughly. "Let's just say I decided to go in another direction."

"Stephen said you got bored and switched to journalism."

Wade felt the familiar pulse begin to tick along his temple, the old anger flaring to life. "Did he?"

"That isn't what happened?"

"No."

"Then tell me what did."

"Let's just say I became . . . disillusioned."

She nodded, pausing to peer out at the steadily falling rain. "I hear that a lot from my writers, particularly after a fresh rejection lands in the in-box. You need thick skin, no doubt about that. But you're back at it now, and you seem pretty focused. What's it about?"

"Not sure really. Over the years, it's sort of gotten away from me. I was nineteen when I started the damn thing." He laughed, a harsh sound that sent Tolstoy scurrying. "I was a dreamer back then. I was going to write the great American novel."

"What happened?"

"That change of direction I mentioned." He drained his mug then dangled it between his knees. "Back in college, the words used to pour out, but journalism uses an entirely different set of writing muscles. I had no idea it would be so hard to find my fiction chops again."

"And have you?"

"Maybe. But they're still pretty flabby. Something's not working, and I can't get past it. I'm stuck."

"At the risk of sounding condescending, I'd be happy to take a look at it, maybe make a few suggestions. Sometimes fresh eyes are all you need. Though given our history, you might feel weird about it."

"I think we're past that, don't you? We've eaten each other's cooking, and I think your cat has a crush on me." He paused, grinning down at the floor where Tolstoy had reappeared and was now turning circles around his ankles. "We're practically family."

She smiled grimly as she collected their empty mugs and headed for the kitchen. "It's ironic, don't you think, that after all these years you'd be the one I'd end up dragging into this thing with Iris? I know you think I've lost my mind. Maybe I have. It certainly feels like I have."

"You haven't lost your mind," he assured her as he gathered the remaining utensils from the table and dropped them into the sink. "You're human. And much stronger than you think. Maybe the next time you feel like beating yourself up you should remember that. Now," he said, grabbing the dish towel, "whose turn is it to dry?"

Neither spoke as they worked, Christy-Lynn wielding the sponge, Wade the towel, and yet there was a strange comfort in the rhythm, a kind of domestic ballet he found pleasing, the accidental brush of hips, the touch of wet fingers. Not a sensual connection—not exactly—but intimate somehow. It was about a simple moment shared, the comfort of another person standing beside him. It made him realize just how isolated his life had become over the last year. Safe but empty. But wasn't that what he'd been looking for when he came running back to Sweetwater? Now, suddenly, he wasn't so sure.

When they finished, she walked him to the door and out onto the porch. The rain was coming down hard now, billowing in ragged sheets across the yard. The ride home was going to be tricky, but first he had to get himself off the porch, and suddenly his legs didn't want to move.

"So . . . thanks for dinner," he said awkwardly.

"Thanks for coming. And for listening."

"What are friends for?"

"Yeah, well." She was shifting from foot to foot, staring down at her bare toes. "I'm still pretty new at the friend thing."

He studied her a moment in the dim porch light, her face nearly lost in shadow. "I don't think I've ever heard anyone say that before—they're *new* at the friend thing."

"I guess it would sound funny to most people, but I learned to keep my distance at an early age. A survival mechanism, you might say. I'm working on it, though. Another thirty years and I should about have it mastered."

She smiled then, a genuine smile that chased the shadows from her face, and for an instant, he was reminded of the time he'd gone cliff diving in Mexico, the dizzy, breathtaking moment he'd kicked away from solid ground and fallen out into space—praying the whole way down.

"I'm willing to wait," he said quietly.

Her smile flickered and went out. "I'm not sure I'm worth the wait. In case you hadn't noticed, I'm a bit of a wreck right now. Lots of baggage."

He leaned in then, pressing a kiss to her forehead. "I'll risk it."

# THIRTY-FOUR

*Sweetwater, Virginia*
*July 4, 2017*

With the exception of Christmas, Independence Day was by far Sweetwater's favorite holiday, and this year, Christy-Lynn found herself smack-dab in the middle of the festivities. It was hard not to get caught up in the enthusiasm as she scanned the crowd gathered on the drilling green to witness the annual reading of the Declaration of Independence.

She was looking for Missy and the boys when she spotted Wade just a few yards away, his phone to his ear. He ended the call when he spotted her, smiling as he made his way over.

"Fancy meeting you here." He nodded toward her American flag tank top. "I see you dressed for the occasion."

"I did." She smiled as she surveyed the crowd. "It's nice, isn't it? Taking time to remember what it's all about, hearing the words read aloud. Even the kids seem to love it."

Wade nodded as he followed her gaze. "I'd forgotten how much this town loves the Fourth. My grandfather used to bring me when I was a kid. I'd pretend I was bored, too cool for parades, but I loved it. I think he knew. Not much got past the old man."

They were meandering toward the sidewalk now, flowing with the throng of families scouting shady spots to watch the parade. Christy-Lynn grinned as a pair of twins wearing matching yellow sunglasses scampered past. "Did you come from a big family?"

"Not big. One sister, but we were close. My father died when I was three. I don't really remember him. My mom still has pictures of him everywhere, so I have a memory of his face, or at least what feels like a memory."

"I'm sorry."

Wade shrugged. "You can't miss what you never had."

She shot him a quick glance. "You don't think so?"

Another shrug. "Maybe it's because I had my grandfather. He stepped in when my mother went back to work and sort of took me under his wing. What about you? What was your family like?"

"I didn't have a family," she said bluntly. "It was just my mother and me."

"Two people can't be a family?"

She could feel his eyes and knew he was waiting for an explanation. Instead, she pointed across the street where a vendor with a shiny metal cart was hawking frozen lemonade. "I'm hot. How about you?"

She didn't wait for an answer before dashing across the street, winding her way through the throng until she reached the cart. She ordered two and handed one to Wade. "Happy Fourth of July."

As if on cue, the Sweetwater High School marching band began moving down the center of Main Street, kicking off the parade with a warbling rendition of "The Stars and Stripes Forever."

Stephen had taken her to see the Macy's Thanksgiving Day Parade once, not long after they were married. She had been dazzled, overwhelmed by the seemingly endless sights and sounds. But now, as she watched Sweetwater's homegrown procession of toilet paper floats and sequined majorettes move past, she couldn't remember ever feeling such delight. In fact, she almost hated to see it end, cheering and clapping along with the rest of the crowd as the parade moved off down Main Street.

"That was so much fun!"

Wade took her empty cup, tossing it into a nearby trash can. "What are you doing later?"

Christy-Lynn shielded her eyes as she looked up at him. "I've been toying with starting a book club at the store. I was going to work on a flyer to help gauge interest. Why?"

"I've been thinking about your offer to look at my manuscript, and I think I'd like to take you up on it. You could come by a little later. It's my turn to cook."

The invitation took Christy-Lynn by surprise. When she made the offer to look at his manuscript, she hadn't really thought about what might happen if he accepted. Nor had she considered the possible fallout if the book turned out to be bad. She'd been coaching writers long enough to know that many who claimed to want the truth actually wanted anything but.

"In the interest of full disclosure, you should know I have a tendency to shoot from the hip," she warned. "Are you sure that's what you're looking for?"

"If I was looking for a pat on the back, I'd just send it to my mother. I need to know if I'm wasting my time. And I promise to let you off the hook if you decide it's just too terrible to read. At least you'll get a meal out of it."

"All right. I'll be there around six. That'll give me a few hours to work on the flyer. Should I bring anything?"

He grinned sheepishly as he stepped off the curb, preparing to cross the street. "An open mind."

~

Christy-Lynn was still feeling anxious as she pulled into Wade's driveway. Stephen had made no bones about the fact that Wade was talented—or had been back when they were in college. But that was twenty years ago. Wade himself had admitted struggling to get his chops back. The question was had he succeeded, and if not, did she want to be the one to tell him?

"Come on through. I'm out on the deck."

Wade's voice startled her, bleeding through the screen door before she could lift a hand to knock. She left her purse on the kitchen table and stepped out onto the deck where he was scrubbing a grill grate with a wire brush and a bucket of soapy water. He was barefoot, wearing a faded University of Virginia T-shirt and jeans that were drenched from the knees down.

"Excuse the mess. I thought I'd give the thing a good cleaning since I was having company."

"Can I help?"

"Not unless you want to ruin those white pants. You can go in and get us something to drink, though. I'll take a beer."

A few minutes later, she returned with a bottled water and the requested beer. Wade dropped the brush into the bucket and grabbed his beer with wet hands. "Listen, I started thinking about it on the way home, and I realized you were probably just being polite the other night. I don't want to be the writer who foists his work on everyone he meets, so if you want to back out, no worries."

"You aren't foisting anything on me. I volunteered."

"I saw your face this afternoon. You looked as if you'd just stepped into oncoming traffic."

"I think I was surprised that you actually want my feedback. Stephen stopped asking a long time ago."

"I would have thought it rather handy to have you around. A second set of eyes, someone to bounce ideas off."

Christy-Lynn looked up from peeling the soggy label from her water bottle. "Stephen never thought much of what I do—or the writers I do it for. As far as he was concerned, if you weren't with one of the Big Five, you should be doing something else. In his eyes, it wasn't real editing because my clients weren't real writers."

Wade took a pull from his beer then stood looking at her with something like bewilderment. "Can you help me with something? Because I've been wondering about it for the last four years. How did a jackass like Stephen ever manage to snare someone like you?"

The intensity in his tone surprised her, but not as much as the words themselves. "You've been wondering that for four years?"

"I guess it's more like five now, but yes. That night at the alumni dinner, when you got in my face, all I could think was *he doesn't deserve her.*"

Christy-Lynn felt her cheeks go pink but said nothing.

"Were you happy? Back then, I mean."

She thought about that a moment—and about her *need* to think about it. *Shouldn't the answer be obvious?* It wasn't, though. Like everything else in her life the truth lay half in shadow, perhaps because that was how she preferred it. Things tended to be less messy that way.

"I think I was numb," she said at last. "Not happy. Not unhappy. There were signs, I suppose, that it wasn't Shangri-la, but there wasn't any one thing. It was gradual, you know? Insidious. It wasn't until he was gone that I realized I'd been married to someone I barely knew. I was holding on so tightly I never realized how much we'd both changed. Still, it wasn't enough to leave. At least I didn't think it was."

Wade came to sit in the chair beside her, beer balanced on one knee. "Were you still in love with him? I asked once before, and you never did answer."

Christy-Lynn looked out over the lake, watching the light play over the mercury-smooth surface. "I'm not sure I *ever* was," she answered finally, realizing, perhaps for the first time, what she had never let herself see. "How's that for an admission?"

"Then why marry the guy?"

"I was in awe of him," she said with a shrug, not even sure *she* understood it. "And it's what respectable people do, isn't it? Grow up and get married? Respectability was important to me back then. Which is probably why I always gave up what I wanted—so I could be who and what *he* wanted. But after a while, the shine started to wear off. It was like going backstage after a play and seeing the star without his makeup."

"But you stayed."

Christy-Lynn looked at her hands, smoothing her nails one at a time. "It wasn't because of the money."

"I knew that," Wade said quietly.

"Or the status."

"I knew that too."

"I don't know. He was this larger than life guy, always so sure of himself. And back then, I wasn't sure of anything. It was . . . attractive. And it made him the perfect place to hide."

"From what?"

She met his gaze evenly. "Myself. And it worked. The day I became Stephen's wife I stopped being Christy-Lynn Parker. And for a while, I was okay with it. They say ignorance is bliss, and I guess it was, because I never bothered to ask myself who I'd be if I *wasn't* his wife."

"You said you gave up what you wanted. What did you want?"

They were silent for a moment, sipping in unison as they watched a pair of egrets lift away from the shore. "I used to think about writing sometimes," she said, finally breaking the quiet. "Not the great American novel, but something. I had a couple of ideas I pitched to Stephen, but he always squashed them. He said telling someone else what they're doing wrong isn't the same as being able to do it yourself."

Wade eyed her stonily. "So that's it? You just abandoned your dream because he said so? Stephen gets what he wants and to hell with your dreams?"

Christy-Lynn screwed the cap back on her water bottle and set it on the railing. It was true. Well, mostly true. She wasn't sure writing had ever been a lifelong dream, but it was something she had toyed with—and given up. On Stephen's say so. But at the moment, she was more intrigued by the anger she saw banked in Wade's eyes.

"What happened between you two?"

He shrugged, rolling his empty beer bottle back and forth between his palms. "It was years ago."

"Maybe, but it still bothers you. It's there every time you talk about him, the same tamped-down fury that's coming off you right now. So what was it?"

"We were friends. Or I thought we were. Stephen didn't have many friends back then. He had a tendency to suck up all the oxygen in the room. But there was another side of him, one he kept to himself until no one else was around, like when we'd come up here to study. He was different then, laid-back, maybe because there was no one around to impress. But then we'd get back to Charlottesville, and it was like he'd flip a switch. All of a sudden the big man on campus was back."

Christy-Lynn nodded. She knew exactly what he was talking about. "And what else?"

"He was lazy."

"That's it?" She wasn't sure what she'd been expecting, but criticizing Stephen's work ethic hadn't been on the list. "You think cranking out a book a year is lazy?"

"I meant his writing was lazy. He had talent but never bothered to hone it. He was happy just turning out stock stories that leaned on sex or violence to sell. There was never any emotion in his work, never any of himself. That's the hard part, spilling your guts out onto the page, tapping into the stuff that scares you, crushes you, breaks you wide-open. Stephen couldn't be bothered."

Christy-Lynn sat mulling his words, certain there was more to the long-standing rift than he was letting on, something more personal, more painful. "You're saying you've been angry for twenty years because Stephen didn't live up to his potential?"

"I was laying the groundwork," Wade replied tightly. "I'm not the only one who thought Stephen was lazy. Our professors saw it too. They started leaning on him, challenging him. It was getting harder and harder for him to slide. At the end of our sophomore year, we had a course project due, a short story that counted as a large part of our grade. Stephen knew what he was working on wasn't good. He asked me to help him fix it, so I gave him some ideas, all of which required pulling the story apart. Rather than doing the work, he went into my desk and found a piece I'd written the previous year. He retyped it minus my edit notes and handed it in as his own. He got an A and passed the class. Unfortunately, the professor passed it along to the editor of the *Meridian*, who ended up printing it. That's how I found out—when I saw my story in print with his name on it."

Christy-Lynn went still, numbed by the revelation. "He just . . . stole it?"

"*Borrowed* was the term he used. He said he just needed to pass the class, and it wasn't like I was ever going to do anything with the story, so what was the big deal?"

"I can't even—" She paused, dragging both hands through her hair. "What happened when you told the professor it was your story?"

"Nothing happened. I didn't tell him."

Christy-Lynn gaped at him. "I don't understand. He stole your story and got a publishing credit for it, and you just let him get away with it?"

"It would have been my word against his, and I knew better than to think he'd ever cop to plagiarism. The bastard couldn't even bring himself to apologize. Suffice it to say, we were through as friends. It wasn't just that he stole my work and passed it off as his. It was that he could screw over a friend when he knew damn well I was willing to help him."

"I'm so sorry, Wade."

"For what?"

"That night at the alumni dinner. I thought it was sour grapes, and all the time you were sitting on this."

"You called me bitter and jealous."

"I'm sorry."

Wade forced a smile. "Forget it. You didn't know. Besides, you were right. Or at least half-right. I was pretty bitter. But it's water under the bridge now."

Christy-Lynn pushed to her feet and crossed to the opposite side of the deck, more shaken than she wanted to admit. Who had she married? A man who kept a mistress, who fathered a child he barely saw and had neglected to provide for, who plagiarized a story written by his best friend. It was unfathomable. But really, it wasn't. And that made it worse somehow.

She didn't hear Wade leave his chair, but suddenly he was standing beside her, his fingers warm as he reached for her hand on the railing. "You okay?"

Christy-Lynn kept her eyes averted, watching the breeze push a series of ripples across the lake's silvered surface. "I honestly don't know. I keep learning things about a man I thought I knew, terrible things. It makes me wonder."

"Makes you wonder what?"

"How I could live with someone for so long and still not have a clue who he was."

# THIRTY-FIVE

Christy-Lynn had been only too happy to change the subject when Wade suggested they start dinner. He had grilled salmon steaks and skewers of fresh summer vegetables, which she'd helped him prepare. Now, as they sat on the deck, eating strawberry ice cream and watching the sun slip behind the trees, she felt herself finally starting to relax.

"Refill?" Wade asked, holding up his empty bowl.

"God, no. I'm stuffed. But I think I could sit here all night looking out over this lake. It's so peaceful, like a church without walls."

"My grandfather built this place with his own hands. He loved it up here."

Christy-Lynn closed her eyes and pulled in a lungful of air. "I can see why. It's the perfect place to forget all your cares."

"That's why I came."

Christy-Lynn opened her eyes. "Did it work?"

Wade shrugged. "Jury's still out. Oh, hey. I almost forgot why I lured you here in the first place. Be right back."

He appeared a short time later carrying a thick sheaf of papers. "It's not finished," he told her sheepishly. "I threw up my hands around page three-twenty, when I realized something wasn't working. I printed you off a hard copy, but I can send an electronic copy if you prefer. I plan to pay you, by the way. I'm not asking for a freebie."

Christy-Lynn eyed the stack of pages in his hand with something like dread. She was half hoping he'd forget. "I prefer paper for my first pass. And don't be silly. I'm not taking your money. What's the title?"

"*The End of Known Things.*"

She let the words roll around in her head, dark but intriguing. Perhaps a bit dystopian, but that wasn't necessarily a bad thing. "And your premise?"

Wade dropped back into his chair, the pages in his lap, and propped his feet up on the railing. "The main character is Robert Vance, a big-shot business type who thinks he's got it all figured out. He's had a plan since he was fourteen, and nothing's getting in his way. Until something does, and his life is completely turned inside out. He realizes the only way he's ever going to be happy is to lay himself open. I just can't seem to get him there. And before you ask, no, it isn't autobiographical."

Christy-Lynn smiled. "Not even a little?"

"I was nineteen when I started it. I thought I knew everything."

"And now?"

"Now?" He looked away, his gaze lost on the horizon. "Now, I'm not sure I know anything at all. Why things turn out the way they do. How the world works." He shrugged then turned to face her with a thin smile. "A classic case of the nice guy finishing last, I suppose."

Christy-Lynn could see that she'd stumbled onto a sore subject. Hoping to steer the conversation to safer waters, she held out a hand. "Give me the pages. I'll dig in, make some notes, and then we can talk."

Wade was about to pass her the pages when he paused, frowning. "What's this?" He had captured her upturned wrist and was pointing to the small cluster of half-moons. "They look like scars."

Christy-Lynn jerked her hand away, tucking it between her knees. "They are."

"I've never noticed them before. How'd you get them?"

She shrugged. "I don't remember. It was a long time ago."

When Wade's gaze lingered, she pushed up out of her chair. She needed to put some distance between herself and those shrewd journalistic eyes. But Wade was soon beside her at the rail, his silhouette outlined in the thin twilight.

"Everything all right? You seem jumpy all of a sudden, like I made you uncomfortable. I meant what I said before, Christy-Lynn. If you feel weird about the manuscript, I understand."

"It's fine. I'm fine." But she couldn't meet his eyes as she said it. "And I don't feel weird. It's just . . . my head's so full right now."

"You've decided, haven't you? To go through with the trust?"

"Yes." She'd been wondering when he'd get around to asking. "I know you think it's a bad idea. But it feels right."

"So things are moving along?"

"I've asked the attorney to draw up the paperwork. When it's ready, I'll set up some time to talk through it all with Rhetta."

Wade had his enigmatic face on again, but she could see the wheels turning behind those amber eyes, assessing risks, weighing the what-ifs. "Are you sure she's going to be able to handle that kind of money?"

"She won't *be* handling it. At least not all at one time. Peter's setting it up with me as trustee, which means the principal remains under my control with a kind of monthly allowance being paid to Rhetta."

"You're sure about this?"

"No. But I'm doing it anyway. I have to."

He nodded. "I know."

Except he'd said it in a way that made Christy-Lynn wonder if he really did. He told her once that he believed in clean breaks—in walking away and burning your bridges. And she had for the most part. She'd left Clear Harbor, sold the house, opened the store, and put down roots in Sweetwater. But this was different. How did you burn a bridge when there was a child standing on it?

She was still trying to come up with a response when Wade surprised her by changing the subject. "Are you up for fireworks? If we hurry, we can get out there in time."

Christy-Lynn checked her watch, but it was already too dark to read the time. "I thought they started at nine. It'll take at least twenty minutes to get downtown and find a place to park."

"Who said anything about downtown?"

"Seriously?" Christy-Lynn tipped back her head. "You can actually see them from here?"

Wade surprised her again by taking her hand and leading her down the deck stairs. "Come with me."

"Where are we going?"

"Out there," he said, pointing toward the lake.

"In the dark?"

Wade stepped into the canoe and held out a hand. "It's the best way to see them. Come on. You'll be fine."

Christy-Lynn smothered a sigh. He was already seated, the paddle resting across his thighs. "All right, but if I end up in the drink, the markup on that manuscript of yours isn't going to be pretty."

He chuckled warmly in the dark. "I'll take my chances. Just stay low like I showed you and hold on to both sides."

Breath held, she stepped over the side and into the canoe. Climbing into a boat was tricky enough for a novice, but doing it in the dark was downright scary. Finally, she eased down onto the empty seat and was able to breathe again.

"This better be good."

"Would I lie?"

Christy-Lynn considered the question, knowing full well it had been rhetorical. And yet somehow she knew the answer. "No," she said quietly, wishing she could make out his face in the dark. "I don't think you would."

Wade said nothing as he pushed off and began to paddle, smooth, easy strokes that barely made a sound against the quiet. Eventually

Christy-Lynn felt herself relax. She let go of the sides, gazing up into the indigo sky as they glided soundlessly over the water.

"Okay," she said grudgingly. "This is nice."

"My grandfather and I used to come out here every year for the fireworks and for the Perseid meteor shower. There's less ambient light so everything looks brighter."

"Sounds like you and your grandfather made a lot of great memories."

Wade stopped paddling, letting the canoe drift. "We did. In fact, we built this canoe together. Took us three summers. The old man was a stickler for detail, a real perfectionist. But thirty years later, here we are, out on the lake watching another set of fireworks."

As if on cue, the first plumes of color erupted overhead, illuminating the night sky with a burst of red-and-white fire. Seconds later, a boom punctured the quiet, the percussion palpable in the heavy night air. Christy-Lynn's breath caught, then caught again as a single missile arced into the darkness, followed by a profusion of pink, white, and gold that echoed like diamonds in the lake's mirrorlike skin.

She wanted to tell him he was right, that she'd never seen anything so wonderful, but there wasn't time. One after another the volleys continued, each explosion bigger and brighter than the last. She barely noticed when Wade's hand closed over hers, her eyes locked on the sky, reveling in the hypnotic pulses of color and sound, flecks of gold and silver tumbling down around them like falling stars.

Finally, she snuck a glance at Wade, surprised to find his attention on her rather than the sky. "You're not watching the fireworks."

"It's okay. I can see them in your eyes."

The words threw her off balance, smoky and warm, the way she imagined a shot of whiskey might feel as it snaked its way into the bloodstream. Her pulse ticked up as his fingers twined with hers and the sky continued to explode overhead. And then he was pulling her toward him. Something fluttered in her belly, like a pair of soft wings lifting off. He was going to kiss her, and she was going to let him. Because suddenly she wanted him to very badly.

His mouth opened against hers with maddening slowness, a velvety assault on her long-starved senses. She stiffened briefly as his arms came around her, startled by her body's sharp and visceral response. She had nearly forgotten this part—the urgent mingling of breaths, the blending of bodies, the languid, bone-deep sense of surrender. How easy it would be to let this—whatever this was—happen, to sweep caution aside and yield to this startling new ache. It was a heady thought. And a dangerous one.

She pulled back abruptly, causing the canoe to skitter. "We can't," she blurted. "I can't."

"I thought—"

Christy-Lynn's fingers felt bloodless as she gripped the sides of the canoe, thankful for the darkness. "I know what you thought. I must have thought it too. But I'm not . . . I can't."

"Did I read it wrong?"

"No. I did."

"You felt it too, then?"

Yes, she'd felt it. And for a moment, she'd nearly let it consume her. She glanced at the sky, empty now but for a scatter of stars. The fireworks had ended, and the quiet felt unsettling, as if all of a sudden there was nowhere to hide. "I'm sorry. I wasn't . . . thinking."

"Apparently, neither was I. I don't want to be the guy who makes a move on a friend when she's vulnerable."

His words brought her up short. "You think I'm vulnerable?"

Even in the dark, she could sense his astonishment. "You don't?"

*Vulnerable.* It wasn't a word she liked the sound of. It was a weak word. A needy word. And she didn't want to need anyone. But now there was Wade. Strong, kind, and more than willing to be a shoulder in her time of need. How had she not seen it coming? She had gotten caught up in the moment, foolishly opening a door she wasn't remotely ready to walk through. And had nearly ruined a friendship in the bargain.

"I honestly don't know what I am," she answered finally. "A mess, I suspect. But you're not that guy, Wade. This was my fault. You've been a friend. A good friend, and that's where we need to leave it."

He said nothing as he reached for the paddle and turned them about. Christy-Lynn was quiet too, studying the angular set of his shoulders as he maneuvered the canoe back toward shore. She had hurt him. Or at the very least confused him. She should have been more careful—for both their sakes. Instead, she had chosen to ignore the danger signs that had apparently been smoldering for some time. It was Wade she had turned to for help, after all, Wade she'd wept her heart out to when she learned about Iris, Wade she felt drawn to whenever she found herself needing a shoulder. But that had to do with his connection to Stephen—didn't it?

Wade wasted no time climbing out of the canoe when they reached shore, offering a brief hand as she followed clumsily. He took the deck steps two at a time, not bothering to look back as he disappeared through the open sliding glass doors. Christy-Lynn was happy to lag behind, relieved to have time to rein in her emotions.

The kitchen was empty when she finally stepped back into the cabin. Wade's manuscript was lying on the counter beside their empty ice-cream bowls. She picked it up along with her purse, wishing she knew what else to say.

She found Wade in the living room, busily reshelving a stack of CDs. He looked up when she entered the room, his expression dark but unreadable. "Why?"

She stared at him, baffled. "Why what?"

"Why do we have to leave it there?"

She sighed, wishing she could make him understand. "Because we do. Because *I* do. I'm just getting my feet back under me, Wade. I'm not ready for complications. And that's what you'd be. I know that sounds harsh, but I've basically had one adult relationship in my life, and it didn't end well. I don't need another failure on my record."

He stood with his legs braced wide apart, his arms stiff at his sides. "My feet aren't exactly firmly planted either, Christy-Lynn, but there's something here, something we both felt tonight. Maybe it's just physical—and maybe it isn't—but our paths keep crossing. Maybe that means something."

Christy-Lynn clutched the manuscript to her chest, as if to shield herself from the pull of his words. "You're right. There is a connection. It's there, and it's real—but it's Stephen. It's all the damage he's done, all the ways he cheated and lied and screwed us both over. That's what we have in common. My dead husband. But that's a therapy session not a romance. I can't afford to get the two confused."

Wade folded his arms, his face suddenly closed. "So where does that leave us?"

She would have touched him then, if she thought she could trust herself. Instead, she reached for a smile or what she hoped passed for one. "Where we've always been, I hope—friends."

"Does that ever work? Going back to being friends?"

"It was a kiss, Wade. We don't have to let it get weird."

"Right," he said, though his nod was less than convincing. "No weirdness."

"Exactly. Look, I'm going to go." She held up the manuscript. "I've got reading to do."

He followed her to the door, hands shoved awkwardly in his pockets. "For the record, when I asked you over tonight, I wasn't planning some big seduction scene."

"I know you weren't. And it might be better if we just pretend the whole thing never happened."

Wade held her gaze as he pulled back the door. "I'm not sure that's going to be possible for me."

Christy-Lynn said nothing as she stepped onto the porch, the memory of Wade's lips on hers still much too fresh. She wasn't sure it was going to be possible for her either.

# THIRTY-SIX

*Sweetwater, Virginia*
*July 12, 2017*

Christy-Lynn flipped her pillow over, giving it another sharp punch. She'd been lying awake for nearly an hour, though this time her insomnia had nothing to do with bad dreams. Her thoughts kept returning to her upcoming trip to Riddlesville, rehearsing ways to convince Rhetta to accept her help. If a check for $10,000 had spooked her, she was really going to slam on the brakes when she found out what kind of money they were talking about now.

Resigned, she sat up and clicked on the bedside lamp. If she wasn't going to sleep, she might as well work. She still hadn't finished the book club flyer for the store, and her in-box was out of control.

She was reaching for her laptop when she spotted the stack of pages Wade had given her more than a week ago. She had yet to touch them. Not because she'd been too busy, but because they were an awkward reminder of their impromptu kiss. Yes, she was the one who said it didn't have to get weird, and she meant it, but for a while at least, it seemed wise to keep her distance. And that included his manuscript.

Not that he'd been around much since that night. In fact, he seemed to be keeping enough distance for the both of them. But maybe that was for the best. Maybe he was right. Maybe going back to being friends really didn't work. Maybe once you crossed that line you were either all in or all out. And if that was the case, she had no choice but to opt for all out.

She couldn't deny that the temptation was there but so was the potential for disaster. Like a parched forest and a stray bolt of lightning, the chance of conflagration was all too real. And if marriage to Stephen had taught her anything, it was that she wasn't cut out for the love-and-marriage paradigm. Yes, she had belonged to Stephen, legally and perhaps even emotionally for a time. But belonging to someone and giving yourself to them were two very different things. One formed out of need, a tidy arrangement mutually beneficial to both parties, while the other involved laying yourself bare—something she'd never been very good at.

She eyed the manuscript again with a lingering pang of guilt, then grabbed her laptop. She'd get around to it—eventually. But for now she was playing it safe. She went to her in-box first, pleasantly surprised to find a request from Kimberly Ward, a women's fiction author, inquiring about a possible signing for her debut novel. She had included several links, one of which took her to the author's website.

A pretty redhead smiled back at her from the landing page, a thirtysomething with long copper hair and a dusting of freckles across the bridge of her nose. Her bio was brief but friendly—a mother of two boys and two tricolor shelties; a lifelong native of Beaufort, South Carolina; a southern lit junkie who'd cut her teeth on *The Prince of Tides* and *To Kill a Mockingbird*.

Christy-Lynn liked her already. But it was the montage of photos on the About Me page that intrigued her most: ancient oaks dripping with silver-blue moss, historic downtown streets lined with palmettos, a sliver of sun sinking into gilded water. It was all so lovely, so charmingly old South. And yet it was nothing like the South Carolina she'd grown up in.

Without warning, Charlene Parker's face drifted into her head. Not the stitched-up ruin she had glimpsed that last night at the hospital, but the face of the woman she'd been before the drugs and booze had taken hold. She'd heard from her only once in twenty years, a phone call out of the blue six or seven years back, and then nothing. Whether she was still alive was anyone's guess. Women like Charlene Parker, who engaged in what psychologists referred to as high-risk behaviors, had a habit of dying young.

On impulse, Christy-Lynn opened a new window and typed the words *people finder* into the search bar. When a list of sites popped up, she clicked the first one and typed in her mother's name, birth date, and last known city and state. The screen blinked then popped up with a list of names and addresses. And there she was, third down on the list: Charlene Kendra Parker, 1710 Proctor Avenue, Apartment 13, Walterboro, South Carolina. Last reported at the given address seven months ago.

Alive then, after all these years.

There was no phone number listed, but that was hardly a surprise. When times got tough—which they always did—the phone had always been the first thing to go. Not that Christy-Lynn would have used a number if there had been one. After so many years, so much anger and resentment, what was there to say? But the answer came back almost before the question had formed. There was plenty to say. Plenty of blame to lay. Plenty of fingers to point. And maybe some of those fingers would be pointed back at her. For the kind of daughter she'd been. The kind who left a mother in trouble and never looked back.

Five hours. Six at most. She could make the trip in a day. But why? There was no way of knowing if she was even still there. And what if she was? There was no way to patch it up now, no way to fill the empty places Charlene Parker's brand of motherhood had carved out in her.

And yet she found herself opening the drawer of the nightstand, reaching for the familiar dog-eared envelope.

Dar's words rose like a specter. *Let the memories catch up to you.* Except she didn't want to let them catch up. Not tonight. Maybe not ever. Instead of opening the envelope, she dropped it back into the drawer. She'd been doing just fine keeping her past under lock and key. Okay, maybe not fine, but she was managing. She saw no need to relive it all again. Once had been quite enough.

# THIRTY-SEVEN

*Clear Harbor, Maine*
*March 12, 2011*

*Christy-Lynn is walking through the door with an armload of groceries when she hears the phone ringing. After dumping the bags on the counter, she reaches for the phone. The caller ID displays an 843 area code—South Carolina. Her stomach clenches.*

*"Hello?"*

*There's a brief silence and then, "Sorry, wrong number."*

*The voice is familiar, unnerving after more than ten years—the voice of a ghost. "Mama?"*

*She can hear breathing over the line and in the background what sounds like* The Price Is Right. *Her mother had always loved* The Price Is Right.

*"Mama—is that you?"*

*There's the sound of a lighter flicking, the pull of breath, the release of smoke. "You sound different," Charlene Parker says finally. "All Yankee-fied."*

*Christy-Lynn's legs feel bloodless as she sags against the chilly granite countertop. "How did you get this number?"*

*Charlene ignores the question. "I was glad to hear about your marriage and to a real up-and-comer too. Looks like my baby girl's landed herself in high cotton. But then I always knew you would. You were always so smart, so . . . good."*

*Christy-Lynn doesn't ask how she knows about Stephen. The publicity photos had made the usual rounds. She remains quiet for a time, letting her mother's words hang between them on the line. Was it sadness she heard? Bitterness? Accusation?*

*"The number, Mama. How did you get it?"*

*"Some woman named Sandra at your old job. I told her there was a family emergency, and I needed to get in touch with you as soon as possible."*

*Christy-Lynn smothers a groan. "Why did you need to get in touch with me?"*

*"Oh, a bit of trouble. You know . . ."*

*Yes. She knew. "What kind of trouble?"*

*"I'm a little bit short, sweetie. I still owe last month's rent, Dave says the car needs some kind of pump, and I . . . I lost my job at the Quick Stop."*

*Christy-Lynn is about to ask who Dave is and why she lost her job, but decides she doesn't want to know. "How short?"*

*"They're saying four hundred for the pump thingy, but there's the rent too." There's a pause, the rasp of smoke being exhaled. "I know it's a lot, sweetie, but a grand would really get me back on my feet. And then I promise, I won't bother you again."*

*A thousand dollars.*

*Christy-Lynn closes her eyes, forcing herself to take slow, even breaths. It's a small price to get her off the phone—and back out of her life. "Where should I send it?"*

*Charlene rattles off an address somewhere in Walterboro. Christy-Lynn jots it down on the notepad she keeps on the fridge.*

*"Thank you." Her voice seems to wobble, and there's a long pause. "Are you . . . are you happy, baby girl?"*

"Yes," Christy-Lynn tells her. Her voice is clipped, almost defiant. "Yes, I am."

It occurs to her as she doodles a sad face on the notepad that she should ask her mother the same. But the truth is she isn't sure she can bear the details.

"I'll mail the check today," she says instead. "It should be there in a few days."

"Thank you, baby." It's little more than a whisper, thready and desperate. "Thank you so much." And then, abruptly, the line is dead.

Christy-Lynn stares at the phone, and for a moment, the old guilt rears its head. Would things have gone differently for Charlene Parker if her daughter hadn't deserted her? It's hard to imagine. If those terrible years had taught her anything, it was that time didn't change women like her mother. It merely hastened their decline. Still, the question lingered. Could she have made a difference?

She drops the phone into its cradle and goes to her purse to find her checkbook. Her hand shakes as she makes it out—$3,000. It's more than her mother asked for, but guilt has a way of making people generous.

She drops the checkbook back in her purse. It's her personal checkbook, of course. There's no reason for Stephen to know about the call. As far as he knows, her mother is dead—and until a few moments ago she had assumed the same.

# THIRTY-EIGHT

*Sweetwater, Virginia*
*July 19, 2017*

Christy-Lynn propped her feet up on an unopened carton of books, eyeing the stack of papers awaiting her attention. There were invoices to pay, next week's schedule to finish, and the back-to-school sale to plan, but at the moment, she was too distracted to tackle any of it.

She had green-lighted the trust paperwork with Peter Hagan six days ago. At the time, he had promised they would be ready in a week, two at the most. Now he was saying it was looking more like three—something about needing more time to make sure the necessary safeguards against abuse were in place. She appreciated his diligence on her behalf, but in the meantime, her life seemed to have slipped into a kind of limbo, her thoughts consumed with the logistics of the thing. She never imagined giving money *away* could be so complicated.

And there was still Rhetta to convince. Despite their complicated and inexplicable ties, they were little more than strangers. And here she was, the well-heeled widow preparing to swoop in like some kind of lady bountiful. Would Rhetta think the offer presumptuous? See it as meddling in something that was none of her business? Both were not only possible but likely.

She had planned to broach the subject with the paperwork in front of her, hoping that laying it all out in black and white would help put Rhetta at ease. But she wasn't sure she wanted to wait three weeks. She'd seen firsthand how stubborn the woman could be when it came to accepting help. Perhaps it would be wise to reach out now and get her used to the idea.

Christy-Lynn reached for her cell, pulled up Rhetta's new number, and hit "Send." Rhetta's voice came wheezing over the line after three rings.

"Hello?"

She sounded tired and almost startled, as if she was surprised the phone had rung at all, which Christy-Lynn guessed it rarely did. "Rhetta, it's Christy-Lynn. Are you all right? You don't sound well."

"Just . . . winded is all. Is anything wrong?"

"No. Nothing's wrong. I was just wondering if you were going to be home this weekend. There's something I'd like to discuss with you."

The television was on in the background, a talk show with lots of hooting and applause. Rhetta raised her voice over the din. "Are you sure there's nothing wrong?"

"Yes, I'm sure. I just have something . . . I have an idea I'd like to talk to you about, a way I think we can both help Iris, but I'd like to do it in person if possible. I could come on Saturday."

"Well, I've got nowhere to go, so that would be fine, but I hate for you to drive all that way."

"I don't mind really. It's a little complicated, and I think it would be better if we talked about it face-to-face. Would that be all right?"

"Well, yes. I guess so." She sounded confused, perhaps even leery.

"It's a good thing, Rhetta. I promise. I'll see you on Saturday."

Christy-Lynn was tossing her phone back into her purse, pleased to have at least gotten the ball rolling, when she realized she had made plans to go out of town without a thought to store coverage. She was going to have to ask Tamara for a favor.

Tamara was behind the café counter brewing an espresso when Christy-Lynn stepped out of the back room. She looked up, smiling sunnily across the pickup counter. "What's up, boss?"

"I need a favor."

"One of my spectacular triple shot lattes?"

"No. I don't need coffee. I'm in a jam. I have to go out of town Saturday, and I was hoping you could close with Aileen. I hate to spring it on you last minute, but it's important."

Tamara disappeared briefly to deliver her espresso then quickly reappeared. "No worries. Do what you have to do. Wait. Don't go. You skipped lunch. At least let me make you a latte."

"Thank you. You're a lifesaver. But only a single shot in the latte."

She was tidying napkin stacks and coffee stirrers, waiting for Tamara to finish brewing her latte, when she spotted Wade standing in the order line. It was the first time she'd seen him since the fireworks in the boat. God, that sounded bad. Maybe she'd just wait in the back room.

"Christy-Lynn."

*Too late.*

"Oh, hey!" Christy-Lynn pasted on a smile, scrambling for something to say. "I didn't see you there. Sorry. It's been a crazy day—well, a crazy couple of weeks actually." She paused to throw in a laugh. It came out sounding forced and slightly deranged. "I'm still trying to get the book club organized and line up events for the fall. I feel like all I do is work. It's crazy, crazy."

Wade nodded knowingly. "I know what you mean. I've been crazy busy myself. I just popped in to grab coffee, and then I'm on my way to Harmon's for some two-by-fours. I've been working on the deck, replacing some rotted wood. Then I'll have to restain it all. Hopefully the weather holds."

Christy-Lynn was still nodding when Wade's words ran out. There was a gaping moment of quiet, the awkward abyss that descends when two people run out of small talk. So much for it not getting weird.

"Here ya go, boss," Tamara said mischievously as she pushed an oversize mug across the counter. "Steamy and hot . . . just the way you like it."

Christy-Lynn shot Tamara her best scary boss face, but Tamara wasn't finished making mischief. Smiling sweetly, she set a mug of freshly brewed Sumatra on the counter.

"And here's your coffee, Wade. One sugar already in."

"I believe Wade wanted his coffee to go, Tamara," Christy-Lynn pointed out tightly, though she was sure Tamara already knew this.

Wade stepped in, grabbing the mug before Tamara could retrieve it. "No, it's okay. I can hang out a minute if you're going to sit."

Christy-Lynn had no choice but to follow Wade to his usual table. To make an excuse and slink away wouldn't just be rude; it would be glaringly transparent. She just hoped he didn't ask about the manuscript. She didn't want to tell him she hadn't even picked it up—or to lie about why.

"So . . . you're going out of town," he said as soon as they were seated. "I couldn't help overhearing you talking to Tamara. Anywhere fun?"

Christy-Lynn narrowed her gaze at him, certain he knew exactly where she was going and why. "I have an appointment to see Rhetta. The paperwork isn't finalized yet, but I thought I'd drive over on Saturday and see what she thinks."

Wade lowered his mug, brows raised. "Sounds like you're pretty optimistic if the lawyer's already drawing up the papers. Have you considered that there could be some pushback from the family?"

"It's Rhetta I'm worried about convincing, not the family. And why should they push back? I'm giving money away, not asking for it."

"People are funny when it comes to money. Not everyone's keen on taking a handout."

"Except that's not what this is. The money already belongs to Iris. I'm just making it legal."

"You don't have to convince me. I'm just asking the question. I'm curious about where the grandson will stand on all this."

At the mention of Ray Rawlings, Christy-Lynn felt her face go hot. "I don't care where he stands. Iris is the one I care about—and Rhetta. As soon as the documents are drawn up, the lawyer will send her a copy to look over. When I'm sure she understands everything, we'll sign the papers. After that, the funds will be released. I know she hasn't said yes yet, but she will. I'm determined to make her see that this is the best thing for everyone."

"Does that include you?"

The question seemed to come out of left field. Not just the words, but the way he'd said them, as if he knew something she didn't. "I don't really have anything to do with it."

"I think we both know that's not true. From the moment you laid eyes on that girl, you've been consumed. It's like you think by fixing this you can fix all the other stuff."

Christy-Lynn felt her hackles rise. "What other stuff?"

"Stephen cheating on you. Stephen lying to you. This crazy idea that it's all your fault. Or maybe it's something else. I just know this isn't some casual cause for you. Something's going on, and I'm not even sure *you* know what it is."

She was silent a moment, sipping her latte. Of course something was going on. Every time she looked at Iris, she saw herself, the child she'd been trying to outrun for years, reflected back in sharp, heartrending fragments. A selfish, emotionally absent mother, the grim sense of uncertainty, a childhood on the brink of collapse.

"Can't it just be about doing the right thing?" she asked finally. "About helping because I can?"

"Yes, it can be. But I don't think it is. And I don't think you do either. I'm not saying don't do it. I'm just saying don't pretend it's not a big deal when it obviously is. You're probably the kindest, most generous person I've ever met, but this isn't just kindness."

"What is it then?"

"I don't know." His voice was gentle, thoughtful. "Something else. Penance maybe. Or atonement."

"Atonement?"

He let out a sigh. "Okay, maybe that's not the right word either, but I see you shutting down, keeping everything and everyone at arm's length. Except this little girl."

Christy-Lynn peered over one shoulder, making sure Tamara was out of earshot. "So this is about the other night? About what happened in the boat?"

"No," he countered defensively. "Okay, maybe, but not the way you think. I know what it looks like when someone's pushing the whole world away and how much you can lose while you're doing it. And yes, I know I sound preachy right now, but this isn't about me and what I want. It's about you. Do you even know what you want?"

The question made Christy-Lynn squirm. Yes, she knew what she wanted. She wanted to go back, to clean it all up, to rewrite her story without all the dark parts, to unknow the things she knew, to unsee the things she'd seen, to live without her memories, her shame, her regret. And maybe that *was* a kind of atonement, after all. But none of those things were possible.

"Christy-Lynn?"

Her head came up sharply. Wade was still staring, still waiting. "Hmmm?"

"I asked if you knew what you wanted."

Christy-Lynn reached for her latte, sipping slowly as she fumbled for an answer. In the end, she decided the best she could hope for was a change of subject. "Well, I could use someone to cat sit while I'm out of town. Interested?"

Wade's brows shot up. "Did you say 'cat sit'?"

"It's only two days, but I've never left him alone before. I don't want him to feel abandoned. And the two of you did seem to hit it off."

Wade seemed to be holding his breath, as if searching for a way to steer the conversation back to more serious matters. Finally, he let out a resigned sigh. "Sure. I'll be your cat sitter."

His response caught her off guard. "Seriously?"

"Why not? No diapers. No cooking. How hard can it be?"

"It's just Saturday and Sunday, and I'll leave food down and everything. All he'll need is someone to check his food and give him a little pet for reassurance."

Wade emptied his mug and set it down with a grin. "I told you, animals have a thing for me. It's the grown-ups I can't seem to win over."

Something caught in her throat, a protest or an admission. She wasn't sure which. "Wade—"

"Go to West Virginia," he said softly, cutting her off.

"Thank you. I'll leave a spare key with Tamara."

"Do me a favor?"

She smiled, feeling shy suddenly. Was he flirting? Was she? "Well, you're watching my cat, so I guess I owe you one." God, she *was* flirting.

"Come back safe?"

And now he was flirting back, all scruffy smile and brooding charm, like one of those guys on the Hallmark Channel. This had to stop. This had to stop right now. And yet she was still smiling as she pushed back from the table and stood.

"All right. I can do that."

# THIRTY-NINE

*Riddlesville, West Virginia*
*July 23, 2017*

Rhetta pressed a hand to her lips, papery lids clenched tight. Across the kitchen table, Christy-Lynn waited for the moment to pass, pretending not to notice Iris standing in the doorway clutching her tattered teddy bear for dear life.

Several moments passed before Rhetta managed to find her composure. "I don't know what to say. Are you sure about this? It's . . . so much."

Christy-Lynn smiled. It had taken more than two hours to explain the ins and outs of what she was proposing, but Rhetta finally seemed to be warming to the idea. "Yes, I'm sure. Stephen should have taken care of this when Iris was born, but he didn't, so I'm doing it for him."

"But it's your money now. Legally it belongs to you."

"Look at me, Rhetta." Christy-Lynn waited until Rhetta's hazy blue eyes lifted to hers. "I want to do it. In fact, I need to."

"Why?"

Christy-Lynn thought back to her conversation with Wade, to his theories about penance and atonement—about her trying to fix the past. But whose past? Hers? Stephen's? Or was this about Charlene Parker, who, like Honey, had turned her back on her daughter? Perhaps Wade had been closer to the mark than she wanted to admit.

"My reasons aren't important, Rhetta. But Iris is. We agree on that, don't we?"

Rhetta nodded mutely.

"Then you're saying yes? You'll let me do this for you?"

Rhetta nodded again, with a little gulp, then buried her face in her hands.

Iris was instantly at her side, a tiny arm wound about Rhetta's neck. "Nonny, don't cry."

Rhetta sniffed loudly and managed a smile. "Nonny's fine, baby. Sometimes grown-ups cry when they're happy. That's what I'm doing. I'm crying because I'm happy."

Iris shifted her gaze to Christy-Lynn and then back again, clearly perplexed. Rhetta took hold of her shoulders, turning her to face Christy-Lynn squarely. "You remember Miss Christy-Lynn, don't you? You liked her so much you gave her a fish, and she put it on her icebox."

Iris nodded almost dreamily.

"And now she's come back to do something nice for you, like an angel sent from heaven. Can you tell her thank you?"

Christy-Lynn dropped her eyes uncomfortably. She wasn't an angel; she was merely trying to right a wrong. But Iris had clearly taken her great-grandmother's words to heart. Hesitant at first, she broke from Rhetta's side, eyes lowered as she approached. And then, with a shy smile, she laid her teddy bear in Christy-Lynn's lap.

She was gone in an instant, scurrying from the kitchen in her stockinged feet. Christy-Lynn met Rhetta's eyes. They were moist again.

"She likes you," Rhetta said softly, her voice full of emotion.

Christy-Lynn dipped her head. "I like her too. And she deserves a good life. Hopefully this trust will help give her one."

Rhetta shook her head, dashing away a tear with the back of her hand. "I don't know how to thank you for your generosity. After what Honey did, I can't imagine what would make you want to help her little girl, but I can't find it in my heart to say no. Things have been so hard, and now . . ."

"Now they'll be better."

Rhetta looked down at her hands, studying nicotine-stained nails. "Yes," she said, as if trying to convince herself. "They'll be better."

"You'll be able to afford a new house. One with lots more room and a yard for Iris to play in. It would be nice to be closer to town, don't you think, and not be so far away from everything? And I can help you look for a good school when it's time."

"School," Rhetta said, as if rolling the idea around in her head for the first time. "I'd like her to go to a good school, to make something of herself someday."

Christy-Lynn was hesitant to bring up another matter, but at some point, Rhetta's health—or lack of it—was going to become a factor. "I'd like to help in other ways too, if you'll let me. I'd like to try to find you a new doctor, a pulmonary specialist who might be able to help you breathe better and feel better."

Rhetta abandoned the study of her hands, meeting Christy-Lynn's gaze head-on. "No need for all that. My doctor's no specialist, but he knows what's what. Can't erase fifty years of cigarettes, any more than you can erase any of my other mistakes. But there is something else you could do for me. For us."

"What's that?"

"Take us to the cemetery."

Christy-Lynn blinked at her uneasily. "The cemetery?"

"Iris didn't go when her mama was buried. No one did but me. Ray didn't want his sister buried at his church. He paid to have her shipped home, and for the box and marker, but there wasn't a funeral. I just buried her at the cemetery on the edge of town like he told me to. Hardly anyone goes there anymore."

"And you want me to take you there now—with Iris?"

"It's the dreams," Rhetta said with a hitch in her voice. "They're so hard on her. Started right after the accident—Honey calling her name."

A cold prickle traced its way down Christy-Lynn's spine. "She can . . . hear her?"

Rhetta nodded ruefully. "Claims to. Poor thing wakes up in a panic, and then she's looking all over the house, trying to find her mama. I've tried explaining that she's with the angels, but she doesn't understand that—or that Honey's never coming back. I thought if she saw the grave . . ."

Christy-Lynn's loathing for Ray Rawlings ticked up a notch when she pulled through the sagging chain link gates and saw the sign for Green Meadows. It was a stunning misrepresentation of what lay before them. Perhaps there had been grass once, to make it green and meadowlike, but at the moment, it was nothing but a treeless patch of dun-colored ground studded with listing headstones and an assortment of dead leaves and blown trash. What kind of man would bury a dog in such a place, let alone a sister?

Rhetta pointed to the northeast corner of the cemetery. "She's at the back, out of the way."

Christy-Lynn followed the pocked ribbon of pavement until it ran out, then parked the Rover and went around to help Rhetta unfasten her seat belt and climb down. By the time her feet touched the ground she was wheezing openly, her lips faintly blue.

"Maybe this isn't such a good idea," Christy-Lynn said, eyeing her dubiously.

"Maybe not, but it needs doing."

In the back seat, Iris sat clutching her teddy, her tiny brow knitted in confusion. Rhetta pulled open the door and held out a hand. "Come on, baby girl. There's something Nonny needs to show you."

Iris scrambled from her car seat and took Rhetta's hand. Christy-Lynn felt awkward suddenly and hung back, content to watch from a distance. But Iris had other ideas, thrusting a tiny hand at her.

"Come too."

Christy-Lynn swallowed her protest. When a three-year-old held out her hand, you took it.

They walked about twenty yards, over crackling dead leaves and sun-bleached weeds, to a small marker tucked back near the corner of the fence. The headstone was a plain one, the simple slab of granite glaringly new beside its dingy neighbors. The inscription was plain, conspicuous in its lack of endearments.

## HONEY ROSE RAWLINGS
## 11/19/91–11/19/16

Christy-Lynn stared at the dates with a pang of realization. "She died on her birthday."

Rhetta nodded, her weathered face somber. "Twenty-five." She reached out then, grasping the top of the headstone, though whether out of grief or a need for support Christy-Lynn couldn't say. "I saw her a few days before. She said Stephen was taking her somewhere special. Foolish girl."

The heartache behind the words was unmistakable, but her eyes were surprisingly dry as she turned to Iris. "Come here, baby. I want to talk to you about your mama."

Christy-Lynn took several steps back as Iris moved to Rhetta's side, giving them some space. It was hard to imagine feeling more out of place than she did at that moment. She had never considered where Stephen's lover might be buried or what her funeral might have been like, that somewhere in the world family and friends might have mourned her.

Except no one really had.

Her thoughts drifted to Stephen's memorial, to the call she had received about how to proceed in light of the fact that almost no one had shown up—including her. Apparently, both Honey and Stephen had departed the world uncelebrated and unmourned.

A bit of movement suddenly caught her eye. She glanced up to find Rhetta back at her side, her cheeks blanched of color and slick with tears.

"She understands now, I think," Rhetta said hoarsely. "She knows her mama isn't coming back."

Christy-Lynn nodded, not sure how to respond. She turned to look at Iris, still standing in front of Honey's grave, her blonde head lowered. The sight made her throat go tight. "Is she going to be all right?"

Rhetta sighed, a rattling, phlegmy sound. "I hope so. I told her she could talk to Honey anytime she wanted, that all she had to do was talk to the angels, and they'd make sure her mama could hear her. That's what she's doing now—talking to the angels. Would you stay with her? I said she could stay as long as she needs to, but I'm afraid this trip has taken it out of me."

"Can you make it back to the car on your own?"

"I'll be fine. Just . . . stay with her."

She watched as Rhetta picked her way through the weeds on her way back to the Rover, already fumbling in her dress pocket for the pack of cigarettes she kept there. Christy-Lynn didn't realize Iris was approaching until she felt the air stir behind her.

"Mama's with the angels," she lisped softly. "She's not coming back."

"No," Christy-Lynn managed thickly. "She isn't."

Iris said nothing for a time, looking up thoughtfully with one eye squinted. And then, before Christy-Lynn realized what was happening,

Iris's hand had stolen into hers, fingers small and slight weaving with her own.

"Nonny says you're my angel. She says Mama sent you."

Christy-Lynn stared down at Stephen's daughter, so beautiful and sad, and could think of nothing to say. It was the longest string of words she'd ever heard her speak, and she felt each one like a knife. She wasn't an angel. Not Iris's or anyone else's. But how did she say that to a child? To *this* child, who'd just been told otherwise?

She looked away quickly, clearing her throat. "I should take you home now. And then I have to go home myself."

Iris's chin began to quiver. "Will you come back?"

"Yes, in a few weeks."

"Promise?"

Christy-Lynn swallowed past the jagged place in her throat as she stared at their entwined fingers and remembered Rhetta's words. *She never knows who's coming back and who's not.*

"Yes, honey. I promise."

# FORTY

Tolstoy made a beeline for Christy-Lynn the moment she stepped through the door, squalling balefully in what she suspected was a scolding for leaving him for two days. She abandoned her bags and bent to pick him up, snuggling him against her cheek. It was nice having someone to come home to, even if that someone did have four legs and a tail.

He protested when she put him down and nearly tripped her twice as she made her way to the kitchen. As she rounded the corner, she felt something soft and squishy beneath her shoe. A tentative inspection revealed a gray felt mouse with a feather for a tail—obviously a present from Wade. There was another under the kitchen table and a third lodged under the fridge door. She gathered them up and deposited them at Tolstoy's feet.

"Looks like someone has an admirer."

She watched him a moment, batting the toys about, then turned to grab a bottled water from the fridge. She had to squint to read the handwritten note tacked up beside Iris's fish.

*Check the microwave. I thought I'd give you a second chance since you missed out last time. Welcome home.*

Curious, she opened the microwave to discover a plastic leftover container. She found herself smiling as she peeled back the lid, delighted by the mingled aromas of tomato sauce and Italian herbs. Spaghetti. The man was full of surprises.

In the living room, she retrieved her cell from her purse and pulled up Wade's number.

"You're home," he said in lieu of hello, as if he were simply picking up the thread of their last conversation. She found it strangely comforting.

"Yes, I'm home. Safe and sound, as promised."

"How was it?"

Christy-Lynn pulled in a breath then let it out slowly. "Emotional."

"But you got Rhetta to agree?"

"After two hours of arm twisting, yes. I still don't think she's grasped how much this is going to change their lives."

"No second thoughts?"

"About the trust? No. About everything else . . ." She let the rest dangle, not sure she wanted to go there with Wade. He had warned her, after all.

"What's everything else?"

"Nothing, really. It's just that I'm starting to see that I'm going to need to be more involved than I thought. At least in the beginning. There's so much they both need, so many details to take care of, and I'm not sure Rhetta's up to handling it by herself. She doesn't even have transportation. She asked me to take her and Iris to the cemetery to see Honey's grave."

"And did you?"

Christy-Lynn held her breath a moment. She hadn't meant to tell him about the cemetery, but it was out now. "What else could I do?"

Wade was quiet for a moment, as if weighing his next words very carefully. Christy-Lynn braced for an *I told you so*. Instead, he surprised her by changing the subject. "You sound tired."

"It's been a long two days. I'm going to eat your spaghetti, and then I'm going to take a long hot bath and climb into bed. And thank you by the way. That was . . . thoughtful."

"Get some rest. I'll drop the key by tomorrow."

After dinner, which turned out to be delicious, she filled the tub and indulged in a long hot soak, then crawled between the sheets with the latest Barbara Claypole White novel. All she wanted at the moment was to lose herself in someone else's story and not think about the tangle of emotions she'd brought back with her from West Virginia.

She was reaching for the crisp new novel when she saw Wade's manuscript, still untouched and gathering dust on the nightstand. She picked it up, propping the stack of unbound pages against her knees, and began to read. Not because she felt guilty, but because she was suddenly curious about the man who bought mouse toys for her cat and left homemade spaghetti in her microwave.

It was 2:00 a.m. when she finally forced herself to set the manuscript aside, her eyes too tired to focus on one more sentence. She was only halfway through the stack but had already scribbled several pages of notes. *The End of Known Things* had the potential to be a beautiful story of growth and redemption. The premise was largely sound, and the prose was gorgeous, woven in a way that managed to feel both lush and spare. It was his main character—Vance—that was the problem. Midway through the second act, he had simply fallen flat, as if Wade had suddenly forgotten who he was writing about. Or had never known to begin with.

It wasn't a fatal flaw or even serious as long as he was willing to work on it, but as she flicked off the light and slid under the covers, she couldn't help wondering what had caused the sudden rift in Wade's writing. Perhaps he'd simply lost touch with the story he'd started twenty years ago. A lot could happen to a person in twenty years, and from what he'd told her, a lot had—a career ended, a love lost. Was it possible that in closing the door on that part of his life he had also closed the door on his creativity? It wasn't hard to imagine. There was certainly plenty in her own past that she was reluctant to look at.

Because looking made it real.

Christy-Lynn was returning from lunch with Missy and Dar when she saw Wade's Jeep parked outside the store. She found him in the café, seated at his usual table, banging away at his laptop.

"Looks like you're on a roll."

Wade pecked out a few more words, then looked up and smiled. "Hey, you. I came to drop off your key."

Something about that smile, all white teeth and scruffy jaw, always took her by surprise. He was the only man she'd ever met who could leave the house without shaving or combing his hair and still look like he was ready for a *GQ* photo shoot.

"Sorry. I ran out to meet Missy for lunch."

Wade fished the key from his shirt pocket and handed it to her. "No worries. I got some work done while I was waiting."

Christy-Lynn could feel Tamara peering furtively around the espresso machine, no doubt drawing her own conclusions about the key exchange she had just witnessed. She'd be sure to set her straight the moment Wade was gone.

"Tolstoy asked me to thank you for the mice. He's crazy about them. In fact, he batted them around the house half the night."

"It's the catnip. It's like kitty pot. Makes them frisky and then really mellow."

"That explains a lot."

"You still look pretty tired. Did you manage to get some rest?"

"A little. I was up until two, reading your manuscript."

Wade winced visibly. "And?"

"I made lots of notes. We could go over them if you want. Or we can wait until I get through the rest of the pages."

Wade scrubbed at the scruff on his chin with a pained expression. "No time like the present, I guess. Are you free for dinner?"

"Hmmm, dinner with my cat's dealer. I'm not sure that's a good idea."

"Come on. Take a walk on the wild side."

There was that smile again. He was making it difficult to say no, and she was pretty sure he knew it. "Let me guess—you have spaghetti leftovers you need to unload."

"Actually, I was thinking the Cork and Cleaver around seven?"

Christy-Lynn felt a skitter of nerves. Dinner. Out. Probably not a good idea. But it was business, wasn't it? A business dinner. With a client. In a public place. How dangerous could it be? "Okay, then. I'll run home for my notes when we close and meet you there."

Christy-Lynn waved as she stepped into the lobby of the Cork and Cleaver. Wade was seated at the end of a long oak bench, looking handsome and crisp in dark slacks and a light-blue oxford. He stood when he saw her, wrapping up his chat with Queenie Peterson, who, in spite of owning the restaurant, appeared to also be playing hostess.

Queenie's face brightened when she spotted Christy-Lynn. "Well now, Wade didn't say it was you he was meeting. How lovely."

"Just a little business," Christy-Lynn assured, not liking the matchmaker gleam in Queenie's eye. "Wade asked me to give him some feedback on his novel."

Queenie leaned close, voice lowered. "Are you sure? He's awfully dreamy."

"He's a client, Queenie. We're here to talk about his book, and that's it."

"Fine." Queenie sighed, reaching for a pair of menus from the hostess stand. "But for the record, I think you're crazy."

Wade trailed behind as Queenie led them to a dimly lit corner table. He held out Christy-Lynn's chair before settling across from her. "I'm a client?" he asked with raised brows.

"I needed to set the record straight. She tends to go off the rails when there's a good-looking guy around."

"You think I'm good-looking?"

He had opened his menu, so that only his eyes were visible, but she could tell by the tiny creases at the corners that he was smiling. She fought a smile of her own as she spread her napkin in her lap. "Don't beg for compliments. It isn't attractive. Now let's decide what we're eating so we can get to work."

Wade grunted. "All work and no play—"

"Makes Wade a better writer," Christy-Lynn finished primly. "Let's do the crab dip. It's delicious."

By the time dessert arrived, she had checked off most of the large ticket items on her notepad. Across from her, Wade sat pushing a bite of cheesecake around his plate, his face stony. She wished she could read him better, but he had a way of closing down that made it impossible to guess his mood.

"Look, I know no one likes negative feedback, but it's part of the gig. And I'm not saying it isn't good. Quite the opposite, in fact. You have a wonderful voice, fresh and clean, stripped down but still evocative. And the story mechanics are strong in the beginning. The problem is your main character. I haven't read all the pages you gave me yet, but as a reader, I'd have probably put the book down about halfway through. I just . . . stopped caring."

"Wow." Wade put down his fork and looked at her. "I really am a client."

Christy-Lynn felt a pang of sympathy. She wasn't used to dealing with writers face-to-face. Her clients were spread from Nova Scotia to Scotland, which meant she gave most of her feedback by e-mail or phone. It was different when you had to look someone in the eye and stomp all over their heart's work.

"Come on," she said, trying to keep it light. "You didn't really ask me to read it so I'd fawn all over you. You wanted to know what wasn't working, and I've told you—or at least given you my opinion. And it's not like any of it's fatal. You just need to know your characters better. Do a little psychoanalyzing."

Wade glowered over his wineglass. "On my characters or myself?"

"Sometimes it's the same thing."

"You think I'm Vance?"

"I have no idea *who* Vance is based on or if he's based on anyone. In fact, all I know about him is he's an angry guy with a past, and anyone can write that guy. Tell me where he's vulnerable. Show me what makes him bleed. Because if he doesn't bleed, no one's going to care if he gets the girl."

Wade was quiet as he signed for the check, leaving Christy-Lynn to wonder what he was thinking. Was he nursing a bruised ego? Digesting what she'd said? Already pondering how he might apply her suggestions? Judging by his grim expression as they made their way to the lobby it could be all of the above—or none.

After the close atmosphere of the restaurant, it felt good to step out into the cool night air. They were quiet as they crossed the parking lot, feet crunching on the pea gravel, shoulders brushing occasionally.

"You're quiet all of a sudden," Christy-Lynn said when they reached the Rover. "I can't tell what you're thinking, but I hope you're not miffed because of anything I said in there."

"No," he said, stuffing his hands in his pockets. "I'm not miffed. I'm just trying to figure out if it's worth the trouble. Maybe Simone was right. Maybe it's all just a big pipe dream."

"It isn't a pipe dream, Wade. The book has real potential. In fact, with a little tweaking, you might really have something."

"I can't tell if you're being a friend now or an editor."

She smiled at that. "One doesn't necessarily preclude the other. And I meant every word. Just show your readers that there's more to Vance than anger. Give them some layers to peel back. Show the chinks in his armor. He can be mad as hell at the start of the book, but at some point, we need to see that there's a way out of all that darkness."

"And if there isn't?"

Christy-Lynn was fumbling in her purse for her car keys. The sudden gravity in his tone made her look up. "There's always a way out."

"You say that like you believe it."

She looked up through her bangs to meet his gaze. "I have to. Otherwise you don't have a book—or a life."

"Was that for you or for me?"

She shrugged. "Both, I guess. The other day Missy said something that got me thinking. She said the word *never* represents all the doors we keep closed, that when we say *never* we close ourselves off from the hope that things can ever be different."

Wade tilted his head to one side, studying her in a way that made her want to look away but made looking away impossible. She felt rooted to the spot, paralyzed by something she could feel but not name. Finally, he reached up to brush a stray lock of hair from her eyes, tucking it behind her ear.

"Are there things you'd like to be different, Christy-Lynn Parker?"

His touch was warm and unsettlingly familiar, and for an instant, Christy-Lynn felt one of Missy's closed doors nudge open. But it was a door almost certain to lead to heartache—for both of them. She took a step back and would have taken another if she wasn't already pressed against the car door. "Please . . . don't do this. Don't try to get in my head and figure me out. I promise you, it isn't worth it."

"It was just a question." He was standing so close his voice seemed to vibrate in her chest. "Do you know the answer?"

She sighed, dropping her head. "Sometimes it just is what it is, Wade. There are things we can change and things we can't. The key is knowing the difference."

"Wait. Weren't you the one just lecturing me about the word *never*? Maybe you should take your own advice."

"Actually, it was Missy's advice. I was just thinking out loud." Christy-Lynn glanced about helplessly, wishing there was some way to escape without making a fool of herself. The longer they lingered, face-to-face in the nearly deserted lot, the more vivid the memory of their brief kiss became, stirring impulses she didn't dare trust. She cleared her throat, fidgeting with her keys. "Look, I need to get home. It's getting late, and I've got a ton of e-mails to answer."

Wade took a quick step back. "I did it again, didn't I?"

"Did what?"

"Pushed you. Scared you. I didn't mean to."

She shook her head, smiling sadly as she unlocked the door and slid behind the wheel. There was no way to explain what she was feeling. It was like standing at the edge of a cliff, longing, inexplicably, to hurl herself off, knowing she'd never survive the fall. She wasn't cut out to be the other half of anything, no matter how tempted she was—and she *was* tempted.

"You didn't scare me," she said, reaching for the door handle. "I scared me."

"Wait!" Wade grabbed the door before she could pull it closed. "I don't know what that means."

"You don't have to know," she said, letting the smile slip. "As long as I do."

# FORTY-ONE

Christy-Lynn turned the freshly delivered FedEx envelope over in her hands. Peter had called yesterday to let her know he was finally overnighting the trust papers, asking her again if she was sure she wanted to proceed. Nothing was final until the papers were signed. But after weeks of weighing the pros and cons, she saw no reason to change her mind.

It wasn't like there'd be a lot of personal contact. Peter had strongly urged her to name him as point person, expressing concerns that in the event of an "irregularity" she might prove less than objective. She agreed, not because she didn't trust her objectivity, but because keeping a little distance might be a good thing. Once she'd helped Rhetta settle the housing and school questions, her duties would amount to little more than reviewing the monthly statements. But her conscience would be clear.

She slid the pages free, staring at the words on the top sheet: *Revocable Living Trust.* She leafed through the rest, noting the tiny green and yellow flags strategically placed near the lines to be signed by each party, then realized she'd better call Rhetta and let her know her copies would be arriving in the next day or so.

It took three rings before Rhetta finally picked up. As usual, she sounded breathless and worn to the nub. "It's Christy-Lynn, Rhetta. How are you?"

"Fine. Just outside on the porch with Iris. Is something wrong?"

It was the same question she always asked, as if she was always expecting trouble. "Nothing's wrong. I was just calling to tell you my attorney sent out your copies of the trust paperwork, and they should arrive in a day or two. I asked him to send them so you'd have time to look everything over ahead of time."

"That wasn't necessary. And I'm not likely to understand a word of it."

"You could have Ray look at it. Or if you'd like, I can have my lawyer call you and go over them. I want to make sure you understand how the trust is funded and exactly how those funds will be released to you."

"No. Not Ray," she answered abruptly. "And I've got no reason to check up on you. Any woman who'd do what you're doing for Iris doesn't need to be questioned. Besides, you already explained it all. I won't have to come to Virginia to do the signing, will I? I don't see how I could manage that."

"No. I'll come to you. I explained your situation to my attorney. All we have to do is make an appointment with a notary, sign the papers, and then mail them back. Once he's looked them over, he'll send us each a finalized copy. Would Saturday be okay, or would you like a little more time? I don't want you to feel pressured."

"I don't feel pressured, and time is something I'm running a little short on these days. Saturday will be fine."

Christy-Lynn drained her coffee mug and zipped her overnight bag closed. Tolstoy looked on with an air of disapproval. He had already attempted to stow away three times and was clearly put out at being denied another opportunity. She'd be glad when things with the trust were finalized, and she could handle things from a safe distance. It wasn't so much the trip she minded, but the emotional hangover that tended to linger afterward, sometimes for days.

She was about to drag the overnight bag up onto her shoulder when she heard what sounded like a car pulling into the drive. Frowning, she peered through the curtains, surprised to see Wade climbing out of his Jeep, a red to-go mug in his hand.

"Morning," he said brightly when she pulled back the door.

"What are you doing here? It's seven—" She broke off when she spotted a dark-green satchel sitting in the drive. "Is that a suitcase?"

"It's a duffel, actually. You said last week that you were leaving this morning, and I've decided to be your wingman."

"You just invited yourself?"

"Yes."

"Why?"

He tipped back the to-go mug and took a quick swallow. "Think of me as your bodyguard."

Christy-Lynn cocked an eye at him. "You think I need a bodyguard to meet with an eighty-year-old woman?"

"Okay then, I'm your chaperone. Your entourage. Your posse."

"Except none of those things are necessary."

"I don't like the idea of you driving all that way on your own."

"I've done it three times now."

"And each time you've come back looking like a zombie. This way I can do some of the driving and you can sleep. Or read the rest of my manuscript if you're so inclined."

Christy-Lynn opened her mouth to protest, but Wade was one step ahead of her. "I promise you'll be perfectly safe. Separate rooms. Separate checks. Separate everything."

She eyed him warily but felt a little ashamed too that he'd been able to read her thoughts so easily. "It isn't that. Really. It simply isn't necessary. It's just some paperwork, a couple of signatures. As soon as I'm done, I'll check into the Days Inn, then drive back on Sunday. I don't need a . . . wingman."

"I know this is going to come as a nasty shock, Christy-Lynn, but you're not Wonder Woman. You may not see the toll this has taken on you, but I do. You're exhausted and distracted, which isn't a good combo when you're about to get on the road. I'd like to help, if you'll let me."

"I've got this. Really I do."

"Is it because you don't trust me?"

Christy-Lynn felt herself flush when she thought of their strained parting after dinner the other night. She had acted like a flustered schoolgirl. "Don't be ridiculous. Of course I trust you."

"Then say yes. It'll be like *Thelma and Louise*—but without the cliff thing."

Christy-Lynn couldn't help laughing. She had to admit, having company on the long ride to Riddlesville wasn't a wholly unwelcome idea. "All right. But I pick the music, and you don't get to complain."

It was nearly two o'clock when they finally pulled into Riddlesville. Wade said nothing as Christy-Lynn drove through the center of town, his expression grim as he took in the empty storefronts and boarded windows. The view didn't improve much as they headed west toward the outskirts of town, the pocked streets lined with listing houses and weed-choked yards. It wasn't until she slowed to make the turn into Rhetta's drive that he finally spoke.

"Jesus." It was barely a whisper, the natural reaction to finally seeing what she'd been talking about all these weeks.

"I know," she said softly.

"It looks like ground zero."

*Now do you see?* she wanted to say but didn't. In fact, there wasn't time to say anything. Rhetta suddenly popped up out of one of the chairs on the front porch, a half-smoked cigarette caught between her fingers. Christy-Lynn waved as she stepped down out of the Rover.

"Hey, Rhetta."

"I thought I heard a car coming up the road. I wasn't sure what time to expect you, so I thought I'd sit out awhile." It wasn't until Wade threw open the passenger side door that Rhetta seemed to realize Christy-Lynn wasn't alone. "Who are you?"

"This is Wade Pierce, Rhetta. He came to help with the driving. He was a friend of Stephen's."

Rhetta looked him up and down, her cloudy eyes suddenly sharp. When she finished her inspection, she ground out her cigarette in the plastic ashtray on the railing and looked hard at Christy-Lynn. "You're not sick, are you? You look a bit wrung out."

Christy-Lynn felt rather than saw the pointed glance Wade threw in her direction. She chose to ignore it. "I'm fine, Rhetta. Just a little tired."

"Well, come on in. I've got a fresh pitcher of tea in the fridge. Are you hungry? I could fix you something."

"No, thank you. We stopped for lunch. But some tea would be wonderful."

They followed her up onto the porch and then into the house. The air was hot and close and still smelled of this morning's breakfast. The TV was on—an old rerun of *Gilligan's Island* with the sound turned way down. Rhetta clicked it off.

"I've just put Iris down for a nap." She was tidying as she moved about the living room, gathering socks, barrettes, scrunchies, and stuffing them into the pockets of her yellow gingham housedress. "Poor thing had another bad night. Oh, be careful there," she warned Wade, pointing to the floor littered with crayons. "You'll break your neck if you step wrong. I'm afraid I learned that one the hard way."

Rhetta ran an eye around the room while Wade navigated the mine-field of crayons. She hadn't been counting on him, and Christy-Lynn could see that she was wary. "I'm not sure how long she'll be down, but she sleeps so poorly these days I don't expect it'll be long. We can head over to the notary with the papers as soon as she's up. In the meantime, I'll pour the tea."

Christy-Lynn picked up a well-thumbed copy of *Reader's Digest* from the couch and set it on the end table before taking a seat. Wade dropped down beside her, his knees nearly up to his chin as he sank into the rump-sprung cushions. His eyes met Christy-Lynn's as Rhetta shuffled out of earshot, but he said nothing.

A few minutes later, Rhetta reappeared with a pair of glasses and handed one to Christy-Lynn. "I hope you like it good and sweet. Only way I know to make it. And I'm sorry—" She paused as she handed Wade the second glass. "I've already forgotten your name."

"It's Wade, and I was weaned on sweet tea. Thank you."

"Wade," she repeated, as if trying to commit it to memory. "You were Stephen's friend?"

"A long time ago. We were roommates in college, but we, uh . . . lost touch."

Rhetta nodded vaguely, as if it had nothing to do with her, then disappeared into the kitchen again. She returned moments later with her own glass and took a seat in the worn green recliner beside the couch. She looked vaguely distracted, bone-thin fingers clutching her tea glass, eyes darting furtively in Wade's direction.

When the silence began to grow awkward, Christy-Lynn reached for the FedEx envelope but didn't immediately remove its contents. "Did you have a chance to look at the paperwork my attorney sent?"

Rhetta nodded. "More or less. The money will go into an account every month for Iris. That's right, isn't it?"

"And for you, Rhetta. Remember, we talked about getting you some help and finding you a better place to live, somewhere close to your doctor and good schools. And I'm going to help you with all of that when it's time. You'll receive a check each month to use for whatever you and Iris need—like an allowance. And that's it really."

Rhetta nodded, fishing around in the pocket of her dress for a tissue. She blotted her eyes then blew her nose. "Don't mind me. I'm just a foolish old woman."

It suddenly struck Christy-Lynn just how daunting all this must seem to a woman who had probably never signed a legal document in her life. "I know this is a lot to digest. Are you sure you don't have any questions?"

"Will I need to save receipts or anything?"

"No. You won't need to account for how you spend the money. But in case something does come up, something out of the ordinary, I'm going to leave you my attorney's card. His name is Peter Hagan. That's who you'll call."

Rhetta put down her glass very slowly. "Not you?"

Christy-Lynn exchanged a quick look with Wade. They had discussed this particular stipulation while on the road. Wade approved of the idea, glad she'd be able to maintain some distance, but she was already having second thoughts. Peter Hagan might be a highly skilled attorney, but he lacked anything like the legal equivalent of a bedside manner. He could be gruff and intimidating, and though he'd never come right out and said so, he had formed his own opinion of the Rawlings family.

"Of course I'll always be here to help you, Rhetta, but Mr. Hagan is better equipped to handle the legal stuff. You'll have—"

Christy-Lynn broke off abruptly, the hair on her arms prickling to attention as an earsplitting wail suddenly careened down the hall. She knew the sound only too well, the blind panic of a child caught between sleep and waking. Rhetta was on her feet in an instant, scurrying as fast as her legs could carry her. It was a relief when she closed the bedroom door behind her, muffling the terrified shrieks.

Wade was clearly spooked, perched on the edge of the couch, ready to spring into action should it be required. "What's happening? Should we be doing something?"

"Night terrors," Christy-Lynn told him grimly. "And there's nothing *to* do, except wait until she comes out of it. Rhetta says she has them pretty often. The good news is that at her age she probably doesn't remember."

"You sound like an expert."

"I had them until I was seventeen."

Wade's eyes widened, and for a moment, he looked at her as if he was seeing her for the first time. "But not anymore?"

"No. Not anymore." It wasn't a lie. The dreams she'd been having since Stephen's death had nothing to do with night terrors, which tended to diminish with the onset of adolescence. "I was an unusual case. Most kids grow out of them around seven or eight." She paused, cocking her head. "Listen—it sounds like she's starting to come out of it."

A short time later, the bedroom door opened, and Rhetta appeared with a dazed Iris in tow. "It was a short one, thank the Lord." She sagged into her chair and pulled Iris onto her lap. "Sometimes they go on for half an hour. This one wasn't so bad. Can you say hello to Miss Christy-Lynn, Iris?"

Iris seemed not to hear. She was sticky with sweat or tears or both, her face mottled with angry red splotches. But it was her eyes, glassy and vacant, that held Christy-Lynn's attention, too reminiscent of her mother's that night at the morgue.

"It takes her a while to come all the way out," Rhetta said, patting Iris's back in a steady, comforting rhythm. "And then sometimes she doesn't come out at all. She just drops back to sleep like nothing happened. I never know which it will be."

Wade seemed unable to take his eyes off Iris. "How often does she have them?"

"Sometimes it's every night. Sometimes she goes weeks and nothing."

"Has she been to a doctor? Maybe there's something they can do."

Rhetta shook her head. "I took her when they first started. They printed some pages off the computer and told me to read them. It basically said there was nothing they could do, and that she'd eventually grow out of it."

Christy-Lynn wondered if Rhetta had any idea just how long that might take but decided to let the subject drop. "Look, we don't have to go to the notary today. We can come back tomorrow when Iris is feeling better. We're staying over anyway."

Rhetta was about to respond when the heavy thump of feet sounded on the front porch. There was no knock, no greeting of any kind as Ray Rawlings came through the door. Rhetta's arms tightened almost imperceptibly around Iris, her face suddenly chalk white. "What are you doing here, Ray? I have company."

Ray barely glanced in his grandmother's direction, locking eyes with Christy-Lynn instead. He wore a shiny gray suit that fit too snugly at the waist and a red tie that had seen better days. "Mrs. Ludlow, nice to see you again."

Christy-Lynn fought down a shudder. His smile reminded her of a small rodent, hungry and sharp-faced. "Reverend."

"Rhetta mentioned you'd be by. Nice of you to come all this way for our Iris."

Christy-Lynn stared at him. *Our Iris?*

Wade was suddenly on his feet, shoulders squared and clearly bristling. "I don't believe we've been introduced, Reverend."

Ray studied Wade but made no move to extend a hand. "I'm Iris's uncle. And you are?"

"A friend of Ms. Parker's."

Christy-Lynn shot Wade a sidelong glance. His fists were knotted tightly at his sides, the telltale muscle at his temple ticking ominously. Clearly, his gut reaction to the honorable Reverend Rawlings aligned perfectly with her own.

Ray was either oblivious or unimpressed, dismissing Wade with an icy glare before turning his attention to Iris. Crouching down on one knee, he held out his arms with a greasy smile. "Come to Uncle Ray."

Iris was having none of it. She drew back against Rhetta, her chin tucked into her chest like a turtle trying to retreat into its shell. He tried again. This time she turned her head, burying it in the crook of her great-grandmother's shoulder.

Rhetta flashed her grandson an imploring look. "She's just had one of her nightmares, Ray. You know how she is after. She doesn't—"

Ray silenced her with a look, clearly bent on having his way. "Iris," he barked again. "I'm talking to you."

It was Christy-Lynn's turn to bolt to her feet. Ray Rawlings might be Iris's uncle, but she wasn't about to sit there and let him browbeat a little girl. Before she could open her mouth, Iris had scrambled off Rhetta's lap and ducked behind her legs.

Ray feigned amusement, but his patience was clearly wearing thin. He cleared his throat, his cajoling smile beginning to fray. "Now, sweetheart, there's no need to be shy. Don't you want to see your uncle Ray?"

Christy-Lynn found herself gritting her teeth. Who did he think he was fooling? Certainly not Rhetta, who was sitting frozen in her chair. Or Iris, whose grip on her legs grew tighter with every word her uncle uttered.

Ray glared menacingly. "When someone tells you to come, young lady, you come."

Christy-Lynn bent to scoop Iris up into her arms. It was the last straw. Apparently it was the tipping point for Wade too. He took an abrupt step forward.

"That'll do, Reverend."

Ray puffed out his chest, his face the color of a ripe plum. "Who the hell are you to tell me what *will do* in my own house?"

Wade didn't blink. "I'm a guy who's smart enough to know when a kid's being bullied. And I believe this is Rhetta's house not yours."

Rhetta fixed her grandson with pleading eyes. "Please, Ray. You're scaring her."

And just like that, Ray's bluster vanished, as if he'd suddenly remembered the part he was supposed to be playing.

"Forgive me," he said softly, folding his hands before him. "It's been a trying time. But I've come to share some news with Rhetta, and

I suppose you should hear it too. After much prayer and soul searching, my wife and I feel led by the Lord to take my sister's child into our fold, to love and raise as our own."

Christy-Lynn wasn't sure if she was more stunned or horrified. "You feel led . . . by the Lord?"

Ray dipped his head piously but said nothing.

Christy-Lynn laughed, a brief, sharp chuckle. "I must say I find your sudden change of heart a bit surprising, especially for a man who, two weeks ago, was throwing around words like *abomination*."

"The Lord works in mysterious ways, Mrs. Ludlow. As a man of God, I'm bound to do my Christian duty and to do it with a glad heart."

"That glad heart wouldn't have anything to do with the fact that your niece is about to come into an inheritance, would it?"

Ray took an abrupt step forward and would have taken another had Wade not checked him. "Exactly what are you accusing me of, Mrs. Ludlow?"

"Just what you think I'm accusing you of, *Reverend*. I can't help wondering if you'd still be eager to do your Christian duty if I were to change my mind and tear up the trust papers. Somehow, I don't think so."

Ray's man-of-God facade abruptly fell away. "In that case, I suppose we'd have to see what the courts have to say on the matter. I've spoken to a lawyer, and he feels the girl has a claim in her own right, which means your husband's money isn't yours to dole out as *you* see fit. Judges tend to frown on strangers poking their noses where they don't belong. Family should look after family."

"Except you *refused* to look after her!" Christy-Lynn shot back, eyeing him with open contempt. "Now, suddenly, you're willing to bear your sister's sins dutifully. Forgive me if I find your sudden compassion suspicious."

The corners of his mouth turned up slowly. "The Lord has shown me the error of my ways, Mrs. Ludlow. Like Saul on the road to Damascus."

"Spare me the Sunday school lesson, Reverend. And know that I meant every word I said just now. Iris will be taken care of, if it means I have to pay for every barrette and ice-cream cone myself, but my attorney will make sure you never touch a dime of Iris's money. Still, if you want to go to court and air all of this publicly, I'm happy to take my chances."

Rhetta looked at her with wide eyes, visibly horrified by the prospect of a court battle. But Ray seemed to be considering the words carefully. After a moment, he cleared his throat, his expression back to the chilly shrewdness Christy-Lynn had glimpsed earlier. "Perhaps an agreement might be reached. A sort of . . . compromise?"

"A compromise?" Christy-Lynn echoed warily, wishing she had listened to Wade's warning about unscrupulous relatives. She had misjudged the reverend—or at least misjudged his motives. He wasn't just a pious ass; he was a sharp and cunning bastard.

She'd been a fool not to see it or to think a handful of papers could right all the wrongs in Iris Rawlings's life. Poverty was hard on a child, but it didn't compare with the pain of being invisible, unwanted, unloved. And for Ray Rawlings, Iris was all three.

Christy-Lynn fought down a shudder of revulsion. He was watching her now, through narrowed eyes, trying to read her thoughts and planning his next move. "I might—" He paused, clearing his throat, then flashed a wheedling smile. "That is, my wife and I might be open to some form of compensation."

"You mean money," Christy-Lynn flung back.

"I mean a token of goodwill. Iris is, after all, the only child of my dear departed sister. Surely that's worth some small consideration, a modest sum agreed on by both parties—paid discreetly, of course—for the loss of our darling little niece?"

Christy-Lynn stood speechless, still clutching a confused and terrified Iris. Rhetta looked equally speechless, though not quite surprised by her grandson's suggestion. "Why do I have the feeling this was where this was heading all along? You knew I'd never give you control of the trust, so you put on this little show, hoping I'd pay you to go away. Am I right?"

Ray dipped his head, not quite an acknowledgment but close enough. "Come now, Mrs. Ludlow, it isn't the means but the end that matters. This way everyone is happy. Rhetta keeps the girl and the bulk of the money, and I go away a few dollars richer for my sacrifice."

Christy-Lynn was sickened to realize she was actually considering the proposal. "How do I know that's the end of it, that you'll just . . . go away?"

Ray smiled, exposing small, sharp teeth. "I'm a man of God, Mrs. Ludlow."

It was Wade's turn to react. He stepped past Christy-Lynn and grabbed Ray by the arm.

"Why don't we finish this outside, Reverend?"

"Get your hands off me!"

Christy-Lynn took an abrupt step forward. "Wade, don't!"

But Wade was already shoving the good reverend toward the door, his expression one of barely suppressed fury. If she didn't step in, there was a good chance Ray was going to end up in an ambulance and Wade in the back of a police car. By the time she handed Iris off to Rhetta and caught up, Wade was already jerking the reverend down the steps and out into the yard.

Ray's face was the color of a beetroot, his arms swinging wildly without landing a single blow. "You'll end up in jail for this!"

To Christy-Lynn's surprise, the very pregnant Mrs. Rawlings suddenly emerged from the family van, loping toward the fray as fast as her swollen belly would allow. "Let him be!" she bellowed sharply. "That's a man of God you're assaulting!"

But no one was listening. Nor were the words spewing from Ray's mouth particularly godly as he continued to flail, spittle flying like a rabid dog as he tried to shake Wade's hold. As far as Christy-Lynn could tell, Wade had yet to throw a punch, his intent to restrain rather than harm. She was almost disappointed.

Finally, Wade gave Ray's arm one last vicious yank, releasing him so abruptly he nearly toppled over. "You're a big man," he said through gritted teeth as Ray stood wiping flecks of spit from his chin. "Big on threats. Big on bullying. So yes, by all means, let's go to court. But I don't think a custody battle was ever your intent. In fact, I think that's the last thing you want. You see I've done a little homework, Reverend. There's a rumor—though I'm betting it's more than just a rumor— about a certain cheerleader from Riddlesville High School. Her name is Tina Gibson, a member of your congregation, I believe. Sings in the youth choir. Ring any bells?"

Ray dropped his arms, suddenly still.

Ellen took a step forward, a hand on her belly. "Ray?"

But Ray wasn't looking at his wife. "You don't know what you're talking about."

"Let's see if I do," Wade responded coolly. "According to my source, Tina had to go away for several months last summer after a visit to a certain nurse over in Wheeler almost killed her—a visit you not only drove her to but allegedly paid for. I couldn't verify that last part, but let's run with it anyway, shall we?"

Christy-Lynn stood openmouthed, gaping at the drama unfolding before her. How on earth could he possibly know those things? And yet it was obvious he did know because Ray had gone a terrible shade of gray, as if all the blood had drained from his body. He stood glaring at Wade, half of his shirt untucked.

"It's a lie!"

"Not according to Tina's boyfriend. Doug Simpson, I believe his name was. Captain of the wrestling team and very angry with you apparently. He couldn't wait to spill the details. In fact, I'm pretty sure he'd be willing to spill them to anyone who'll listen—including a judge if you're still inclined. But then, I'm betting you're not. I'm no expert, but I don't think there are a lot of judges who'd hand over a three-year-old girl to that kind of scum. I could be wrong though. Ball's in your court."

Ellen Rawlings hadn't moved a muscle during the exchange, but there were twin spots of color on her cheeks now. In three long steps, she closed the distance between herself and her husband, clearly seething. "You said it wasn't true. You swore!"

Ray rounded on his wife, fists knotted at his sides. "Shut up, Ellen!"

Wade was smiling now, but his eyes were hard, devoid of anything like humor. "Here's the long and short of it, Ray. If you pursue this scheme of yours, if you so much as think about coming after that child or her money, or harassing your grandmother for so much as a penny from that trust, I'll make sure every person in this town knows what you are. The cheerleader. The check fraud. The real estate scheme. All of it. And that'll be the end of your precious congregation—and the collection plate that goes with it."

Ray's mouth worked mutely as he sawed at his tie. After a moment, he pivoted toward the van and stalked away, leaving his pregnant wife to trail after him.

Christy-Lynn held her breath until the van had pulled out of sight, then turned to look at Wade. "What just happened?"

"I think I've just gotten rid of the reverend for you."

Christy-Lynn nodded, a blend of confusion and relief. "Yes, I got that part. But how did you know about the cheerleader?"

"Like I told Ray, I did some homework."

"You made another call."

"I had a hunch, and it turned out to be right. Man's got quite a past if you talk to the right people. Even had a couple of arrests way back that I doubt his flock knows about. You were right. He was never going to court—not with his past—but he was banking on you not knowing that."

"That's why you wanted to come," she said, suddenly understanding. "You wanted to be here in case he showed up and tried to pull something. But how did you know he would?"

Wade shrugged. "I didn't. But guys like that don't change their stripes. I wasn't about to let you get blindsided."

For a moment, Christy-Lynn wasn't sure she could speak, the lump in her throat suddenly threatening to cut off her words. He had done this for her. Not for Iris, who until today he had never met, but for her, because he knew how much it mattered. "I honestly don't know what to say. Except thank you, of course. I don't know what would have happened if you hadn't been here. I might have actually paid him. The thought of Iris living with that—" She broke off, not wanting to finish the thought. "I guess we'd better go back in and let Rhetta know no one's dead."

# FORTY-TWO

Rhetta was weeping quietly when they walked back into the house, cradling Iris and crooning some indecipherable tune. She glanced up, blinking to clear her vision. "Where's Ray?"

"I don't think he'll be around for a while," Wade said gently. "We had a conversation. I think he understands that Iris is better off here with you."

Rhetta nodded, though she was clearly bewildered. She closed her eyes briefly, heaving a shaky breath. "I need to smoke. Can you look after her while I'm outside?"

Christy-Lynn turned to Wade. "Can you? I'd like to talk to Rhetta a minute."

Rhetta planted a kiss on Iris's pale head. "Nonny needs to go out on the porch for a few minutes. Can you stay and color with the nice man?"

Iris turned wide eyes toward Wade.

The hard angles disappeared from Wade's face as he bent down to meet Iris's gaze. "Christy-Lynn showed me the fish you colored for her. She has it on her refrigerator so all her friends can see it. Do you think you could color one for me? Maybe a blue one?"

Iris eyed him warily but took his hand when he extended it. Christy-Lynn watched as he led her to the coloring books scattered in the corner and settled down beside her on the rug, as if coloring with a three-year-old was something he did every day.

Rhetta struggled up out of her chair, already patting her pockets for her cigarettes. She moved slowly, almost brokenly, as she stepped out onto the porch and groped her way to her chair. Her hands trembled as she plucked a cigarette from the crumpled packet. It took three tries to light it.

She was quiet for a time, pulling in smoke, pushing it out. Finally, she turned to Christy-Lynn. "I'm sorry about my grandson. He's . . . not a nice man."

"You knew, didn't you? That's why you didn't want to show him the papers. Because you were afraid he'd try something like this."

Rhetta nodded wearily as she blew out a lung full of smoke. "I knew he'd get his hands on the money if he found out, so I kept it quiet. But he showed up one day, and the papers were on the kitchen table. He doesn't give a damn about that girl. Neither does Ellen. They just see dollar signs."

"Why didn't you tell me?"

"He told me not to." She closed her eyes, her lids blue-veined and paper-thin. "He's got an awful temper."

"Are you afraid of him, Rhetta?" Christy-Lynn asked, already knowing the answer.

"It isn't just that. He and Ellen are the only family I have—the only *help* I have. They do my shopping and my errands, run me to the doctor when I need to go, pick up my medicine. I don't know what I'd do if they quit. But that isn't the worst of it." She paused, crushed out her cigarette, then fumbled to light another. "One day I'll be gone. And then what? They were my only hope for Iris, which is why I've been so torn. Part of me hoped the money might bring them around. But then today, when I heard him saying those things and saw the look on Iris's little face, I knew I couldn't let him anywhere near her. I'd rather let the county have her. At least she'll have a chance."

Christy-Lynn felt the words like a physical shock. They had been Missy's words too. But they weren't true. She of all people knew that. "You don't mean that. You can't. There must be some local family who'd be willing to take her—a decent family. My lawyer could help arrange the adoption."

"With who?" Rhetta countered, near tears now. "There's no one. Unless . . ."

Christy-Lynn lifted her eyes, waiting.

"You could take her." She'd said it softly but quickly, like the snick of a trap springing shut. "You could take her away from here, give her a better life—a real life."

There was a dull buzzing in Christy-Lynn's head, a sudden weight at the center of her chest. "Rhetta, I can't."

"She needs you, Christy-Lynn. I've thought so for a while, but I knew it for sure when I saw the two of you at Honey's grave. And you need her."

Christy-Lynn pushed to her feet and moved to the railing, as far from Rhetta as she could get on the tiny porch. "It isn't possible, Rhetta. I can't say why, it just . . . isn't."

"Because of Honey?"

"Because of me. There are a million reasons I can't do what you're asking, but none of them have to do with Iris—or with Honey. Iris needs a mother, and I'm not mother material. It's why I never had children of my own."

"People change," Rhetta told her gently. "They grow. One day something happens, and all of a sudden everything's different."

Christy-Lynn shook her head, unable to bear the naked plea in Rhetta's eyes.

"That girl needs a mama, Christy-Lynn. And you need something to do with that great big heart of yours. You need each other. And that stuff about not being mother material—that's nonsense."

Christy-Lynn turned finally, arms crossed as if to ward off this terrible thing she was being asked to do. But then it had always been inevitable, hadn't it? That Rhetta would at least make the suggestion? Because she didn't know—*couldn't* know—that handing her great-granddaughter over to Christy-Lynn would essentially be trading one disaster for another. And the last thing Iris needed was one more disaster in her life.

"I know you're desperate, Rhetta. And I'll help in any way I can, but I can't do what you're asking." Her voice began to fracture as tears threatened. "I'm so sorry."

The door opened. Wade stepped out onto the porch. "She's asleep," he said softly, before noticing Christy-Lynn's stricken face. "What's wrong?"

"Nothing's wrong." Christy-Lynn swiped at her tears before they could fall. "I just . . . I need to go. Can you bring me my purse from inside?" She was already making her way down the steps, moving blindly toward the Rover. "I'm sorry, Rhetta. I'll call you. I just . . . I have to go."

Wade said nothing as he held out his hand for the car keys. He had no idea what just happened, but one look at Christy-Lynn's face was enough to tell him she had no business behind the wheel.

Her eyes were blank as she climbed up into the passenger seat, her movements heavy and deliberate, like someone trying very hard not to fall apart. She said nothing as they pulled away from the house, nothing as they headed back through Riddlesville's dismal downtown, nothing as they merged back onto the highway. Finally, he had to ask.

"Can you tell me what happened back there?"

"I don't want to talk about it." She turned away then, angling her body toward the window and effectively ending the discussion.

Wade fought the urge to press for an answer. There was still so much about her he didn't understand, but he had learned that pushing would get him nowhere.

She slept for a time. At least he thought she was sleeping. It wasn't until they had crossed over into Virginia that he realized she was awake—and quietly crying. He took the ramp for the next rest stop, pulled into a space near the picnic area, and cut the engine.

Christy-Lynn sat up abruptly, wiping both eyes with her fists. "What are we doing?"

"I thought maybe you'd like to splash some water on your face. I'll get you a drink from the machine."

"Thanks," she said thickly. "But I'm good."

For the second time since climbing back into the Rover, Wade found himself swallowing his first reaction, which was to point out that she wasn't anything close to good. Instead, he reached for her hand. "What *can* I do?"

She looked away. "Nothing. You can't do anything."

"I'd like to help."

For a moment, the tension in her body seemed to ebb, and her hand relaxed in his. And then, before he realized what she was up to, she had unfastened her seat belt and was bolting from the car. He scurried out after her but tangled briefly in his own seat belt, giving her a head start. She ran like a wild thing, panicked and stumbling as she scrambled down the overgrown trail and disappeared into the trees.

He didn't bother calling out; she wouldn't have stopped anyway. Instead, he focused on closing the distance between them, pounding down the path until he was close enough to grab her arm and jerk her to a halt.

"Where are you going?"

She rounded on him, face splotched and tear-streaked. "Leave me alone!"

"I can't do that. You're upset, and you have no idea where you're going." He stepped back, giving her some space, but remained alert, in case he needed to sprint after her again. "Talk to me, please. Let me help."

He was expecting another sharp retort, but suddenly all the fight seemed to go out of her. Like a balloon with a slow leak, she went limp, sagging against him with a choking sob. He led her back down the trail toward the parking lot, steering her toward one of the concrete benches, and for a few moments, they sat in silence.

"I'm sorry," she said after several minutes. She had stopped weeping, but her voice was thick and congested. She dragged a sleeve across her face, mopping her eyes. "I didn't mean to lose it like that."

"Don't be sorry. Just tell me what happened."

She looked down at the ground, hacking at the dirt with the heel of one boot. "Rhetta asked me to take Iris—permanently."

Wade's eyes shot wide. "You mean adopt her?"

"Yes."

It was little more than a whisper, barely audible, and as he studied her face, he was reminded of the disaster victims he had interviewed over the years—stunned into silence, as if she had survived some terrible calamity and was only now coming to terms with the devastation.

He fought to keep his face neutral. "That's a pretty presumptuous thing to ask someone you hardly know."

Christy-Lynn blotted her eyes again then shook her head. "Not presumptuous. Desperate. She's terrified that when she dies Iris will end up in foster care—or with Ray."

"You've already gone above and beyond, Christy-Lynn."

"I know."

"Then why are you crying?"

"Nothing. It's nothing."

"It's not nothing, Christy-Lynn. I just had to chase you into the woods."

She was quiet for a time, her gaze distant and clouded. "I know what it's like," she said finally. "To have no one, to be on your own in the world. I know what that's like."

Wade reached for her hand, then thought better of it, afraid he might spook her again. "How old were you when you lost your mother?"

She blinked at him. A fresh pair of tears slid down her cheeks. "I didn't lose her."

"But I thought—"

"Th . . . that she was dead, yes. It's what I wanted you to think."

Wade wasn't sure what he expected, but it sure as hell wasn't this. "Why?"

"Because I *wanted* it to be true," she said with a watery hiccup. "And because as far as I was concerned it was. I was sixteen the last time I saw her. She was in the hospital, under arrest for smashing her boyfriend in the mouth with a bottle after he sliced her face open with a paring knife—and for being a thief and a junkie. She went to jail, and I went to foster care."

The news landed squarely in the center of Wade's solar plexus as the pieces fell into place. One vital element of the story, and suddenly everything made sense; her obsession with Iris, her resolve to correct a parent's neglect, her determination to safeguard Iris's future. It all finally added up. And it was a gut-wrenching picture.

"I don't know what to say. I guess I get why you've been torturing yourself over all this. How long were you in foster care?"

"Not long. I ran away. I lived on the street for almost two years."

Wade went quiet, absorbing the full weight of her words. Two years on the streets, and little more than a child. The urge to wrap his arms around her was suddenly overwhelming.

"Foster care was that bad?" he asked instead.

"It was for me. And when I think of Iris going through what I did, I just . . ." The words trailed off. She shook her head. "I can't bear it."

She was rocking back and forth now, drawn in on herself, worrying the underside of one wrist repeatedly with the ball of her thumb. Wade locked on the gesture, frowning as he tried to pull up a memory. And then he had it—the night on the deck when he'd asked about her scars. At the time, it had seemed like nothing—three small scars whose origins she claimed not to remember. Now, he wasn't so sure.

He reached for her hand, surprised when she didn't resist. "I asked you about these once," he said, tracing a finger over the trio of crescent-shaped marks. "You said you didn't remember how you got them, but I think you do."

She nodded, and the tears began again. Wade had no idea what to say, no clue how to stem her pain, and so he said nothing, holding her hands instead and simply letting her cry. She had a right to her grief, a right to shutter whatever private hell she had endured, and to keep it shuttered if she so chose.

And then, without any prompting on his part, the whole of it came pouring out.

# FORTY-THREE

**Goose Creek, South Carolina**
**July 18, 1998**

*Christy-Lynn cracks open the bathroom door, checking to make sure the coast is clear before slipping out into the hall in her towel. After two months at the Hawleys, she still feels like an intruder, the new kid everyone watches while pretending not to watch. She can hear the television downstairs, the eleven o'clock news punctuated by the steady sawing of Dennis Hawley's snores. He was usually asleep by now, aided in part by the six-pack he killed each night while his wife worked the nightshift at Charleston Memorial.*

*She reaches for the knob of her bedroom door, trying to remember closing it in the first place. She can't but isn't surprised. She's been in such a fog lately, still sleepwalking through most days. The room is dark. She tries to remember shutting off the lamp beside her bed. That's when she feels the first prickle of warning crawling along the back of her neck.*

*There's a whiff of stale smoke, of sour sweat and old beer. She barely has time to register that she isn't alone when she feels a hand wind through her damp hair, and she's yanked backward. As she gathers her breath to scream, a second hand clamps down over her mouth and nose, cutting off her air.*

*She kicks and flails, but it's no good. She's being dragged across the room, her towel lost somewhere in the dark.*

*Her head slams against the headboard as she's shoved down onto the bed, and a burst of blue light blooms inside her skull. And then there are more hands—fastened over her mouth, pinning her wrists, prying her legs apart. There are two of them, she realizes sickeningly, two sets of hands pawing at her. The reality of what's about to happen—of what is happening—is almost too much to grasp. She can't move, can't breathe, can't scream.*

*Someone is on top of her, a faceless shadow in the darkness, crushing the breath from her lungs as a sweaty hand fumbles between their bodies. And then there's a piercing between her thighs, a rend up the center of her that feels as if she's being split in two. For a moment, she's terrified she'll be sick, that she'll choke on her own vomit because of the hand over her mouth. There's a brief battering, a sickening spell of gasping and bucking, and then finally, a collapse of heavy, sticky flesh against hers.*

*She has no idea how much time passes as she lays there, pinned to the mattress, trying to breathe through the fingers still pressed to her face, but eventually the weight lifts away. There's a rasp and then a flare of light, the brief flame of a disposable lighter, and for the first time, she can make out Terry Blevins's face hovering above her, slack-jawed and slick with sweat.*

*"You want a turn, bro?" he asks thickly, still straddling Christy-Lynn as he smokes. "I'll hold her."*

*"Let's just get out of here before the old man wakes up." It's Todd, the younger brother, the one who has her mouth covered and her wrists pinned. He sounds scared, as if he's just realized what they've done.*

*"Come on, man. She's right here. Or are you scared?"*

*"Ain't scared," Terry grunts sullenly. "Just don't want to."*

*There's a moment, a fraction of an instant when the pressure over her mouth goes slack. She wrenches her head free and opens her mouth to scream. The sound is cut short as an open palm connects with her cheek. Lights dance, and she tastes blood.*

"*Hold her still, dumb ass,*" Terry growls at his brother. *He sucks on his cigarette again, then aims the smoke at Christy-Lynn's face.* "*As for you, you stuck-up little bitch, you're going to lay there and listen. Got it?*"

*The grip on her wrists tightens again, and her fingers begin to go numb. She lies still and dazed, tears leaking from the corners of her eyes.*

"*You ain't gonna tell anybody about this,*" Terry says with vicious softness, his face so close she can smell the beer on his breath. "*You're gonna pretend it never happened. 'Cause if you don't, if you even think about making any trouble, we're coming back.*"

*He leans closer then and takes another pull from the cigarette. The tip glows hot orange in the dark, sinister and coming closer—so close she can feel the heat of it against her cheek. She closes her eyes and struggles to pull away. She isn't expecting the blinding sting that suddenly sears the underside of her wrist. She begins to buck and thrash, anything to get free, but there's another slap, and then another sting as he presses the cigarette to her flesh again. Somewhere above her head Todd lets out a groan.*

"*Jesus, Terry . . . leave her alone. You got what you wanted.*"

"*Shut the hell up, boy,*" Terry barks. "*I ain't done.*" *He leans in then, crushing the cigarette out against her wrist, holding it there until the reek of burning flesh fills her nostrils.* "*Now, you remember what we talked about,*" *he slurs menacingly close to her ear.* "*Not a word. Or I'll be back—and next time I won't be nice.*"

*When Christy-Lynn finally eases herself up off the bed, she isn't sure if one hour has passed or four. She has wept herself dry and knows what she has to do. She has seventeen dollars to her name, the last of her tips from the doughnut shop. Not nearly enough. But she can't stay.*

*She dresses in the dark, ignoring her wrist and the dull ache between her thighs. She empties her backpack—she won't be needing her schoolbooks—then rolls up a pair of jeans, a T-shirt, and a denim jacket and stuffs them inside. It's all she can fit in the backpack, but she's afraid her duffel will be too heavy. And too conspicuous.*

*Her hand is on the knob when she remembers the envelope in the stand beside her bed. It's a silly thing to care about at a moment like this—a meaningless trinket—but somehow she can't bear to leave it behind. After retrieving the envelope, she folds it into her back pocket, slides her pack up onto her shoulder, and steps out into the hall.*

*She holds her breath as she creeps down the stairs. In the living room, Dennis Hawley is still snoring in his faux-leather recliner, his face flickering an eerie shade of blue in the glow from the TV. She eyes the front door then decides not to risk waking him. Instead, she turns down the hall and tiptoes into the Hawley's bedroom.*

*On the dresser is a wallet, a handful of change, a set of car keys. For a split second, she thinks about the Pathfinder parked in the garage but quickly discards the idea. She settles for the wallet instead, hoping it contains some cash, then moves to the window near the bathroom. It takes only a moment to slide the sash up and kick out the screen, then throw a leg over the sill and drop down into the hydrangeas.*

*In the east, the sky has gone pink, the stars already winking out. The sun will be up soon, and by the time it is, she'll be far away from the Blevins brothers.*

# FORTY-FOUR

Christy-Lynn stared down at her hands, clenched and bone-white. "I've never told anyone about that night. Not even Stephen. I thought I was past it. Then I met Iris. When Rhetta told me she could end up in foster care, it was like someone kicked in the door to my memory. Everything started seeping back in, only this time, my story was all jumbled up with hers, until I couldn't tell the two apart. My past seemed like her future."

"And you felt like you had to fix it," Wade said gently.

"Yes. I wanted to believe the trust would be enough, that Stephen's money would protect Iris from the things I'd gone through. But today, when Ray showed up, I realized money won't change anything. She'll have nice things and go to a good school, maybe even an Ivy League college if that's what she wants, but all the money in the world won't buy her what she really needs."

"What's that?"

"A mother." The ache was back in her throat, guilt mingled with a bottomless grief. "I've been in Iris's shoes. I know what it's like to be a little girl and have that empty place in your life. That's why I fell apart when Rhetta asked me to take her. Because I can't give her that. I can't *be* that."

Wade's hands closed over hers, warm, firm. "I don't know a woman who could. Not under these circumstances."

Christy-Lynn's head lifted sharply. "It isn't about that—about Honey or Stephen or any of that."

"Then what is it about?"

"A promise I made a long time ago—to myself. I've always known I wasn't cut out for the soccer mom thing. Mothers like mine make lousy role models, and then there's the whole genetic crapshoot. Either way, I wasn't risking it."

"If it's any consolation, I think you were worried for nothing."

"Maybe, but the statistics aren't good. And I'm not wired to feel things the way other women do. It's like I skipped that line at the factory."

Wade stared at her openmouthed. "You can't be serious."

"Why can't I?"

"Because in my entire life I've never met anyone wired to feel things *more* deeply than you do, and I'm absolutely stunned that you don't know that about yourself. I might buy that you're *afraid* to feel things deeply, but you can't help it. You're one of the most caring people I've ever met. Maybe too caring, if there's such a thing."

"Now maybe," Christy-Lynn said, her eyes sliding away. "But not always. Not with my mother. I did what I could. I made sure we ate and had clean clothes. But she got to where she couldn't keep a job. She started taking money from work, picking up men and bringing them home. When they arrested her, something in me shut down. I was just . . . done. But she's my mother. I should have toughed it out or at least gone back."

Once again, Wade looked stunned. "How can you say that? You were a kid, for God's sake. Living a kind of hell most of us can't even imagine."

"I was supposed to keep her from self-destructing, and I did for a while. Maybe if I had stayed—" She paused, briefly closing her eyes.

"The judge said I could go back if she cleaned up. That's why I stayed gone. Because going back seemed worse than anything that could happen to me on the streets. So I disappeared. I never called, never wrote, nothing. I did a search for her a few weeks ago. Before that, I didn't know if she was alive or dead."

Wade let out a long breath. "I'm starting to realize why you think it's your job to fix everything. You've been carrying the world around on your shoulders since you were a kid, and you're still doing it."

Christy-Lynn hiked a shoulder. She didn't know if it was true or not, but if it *was,* she had certainly failed in spectacular fashion. Despite all her legal and financial maneuvering, Iris's future hadn't been improved in any meaningful way. And to top it all off, she had just run out on Rhetta in a full-blown panic.

She lifted her eyes to Wade's, suddenly exhausted. "What can I say? I'm a profound and irreversible mess."

"You're not a mess, profound or otherwise. You're just overwhelmed and rightly so. It's been a bit of a day. We can either find a hotel close by so you can get some sleep, or I can take you home. Your choice."

"Home," Christy-Lynn said without hesitation. "I want to go home."

It was almost midnight when Wade finally pulled the Rover into the driveway. Christy-Lynn was almost too exhausted to get out and go into the house. She had tried to sleep on the way back, but every time she closed her eyes, Rhetta's words would float into her head.

*You need each other.*

It wasn't true. Iris needed a mother, someone who could mend a broken childhood. That wasn't her. In fact, it was becoming clear that she was still in need of mending herself.

Wade grabbed her bag from the back seat then came around to open her door. She felt strangely detached from her body as she got out, as if she'd left a part of herself back in Riddlesville.

"You don't need to walk me to the door," she protested when Wade took her arm and steered her toward the porch. "I'm fine."

"Hush." He unlocked the door and let her overnight bag slide to the floor. "Why don't you take a bath while I go scrape us up some dinner?"

Christy-Lynn checked her watch. "It's almost midnight, and you drove the whole way back. You've got to be exhausted."

"Maybe so, but as I recall the last time either of us ate was twelve hours ago. I'm not getting in my Jeep until you've been fed. Now go start the water, and let me do my job."

"Your job? What job?"

He smiled. "Taking care of you."

It was true. He'd been taking care of her all day. And long before that if she was honest. "Why do you do that?"

"Because you don't. And someone should."

There was a softness to his tone that unsettled her, a kindness that threatened to melt her into a puddle. It would be so easy to lean on him, to let him become a part of her life. But then what? How long before he realized he'd gotten involved with an emotional charity case and it all came apart? Because it would. Of course it would.

"Look, I know you're trying to help and all, but I'm fine. Really. I don't need looking after."

"Well, I do," he said, dismissing her words with a crooked grin. "I'm starving, which is why I'm off to ransack your kitchen."

A half hour later, Christy-Lynn padded back down the hall in a robe and a pair of slouchy socks. Wade had set up a pair of trays in the living room and was carrying two plates heaped with scrambled eggs and toast from the kitchen. He'd even made two mugs of tea. Her throat tightened absurdly at the sight. She couldn't remember the last time someone had fixed her scrambled eggs. Or anything really.

"You didn't have to do this," she told him, feeling self-conscious. "I know you think I'm this big helpless mess, but I've actually been taking care of myself for a long time."

"Yes. Too long, as a matter of fact." Wade dropped down onto the couch and picked up his fork. "And I don't think you're helpless. But it's okay to let someone help you once in a while. Now eat. I tried to find a chick flick, but at this time of night, it's either the late-night shows or infomercials."

"Thanks. I think I'd just as soon have the quiet."

They ate in silence, Tolstoy purring contentedly between them on the couch. After the turmoil of the day, it felt slightly surreal to be doing something as mundane as eating eggs in her living room. She stole a glance at Wade, absently munching his toast, and thought about the way he had threatened to expose Ray if he so much as blinked in Iris's direction. She had never believed in white knights, but at that moment, Wade had become one. Tomorrow she would have to call Rhetta and make her understand the impossibility of what she was asking, but for now, it was enough to simply eat her eggs and not think about tomorrow.

When she had eaten her fill, she carried the dishes to the kitchen, then returned to fold up the trays. Wade lay slumped against the arm of the couch, head lolled back against the cushions. She stood looking at him, taking him in detail by detail, the slow rise and fall of his chest, the dusky stubble shadowing his jawline, the way the tiny lines around his eyes went smooth when his face was relaxed.

As if he could feel her there, his eyes opened, heavy lidded and golden. He said nothing as he looked at her. Neither did she, pinned by his gaze and the unsettling whirl of emotions that suddenly crept over her: warmth, gratitude—and trust. It was unfamiliar ground for her, and yet it couldn't be denied. Somehow, while she wasn't paying attention, this man had become part of her life, her safe port in a storm.

"Thank you," she whispered, easing down beside him. "I don't know what I would have done without you today. Or through any of this really. I've never been good at letting people in, but somehow you're here, and I'm glad."

"I'm glad too."

She didn't resist this time when Wade reached for her hand and turned it palm up. She watched as he traced a finger over the trio of small scars then softly touched his lips to them.

"I'm sorry you've been through so much, but I'm glad you felt you could share it with me. In case no one's ever told you, you're quite remarkable."

The words had a strange effect on Christy-Lynn, as if some invisible lock somewhere had suddenly sprung open, a sense of letting go, in this moment at least, of the fears that had kept her in check until now. But then there had always been an inevitability to this moment, a bone-deep knowing that there would come a time when what lay between them would be forever changed.

She groped for something to say, for some quick words to fill up the moment, to check the reckless direction of her thoughts. When she couldn't think of anything, she kissed him, tentatively at first, and then more deeply, unspooling all the pent-up emotions of the day. He felt warm and solid, safe. It was a heady mix—and a frightening one. And yet she felt herself yielding to it, reaching for the thing she'd been holding at bay for so long.

It was Wade who broke away, an abrupt severing that left Christy-Lynn feeling suddenly unmoored. She stared at him, dazed. "What . . ."

"This is a bad idea, Christy-Lynn," he said evenly, holding her at arm's length.

"Why?"

"Because you're tired and you're emotional. And because I'm afraid you're confusing gratitude with something else right now."

"I'm not."

"I think you are. You might not remember, but the last time we went down this particular road, you made it abundantly clear that you weren't ready. And I made it clear that I don't want to be the guy who takes advantage of a friend. I don't think either of those things have changed, do you?"

"I don't know," she said softly. "I wish I did. But I know I want to be with you tonight."

"Christy-Lynn . . ."

"Stay."

"I shouldn't."

She leaned in, past the wavering defense of his outstretched arm, and gently grazed his lips. "Please."

With that simple word, all Wade's reservations seemed to fall away. His arm went round her, pulling her tight against him, his mouth moist and hungry as it closed over hers. After a moment, he pulled back, breath coming hard as he probed her gaze one last time. "You're sure?"

"I'm not sure of anything, except that I want this . . . want you . . . now."

Neither spoke as Christy-Lynn led him to her bedroom. Her hands trembled as she loosened her robe and let it slip from her shoulders. The seconds ticked heavily as she stood there, naked and trembling in the wash of moonlight from the open window, reveling in the feel of Wade's gaze moving over her.

And yet there was a prickle of indecision too, a tiny voice reminding her that it wasn't too late to stop this. Now, before things went too far. Was she testing herself? Testing Wade? Or was it only forgetfulness she craved, a place to hide for the night, as she had once hidden herself in Stephen? She didn't know the answers, but suddenly it didn't matter.

She was reaching for him and he for her. There was no more time for second-guessing.

The contact came as a shock at first, all warm skin and hard angles against her bare flesh. She heard Wade's sharp intake of breath and knew he felt it too. They had crossed that line, that fraction of an instant when it was still possible to retreat. She was clinging to him now, breath held, head thrown back, surrendering to the dizzying assault of his mouth along the ridge of her collarbone, the hollow at the base of her throat. Slowly, maddeningly, he teased his way up to her lips.

Christy-Lynn rose on tiptoe to meet the kiss, unable to ignore the sweet ache spreading through her limbs. She breathed his name and heard hers in return. A plea. A promise. And then suddenly they were falling, spilling onto moonlit sheets, a tangle of straining limbs and unleashed need.

They lay quietly afterward, touching but not talking, slick but sated in a tangle of damp sheets. Christy-Lynn lay with eyes closed, listening to the thrum of blood in her ears. Beside her, Wade's breathing was deep and even as he drifted toward sleep, the warmth of their lovemaking still radiating from his skin. He had touched her in a way she'd never been touched before, as if he'd been given a key to all the hidden places she'd been guarding so carefully, had broken her open and laid her bare. And now, as she lay reliving each exquisite moment, she knew she had made a terrible mistake.

It was only a matter of time before Wade knew it too. She'd been willing but not ready, desperate to believe things had changed, that *she* had changed. But it wasn't true. The day's events had dredged up her past like slime from the bottom of a stagnant pond, a glaring reminder that trust was a dangerous thing. Her mother. The Hawleys. Stephen. A trail of betrayal and broken promises. And now there was Wade. Except, in Wade's case, she was the one likely to prove dangerous, weighed down with emotional baggage and a flight risk by nature.

Without warning, Charlene Parker's face appeared, floating behind her closed lids like a specter on a movie screen. Dar's words were there too, disembodied in the darkness. *Let the memories catch up to you . . .*

Perhaps it was time she did just that.

She waited until she was sure Wade was asleep before pushing back the covers and easing the bottom drawer of the nightstand open. In the moonlight, the envelope glowed an eerie white. She took it out, hesitating only a moment before grabbing the clothes she had discarded earlier and slipping out of the room.

In the kitchen, she scribbled a hasty note and left it on the table. There was no nice way to explain leaving him in the middle of the night, but she had to say something.

*Wade—*

*You were right. I wasn't ready. I'm so sorry—about every-thing. There's something I have to do. Please forgive me.*

*CL*

It seemed terse when she read it back, cold and dismissive, but she didn't trust herself to wait until morning to explain where she was going. He might try to talk her out of it, and maybe he should, but this was something she needed to do, even if it came to nothing, which it probably would. It was time to stop hiding and face her past head-on, to lance the old wounds if she could and drain thirty years of poison.

Scooping the still-packed overnighter from the living room floor, she slipped out into the night, trying not to think about the moment Wade would wake up and find her gone.

She stopped for coffee in Raleigh sometime around nine, then dug out her phone to pull up the site she'd used to find Charlene Parker's last known address. She groaned when she typed the information into her GPS. Still three hours to go. Suddenly she began to question the sanity of what she was doing. She hadn't spoken to her mother in six years, hadn't seen her in more than twenty. What did she hope to gain by poking at her past with a sharp stick? The smart thing—the *sane* thing—would be to go back to Sweetwater and clean up the mess she'd made with Wade.

As if conjured, her cell phone rang. Wade's number flashed on the screen. She cringed, briefly considering letting the call go to voice mail. But that was the coward's way out.

"Hello, Wade."

"What's going on, Christy-Lynn? Where are you?"

"In Raleigh, on my way to South Carolina."

"You left me in your bed in the middle of the night to drive to South Carolina?"

"I'm sorry."

"So your note said."

Christy-Lynn blinked against the sudden sting behind her lids. "I wish I knew what else to say, some other way to do this."

"To do what? What are you saying?"

"I'm saying we made a mistake, Wade. That *I* made a mistake. You were right. I wasn't ready. I'm never going to *be* ready."

"I'd say it's a bit late to be figuring that out."

"I didn't just figure it out. I've known it for a long time. In fact, I tried to warn you the first time you kissed me."

"Yes, you did," he replied stiffly. "Must learn to pay better attention. Though to set the record straight, it was you who made the first move last night, not me."

Christy-Lynn smothered a groan, keenly aware of the irony. "You've been a good friend, Wade. A true friend. I don't know what else to say, except that it never should have happened."

"A friend," he repeated coolly. "Right."

His tone, clipped and frosty, stung more than she expected, not that she hadn't deserved it. "I didn't mean it like that. I just meant . . . I never meant to hurt you, Wade."

"What's in South Carolina?"

The abrupt change of subject should have come as a relief but didn't. "Answers maybe. Or nothing at all. I don't know yet."

"You're going to try to find your mother, aren't you?"

"Yes."

"After twenty years and all by yourself." There was another long pause, as if he were taking time to frame his next words. "I would have gone with you, you know. All you had to do was ask."

"All by myself is what I know, Wade. It's what I'm good at. Say what you want about Stephen, but even he figured that out. And it isn't about fixing anything. It's too late for that. It's about looking her in the eye—looking all of it in the eye—so I can finally stop reliving it and blaming myself for it. I know that doesn't make sense to you. You don't believe in looking back. And I tried that approach for years. But it hasn't worked. So I have to try something else. If I don't, nothing's ever going to change for me."

"Are you sure you want things to change?"

"Of course I do. You think I like the way things are now, the way I . . . am? Afraid of making another mistake? Of hurting someone else? Of hurting you?"

"Let's leave me out of the equation for now, since you've apparently already done that. I just want you to think about what you're doing—and why you're doing it. This trip seems like a pretty spur-of-the-moment thing. Have you given any thought as to what happens when you get there? What you'll say to her if you find her?"

"I have no idea."

"Maybe you're not as ready to do this as you think." The hard edges were gone from his voice now, replaced with something softer.

"If I don't do it now, I never will."

"Look, I know you feel like you have to work through all of this on your own, Christy-Lynn, and maybe you do, but I told you once that I'd wait. That hasn't changed."

Christy-Lynn closed her eyes, hating the words she was about to utter. "And I told you I wasn't worth the wait. That hasn't changed either."

"Christy-Lynn—"

"I come with too many *nevers*, Wade, too many doors it's too late to open."

"And I'm behind one of those doors?"

"Yes," she said softly. "I'm sorry."

"Will I see you when you get back?"

Christy-Lynn swallowed past the fist-size lump in her throat. She was trying to do the right thing, but he wasn't making it easy. She needed him to understand once and for all that they were a bad idea—that *she* was a bad idea. "Sweetwater's a small town," she said finally. "We're bound to run into each other."

"Right."

"Wade—"

"Never mind. I get it. Good luck with your mom."

She felt a strange hollowness as she ended the call, as if she had just burned a bridge she might want to cross in the future. She tried to shake the feeling as she put the Rover in gear and pulled back onto the highway, telling herself it was for the best. There simply wasn't room in her heart right now for one more ache.

# FORTY-FIVE

The Dixie Court apartments weren't quite as depressing as Christy-Lynn had imagined them, but they were close. The treeless grounds wore a vaguely blasted look, as if a bomb had been dropped years ago and the place had never recovered, and the squat, squarish brick buildings reminded her of a prison. It was Sunday, and the parking lot was nearly full, populated with older-model cars pocked with rust or sporting mismatched fenders. At the far end of the lot, a grimy dumpster overflowed with trash, a cloud of flies humming greedily in the late August heat.

Slowing the Rover to an idle, she scanned dirty apartment doors until she located number thirteen. Strains of Blake Shelton's "Kiss My Country Ass" drifted down from one of the upper-story windows. It took everything she had not to restart the engine and pull away.

A little girl in a stained dress and bare feet stared at her wordlessly as she approached the door and lifted her hand to knock. The front windows were open, the curtains wadded into knots to let in the spongy summer air. She tried to peer in but could see nothing. The TV was on, the volume turned way up—old *Matlock* reruns. She knocked again, harder this time, not sure her first attempt had been heard over the TV.

Seconds later, the door pulled back a few inches. A pair of shrewd eyes peered out. "Yeah?"

There was a moment of disorientation, of fractured memories coalescing around the cigarette-gruff voice and warily narrowed eyes. It was how she used to open the door when the rent was due or when she owed money to one of her dealers.

"Mama?"

The door pulled back another few inches. "Christy-Lynn?"

It was the scar she noticed first, a puckered pink gash running from her right eye down to the corner of her mouth, tugging her upper lip into a perpetual half smile. It was all Christy-Lynn could do not to take a step back.

"Yes, Mama, it's me."

The door pulled back the rest of the way, a pong of stale cigarette smoke drifting out to envelop her. "What in God's name—"

"I came to see how you were."

"Why?"

Christy-Lynn stared at her, baffled by the one-word response, but the truth was she didn't have an answer. "I honestly don't know."

"You drove clear from Maine for no reason?"

"I live in Virginia now. Are you going to let me in?"

Charlene seemed to give the question serious thought, but finally pulled back the door and stepped aside. It took Christy-Lynn's eyes a moment to adjust to the dimness, but gradually she made out a small living room with an even smaller kitchen and dinette off to the side. The furniture was worn and mismatched, the couch covered in a faded orange sheet. There was a box fan perched in one of the side windows, circulating sticky air in the cramped space.

A cigarette fumed in a chipped glass ashtray overflowing with butts. Charlene reached past Christy-Lynn to stub it out, then whisked a

Natural Light can from the end table before clicking off the TV. Her eyes darted anxiously, as if seeing the place through her daughter's eyes, and for one terrible moment, Christy-Lynn was reminded of the day she'd brought poor Linda Neely home.

"I've just made some tea," Charlene blurted awkwardly. "I'll get you a glass."

Christy-Lynn followed her to the kitchen, where the smell of old beer and even older food greeted her. She tried not to count the empty beer cans in the sink, scattered among what looked like last night's dishes. There were nine.

"They're not all mine," Charlene told her, noting the direction of her daughter's gaze. "Some of them are Roger's. I'd have tidied up if I knew you were coming."

"I'm sorry," Christy-Lynn said, dragging her eyes from the sink and then from the overflowing trash can in the corner. "I couldn't find a phone number for you."

"You know I never could stand a phone."

*No. Especially when the bill collectors were calling.*

"Who's Roger?"

"He's my . . . we live together. Going on two years now. Works for Tilden Lumber over in Ravenel." She handed Christy-Lynn a glass of tea. "He's . . . steady."

Christy-Lynn's brows lifted. Two years. And a job. As far as she knew, it was a first for both, so by her mother's standards he probably was steady. Still, she refrained from voicing her thoughts.

Charlene turned a hard eye on her. "Why are you here, Christy-Lynn? After all these years?"

"You're my mother," she said coolly.

Charlene snorted as she turned away, heading for the living room and the half-smoked cigarette in the ashtray. She fumbled in her pocket for a disposable lighter and lit the crumpled end. "I've always been your mother," she said, blowing a plume of smoke at the ceiling. "Never brought you around before."

There had been no indictment in the words, only a wary curiosity. For the first time, Christy-Lynn allowed herself a closer study of her mother. She wore slippers and a limp cotton housedress, the missing top button exposing several inches of blade-thin collarbone. Her once dark hair was dull and brittle now, shot through with threads of gray, and her skin was deeply lined. But it was Charlene Parker's eyes that told the real tale. Once a deep and startling green, they had faded to a washed-out gray, as if the light in them had guttered out. Christy-Lynn did the mental math—fifty-two or thereabouts. Far too young to look so used up. She'd been beautiful once, the kind of beautiful that turned heads. A million years ago.

"I know it's been a long time, Mama."

"Twenty years."

Christy-Lynn dropped her eyes. "Yes."

"So why now?"

"I've been trying to forget you."

The words had tumbled out unchecked; Christy-Lynn regretted them the moment they were out. She watched as they hit their mark, the brief flash of pain in the dull gray eyes, the quick look away as her mother sank into a shabby velour recliner.

"That's what I get for asking, I suppose."

Christy-Lynn perched on the edge of the couch with her tea. "I didn't mean it the way it sounded. My husband died, and I've been dealing with some things. A lot of memories keep coming up."

Charlene reached for her hand, then drew back, as if she'd thought better of it. "I saw the news about your husband on TV. And in the papers." She shook her head as she stared at the dirty shag carpet between her slippers. "Nasty business with that woman and all. Do you have . . . are there children?"

Christy-Lynn shifted uncomfortably. "No. No children."

"Was that by choice?"

"Yes."

"Because of me?" she asked quietly. "Because of . . . how I was?"

"Because I was afraid of how I'd be. I was afraid I'd . . ."

"End up a drunk?"

"Yes," Christy-Lynn replied, holding her mother's gaze without flinching. "Or worse. I swore I'd never put a child through that."

It was Charlene who looked away first, sighing as she shifted her attention to the glowing tip of her cigarette. "You were never like me. You were always good . . . responsible. I'd have given anything to be a better mother to you."

"No, Mama, you wouldn't. Not anything."

"No," Charlene admitted, nodding. "Not anything."

Christy-Lynn put down her tea and reached into her purse for the envelope she had taken from her nightstand. Charlene looked on as she spilled the contents into her lap, then picked up the photo and held it out. "Do you remember that day? You took me to the fair."

"I remember."

"And this?" Christy-Lynn held up the tarnished necklace, letting it dangle slowly from her fingers. "Do you remember this? You're wearing one just like it in the picture."

"The other half of mine." Her voice had fallen to a near whisper. "You kept it all these years?"

Christy-Lynn ignored the question. "Do you remember what you said when you put it on me? You said we'd never take them off. But you did take yours off."

"I didn't realize it meant so much to you. It was just a cheap trinket."

"It wasn't the necklace, Mama. It was the promise you made when you gave it to me. The promise you broke when you pawned it." She paused to gather up the contents of the envelope and tuck them away. "That's when I knew the drugs were more important than me—and how easy it is to make promises you don't intend to keep."

323

Charlene nodded dully. "I see. It's judgment day. Go on then. I can take it."

"This isn't about judging you. It's about wiping the slate clean. My slate. For years I managed to keep all the bad stuff locked away, to pretend it happened to some other girl, someone who didn't exist anymore. But some things have happened lately, things that make me realize I can't do it anymore. It's like a door opened, and all the stuff—the way you were, the way we lived—all came spilling out. The drugs, the evictions, the men. And then seeing you in the hospital with your face all stitched up. You going to jail, and me shipped off to the county." She broke off abruptly, reaching for her tea. She wasn't thirsty, but she needed something to hide behind.

"Foster care," Charlene said, drawing the words out slowly. "Was it . . . terrible?"

Christy-Lynn took another sip of tea, staring at the twenty-year-old burns on her wrist. She had come to exorcise her demons, to force her mother to own her past and acknowledge the damage she had done. But suddenly the words wouldn't come. What would it serve to dredge up Terry Blevins now? Except perhaps to pass her demons on to her mother. And it was clear that Charlene Parker still had enough demons of her own.

"I ran away," she said finally, leaving out the why. "I lived on the street for two years until I turned eighteen."

Charlene's eyes filled with tears, the scarred corner of her mouth puckering in a lopsided grimace. "They told me. When they couldn't find you, they came to me. They thought I might've heard from you. They should have known I'd be the last person you'd come to."

Christy-Lynn wasn't sure why her mother was crying. Were they tears of self-reproach or self-pity? The line between the two had always been blurry, and the years had done nothing to make that line clearer.

"I didn't come here to make you cry. Or to make you apologize. In fact, today isn't about you at all. It's about me looking you in the eye and facing what happened back then, about reminding myself what I've been through, and that I was strong enough to survive it. I'm here because I want closure, because I *need* it. So I can finally stop punishing myself."

Charlene had been about to light another cigarette. Her head came up as the lighter fell from her hand. "Why in God's name would you punish yourself?"

"For leaving you," Christy-Lynn said thickly. "For running away and leaving you alone all those years ago. I never knew if you were . . ." She looked away, blinking back tears she had vowed not to shed.

Charlene shifted in the recliner until she was facing Christy-Lynn, her cigarette forgotten. "Now you listen to me, baby girl. You did right to leave. And you did right to stay gone. Look at you, where you've ended up, what you've made of yourself. Strong, respectable, beautiful. Do you think for a minute it would have turned out like that if you'd stayed around to babysit me?"

Christy-Lynn dragged in a breath. "There's no way to know."

Charlene's gray eyes flared. "Yes, there is, and we both know it. You think I don't know what it was like for you, having to take care of me when it should have been the other way around? You think there's a day I don't remember coming home drunk out of my mind, stoned out of my mind, passing out or worse? I do. I remember it all. It's amazing what comes back to you when you lay off the stuff. Things you wish to God you *could* forget. Hell, you were better off on your own than with a mother like me—a boozer and a junkie. It's not an easy thing to say, especially to your own daughter, but there it is."

Christy-Lynn stared at the rapidly melting ice in her tea as she waited for her emotions to right themselves. "Are you . . . ?"

"I'm off the drugs. All of it."

"But you're still drinking."

She smiled grimly. "Old habits die hard. I had to pick one or the other, and I figured I was less likely to kill myself with a bottle than with a needle."

It was a strange conversation to be having. They had never actually talked about the booze and the drugs. They were just a fact, something to be tiptoed around whenever possible.

"Was it after you got out of jail? Is that when you got clean?"

"No. Not then. Not even to get you back. I wanted to. I did. I just . . . couldn't. I've only been clean about four years. So you see, hanging around waiting for me to become mother of the year would have been a waste of time. For a long time—years—I wondered what had happened to you, if you'd turned out all right. And then one day I saw your picture in one of those celebrity magazines—married to some hotshot writer—and I knew you'd be fine. No thanks to me, of course, but I was so proud and happy for you. And so ashamed when I had to call and ask you for money that time. I said it was for rent, but it wasn't."

"You used it to buy drugs?"

"No." Charlene shook her head as she fumbled in her lap for her lost lighter. "But I used it to pay off my guy, which amounts to the same thing. But that was the last time. That's when I decided to get clean. Not because I was afraid of ending up dead in an alley somewhere. Because I couldn't bear the thought of ever having to dial your number again."

There were tears in her eyes. She blinked, and they spilled down her cheeks, leaving a pair of shiny tracks down her ruined face. Christy-Lynn was quiet for a time. In spite of everything, all the recklessness and neglect and shame, it was hard to see her mother this way.

"Do you need money?" she asked quietly. "Or . . . anything?"

Charlene managed the ghost of a smile. "No, honey, and even if I did, I couldn't take it from you. Things are tight, and this is no palace, but we manage. And you . . ." She reached for her cigarettes only to find the pack empty. "I know it hasn't been long since the accident, but are you . . . happy?"

"I own a bookstore now. It keeps me busy. And I do some editing on the side."

A crease formed between Charlene's brows. "Busy and happy aren't the same thing. I meant is there someone in your life, someone who *makes* you happy?"

Christy-Lynn shifted uncomfortably. She found her mother's sudden concern for her happiness grating. "You saw the papers," she replied stiffly. "I'm not cut out for happy. Busy is going to have to do. And I prefer being alone. Fewer . . . complications."

The unscarred corner of Charlene's mouth turned down. "You always were a terrible liar."

"It isn't a lie. And I didn't come here for a lecture on happiness."

"No," Charlene said flatly. "I don't suppose you did. Have you said what you came to say then, or is there more?"

Once again, Christy-Lynn's eyes crept to the scars on her wrist. Yes, there was more. Much more. But there was no point in raking through it. She'd done what she needed to do, seen what she needed to see. "Yes," she said evenly. "I have."

Charlene stood abruptly and crossed to the door. "Then it's time for you to go."

Christy-Lynn stared at her, stunned by the curt dismissal.

"It's best for us both really," Charlene said with a fleeting smile. "Roger will be home soon. He works a half day on Sundays, and I don't want to have to explain you. He knows all the rest of it, but I couldn't bear him knowing the kind of mother I was. I've done a lot in my life that I'm ashamed of, but nothing compares to the way I screwed up with you."

Christy-Lynn came slowly to her feet, reaching into the side pocket of her purse for a pen and a business card. "I'll leave you my cell. In case you need anything." She scribbled down the number and held it out, but Charlene shook her head.

"Thank you, but no. We're done, you and I, and have been for a long time. You said it yourself—you came because you wanted to forget me, and now you can. At least I hope you can. Consider it a gift. God knows I've never given you much else. Except maybe a promise I never kept. So go—forget."

There was a heaviness in Christy-Lynn's chest that she hadn't expected as she moved to the door. "But I can't just—"

"Go," Charlene urged, pulling back the door to let in a blast of Carolina heat. "Please. You have a life, Christy-Lynn. Maybe it's not perfect, but it's a life you can be proud of, which is more than I can say. I'm lucky to be alive after the way I've lived mine. I don't deserve to get my little girl back."

"Won't you at least let me do something for you?"

"You were always smart. Be smart now. Go back to Virginia and don't look back. That's what you can do for me."

Christy-Lynn stood there a moment but couldn't think of anything to say. Finally she dropped the card on the coffee table and slipped through the open door. She had come for closure, but as she started the engine and drove away, all she felt was numb, unable to put a name to the dull ache in her throat as she watched the Dixie Court apartments recede in her rearview mirror.

# FORTY-SIX

Christy-Lynn watched as Missy wove her way through the crowd, pausing to throw Marco a wave and a wink. It was Taco Tuesday, and the place was jammed with the after-work crowd, unwinding with cheap tacos and full-priced margaritas. She wished she'd remembered before suggesting it. Her mood was anything but festive.

"My God," Missy said as she flounced into her chair. "You look terrible."

"Gee, thanks."

"You know what I mean. You look like you should be home in bed."

Christy-Lynn reached for a tortilla chip and munched it absently. "My next stop. Promise. Thanks for meeting me tonight. I just didn't feel like being by myself."

"You know I never turn down a margarita. Do you want to do some food? We could order nachos and share."

Christy-Lynn nodded.

Missy waved Marco over and placed their order, then turned back to Christy-Lynn. "So how was it? Your mother I mean. You said you found her."

"It was awful."

"Oh, honey, I'm so sorry."

"She says she's off the drugs, and I think I believe her. But the sink was full of beer cans. She was so beautiful once, the kind of woman men stopped and stared at—but she looked all worn down, like life had broken her."

"I'm not surprised after everything you've told me. At least she's off the stuff. That's something, at least."

"I suppose. She's got a boyfriend—Roger. They've been together two years. That's all I know about him. Oh, and he works for a lumber company."

"So did you talk about . . . everything?"

"I did most of the talking. It was all very civil. No fireworks and not too many tears."

"How did you leave it?"

"She told me to leave and not come back."

Missy blinked several times. "I don't understand."

"I think she was ashamed. It was like she couldn't wait to get rid of me."

"I guess that makes sense. It had to be hard seeing you after all these years, remembering how she was back then. Honestly, I expected her to hit you up for money."

"I offered. She wouldn't take it. She said taking money from me was one of the lowest points in her life. She claims it's why she finally got clean."

"Are you going to do what she asked and stay away?"

Christy-Lynn squeezed her lemon into her tea and gave it a stir. "I don't know. She meant what she said. She really doesn't want me to try and see her again. I left my number, but she didn't even want that."

"Then maybe you should honor that."

"Maybe."

Marco dropped off Missy's margarita, promising to be back soon with their nachos. Missy discarded her straw and took a long sip, licking salt from her lips. "Sounds like she's at least trying to take responsibility for the choices she's made. That's a good thing, right?"

"I guess."

"So are you glad you went?"

Christy-Lynn picked up another chip then put it back down. "I don't know what I feel. Or if I even accomplished anything by going. I felt like I was talking to a stranger. The woman I remember was never much of a mother. She was always too drunk or high or freaked out to think about me. And suddenly there she was, being all noble and self-sacrificing, asking me if I was happy."

"And you told her what?"

"That I had a bookstore that kept me busy."

"Is that the same thing?"

Christy-Lynn rolled her eyes. "Now you sound like her."

"It's a valid question, honey. I know there's a ton going on in your life right now, but at some point, you really are going to have to give the happy thing a try."

The nachos arrived just as Christy-Lynn was about to respond. She waited for Marco to disappear then spread her napkin in her lap. "Speaking of having a ton going on, there's sort of been a development. Well, several actually."

Missy set down her margarita a little warily. "I'm almost afraid to ask."

"Rhetta asked me to adopt Iris."

"To adopt . . . oh my God, are you kidding? Where did that come from?"

"It's a long story, but the short version is that Honey's brother has suddenly decided to play the doting uncle now that his niece comes with a trust fund. He showed up and made a big scene about suing for custody. Rhetta was beside herself. That's why she asked—because she's terrified, and there's no one else."

"What did you say?"

"What do you think I said? I said no. I'm just getting used to the idea of having a cat. Can you see me raising a little girl? *That* little girl?"

"I can actually. And apparently so can Rhetta."

"I can't, Missy. And you know *why* I can't. And it's not about her being Stephen's. Seeing my mother, remembering just how wrong things can go . . . I just can't."

"For the record, I think you're wrong. That child has had a claim on you since the day you laid eyes on her. But I get why you're afraid. So what's the other development if I dare ask?"

"I slept with Wade."

Missy nearly choked on her margarita. "Wait? What? When did this happen?"

"Two nights ago, when we got back from Rhetta's."

"He went with you to West Virginia?"

"Yes. Another long story, but one thing led to another, and he ended up staying the night—because I asked him to."

Missy was leaning forward in her chair, grinning like a schoolgirl. "I knew it! I knew you were holding out on me. So spill. Was it amazing?"

Christy-Lynn struggled to keep her face neutral and to remind herself that ending things with Wade before they went any further had been the right thing to do. "Yes, it was amazing, but there's nothing to spill. I told him I made a mistake, that I wasn't ready for anything beyond friendship. And maybe not even that."

"Oh, Christy-Lynn, please tell me you didn't."

"I had to. He wants more. And maybe I do too, but I don't know how to be *that*."

"*That* being . . ."

"A couple. Half of someone else."

Missy sighed. "You were married for eight years."

"That was different. I didn't need Stephen in my pocket, and he certainly didn't want me in his. In fact, there were times when he seemed to forget I was there at all. And I really didn't mind. It worked for a while.

And then obviously it stopped working. I don't think I could bear that again. Not with Wade."

"Are you saying you *want* Wade in your pocket?"

"No. Maybe. I don't know."

"Talk to me, Christy-Lynn. What's going on in that head of yours?"

"I don't know what's going on. He's a good man, a good friend, a good listener. He brings toys for Tolstoy and leaves spaghetti in my microwave because he thinks I need looking after."

Missy groaned, then drained her glass. "Tell me, please, how any of this is bad?"

"It's bad because I'm starting to depend on him more than I want to."

"You're scared."

"Yes. And realistic."

"Doors," Missy said, staring woefully at her empty margarita glass. "You get that, right? That you're slamming doors on your chances for happiness?"

Christy-Lynn nodded somberly as Marco approached with their nachos. "I do actually, though I prefer to think of them as loose ends. And tying them up is the only way I know to protect the people I care about."

Tolstoy came running as Christy-Lynn stepped through the door, squalling insistently as she went to the kitchen to fill his bowl, then rescued one of his catnip mice from under the fridge. She had just retrieved her purse from the counter when she spotted the note she'd left for Wade crumpled on the kitchen table. She picked it up and dropped it into the trash without rereading it.

*Slamming doors.*

Maybe Missy was right, but it was for the best. Wade had already been hurt by one woman who didn't know how to love him. He didn't need another one.

And there was Rhetta. Tomorrow she was going to have to pick up the phone and make Rhetta understand that adopting Iris was impossible. She'd be only too happy to help place her with a good family and to provide whatever financial support was needed for them both, but that's where it had to end. For her sake as well as Iris's.

She took a quick shower to scrub away the aroma of Taco Loco then brewed a cup of Dar's valerian root tea. She needed sleep desperately, preferably the dreamless kind, but when she stepped into the bedroom, Wade's manuscript was waiting for her on the nightstand—another loose end that needed tying up. She had promised to finish it, and she owed him that much. Whether he would bother reading her notes was another story, but at least her conscience would be clear.

The light was still on, the comforter scattered with manuscript pages when her cell jarred her awake several hours later. She squinted at the clock as she fumbled for her phone. It was after midnight.

"Hello?"

"Christy-Lynn?"

For a moment, she thought she must be dreaming. "Mama?"

"I'm sorry it's so late."

"Is something wrong?"

"No. Look, I know I said I wasn't going to call, and I really wasn't. But then I found the card you left on the coffee table." There was a pause, the sound of smoke being inhaled and then exhaled. "After you left, I got to thinking about . . . well, about everything, and I realized I never said I'm sorry. I may have said the words, I can't remember, but if I did I meant I was sorry for me. It wasn't about you—about how I hurt you—and it should have been. That's why I'm calling."

Christy-Lynn sagged back against the pillows, wondering where this fresh wave of contrition was coming from—and where it might be going. A few hours ago, her mother had shown her the door. Now this. Had she changed her mind about the money after all?

"It doesn't matter now, Mama."

"Yes, it does. And there was more I should have said. So much more. I always swore that if I ever got the chance I'd make sure you knew how much I regretted it all, and then there you were, right in front of me with that necklace in your hand, and all I could think about was getting rid of you. That's why I rushed you out the door—because I was ashamed. I could see what I'd done to you—then and now."

Christy-Lynn said nothing, letting the silence stretch.

"Christy-Lynn?"

"I'm here."

"The thing I should have said—the thing I need to say now—is that I hope you find a way to be happy. I'm sorry I never gave you the kind of life you deserved, sorry I broke my promise to you, sorry about all of it. But please, baby girl, don't let that stop you from making a life of your own."

"Mama—"

"I have to hang up now. I'm at the pay phone on the corner, and I don't want Roger to wake up and find me gone." There was a brief pause then a jagged breath. "I promised myself I'd never ask you for another thing, including forgiveness, but I'm breaking that promise now and asking you for one thing. Please, Christy-Lynn, let yourself be happy."

And then she was gone.

Christy-Lynn stared at the blank phone screen, imagining Charlene Parker standing in her housedress at the corner pay phone, not to ask for money as she had initially suspected, but for forgiveness. And to wish her happiness.

*I could see what I'd done to you—then and now.*

The words seemed to echo in her head—and her heart. Was she such an open book? So glaringly transparent that her mother—a woman she hadn't seen in twenty years—could see through all the careful layers of veneer to the emptiness beneath? It was a daunting thought, particularly when others seemed to be echoing similar sentiments.

*It was time to let herself be happy, to stop closing doors, to make a life of her own.*

It must look so easy from the outside.

From the foot of the bed, Tolstoy eyed her quizzically, stretched out like a pasha amid the strewn manuscript pages. She'd managed to get through the last page before passing out. Now, as she began gathering them up, she realized she'd probably never know how the story ended—unless *The End of Known Things* wound up on a shelf in her store one day. She hoped it would. It was certainly good enough or had the potential to be.

The house was still as she padded to the kitchen with her empty mug, the quiet like a shadow stalking her down the hall. On her way back to bed, she lingered in front of the closed door to the spare room, hand poised above the knob.

*All the things we won't let ourselves have.*

The door seemed to open of its own volition. It hadn't of course. Doors didn't open on their own. You had to *choose* to open them, to consciously cross the threshold and glimpse what lay beyond. She flipped on the overhead light, sighing as she scanned the jumble of half-packed boxes and unused furniture she should have donated months ago. But then it wasn't like she had a real use for the room. Maybe that's why she'd been dragging her feet, because she didn't like the idea of it sitting empty, like a great big glaring hole in her life.

On impulse, she dropped to her knees and began picking through the nearest box. They were Carol's things mostly, items hastily left behind when she moved to Florida: lamps, linens, chipped dishes. She'd held on to most of it—in case Carol changed her mind and wanted it sent. But she hadn't. Maybe because she'd already taken the things that mattered.

Conspicuously absent from the boxed-up castoffs was any trace of personal memorabilia, no scrapbooks, photographs, or family keepsakes. Nothing that represented Carol Boyer's *real* life. Those things she'd been careful to take.

Now, as she thought back to the night she left Clear Harbor, it struck her that the only things she'd been careful to take were an old photograph and a tarnished necklace. That's what she'd chosen to hold on to, reminders of pain and loss, because there were no happy memories to cherish. She hadn't bothered making any. Instead, she'd built a careful life with nothing to look back on and even less to look forward to.

The tears came then, like a dam giving way after a storm, as Wade's words, Missy's words, even her mother's words, crowded in on her. It was a moment of terrible clarity, the kind that usually came at the start of the third act, while there was still time for the heroine to save herself. Sadly, that train had left the station. There was already a big hole in her life.

But if she was being honest—and it was well past time for that— she had to acknowledge that the empty places in her life were of her own making. Not her mother's. Not Stephen's. Hers. She'd been living in a kind of bubble, playing it safe while the world went by, but somewhere along the way, that had stopped working. She wanted more. Was it too late to change, to salvage something after all the lost years? She honestly didn't know. She only knew she wanted to try—and she knew exactly which door to open first.

# FORTY-SEVEN

Christy-Lynn dropped into the deck chair with her phone and her coffee mug, sipping as she checked her messages. So much had happened in the past couple of weeks, so many things she needed to share with Wade, though things on that front didn't look particularly promising. They hadn't spoken in weeks—since the morning she'd left him in her bed to drive to Walterboro—and he had completely stopped coming to the store.

Not that she blamed him after the way she'd left it. She'd been very convincing when she said they'd made a mistake. In fact, she had almost convinced herself. But the truth was she missed him, his smile, his sometimes harsh but always well-meaning advice, his presence in her kitchen—and her life.

She had tried his cell several times, but the calls always went straight to voice mail. Either he'd shut off his phone or he was purposely declining her calls. Finally, she'd sent him a text. Finished the manuscript. Was wondering how to get my notes to you.

It had taken him two days to respond. His tone had been distant, even for a text. Out of town. Don't know how long. I'll let you know.

She had replied immediately. I've made some decisions. Can we talk?

He hadn't bothered to respond.

Now, as she sat watching Sweetwater Creek tumble smoothly past its bank, it occurred to her that some people might be meant to simply pass through a person's life, to touch briefly and then move on. Perhaps that's why she and Wade had crossed paths again after so many years. He had been *her* fresh set of eyes, a new lens through which to see herself, and perhaps rewrite her life. And now that she had, or was at least trying to, he had moved on.

She stood, turning her back to the creek, and carried her mug inside to the sink. She had things to do, a final run of boxes to drop off at Goodwill, the borrowed ladder to return to Hank, the vintage lamp she was having rewired to pick up from the shop.

Two hours later, Christy-Lynn's errands were complete, and she was on her way home, eager to put the final touches on her first ever DIY project. Her heart skittered when she pulled into the driveway and saw Wade's Jeep. He was sitting inside with the engine turned off, scribbling in one of the leather journals he always carried with him. He set the journal aside when he heard her approach but said nothing, his expression unreadable.

"Hi."

He nodded curtly. "Hello."

"I didn't expect to see you. I wasn't sure where you'd gone."

"I went to see my mother for her birthday and decided to stay awhile. I needed to clear my head."

Christy-Lynn wasn't sure she wanted to know what clearing his head might mean. "I have the notes on the rest of the manuscript."

"Yes. I got your text."

"I wasn't sure you had. I didn't hear back after the last one."

"No."

"Why?"

"I thought it best. I wasn't sure I was coming back, and I didn't want to . . . confuse things."

The news that he'd even considered not coming back to Sweetwater made Christy-Lynn's stomach knot. "But you did come back. You're here."

He eyed her coolly, fingers drumming on the steering wheel. "At some point, you have to stop running, don't you? And you still have my manuscript."

"Right. It's inside. Do you want to come in?"

"I'll wait out here."

His abrupt refusal stung. "All right. I'll just be a minute."

Christy-Lynn was more than a little shaken as she unlocked the front door. She was hoping there would be a conversation, a chance to apologize, to explain, but he'd made it abundantly clear that he wasn't interested in apologies *or* explanations.

She hurried to retrieve the manuscript and notes from her night-stand, then started back down the hall, wanting him gone before she made a complete fool of herself. She wasn't expecting to find him standing in the living room holding Tolstoy.

"You left the door open," he explained, setting the cat down on the arm of the love seat. "He was about to stage a prison break."

"Thanks." She handed him the pages and stepped back, not trusting herself to stand too close. "I hope the notes help but feel free to ignore every word if you don't agree. It has to be yours, or it won't work."

He glanced briefly at the pages before tucking them under his arm. "Thank you. I'd be happy to pay you."

The chilly response felt like a slap. "I didn't do it for money. I did it for you."

Wade shifted uncomfortably. "I better get going."

"Wait. Can I show you something? It'll only take a minute." His eyes slid to the door, and she saw that he was about to say no. "Please?"

He nodded, turning to follow her down the hall. Paint fumes wafted out as Christy-Lynn threw open the door to the spare room. Wade stepped inside, pivoting in a slow circle.

"It's . . . pink."

"Yes."

She couldn't help smiling as she surveyed her handiwork, the pink walls and white canopy bed, the delicate rosebuds stenciled in each of the four corners. It had taken her nearly two weeks to finish, far longer than it would have taken Hank, but it had been important that she decorate Iris's room herself.

He looked at her, clearly stunned. "You said yes?"

"I did."

"I guess a lot's changed in two weeks. Did this change of heart have anything to do with seeing your mother?"

Christy-Lynn looked down at her hands, scraping at the specks of pink paint still clinging to her nails. "It had to do with a lot of things, but I think it's been coming for a while. I started realizing how empty my life has been—and how much I stood to lose if I kept on playing it safe."

"It's a big step."

"Yes," she said gravely. "It is. But there are worse things than being afraid, like hurting people you care about. And being alone."

She stood there, waiting for some sign that Wade understood. Instead, he turned away, feigning interest in the wall stenciling. "So . . . when's the big day?"

"I don't have an exact date. I had to hire an adoption lawyer to draw up the papers. It's a little more complicated than setting up a trust, but they should be ready soon. And it took some doing, but I finally convinced Rhetta to move to an assisted-living facility Missy recommended here in town. I told her the only way I'd agree to take Iris was if she came too. I hated to resort to blackmail, but I really want her out of Riddlesville. She's getting to the point where she'll need looking after, and at Pine Brook, she'll have nursing care and still be able to see Iris whenever she wants."

"No trouble from Ray?"

"None. It seems the good reverend has lost interest in his niece."

Wade smiled drily. "Surprise. Surprise."

"I have you to thank for that," she said softly. "You knew he was going to be trouble."

"Journalistic instincts," he said, running a hand over the freshly painted bookshelf near the window. "This is nice. Did you do it?"

Christy-Lynn nodded, beaming just a little. "My first attempt at furniture refinishing. Picking the books was fun too. I loved books when I was a kid. I hope Iris will too."

Wade reshelved a copy of *Green Eggs and Ham* and forced a smile. "Well, it looks like it's all going to work out. I'm happy for you. And for Iris."

She panicked as he turned to go. He was still so angry, and he had every right to be, but she couldn't just let him walk out. "I was wondering . . ." The words seemed to stick in her throat. "I was hoping you'd come with me when I go pick up Iris."

He was scowling when he turned back. "I thought you said Ray had lost interest."

"It isn't Ray. It's . . ." She felt him stiffen when she touched his arm but held on until he had no choice but to look at her. "I don't want to do this alone, Wade. I know what I said before, about being better off on my own, but I was wrong. I want you in my life."

Wade's face went coolly and carefully blank. "I'm not interested in being your wingman anymore, Christy-Lynn. I tried that, and it didn't end well."

She dropped her hand from his arm and moved to the window, peering out through the crisp eyelet curtains she had hung last night. She'd been rehearsing this moment for weeks, not sure she'd ever get a chance to say what was in her heart, and now that the moment had finally come, she found herself tongue-tied, on the brink of losing the man who, against all odds, had found his way into her heart. Why couldn't she just say it? I want you . . . I love you . . .

Wade was still in the doorway, still waiting for some kind of response, though the chill in his gaze told her he wasn't going to wait much longer. She needed to say something, anything, because if she didn't, she would never get another chance.

"Do you remember when we talked about what Missy said—about our nevers being the doors we keep closed?"

Wade shrugged, the barest of acknowledgments. He was going to make her work for this, and she supposed after everything that was only fair.

"Anyway, I've been doing a lot of thinking, and I realized she was right. Being a mother was one of my nevers because I was afraid I'd get it wrong. But that isn't the only door I've been keeping shut. There were others, like letting myself love someone—and letting myself *be* loved. And then you came along, and I was so scared that I *did* get it wrong. But I don't want to get it wrong anymore. I want to figure out how to get it right—with you."

He was standing with his arms crossed now, his face still carefully blank. "So that's it? Just like that, you're ready to turn over a new leaf?"

Christy-Lynn took a step forward, then checked herself. "It isn't just like that, Wade. I've been thinking about this for a while. *You* made me think about it. And I know now that it's what I want, that you're what I want." His face became a blur as her eyes filled. She blinked away the tears. "I can't . . . lose you."

There wasn't a chink in Wade's frosty facade. "You'll forgive me for being skeptical."

She wiped at her eyes again. "Please. I know I hurt you, and you have every right to be skeptical. But you have to know it wasn't on purpose."

"I do know that. I also know it won't be on purpose next time. And there will be a next time, if I let myself believe you."

"You're wrong," Christy-Lynn shot back, closing the distance between them in two quick strides. "Yes, I ran. Because it's what I've always done. But it was because you were trying to make me see things I didn't want to see." She dropped her eyes to the floor, her throat thick with a fresh rush of tears. "I just didn't see them until it was too late."

She was startled when she felt his fingers under her chin, tilting her head back until she was forced to meet his gaze. "It doesn't have to be too late, Christy-Lynn. Not if you really mean what you're saying. I told you once that I'd wait, but I have to know—for sure this time. Do you want this? Do you want . . . us?"

Christy-Lynn dipped her head, afraid to trust her voice. "Yes," she whispered. "I do. But I warned you once—I might not be worth the wait."

"And I told you I'd risk it."

"Even if I'm still scared?"

He pulled her close, his lips feather light as he touched them to her forehead. "*Especially* if you're scared." His words were like honey, slow and warm and unbearably sweet. "I can be brave enough for the both of us until you get good at it."

"How do you know I will?"

"Because you've finally decided to. And because the woman I know is much too strong to let a little thing like being loved scare her for long. You're going to get good at it, Christy-Lynn. I promise. In fact, something tells me you're going to get very good at it."

He kissed her then, so slowly and thoroughly that she felt herself sway against him. It was the delicious surprise of it that made her head swim, the rightness of their bodies melding together, like two halves of the same perfect whole. She was ready. After years of running, of hiding, of punishing herself, she was ready to let herself be happy.

But there was something they hadn't discussed. She pulled away briefly, looking up at him through damp, spiky lashes. "In the interest of full disclosure, I need to inform you that I'm now a package deal—I come with a little girl."

Wade grinned broadly as he dragged her back against his chest. "And a cat," he murmured against her mouth. "Don't forget the cat."

# FORTY-EIGHT

*Riddlesville, West Virginia*
*October 15, 2017*

Christy-Lynn glanced at Wade as he pulled the Rover into Rhetta's drive and cut the engine.

He must have felt her gaze because he turned and reached for her hand. "Ready?"

She pulled in a deep breath, the kind kids took before hurling themselves into the deep end of the pool. "I think so."

Wade gave her fingers a squeeze. "You are. I promise."

Rhetta was at the door before they made it up the porch steps. She looked frailer than the last time Christy-Lynn had seen her, her eyes rimmed with shadows, her face worn. Inside the door, a pair of battered green suitcases waited, along with a pink fleece jacket and Iris's beloved teddy—a child's life stuffed into two avocado-green Samsonite cases. The sight brought a sharp pang of memory, of other moving days, of strange beds and new schools, of having to start all over—again.

*She must be terrified.*

Wade followed the direction of her gaze. "It's okay," he said softly. "This is good. It's right."

Christy-Lynn nodded, noting the trio of half-packed boxes in the middle of the living room floor. Rhetta had been packing, picking and choosing which things to take with her to Pine Brook and which to leave behind. She was glad to see it. Part of her had been afraid she might change her mind at the last minute.

Christy-Lynn nodded at the boxes. "You've been busy."

Rhetta's faded blue eyes moved wearily around the room full of knickknacks, as if wondering where it had all come from. "I'm leaving more than I'm taking. They say I won't even need to bring dishes to the new place. I should be able to finish boxing the things I want by the time you come back." She paused, making another scan of the living room. "I still can't believe I'm leaving this place. I always thought I'd die right here in this house."

Christy-Lynn had no trouble believing that. "Will you miss it?"

Rhetta mulled the question a moment, lips pursed thoughtfully. "I'll be sad to leave Honey all alone in that cemetery," she said finally. "She always hated this town' and now she'll never get out. But Iris will, and I'm glad of that. She deserves better than the little bit I could give her."

"Where *is* Iris?" Christy-Lynn asked, imagining her hiding somewhere, sobbing her heart out.

"She's in her room. I sent her to check her closet one last time. Trying to keep her busy." She paused, gathering a shaky breath, then called down the hall. "Iris, honey. It's time to go."

Christy-Lynn cringed, wondering what those words must sound like to a three-year-old who was about to be yanked up by the roots, torn from the only home she'd ever known.

"How is she? Is she . . . upset?"

Rhetta's lips thinned. "There were some tears when I first told her. But she settled down when she realized she'd be living with you—her *Angel Mama*."

Rhetta loved the nickname, and apparently Iris did too, but it still made Christy-Lynn uncomfortable. It wasn't an easy name to live up to, especially for someone with no maternal skills whatsoever.

Rhetta reached for her hand, her smile teary. "Don't you worry. She's young, and young hearts mend. A year from now she won't remember this place, and you'll be her mama for real."

Christy-Lynn felt the butterflies in her stomach stir to life. "She knows you'll be nearby though, right? That she can see you whenever she wants?"

"Yes, but not too much at first, I think. Having me around in the beginning would only confuse her. That's why I wanted to wait a bit before coming. She needs to get settled in, to know her place is with you now."

Before Christy-Lynn could protest, Iris appeared wearing the sparkly pink sneakers she had brought her the last time she visited. Her eyes went wide when she spotted Wade and Christy-Lynn.

"Baby," Rhetta said gently. "Can you say hello?"

Iris mouthed the word soundlessly, her gaze locked on Christy-Lynn.

Rhetta bent down and smoothed Iris's blonde curls, her gnarled hands skimming over the child's hair, face, shoulders, as if trying to memorize the feel of her. "Are you ready to go on a nice long car trip like we talked about? All the way to Virginia?"

It took a moment, but Iris finally nodded.

Rhetta reached for her hand, leading her across the living room to where Christy-Lynn stood. "And you're going to be a big girl for Nonny, aren't you?" she asked with a sudden catch in her voice. "You're going to be brave and not cry."

It was all Christy-Lynn could do not to turn away, but she needed to be brave too. As much for Rhetta's sake as for Iris's. And it was only temporary, she reminded herself. In three weeks, Rhetta would be with them in Sweetwater, living just a few miles away, a welcome addition to her rapidly growing family. In the meantime, she'd be fumbling her way through motherhood with zero advance training. Not that motherhood ever came with an instruction manual. According to Missy, you learned to be a mother by *being* a mother—one skinned knee and juice spill at a time. She prayed it was true.

"Let's make sure you're good and warm," Rhetta was saying as she zipped Iris into her jacket. "And then it's time to get in the car."

"I'll take the bags out," Wade said, grabbing the suitcases and heading for the door.

Christy-Lynn watched him go, feeling suddenly bereft. He was giving her a few moments with Rhetta, to say whatever needed saying. But what was there to say at this bittersweet moment that hadn't already been said over the past weeks and months?

"Iris," Rhetta said evenly, stooping down with arms extended. "Come say goodbye to Nonny."

Iris melted into Rhetta's arms, her violet eyes brimming as her great-grandmother pressed one last fierce kiss to her cheek, then handed her off to Christy-Lynn. "Take care of each other," she whispered brokenly.

Christy-Lynn stifled a gasp as Iris landed in her arms. The sudden weight of her, warm and slight and already clinging, was sobering. "It would be so much easier if you were coming with us today, Rhetta. For Iris and for me."

Rhetta forced a smile. "Easier isn't always best."

"What if there's something I need to know, like how she likes her oatmeal or what vitamins I'm supposed to buy?"

"We've talked about all that, Christy-Lynn. And if there's something we missed, there's always the phone, though I doubt you'll need it. Aside from the nightmares, she's an easy child, and I expect those will stop soon. She just needs to feel safe, and she will with you. You'll see. Now get gone. You've got a long drive."

"You're not coming out to the car with us?"

Rhetta closed her eyes, throat bobbing convulsively. "I don't think I can. I know I'll see her in a few weeks, but we've never been apart, and it's . . . hard. Just know how grateful I am to you. Everything changed the day you knocked on my door."

Christy-Lynn blinked back tears of her own as she pressed a kiss to Rhetta's cheek. "It's me who should be grateful. We're family now, and that's something I've never had."

Rhetta reached into her pocket, fishing out a tissue. "Stop that talk or you'll really have me blubbering. Now go on. I've got packing to do, and you've got a little girl to get home."

Iris clung to Christy-Lynn's neck, propped on one hip as they stepped off the porch and out into the bright afternoon sunshine. Wade was waiting, the back door of the Rover thrown open, ready to buckle Iris into her car seat. Christy-Lynn met his gaze as she handed Iris over, grateful for the unspoken reassurance she saw there. *She was going to be fine. They . . . were going to be fine.* And in that moment, perhaps for the first time, she knew it was true.

She glanced back at the house as Wade turned the Rover toward home, recalling Rhetta's words of gratitude. *Everything changed the day you knocked on my door.* The thought brought an unexpected sting to the backs of her lids.

Everything had changed for her too.

# EPILOGUE

Iris sat wide-eyed on the edge of the pink princess bed, sparkly sneakers drumming rhythmically against the dust ruffle. Christy-Lynn eased down beside her, a small velvet box tied with silver ribbon in her lap.

Poor thing. She still looked a bit shell-shocked, as if afraid this new world might evaporate at any moment. And why shouldn't she be afraid? When she'd just been whisked away from everything she had ever known. If anyone knew what that felt like, it was Christy-Lynn. But she also knew she could change that for Iris, and she would.

Wade stood watching from the doorway, a shoulder pressed against the jamb. He smiled as Christy-Lynn caught his eye, shooting her a wink that sent a ripple of warmth and gratitude through her. She hadn't expected to feel nervous, but then she never expected to be sitting in a pink bedroom with a three-year-old gazing up at her.

"I have a present for you, Iris," she said softly, holding out the box.

Iris continued to stare, her violet eyes wide pools of uncertainty.

"Would you like me to open it for you?"

Iris nodded then ducked her head, as if suddenly shy.

Christy-Lynn's hands shook as she tugged the ribbon free, then lifted the lid of the box.

Iris's eyes shot even wider as she caught a glimpse of what lay inside—a pair of silver necklaces that when fitted together formed a single shiny heart. But a crease suddenly appeared between her pale brows, her gaze shifting from the box to Christy-Lynn.

"It's broken."

"Oh no, baby—look." Christy-Lynn lifted out both necklaces, placing them side by side in her palm. "They're part of the same thing—two pieces of the same heart. There's one for you and one for me. I'll put yours on if you hold up your hair."

Iris stared at the necklaces with a kind of wonder, then fumbled to rake her hair out of the way, holding very still as Christy-Lynn snaked the silver chain around her neck and fastened it.

"Good girl. Now I'll do mine."

On cue Wade stepped in, taking the remaining necklace from her hand. After several failed attempts, he finally managed to clasp it. Christy-Lynn grinned at Iris, then pointed to the mirror over the dresser.

"See—we match."

Iris gazed at her reflection with enormous eyes, mesmerized as she stroked the necklace at the base of her throat. After a moment, she turned to Christy-Lynn. "Match."

"Yes. You have one half, and I have the other. Because from now on, you're going to be a part of my heart. And I hope that one day I'll be a part of yours."

Iris seemed to weigh what this might mean, her little brow puckered. Finally, she cocked her head to one side, regarding Christy-Lynn quizzically. "Are you my mama now? My *real* mama?"

Christy-Lynn blinked down at her, not sure how to answer, or if she'd even be able to find her voice. "Would you like that?"

Iris nodded, but her tiny face was clouded with questions. "Will you still be my angel if you're my mama? Nonny says God sent you to take care of me."

Christy-Lynn couldn't help thinking of the dreams that had once plagued her almost nightly—dreams that hadn't returned since she agreed to take Iris—and wondered if Rhetta had been mistaken.

"I think Nonny got it backwards, sweetie. I think I'm the one who needed taking care of, and now here you are, my own little angel—just like a dream."

There was no warning, no time to brace for impact before Iris launched herself full force into Christy-Lynn, clinging so tightly that it was impossible to say who was hanging on to whom. But suddenly it didn't matter. Suddenly it felt like the most natural thing in the world, as if this child had somehow always been a part of her life.

Peering over Iris's blonde head, she found Wade again in the doorway, her heart full as their eyes locked. She'd been living with *nevers* for far too long, holding happiness at bay with both hands. But now there was Iris. And Wade.

It seemed *never* had come after all.

# ACKNOWLEDGMENTS

No book is written in a vacuum. There's always a long list of people to thank, ranging from the professionals whose job it is to get a book on the shelves or onto your Kindle, to the helpful contacts who aid us in research, to the loved ones who feed us, make sure there are clean clothes, and otherwise sustain us throughout the process. And so, I will begin my list, praying as always that I don't forget anyone.

As with all my writing projects, there is one person without whom a finished book would never come into being. Her name is Nalini Akolekar of Spencerhill Literary Agency, and she is without a doubt the best agent in the biz. Thank you for all of it: for the books, for the journey, for the guidance, for the smarts, and for the support!

To my amazing editors, Jodi Warshaw and Charlotte Herscher, thank you for believing in this book and helping me get the best version of it out onto the page. And what can I say about the rest of the Lake Union Publishing team, except every good thing I've ever heard is true. Your ongoing commitment to authors makes it a true pleasure to be a Lake Union author. I couldn't be more thrilled to be part of this amazing team of writers and professionals!

To my brothers and sisters of the pen scattered all over the country: Barbara Claypole White, Diane Chamberlain, Laura Spinella, Kim Boykin, Karen White, Terry-Lynn Thomas, Normandie Ward Fisher, Heather Webb, Anita Hughes, Bernie Brown, Matt King, Doug Simpson, Lisa Cameron Rosen, Mitch Richmond, Michelle Hicks, Sheryl Cornett, and so many more, who are never too busy to read, critique, encourage, hand hold, council, blurb, and otherwise prop up a writer in need—my deepest love and gratitude. You will never know what your friendship and support mean to me.

To the *real* Melissa (Missy) Beck, Queenie Peterson, Dar Setters, Carol Boyer, and Doug Simpson, whose names I lovingly borrowed for several of the characters in this book, many thanks for the special place each of you hold in my heart.

To Pat Crawford, mother extraordinaire and world's greatest cheerleader, thank you for your faith in me, for your wonderful example, and for every word of encouragement you've sent my way along this journey. I can't begin to tell you how often you've kept me going when I wasn't sure I could get it all done. Love you. Love you. Love you gobs!

To Tom Kelly, my newly wedded husband and all-around knight in shining armor, it always has been and always will be . . . you and me against the world. Thank you for asking, for waiting, for saying I do, and for all the stuff before and after. I love you more than words can say. (And I know a lot of words!)

I would be remiss if I didn't give a special shout-out to Topher Lee and Carmen Tanner Slaughter, who came to the rescue and actually helped me name Honey Rawlings.

And of course, last but not least, big squishy hugs to all my wonderful readers. Thank you for reading, reviewing, sharing, and encouraging. But most of all, thank you for being part of my extended family. Every word is for you!

# BOOK CLUB DISCUSSION QUESTIONS

1.  What events and/or circumstances in Christy-Lynn's past do you see as contributing to her wariness of strangers and her reluctance to develop close personal relationships? By the end of the novel, what evidence are we given that she is finally ready to overcome those fears and move forward?

2.  In what ways do you see the concept of guilt and self-blame playing out as Christy-Lynn struggles to cope with various events? Do you believe women are more prone to these kinds of guilty thoughts than men? And if so, why?

3.  The themes of friendship and acceptance, particularly within the bonds of female friendship, are heavily woven into the novel. What specific examples of these qualities are we shown, and how do you feel they affect Christy-Lynn's self-image and actions as the story progresses?

4. Missy has a strong dislike of the word *never*, likening it to the doors we close on our own happiness—all the things we won't let ourselves have, do, or be. Can you recall a time in your own life when you suddenly realized you were limiting yourself and chose to stop closing a door to your happiness?

5. As the novel progresses, we learn more and more about the dynamic of Stephen and Christy-Lynn's marriage. In what ways do you see Christy-Lynn's unstable past and poor self-image playing a role in enabling a manipulative and controlling husband?

6. How do you feel about Christy-Lynn's early decision to place the majority of Stephen's money in a trust for Iris? Could you foresee a situation in which you would feel uncomfortable spending money that was left to you under painful circumstances? What advice would *you* have given Christy-Lynn?

7. Several mentions of "burning bridges" appear in the novel, referring to irrevocably severing ties to a person or event from the past. Do you believe it's possible to irrevocably burn all one's bridges, or are there some that no amount of time, pain, or distance can ever completely sever? Do you believe that no matter what has transpired in someone's past there is always a way back?

8. Dar believes that dreams are messages from our deeper selves. Do you believe this, and if so, has there ever been a time in your life when you felt your dreams were trying to send *you* a message? Did you listen and act on it? And if not, do you now wish you had?

9. At one point in the novel, Christy-Lynn opens a for-tune cookie and finds the words: *Salvation lies in doing the thing that frightens us most.* What specific fears has

Christy-Lynn confronted by the end of the novel, and how does each stand to help bring her salvation?

10. Can you identify with Christy-Lynn's lingering sense of guilt over deserting her mother? Had you been in her shoes, would you have gone looking for her after so many years, or would you have been content to remain estranged and live with the what-ifs?

11. Throughout the book, we see Christy-Lynn grapple with the pain of her mother's broken promise, as symbolized by the tarnished half-heart necklace. At the end of the book, we see her give Iris a similar necklace. What do you think this gift symbolizes for Christy-Lynn at that point, and what does it say about her personal growth?

12. By the end of the book, Rhetta has come to believe Christy-Lynn is an angel, sent to care for Iris, while Christy-Lynn believes Iris was sent to take care of her. Do you believe there are people who come into our lives to comfort us in hard times or point us toward a happier future, or do you believe everything that happens to us is random? Can you remember an instance in your own life when someone appeared at just the right time to deliver a much-needed lesson or help you through a particularly difficult time?